The air was tainted with the coppery scent of blood and, underneath, something Kallie had missed earlier—the faint brimstone stink of discharged magic.

Layne swung left and stopped in front of the rumpled and blood-drenched double bed. The color drained from his face. "Gage. No."

The shocked grief on Layne's face tightened Kallie's throat. "I'm so sorry," she said, wishing her hungover brain would toss her words a little less trite.

"You're sorry," Layne repeated, voice flat. "My best friend lies dead in *your* bed. You *should* be sorry, woman."

"Look, I had nothing to do with Gage's death."

Layne spun around and grabbed Kallie by both arms, his road-callused fingers clamping around her biceps. "*Nothing*? Ain't that his blood on your fingers?"

"Get your damned hands off me before I forget you're grieving."

"Or what? You'll hex me to death too?"

"*Too*? Is that what you think? I told you—I *found* him like that."

"I smell spent magic. If you didn't kill him, who did?"

(Turn the page for praise of Adrian Phoenix and The Maker's Song series)

***Black Dust Mambo* is also available as an eBook**

BENEATH THE SKIN

"Lush, sexy, and thrilling, *Beneath the Skin* is another darkly addictive entry in The Maker's Song series. Adrian Phoenix makes her world of vampires, fallen angels, compelling characters, and rich settings come alive. I have two words for Ms. Phoenix: write faster."

—*New York Times* bestselling author Jeaniene Frost

IN THE BLOOD

"Phoenix trips the dark fantastic in this wild, bloody sequel. . . . She keeps the plot thick and the tension high."

—*Publishers Weekly*

"The atmosphere is dark, and treachery abounds . . . white-knuckle reading in the extreme."

—*Romantic Times*

"Adrian Phoenix is fast becoming one of my favorite authors. Her ability to create a dark, edgy atmosphere so real you can see, hear, and taste it, while maintaining a fast-moving, page-turning plot, is simply amazing."

—Jenna Black, author of *Speak of the Devil*

A RUSH OF WINGS

"Hard-charging action sequences, steamy sex scenes, and a surprising government conspiracy make this debut, the first in a series, engrossingly fun."

—*Entertainment Weekly*

"Phoenix's lively debut has it all . . . vampires and fallen angels and a slicing-dicing serial killer. . . . Phoenix alternates romantic homages to gothdom and steamy blood-drinking threesomes with enough terse, fast-paced thriller scenes to satisfy even the most jaded fan."

—*Publishers Weekly*

"Sharp, wicked, and hot as sin."

—*New York Times* bestselling author Marjorie M. Liu

"A thrilling tale of lust and murder that will keep you turning the pages to see what happens next."

—*Gothic Beauty*

"A deliciously dark and seductive tale. . . . The fast pace and creative twists make this action-packed read one to remember, and the steamy romance will have readers eagerly looking for more of the same."

—Darque Reviews

"A dark, rich treat you won't soon forget."

—Romance Reviews Today

"A *Rush of Wings* is a fast-paced ride, its New Orleans setting appropriately rich and gothic, its characters both real and surprising."

—*New York Times* bestselling author Kristine Kathryn Rusch

"A goth urban fantasy that moves as fast as its otherworldly characters . . . decadent, glittering fun, wrapped up in leather and latex."

—Justine Musk, author of *BloodAngel*

DON'T MISS THESE OTHER THRILLING ADVENTURES BY
ADRIAN PHOENIX

A Rush of Wings
In the Blood
Beneath the Skin

Available from Pocket Books

BLACK DUST MAMBO

ADRIAN PHOENIX

POCKET BOOKS
New York London Toronto Sydney

Pocket Books
A Division of Simon & Schuster, Inc.
1230 Avenue of the Americas
New York, NY 10020

First Pocket Books paperback edition July 2010

POCKET and colophon are registered trademarks of Simon & Schuster, Inc.

For information about special discounts for bulk purchases, please contact Simon & Schuster Special Sales at 1-866-506-1949 or business@simonandschuster.com.

The Simon & Schuster Speakers Bureau can bring authors to your live event. For more information or to book an event contact the Simon & Schuster Speakers Bureau at 1-866-248-3049 or visit our website at www.simonspeakers.com.

Text design by Jacquelynne Hudson
Cover design by John Vairo Jr.
Cover illustration by Steve Stone

Manufactured in the United States of America

10 9 8 7 6 5 4 3 2 1

ISBN 978-1-4391-6787-8
ISBN 978-1-4391-6793-9 (ebook)

Dedicated to
the Oregon Writers Network Master Class of 2008

Because y'all are an awesome group of dedicated writers and because, through sleep deprivation and battling with our personal demons while rolling a huge-ass pair of dice, we are writers-in-arms, bonded forever.

Write, then let slip the dice of fate!

ACKNOWLEDGMENTS

Special thanks to the Lincoln City, Oregon, version of a New York editorial office—Dean Smith, Kris Rusch, Steve and Chris York, and Loren Coleman—for giving me a huge shove and for laughing at Porn Squirrel.

Thanks, as always, to Sean and Rose Prescott, Karen Abrahamson, and Dean Smith, my first readers extraordinaire; to my editor, Jen Heddle, for always helping me tell the best story possible; to my agent, Matt Bialer, for your passion and enthusiasm; and to Dr. Mark Fletcher, for an incredible repair job on my ankle and for keeping me breathing!

Big-ass thanks to Mippy Carlson, Nate Gross, Sheila Dale, Louise Robson, Judi Szabo, Cyrene Olson, Annette Stone, Erin O'Connor Fetters (best damned virtual bartender EVER!), and all the awesome members of Club Hell and my street team for your support, enthusiasm, and excitement.

Heartfelt thanks to my sons, Matt Jensen and Sebastian Phoenix, and their partners, Sherri Lyons and Jen Phoenix, and my story-writing little, Kylah Phoenix, for all your encouragement and love; to Sharon and Marty

Embertson, D. T. Steiner, and Lynn Adams, for your friendship and for your tireless efforts in spreading the word.

Musical thanks to C. C. Adcock, for creating music that is original and earthy and damned sexy, and for providing the perfect soundtrack for Bayou Cyprès Noir.

And, as always, thanks to you, the reader, for picking up this book and plunging into a new series set in a world of bayou-steeped hoodoo, hard-bodied nomad conjurers, and deadly mystery. None of this could happen without you.

Please visit me at www.adrianphoenix.com, www.myspace.com/adriannikolasphoenix and at http://www.facebook.com/pages/Adrian-Phoenix/.

BLACK DUST MAMBO

One

Crossed Dead

"C'mon, scoot your gorgeous ass over, Gage," Kallie Rivière whispered, climbing onto the shadowed bed. "I feel like shit. How much goddamned champagne did we—" She froze when her fingers touched the hot, wet sheets.

She blinked in the dawn light filtering into the New Orleans hotel room. Not shadows. She caught a faint whiff of coppery blood. Something else altogether darkened the sheets.

Nausea flipped through her belly. Swallowing hard, she lifted her hand and forced herself to push the blood-soaked sheets back from the man they covered. Gage. The good-looking and hard-bodied nomad conjurer she'd hooked up with last night after the May pole dance.

Playing with him had been a bendy, bouncy, naked trampoline act; a free fall into pleasure. One part Gypsy-style outlaw biker, one part pagan conjurer, and one part hot-blooded explorer—all sexy nomad. Man was *beaucoup* skilled.

Or had been.

Kallie stared at the dead man in her bed. He lay on his belly, his face turned to the side. Blood masked his fine features, glittered in his black curls. It looked like blood had poured from Gage's eyes, nose, mouth, and—given the blood staining the sheets beneath him—from elsewhere, like a spigot turned on full blast. All color had drained from his espresso-brown skin, leaving his swirling blue-inked clan tattoos stark on his muscular back, ass, and thighs.

Kneeling on the bed, Kallie reached over, intending to touch her fingers to his throat and check his pulse, but her hand stopped just a few inches above his blood-streaked neck.

Just a few hours ago, he'd devoured her lips with rough and hungry kisses as they had tumbled together on the carpeted floor, her legs wrapped around his waist—so white against his dark skin. The thought of his skin cold and lifeless beneath her fingers kept her hand in the air, motionless.

His empty, unblinking eyes told her he was dead. Gage was gone. She didn't need to touch him. Kallie stared at her trembling hand, wondering if she even could.

She'd seen plenty of dead things at home in Bayou Cyprès Noir, but never a dead person, let alone one she knew.

Well, hey, Kallie-girl, that isn't quite right, now is it? Shouldn't keep lying to yourself like that.

Memory tugged at Kallie, taking her back to another morning nine years ago.

Mama pulls the gun's trigger and the side of Papa's head explodes in a spray of blood and bone. He slumps down in his chair, a bottle of Abita still in his hand.

Kallie stands in her bedroom doorway, frozen—just like now. Mama turns and faces her, aims the gun carefully between her shaking hands. Her hands shake, but her face is still, resigned.

"Sorry, baby. I ain't got a choice."

Mama pulls the trigger again.

Kallie touched trembling and blood-sticky fingers to the scar on her left temple. Traced the lightning stroke of the bullet's path, just as her gaze traced the contours of Gage's face. Pain and shock had widened his hemorrhaging eyes, had twisted his fingers into the sheets.

How had he died? *When* had he died? While she lay curled on the bathroom floor, sick on too much wine and champagne?

She hadn't heard a goddamned thing.

Kallie reached up and closed her fingers around the pendants her aunt had hung around her neck nine years ago—a tiny onyx coffin marked with a silver X and a medallion for Saint Bernadette—and closed her eyes.

It was too late to call 911, but she needed to contact *someone*. Report this. Maybe the coordinators of the oh-so-exclusive May Madness Carnival would know what to do, especially when it came to dealing with a dead member of one of the freewheeling ain't-bound-by-your-squatter-laws nomad clans.

Maybe, yeah, but she thought a friend's calming advice might be the way to go first. She gave her pendants a quick squeeze for luck before releasing them, then opened her eyes.

Kallie's gaze fell on the small stylized fox black-inked beneath Gage's right eye—the tat naming his clan. She wanted to grab a clean section of the sheet and wipe the blood away, wanted to smooth his eyes shut, but her hands remained knotted on her thighs.

"I'm so sorry," she whispered, the sound of her words hollow and inadequate even to herself. "Eternal rest grant unto him, O *bon Dieu.* And let perpetual light shine upon him. All flesh must come to you with all its sins; though our faults overpower us, you blot them out. Baron Samedi, I ask you please to accept this man into Guinee. Guide him safe from the crossroads and from the land of the living."

Course, it might be nice if God and the *loa* actually *listened* to prayers without needing a rum-soaked bribe first. Kallie sighed. Still, old habits and all that bullshit.

Kallie scooted off the bed and, not sure where her cell phone was, grabbed the room phone. Her finger shook as she punched in the number to Belladonna's room.

"Whazz?" Belladonna slurred, her voice thick with sleep.

"It's me." Kallie cupped her hand around the receiver's mouthpiece like she was trying to keep her conversation private or trying to curl her fingers around something normal and real. "Something bad's happened . . . *beaucoup* bad, Bell. I need you to come over right now."

All the sleep evaporated from Belladonna's voice. "I'll be right there. You alone?"

"Yes and no."

An exasperated snort. "Which is it, girl? Do I need to bring muscle or a spell?"

"Just you, dammit. Please."

The line went dead. Kallie re-cradled the receiver, then sat down on the carpet, amid the wreckage of her clothes and Gage's, her arms wrapped around her bare legs. She shivered, teeth chattering, caught in a cold trembling that vibrated up from her core.

Mama's hands shake, but her face is still, resigned.

"Sorry, baby. I ain't got a choice."

Kallie thought she'd put all that aside, all the darkness and fury and tight-throated hurt, when she'd gone to live with her *ti-tante* Gabrielle; had sworn she'd never let her goddamned mama steal another moment of her life.

Looks like I just broke that promise.

Knuckles rapped against her door, and Kallie's heart jumped into her throat. "Hold on," she said, unfolding her shaking limbs and climbing gracelessly to her feet. Belladonna must not've even bothered to dress, must've just thrown on a robe and hustled her ass into an elevator.

Kallie padded to the door, unlocked it, and eased it open. "Thanks for getting here so—" The words withered in her throat.

Not Belladonna in a robe, but a tall and fine-looking guy wearing a hastily tugged-on sage-green tank, jeans, and scooter boots with painted flames licking up from the soles. Blue-inked Celtic tattoos swirled from beneath the shoulders of his tank and down his arms. Thick, honey-blond dreads coiled nearly to his waist, and sideburns, stiletto-thin and sharp, curved along the lines of his jaw.

A shock went through her as she met his pine-green gaze. For a second, everything quieted inside of her as though he'd pressed a soothing finger against her lips and whispered, "*Shhh*." His eyes widened a little as though he felt the strange connection too; then Kallie noticed the small black fox inked beneath his right eye, and her heart sank.

"Hey, you must be Kallie, Gage's hoodoo honey, yeah? Sorry to bug you so early, but is he still here?" the nomad asked. His gaze slid past her and into the room. "I really need to talk to him."

"Now?" Ice sheared off from the glacier encasing Kallie's heart and flowed into her veins, froze her thoughts.

On pure instinct, she stepped into the hall, pulling the door shut behind her. Too late, she realized she was wearing only her red lace please-undress-me bra and bikini-cut panties. Face burning, she pulled one dangling strap back up onto her shoulder.

An appreciative but teasing smile curved the nomad's lips. "Rosy cheeks to match the undies. You wear 'em well, sunshine. I'm Layne, by the way."

Kallie opened her mouth, unsure of what to say, but knowing she needed to say something, *anything*. But before a single word could emerge from between her lips, the nomad's gaze locked onto her hands. He sucked in a sharp breath. She looked down. Blood smeared her fingers. Her pulse thundered in her ears.

"I don't know what happened," she stammered, looking up at him. "He was dead when I— "

Layne stared at her, all expression gone from his face. "*Dead*?"

Temples throbbing with hangover pain, Kallie nodded, holding his pine-green gaze, unable to think of a single worthwhile word to say.

"You're kidding me, right?"

"I wish I was," Kallie said.

Shoving past her, the nomad pushed open the door and walked into the sunlight-laced room.

"Wait, hold on." Kallie hurried into the room after him. Her belly knotted as she drew in a breath of air tainted with the coppery scent of blood and, underneath, something she'd missed earlier—the faint brimstone stink of discharged magic; scents that seemed to register on Layne too.

He swung left and stopped in front of the rumpled and blood-drenched double bed. The color drained from his face. "Gage. No. Oh, shit. Shit."

The shocked grief on Layne's face tightened Kallie's throat. "I'm so sorry." She desperately wished her hungover brain would toss her words a little less trite, give her a verbal lifeline. But no. The only other thing it coughed up was: *Sorry for your loss.*

"You're sorry," Layne repeated, voice flat. "My *draíocht-brúthair*—my brother-in-magic and my best friend—lies dead in *your* bed. And you're fucking *sorry*?"

"Look, I had nothing to do with Gage's death."

Layne spun around and grabbed Kallie by both arms, his road-callused fingers clamping around her biceps. "*Nothing*? Ain't that his blood on your fingers?"

"Get your goddamned hands off me before I forget you're grieving." Kallie met his eyes, glare for glare, her hands knuckling into fists.

"Or what? You'll hex me to death too?"

"*Too*? Oh, hell, no. Is that what you think? I told you—I *found* him like that. I sure as hell didn't kill him!"

"I smell spent magic. If you didn't kill him, who did?"

"I don't know, dammit!" Kallie wrenched free of Layne's grip, suspecting—given the strength of his hands—that he'd *let* her go. Chin lifted, she held his gaze and pulled her bra strap back onto her shoulder again.

Layne folded his arms over his chest. "So where the hell were you when it happened, anyway? The only blood I see on you is on your hands, so you couldn't have even been in the goddamned bed with him."

"We never made it to the *bed*, per se, not together, because we downed a ton of champagne and wine, and I passed out in the bathroom. When I woke up . . ."

"Passed out. Pretty damned convenient, huh?"

"A damned relief at the time, truth be told, considering all the puking."

"You okay, Shug?" another voice said, all purring velvet tones; a voice Kallie knew well. "Or am I looking at a soon-to-be-dead nomad?"

TWO

BAD BLOOD

"You've already got one dead nomad on your hands," Layne growled, swiveling around to face Belladonna, muscles flexing and hands knotting. "And this one plans to go down swinging."

"Dramatic much?" Belladonna kicked the door shut behind her.

"Might ask you the same," Layne retorted.

Belladonna rolled her eyes. "Nomad, please. I only tell it like it is." She walked into the room, tall and boyishly slim, her skin the color of dark chocolate, her hair a bushy natural 'fro haloing her head in black and midnight-blue curls.

"About time," Kallie grumbled, despite the relief curling through her. "I was starting to think you'd gone back to sleep."

"Like I could do that after you uttered that mythical word *please*. I was stunned you even knew it," Belladonna replied. Her nostrils flared as she caught the room's thickening blood-and-brimstone stink, and although the teasing light faded from her eyes, her expression remained calm.

And that was one of the things Kallie loved most about

her best friend—her composure under fire, a skill Kallie envied and hoped to learn one day. Not that she ever planned to say so. What, and give Belladonna a reason to curve her full lips into yet another cat-licking-up-all-the-cream smile? Please.

Shifting her weight to one black-jeans-clad hip and crossing her arms over the cobalt-blue silk tunic she'd pulled on, Belladonna said, "You've got interesting notions about what 'alone' means, girl. Who's the road-rider?"

"Name's Layne Valin, and I ain't *with* her," he said. "I'm here for *him*." He nodded at the bed. "The man she murdered."

"Murdered?" Belladonna held Kallie's gaze, the morning light transforming her startling hazel eyes from river green to autumn leaf brown.

Kallie stiffened at Belladonna's arched-brow expression. "Not by *me*."

"Well, that's a relief—not the 'murdered' part," Belladonna hastily clarified, glancing at Layne. "I meant the 'Kallie being innocent and all' part."

"Yeah, well, that remains to be seen," the nomad said, shoving his hands into his jeans pockets.

"What's it gonna take to get it through your thick skull that I *didn't* kill him?"

"Mama generally recommended solid whacks with a two-by-four," Belladonna said, walking over to the bed. "Great cure for thickskullitis." Her eyes widened as she took in Gage's still form amid the blood-soaked sheets. "Hellfire, Kallie. What in God's name happened?"

"I don't know." Kallie joined her friend at the bed. "I passed out in the bathroom and when I woke up, Gage was . . ."

"Oh, no. Gage?" Belladonna asked. "The nomad hottie you told me about?"

"Gage Buckland," Layne supplied, his voice husky. "Fox clan."

"What did he die of?" Belladonna asked, frowning. "Looks like he had some kinda dread disease like Ebola . . ." As though just realizing what she'd said, she recoiled from the bed and clapped a hand over her nose and mouth.

"He wasn't *sick*," Layne protested. "He was *murdered*."

Kallie sighed. "Place reeks of magic, not germs, Bell."

"Mm-hmm. And being an expert and all on disease, you'd know what germs smelled like, right?" Belladonna arched an eyebrow.

"Oh, you mean a WebMD expert like you? Then no."

"What the hell is it with you two?" Layne cut in. "*Magic* killed Gage, not the motherfucking plague."

Belladonna glanced at him, her expression softening. "That it did. But it never hurts to look at less obvious possibilities."

Kallie rolled her eyes. "Never hurts, no. Wastes time, however. . . ."

"I promise not to laugh when those words bite you on the ass, Shug." Belladonna reached into the black leather bag slung across her shoulder, pulling out a small glass bottle. She unstoppered it and tapped a pale-green powder into the palm of her hand. The pungent scents of mint and wintergreen sweetened the air.

"What's she doing?" Layne asked.

"Giving us a little protection," Kallie said.

"Saint Michael, hear me. Please fill this room with your protective light and keep all within it that are still breathing safe from evil." Lifting her palm to her mouth, Belladonna blew powder into the air as she swiveled to face each cardinal direction in turn—north, south, east, west.

Layne watched as Belladonna wove protection into the room. "She a hoodoo like you?"

"No, she's training to be a *mambo*—a voodoo priestess," Kallie replied. "Me, I'm a rootworker."

"Rootworker? Ain't familiar with that term."

"It's just another name for us hoodoos—rootworkers and root doctors—since we all work with roots and herbs and all aspects of nature in our conjuring and healing."

"No such thing as *just* anything," Layne said. "People are complicated."

"Yeah. And that's the problem." Kallie studied Gage's bloodied features, searching for clues as to the how and why of his death. The memory of his face awash with pleasure, his dark eyes aflame, was the one she yearned to keep, not this one.

Layne reached back and knotted his dreads away from his face. "You called 911?" he asked.

"No, not yet."

"Don't. We take care of our own."

"I understand that, but we're going to have to let carnival security know—"

"'We' nothing. And it ain't carnival security you need to worry about, sunshine. You need to talk to my clan."

Kallie stared at Layne, her hands knotting into fists again. "Look, I'm sorry Gage is dead and I wish I could change things, but I didn't have anything to do with his death. Hell, even if I had that kind of power—and trust me, I don't—I wouldn't lay a trick like that."

A dubious/cynical expression shadowed Layne's face. " 'Lay a trick'? You saying Gage *paid* for your company?"

Belladonna's soft prayers stopped. "Men, minds always and forever in the gutter." She faced the nomad, a hand on one hip. "To 'lay a trick' means to cast a spell."

"My apologies," Layne said; then a smile ghosted across his lips. "Gotta say, men's minds ain't alone in that gutter you mentioned."

"A good thing too, otherwise y'all would never figure out how to slither out of it," Belladonna murmured, looking him over. Her expression said she liked what she saw. "You really ought to sign up for the wet-boxers contest. I'm one of the judges, y'know."

Layne's honey-blond brows slanted down. "Wet boxers? Could we focus here?"

"Fine. Focus it is," Belladonna replied. "So how come you're here anyway, Layne Valin? I don't think Kallie called you, like she did me. What brought you to her door?"

"He showed up like he already knew something was wrong." Kallie mulled over their initial encounter in the hall. "Said he needed to see Gage. How did you know where to find us, by the way?"

"Before he took off last night, Gage told me about the hot little hoodoo chick he'd met at the May pole dance and hoped to hook up with," Layne said. "Told me about your long, dark hair and blue-violet eyes. Told me your name too. I bribed the clerk at the front desk for your room number."

Kallie blinked. "Bribed? Really? For how much?"

"A ten was all it took, sunshine. Times are tight, and I guess tips ain't been good."

"Ten measly bucks? Goddamn." Kallie shook her head in disgust. "Okay, but that doesn't explain why you're here. What did you need to see Gage about so early in the morning?"

Layne looked bleakly at the blood-smeared bed and the body on top of it. "Doesn't really matter anymore, does it?"

Belladonna sauntered over to the bed, her gaze cool and assessing and focused on the nomad. "Maybe *you* should be the one doing some explaining to your clan, not Kallie."

Layne stared at her. "Me? What the hell for?"

Belladonna shrugged. "Maybe there's been bad blood between you and your clan brother. How do I know that *you* didn't hex him? Set Kallie up as convenient to take the fall?"

"Bad blood?" The nomad held Belladonna's gaze, his good-looking face hard as granite. "I woulda spilled every last drop in my veins for Gage. I owed him my life, my god-damned soul. Who the fuck are you to point a finger at me?"

"You haven't answered my question," Belladonna said, arching an eyebrow.

Kallie remembered the expression on Layne's face when he'd first walked into the room and seen Gage on the bed. Genuine shock and spontaneous grief. And damned hard to fake unless he was an Oscar-caliber actor.

She touched Belladonna's arm. "No, he had nothing to do with Gage's death. I'd stake my life on that. But how *did* you know that something was wrong?"

A muscle flexed in Layne's jaw. "I had a dream. But I got here too late. And now there's nothing I can do to reverse it."

A pang of sympathy cut into Kallie. *Nothing I can do . . .* She understood his helplessness all too well. "Some things you just can't stop."

"Small comfort, that. But true." Sorrow and exhaustion etched years into Layne's face, leaving him looking temporarily older than the twenty-four or so Kallie reckoned him to be.

"Do you know of anyone who wanted Gage dead?" she asked.

"Gage had enemies, sure—what conjurer doesn't? But hating him enough to do *this*?" Layne shook his head, and Kallie caught a whiff of sweet orange and musky sandalwood from his dreads. "Maybe Gage knows. If he ain't crossed over yet, I can ask. But I ain't reeling him back if he's gone. I won't do that to him."

Kallie stared at him, not sure she'd heard right. "Excuse me? What?"

Layne climbed onto the bed and knelt beside Gage's cooling body, not seeming to give a damn about all the blood, then did what Kallie had wanted to do earlier, but hadn't been able to—he closed his clan brother's eyes. "Come back and speak to me, bro," he whispered, bowing his head. "I'm listening."

Power, focused and controlled, electrified the air, prickling the hair on the back of Kallie's neck and goosebumping her skin.

"Hellfire," Belladonna breathed. "He's a Vessel for the dead."

A ghost ship.

Kallie had met mediums, had even participated in séances, and had always walked away disappointed. But she'd never met a Vessel before. A Vessel didn't need ritual or séance or linked energy from the living to call to the dead or to open doors between the mortal and spirit worlds.

A Vessel *was* a living, breathing spirit cabinet. And most Vessels spiraled into madness by their late teens, usually ending their lives in messy and desperate ways.

Very few Vessels lasted into their twenties.

Kallie stared at Layne, wondering if he was actually younger than he looked and wondering how much time he had left before his mind and soul twisted in on themselves. She perched on the bed beside him as dark, deadly, and thorn-sharp magic scraped against her senses. And *this* magic wasn't coming *from* Layne, it was coming *through* him. Black juju. Her blood chilled.

Her gaze darted to the long-fingered hand Layne was resting against his clan-brother's face. If the whole trick hadn't been used up on Gage, then touching him might—

Layne's breath caught roughly in his throat. He stiffened as though snake-bit, his muscles cabling like wire stretched beyond its capacity. His face, tight with pain, paled, chalk-white.

"Let go of Gage!" Kallie barely stopped herself from grabbing Layne's arm and wrenching it away. "Let go! Layne? Can you hear me?"

"Can't . . . let . . ." Blood trickled from his nose, dribbled dark from his ears, and wet the lashes of his clenched-shut eyes.

"What's going on?" Belladonna asked. "Speak to me, girl."

"The trick ain't goddamned done, Bell." Grabbing a blood-spattered pillow, Kallie used it to shove the nomad off the bed, then tossed it aside—magic buzzing against it like hungry flies.

Layne hit the floor on his side, his skull bouncing against the carpet, his dreads snaking out behind him. What little air remained in his lungs whoofed out from between his lips. He lay there, limp and unmoving.

"Dammit, dammit, holy goddammit!" Kallie cried, jumping off the bed and dropping to her knees beside him. She seized his wrist.

Layne's pulse—wild and rhythmless—fluttered. Then stopped.

THREE

VENOM

"*Dere will be times, girl, when all de potent herbs and oils and devout prayers in de whole wide world ain't gonna be enough or even the right t'ing; times when all yo' magic will seem to dry up like mud under de noonday sun, or even make matters worse.*"

"*So what do I do when that happens, Ti-tante? And how will I know?*"

"*You'll feel it in yo' bones, child, you'll feel it deep down. And when you do, den you roll up yo' sleeves and go to work using* beaucoup *elbow grease.*"

"*For how long?*"

"*Until de task be done, girl, and not a moment before, y'hear me? Now hand me my broom. Dat damned gator's back on de porch.*"

Elbow grease. This was definitely one of those times.

Kallie rolled Layne's body—all hard muscles and deadweight—onto his back, then bent over him, locked her hands together, and started pumping against his sternum. As she channeled her adrenaline-fueled strength into each downward press, she both heard and felt several ribs crack.

"Guard us from evil, Saint Michael, protect us from murder," Belladonna murmured as she knelt beside Layne. "Papa Legba, I humbly ask that you turn this one away from the crossroads, send him running back to the living."

"CPR, Bell. Need your help here."

Tipping Layne's head back, Belladonna wiped blood from his mouth with the hem of her tunic. "He'd better not have AIDS," she muttered.

"You can always hex his ass if he does."

With a sigh, Belladonna bent over Layne, pinching his nostrils closed and pressing her mouth over his. She breathed into him as Kallie kept the compressions steady and rhythmic.

Beneath her hands, Kallie felt dark magic coiling around Layne's heart like a water moccasin around a sun-heated rock. Felt venom pouring black and cold through his veins.

She only knew one good way to draw snake venom from a wound, to keep it from reaching a bite victim's heart—suction. But would suction work with magical poison? More to the point, would it work with a heart already poisoned?

Worth a try. His life's gonna be short as a Vessel, and not a goddamned second of it should be stolen from him.

A chant circled through Kallie's mind, glimmering with a pure white light that she tried to channel into Layne with each compression of her hands against his chest: *"Heart beat, heart beat, keep the blood and air flowing neat. Death needs to be cheated, for this man is still needed. Heart beat, heart beat, keep the blood and air flowing neat."*

Kallie imagined white light circling his heart and filling his lungs, imagined it sparking opalescent fire in his mind. With each downward press of her hands, she visualized siphoning the hex's black and oily magic up into her palms, through her body, and into the floor, drained of all power.

"Heart beat, heart beat, keep the blood and air flowing neat. Death needs to be cheated, for this man is still needed. Heart beat, heart beat, keep the blood and air flowing neat."

Kallie shivered. Sweat stung her eyes. "Fight, damn you," she panted. "You still need to avenge Gage. Fight, dammit."

Layne. Something bad's happening to Layne. But ye'll never make it in time; he'll be gone before ye find him, an' his destiny nocht but ash.

Those words, as clear as if whispered from cold lips pressed against the cup of her ear, yanked McKenna Blue up from sleep. She stared into the room's curtained gloom, her heart hammering against her ribs. A ship's low horn vibrated in from outside as if underscoring the words echoing through her mind.

Ye'll never make it.

Aye, right. The hell I won't.

She rolled away from the warm body nestled against hers—Raphael or Ramon, his name escaped her at the moment—and out of bed. She dressed as fast as she could in clothing she snatched up from the floor—jeans, a too-big shirt that most likely belonged to lover boy, and her black harness boots. Pausing just long enough to fetch her Kahr P9 and tuck it into her jeans at the small of her back, she dashed from the room.

A sharp feeling of dread propelled McKenna into the hotel elevator and insisted she push the button for the fourth floor. Once she'd exited the elevator, it led her down the Persian-carpeted hall with its embossed cream walls to a door marked 415.

With a belly full of cold stones, she rapped her knuckles against the door. She thought she heard someone speaking in a low, urgent voice on the other side, but what she thought she heard pricked ice through her heart: *Fight, dammit.* McKenna reached back with her other hand and slipped her gun free of her jeans.

A quick flip of the handle confirmed that the door was locked. Not caring if she woke up the entire bloody hotel, McKenna hammered her fist against the metal door and shouted, "Layne? You in there? Open the bloody door!"

Someone was pounding on the door hard enough to make it shake in its frame. *And* yelling like a madwoman. Belladonna lifted her mouth from the nomad's and glanced at Kallie. But Kallie continued her compressions against Layne's chest, her eyes closed, sweat beading her forehead, as though she heard nothing.

And maybe she didn't. Girl was in the zone, totally focused on the nomad and the rhythm she'd created in hopes of jump-starting his hex-flatlined heart. The air crackled with power and seemed to ripple around her like silk fluttering in a breeze.

Belladonna frowned. *Never seen that before. How much of herself is she pouring into that boy?*

"OPEN THE DOOR!" the madwoman screamed.

Belladonna jumped to her feet, ran to the door, and yanked it open. A pixie of a woman in jeans and a huge Bourbon Street T-shirt stood there, her fist lifted for another door-shaking, hotel-quaking knock. Belladonna's gaze skipped from the pixie's short, black, bed-spiked hair to the blackbird V tattooed beneath her right eye.

Lovely. *Another* nomad.

Oh, and in the pixie nomad's other hand? A gun. Natch.

Belladonna grabbed the woman by the arm and hauled her into the room, slamming the door shut behind her. "What the hell are you thinking, raising a ruckus like that?" Belladonna snapped. She waved a hand at the gun. "Put that damned thing away. We've got trouble enough, and you don't need to be adding to it."

The pixie's doe-eyed gaze skipped to the dead nomad on the bloodied bed, then to just-technically-dead Layne sprawled on the carpet in front of the bed. She sucked in a breath, and the color drained from her face when she took in the sight of a nearly naked Kallie kneeling beside him and trying to stiff-arm life back into him.

Despite all that, the pixie didn't do any of the foolish things Belladonna had been expecting given her performance at the door. No screaming. No fainting. No weeping and wailing or gnashing of teeth.

Instead the pixie nomad snugged her gun into the back of her jeans beneath her whale of a T-shirt. "Wha' can I do?" she asked, a rolling lilt to her words.

"Before you interrupted me, I was breathing into him," Belladonna replied. "You take over, and I'll call for an ambulance."

Without another word, the pixie hurried across the floor and dropped to her knees beside Layne's body, then bent over him and went to work.

Using the phone on the nightstand beside the bed, Belladonna called the Prestige's front desk and requested that paramedics be sent to Kallie's room. Then, realizing what would happen when the medics got a good look at the carnage in Kallie's room with its rapidly rising body count, she asked that the carnival administrators be contacted as well and a representative sent to 415.

Belladonna hung up the receiver and turned around. She opened her mouth, intending to tell Kallie that trouble in all shapes, sizes, and levels of authority was on the way, but when her gaze settled on her trouble-bait best friend, the words piled up in her throat.

A white aura streaked with deep purple and sparkling with pinpricks of full-moon silver crowned Kallie's bowed head and flickered around her body like tiny pearlescent tongues of fire. Power—strong, deep, and pure, and unlike anything Belladonna had ever felt from Kallie before—radiated into the room. But something muddied the light spilling out from underneath Kallie's palms and across Layne's green tank.

Belladonna stepped closer, narrowing her gaze. An inky and virulent blackness seeped up from the nomad's chest and into Kallie's hands—as though she was siphoning the hex into her own body.

Belladonna's heart kicked hard and fast against her ribs. A growing shadow pooled behind Kallie as the hex venom she pulled from Layne trickled from the soles of her bare feet and soaked into the carpet, staining it black.

Oh, that can't *be good—for us* or *housekeeping.*

Belladonna fought the urge to grab Kallie by the shoulders and yank her away from the nomad. She realized it was too late in any case. Whatever damage the hex venom could/would do to Kallie had already happened. The only thing Belladonna could do now was to help her friend conquer and dissipate the nasty trick.

Stepping over to the thickening shadow, Belladonna

reached into her leather bag and felt around for her bottle of uncrossing powder and pulled it free. She drew in a deep breath and centered herself as she focused every ounce of her attention on the tainted juju slicked like oil upon the floor.

The heady scents of sandalwood, five-finger grass, patchouli, and myrrh wafted into the air when Belladonna tapped the dark gold-and-green powder into her hand. "I call upon the powers of Gédé in the names of Baron Samedi and Maman Brigitte and ask for your help in unmaking this unholy trick." She traced a cross over the darkness oozing across the carpet.

A final twist of black wormed out from Kallie's foot and merged with the puddle.

Belladonna knelt beside the shadow, her heartbeat steady despite the fear icing the blood in her veins, and lifted her powder-filled palm to her lips. "Saint Michael, give me courage, and Saint Expedite, give me speed to end this bad trick once and for all before it claims another victim," she whispered. *"Au nom du Père, le Fils, le Saint Esprit, si soit-il."* She blew the powder into the liquid shadow.

The black puddle writhed as though touched by the finger of *bon Dieu*. Thick smoke stinking of bitter wormwood, seared pine, and the rotten-egg odor of sulfur fogged the air. Coughing, Belladonna fanned a hand in front of her face and rose to her feet. When the smoke cleared, the pool of blackness surrounding Kallie had vanished.

"Hellfire," Belladonna coughed.

"That's it, Layne, keep fighting, damn you," she heard Kallie mutter. "Don't you give up."

Belladonna glanced over to see the pixie lift her head and

sit back as the nomad's eyes fluttered open, dried blood flaking from his lashes. His heavy-lidded gaze fixed on Kallie.

"I *am* fighting, woman," he whispered. "Quit pummeling me."

The dark-haired swamp beauty in her red undies—filled out well enough to stop his heart again—quit pounding against Layne's chest and opened her eyes. Just mere pinpricks, her pupils, as though she'd been staring into the sun, her violet eyes gleaming with light and heat—a heat Layne felt inside of him with each renewed pulse of his heart.

She lay a trick on me, or am I just bewitched?

Kallie blinked, her expression perplexed. And for a split second, Layne had the weird sensation that she was thinking and feeling exactly the same things he was—until she spoke, her words suggesting otherwise.

"About time, dammit," she said, brushing sweat-damp tendrils of her dark coffee-colored hair from her face. "I was beginning to think you'd died just to spite me."

"Nope. Don't know you well enough to spite you."

"Give it time," she replied absently, pulling one dangling bra strap back up onto her shoulder.

"Shhh, you need to rest," another voice interjected. "Medics are on their way."

Layne recognized the soft, faded brogue. He turned his head and looked into McKenna's dark eyes. "Hey, buttercup," he said. "Don't think I need medics. Not now. What're you doin' here?"

She cupped her warm palm against his face. "Ye called me, luv. Now shut up and rest." She glanced at the bed, sorrow filling her eyes. "I'll check on our Gage."

As she started to rise to her feet, Layne grabbed her

arm, stopping her. "He's dead," he said, more roughly than he'd intended. "Don't touch him. Just leave him be."

Her dark eyes searching his, McKenna sat back down, crossing her legs underneath her. Layne slid his hand from her arm, the touch of her skin and the soft, palc down on her arm as familiar as his own flesh. And, as always, dammit, soothing.

"Mind telling me why?" McKenna asked. "Wha' happened to Gage and to you?"

"Hexed," Kallie volunteered. "And the trick that killed Gage still had enough juice to knock Layne on his ass when he touched him."

"A hex that's now gone," said a flannel-smooth voice. Layne looked up at Kallie's tall, slim-muscled friend with her halo of black and blue curls. She held up a half-empty bottle of amber dust. A satisfied, catlike smile stretched across her lips.

"Thanks, Bell," Kallie said.

McKenna looked at Kallie and her expression hardened. "And how did both men happen to get hexed in yer room?"

"I didn't lay the goddamned trick, so how the hell would I know?" Kallie replied, sitting back on her heels and meeting McKenna glare for glare.

Layne felt sick as he remembered what he'd felt—or rather what he *hadn't* felt—when he'd touched Gage and had tried to summon his clan-brother's spirit.

Absolutely nothing.

"Gage was more than hexed," Layne said. "I couldn't reach him."

"How is tha' possible?" McKenna asked. "Yer a Vessel and—"

"Maybe he'd already crossed over," Kallie cut in, earning herself another narrow-eyed glare from McKenna in the process.

"No. He hadn't fucking crossed over because there was nothing left of him *to* cross over. Nothing remains of him." Layne's voice was strained even to his own ears. "The hex not only swallowed his life, it ate his soul. Like it tried to eat mine."

FOUR

SOUL EATER

Fear slicked a finger down Kallie's spine. *Soul eater.* That kind of evil, that kind of blackest-of-the-black hex, required incredible power and was spoken of only in guarded whispers for fear of calling it down. She stared at her hands, pulse racing.

How the hell did I manage to reel the goddamned hex out of Layne and through me without it killing both of us, body and soul?

"Holy Mother," the little nomad breathed, distress darkening her eyes.

"Hellfire." Belladonna's gaze settled on the floor just behind Kallie. A muscle ticked near her left eye. "Jesus Christ."

"You sure?" Kallie whispered, meeting Layne's gaze.

"Wish I wasn't." Layne eased up onto his elbows, wincing. He touched his fingertips to his sternum. Winced again.

"I broke a few ribs," Kallie said. "Couldn't be helped."

"I'm alive, so I ain't complaining."

"You're welcome."

A smile brushed Layne's lips.

"Stay down," the little nomad gal said, glaring at Layne as if she were a towering basketball center and not a leprechaun. "Let me check ye over before ye do a man-stupid thing like get up and act like everything's all rosy and never been better."

"Hell, woman," Layne muttered. "You'd think we were still married. You lost the right to boss me around when we got divorced."

"I *never* bossed ye. Not once. Directed, maybe. Guided, sure. But never bossed," the black-haired leprechaun declared.

Layne snorted in reply.

"Hush up, you. Just lie down," the never-bossy ex-wife ordered. "I need to make sure yer all right."

With a resigned grunt, Layne eased back down onto the carpet. He looked at Kallie from beneath his blood-stained lashes. "By the way, this is McKenna. She's a shaman. McKenna, this is Kallie. She's a hoodoo."

"Charmed," McKenna said, her tone anything but.

"Be nice, Kenn," Layne warned.

"Oh, please, not on my account. I wouldn't want her to strain herself." Kallie flashed the nomad leprechaun a sweet-as-fresh-baked-apple-pie smile.

"Strain this." McKenna lifted a hand, then extended the middle finger, an equally sweet smile on her lips.

Looked like the leprechaun had some sass to her. Kallie couldn't help smiling again—but hopefully not in any kind of way that could be misconstrued as friendly.

"Hate to break up a good catfight and all," Belladonna said, her voice once again a velvet purr, "but paramedics and carnival security are on their way up. I suggest y'all get your shit together."

"Lovely," Kallie muttered.

McKenna bent over Layne and touched her fingertips to his temples. Her eyes closed. Kallie felt power flow from the woman and into Layne, power as deep and strong as an ancient river sure of its course. Power deeper even than Gabrielle's—and, until now, Kallie had never felt energy as intense as her *tante*'s.

Just who is this leprechaun anyhow?

Kallie studied Layne's fairy-sized former wife. Her small, sharp features cast the illusion of childlike youth, but now Kallie noticed the crow's-feet at the corners of her eyes and the laugh lines bracketing her sensual mouth. Still young and good-looking (okay, *really* good-looking), yes, but definitely older than Layne, maybe even by a good fifteen or twenty years.

Which one of them had ended the marriage? The way the leprechaun kept touching Layne made Kallie think the divorce was still fresh enough to act as an aphrodisiac—*must have you since you're no longer mine.*

Not that it was any of Kallie's concern. Well, maybe a little, given that she'd just saved the man's life. She frowned. Didn't that make her responsible for him? Not that she needed or wanted the responsibility, since she was still trying to figure out how to handle her own life, but still . . .

She remembered the shock that had tingled through her the first time she'd looked into Layne's green eyes, remembered the inner finger-to-the-lips hush that had followed.

"Here." Belladonna shoved a wad of pink material that smelled faintly of irises and green-tea-scented body lotion under Kallie's nose—Kallie's well-worn and comfy pink bathrobe. "All kinds of officials are going to be here any minute. And you shouldn't look like the stripper hired for a bachelor party."

"A *horror* movie bachelor party," McKenna murmured, opening her eyes and lifting her head. "The stripper of death." The little nomad's expression suggested she wasn't entirely kidding.

"I said be nice, woman," Layne growled. He sat up, pain crinkling the corners of his eyes and tightening his lips. But his pine-colored gaze held only humor.

Kallie snatched the robe from Belladonna's hand. She slid her errant bra strap back onto her shoulder again, then rose to her feet. Chin lifted and holding McKenna's gaze, she belted on the robe. "So how is he? Layne, I mean?"

McKenna shot her a sharp glance. "How do ye mean? In bed, or healthwise?"

Kallie blinked. "Healthwise! I'm sure he's fine in bed." When McKenna's lips parted as though to speak, Kallie hastily held up a hand and blurted, "No. Don't answer that. Totally not necessary."

"Hello, I'm right here," Layne said. "I'm fine. Dandy, even. In all ways. So I've been told."

"He's good, aye." A knowing smile curved McKenna's lips. "Now *healthwise*, I found no trace of foreign magic in him, and everything seems to be in working order. Thanks to you."

Kallie stared at her, decided the nomad's words were sincere, then shrugged one shoulder. "Well, okay, you're welcome, but I didn't do it for you."

"And now it's *your* turn to be nice, Shug," Belladonna murmured. "Give it a try."

"I *am* being nice." Kallie swiveled around to face Belladonna. "I wanna take a look at the bed before everyone swoops in and tosses us out. See if there's anything to indicate who mighta laid this goddamned trick."

Belladonna nodded, her curls bobbing. "Okay. And

may I point out that we're dealing with an enemy that wanted Gage *more* than dead—he wanted Gage erased from existence? That's a very special kinda hating. It also means we're in *way* over our heads."

"We need to contact our clan," Layne said. "This is nomad business. We'll deal with it."

"He's right," McKenna said.

"No offense, but where's your clan at right now?" Belladonna asked.

"Florida," Layne replied.

Belladonna perched a hand on her hip. "I don't think there's a whole lot they can do to help you at the moment. And something needs to be done *now*. Given that this is a murder-by-magic, I requested carnival authority, not the cops."

"Law involvement is the last thing we want," Kallie agreed. "The switched-off may not believe in magic or the supernatural, but they *do* believe in Manson-style madness, and that's how they'll see this. We need to find who did this to Gage and why."

"Oh, we'll find the bastard," Layne said, his voice cold and flat.

"Question is, how did the killer even know Gage would be here?" Kallie asked.

Belladonna tapped a blue-lacquered fingernail against her chin, her gaze on Layne. "If Gage told *you* about hooking up with Kallie, maybe he told someone else too."

"And the word got to the wrong person," Kallie said. "But why kill Gage with a potential witness present?"

"Maybe being passed out in the can saved you from dying too," Belladonna said. "Or maybe it made you convenient to pin the murder on. Did it look like anyone broke into the room? Was the door unlocked?"

Kallie shook her head. "I don't know. Not that I noticed, anyway. Maybe whoever it was had a passkey. Hell, what a mess."

"A *mess?*" Layne repeated. He looked at Gage's body on the bed. A muscle flexed in his jaw. "That what you call murder in your neck of the woods, hoodoo woman? A mess?"

Kallie bit her lower lip, wishing she could take back her poor choice of words. But they were already out there, and she knew from personal experience that more words would only fan the flames into a heart-devouring bonfire.

"Yo' mama wasn't herself, honey-girl. You were de moon at night for her, de sun during the day. Her life done revolved around you."

"Maybe it shouldn't-a. Maybe that's why she pulled the trigger."

"Kallie, no, don't even t'ink dat—"

"No one should ever live for anyone else."

Nothing anyone could say would stitch together a grief-torn heart. Only time eroded the rough edges and smoothed them away, like a river over rocks. But also like a river, time deepened the crevices carved within by violent loss. By betrayal.

"Sorry, baby, I ain't got a choice."

Kallie shut the memory down. Over and done with a helluva long time ago.

"No, I ain't calling murder a mess, Layne Valin," Kallie said, uncurling her fingers from her palms. "That wasn't what I meant, and I apologize."

She felt Belladonna staring at her. "You . . . what was the word you just used? *Apologize*? First 'please' and now 'apologize'? I think I need to sit down."

Cheeks heating, Kallie growled, "We're wasting time here, Bell." She walked around to the other side of the bed and drew back the stiffening sheets. Underneath Gage's body and the bloodstained sheets, she thought she saw something dark smeared on the mattress. Soul-eating juju. Her skin crawled.

Belladonna joined her. "How you wanna do this? We can't touch him without risking the sudden and urgent need for a defibrillator."

"We can use the pillows to push Gage's body away. I don't think we need to move him far."

Layne rose to his knees. "Let me do it. Hand me the pillows."

"No!" Kallie, Belladonna, and McKenna said in unison, a sensurround denial.

A hard rap at the door was accompanied by a metal-muffled request of "Paramedics. Open the door."

"Hurry," Kallie said, grabbing a blood-spattered pillow and tossing the other to Belladonna. Blue-ink tattoos curled along Gage's hips and up his back in curving Celtic designs, and her throat tightened as she remembered how she'd traced her fingers along some of them just a few hours ago.

Together, she and Belladonna pushed Gage's body a couple of feet away from the drying maroon stain beneath him.

"Open the door! Paramedics!" The knocking intensified.

Tracing a symbol for protection in the air, Kallie grabbed one corner of the fitted sheet and pulled it free of the mattress.

"Be careful, girl," Belladonna whispered.

"Totally my intention."

Kallie rolled the sheet down until a line of black dust appeared. Her mouth dried. A rotten-egg-and-burned-bone stench wafted into the air, mingling with the fresher odor of Gage's blood. She pushed the bloodstained material aside, revealing the hex in its blackest-of-black glory: a smudged two-foot-wide *X* traced across the mattress in deadly black dust.

Snake scales glittered in the powder, a powder in all likelihood composed of graveyard dirt, black salt, ground sulfur and bones, and rattlesnake skin with magnetic sand, blood, and, most likely, pigeon shit added into the mix.

Gage's enemy had been a hoodoo or maybe a voodoo *bokor,* and had laid down the nastiest of tricks using goofer dust—a trick designed to kill an enemy. But not a soul-eating spell, unless something new had been added.

Something that I funneled through my body.

"Layne, did Gage piss off a hoodoo or anyone with ties to voodoo?" Kallie asked, unable to tear her gaze away from the murderous trick dusting the bed.

"Not that I know of," Layne replied.

"Y'know, Shug, I hate to say this," Belladonna said quietly, "but I got a feeling that hex wasn't designed for Gage. It was designed for you."

FIVE

DEAD IN ALL WAYS POSSIBLE

"What? Me?" Kallie jerked her gaze up from the body-smudged lines of black dust on the mattress and stared at Belladonna. "Designed for *me*?"

"And a good man died because it fooking well missed," McKenna muttered, her brogue thickening, as she walked to the door and opened it.

Two grim-faced male paramedics in blue slacks and white shirts hurried into the room, carrying a defibrillator and other equipment. They beelined for the bed and the motionless man half-buried in pillows.

"No!" Kallie cried. "He's dead. Don't touch him!" She pointed at Layne still kneeling on the floor and looking pale and drawn. "He's the one you need to check over. He suffered a cardiac arrest."

Layne's dreads slipped free of their knot and swung against his back when he shook his head in denial. He opened his mouth to protest, but the paramedics knelt on either side of him and one started firing questions—"What's your name, podna? How old are you? Any history of heart problems?"—while the other wrapped a blood pressure cuff around Layne's well-defined biceps.

"Dammit," Layne grumbled. "This ain't necessary. I'm okay."

"It *is* necessary," Kallie said. "His heart stopped, and he quit breathing. We had to perform CPR."

The medic asking questions switched his attention to Kallie. "How long before he started breathing again?"

Kallie shook her head. "I'm not sure, to be honest. It seemed like forever, but it was probably only a couple of minutes. Oh, and I think I broke a few of his ribs in the process too."

Layne arrowed a dark look her way. "I *said* I'm okay. I've broken ribs before."

"Yer being man-stupid again," McKenna said, joining the small huddle on the floor. "Let them look you over."

"*You* checked me. I'm fine." Layne peeled the blood pressure cuff from his arm, the ripping sound of Velcro silencing his ex-wife. "I'm refusing treatment."

"Man-stupid."

"That's right. And proud of it."

"Kallie?"

"Hmmm?" Kallie pulled her gaze away from the nomad-to-nomad glaring match and looked at Belladonna.

"Nobody sneaked into your room and did this while you were passed out on the floor," Belladonna whispered. "This was done much earlier, maybe when housekeeping was tidying your room. *Before* you hooked up with Gage. Whoever did this was trying to kill *you*."

"And Gage climbed into bed while I stumbled off to the bathroom," Kallie whispered. "Shit, shit, goddamn." She dropped the sheet back over the hex, then sank to her knees on the carpet, her pulse pounding at her temples. Her headache reawakened. She closed her eyes.

A dark voice, one that sounded like Mama's, whispered: "*See? I'm not the only one who knows you need to die, baby, and it looks like I'm not the only one willing to do what's necessary.*"

Kallie caught a whiff of patchouli as Belladonna crouched down beside her. She felt the strength in her friend's slender-muscled arm as it laced around her shoulders.

"I know what you're thinking," Belladonna said, voice low, "but security's pretty tight at Saint Dymphna's. Your mama couldn't—" She stopped speaking, and Kallie opened her eyes.

McKenna stood on the other side of the bed, her weight on one hip, her arms crossed over her chest. "So who wants you dead in all ways possible, Kallie Hoodoo?"

Good question, and one Kallie didn't have an answer for. At least, not an answer she cared to voice aloud. Slipping free of Belladonna's embrace, she rose to her feet, then offered her friend a hand up.

"What about that ex-boyfriend stalker you laid the shriveling trick on?" Belladonna grasped Kallie's hand and uncurled her slender and elegant body up from the floor. "Whenever he got within a hundred yards of you, his goodies withered up like old prunes."

"That trick was better than any restraining order," Kallie said, smiling grimly at the memory. "Tommy was no conjurer, though. He couldn't've done this."

"He could've hired one," Belladonna said, squeezing Kallie's hand before letting go of it. "You don't mess with a man's junk like that."

"You do if he deserves it," Kallie retorted. "But even so, you hire someone to put a hurting on me, you don't hire someone to kill my soul along with my body."

"Most men, aye," McKenna said. "But I've known a

few in my time who wouldn't've hesitated to rip a lass's soul from her body just fer refusing their touch."

In my time? McKenna spoke like she truly was an ancient leprechaun and not a woman in her mid-thirties or forties. Kallie shook her head. "Tommy was obsessive, not homicidal, and I doubt he would've even known such a thing was possible."

"Hate to say it, Pix—um . . . McKenna, but it sounds to me like you've been looking for love in all the wrong places," Belladonna commented, her gaze sweeping the nomad from head to foot—a very short trip.

"Thanks," Layne growled, rising to his feet. He pushed his dreads back from his face—a handsome face, really, with those sharp cheekbones and that mouth made for kissing—with both hands, then turned to face the bed and all that remained of his best friend. Sorrow reawakened in his eyes.

"Excuse me, but what is the situation here?" A plump woman in a charcoal-gray business suit, her auburn hair tucked into an unraveling bun, whisked into the room. A name tag on her jacket read: *Maria Conti, Prestige Manager*.

Rising to his feet, one of the paramedics nodded at Layne. "He refuses treatment. And the other one is dead."

"Dead?" The manager's gaze landed on the bed. Her eyes widened. "Holy Mother of God," she whispered.

"I have a feeling, Mrs. Conti, that the Sainted Mum's voicemail box is full," a male voice said, smooth and dry and very British. "And at the very least she and her holy Son are screening their messages."

A tall man in his late thirties or early forties wearing a pale gray suit and a slim cobalt-blue tie eased past the manager's motionless form and sauntered into the room, one hand tucked into his front trouser pocket as though he were taking the air during a morning stroll.

For reply, the grim-faced and now pale Prestige manager crossed herself.

The Brit brushed a wavy lock of nutmeg-brown hair away from his deep-set gray eyes with a practiced sweep of a long-fingered hand. His gaze landed on Layne and lingered for several moments before shifting to scrutinize Gage's body on the bed.

"Wouldn't you agree, Ms. Rivière?" the Brit asked, lifting his eyes to Kallie.

"Depends on the god," Kallie said. "Most are pretty damned fickle and more than likely to hit the Delete button instead of returning calls."

"Indeed." Something between a smile and smirk twisted up one corner of the Brit's mouth.

The fact that this official-looking stranger not only recognized Kallie but also knew her name didn't leave her feeling all warm and fuzzy with joy. She lifted her chin. "Excuse me, you are . . . ?"

"Lord Basil Augustine," Layne answered in a low drawl. "Master of the Hecatean Alliance."

One of the Brit's dark eyebrows quirked up at Layne's words. His gaze swept the nomad from head to toe. Again. "And here I thought nomads refused to acknowledge any kind of authority. Or even bother to learn what it might be."

"Ain't acknowledging," Layne replied, rolling his shoulders back despite the pain it must've cost him. "Just naming."

"Hellfire," Belladonna breathed. "Lord Basil Augustine."

Goddamned hellfire, indeed. Kallie was pretty damned sure Belladonna had the right of it. Gabrielle's words about the Hecatean Alliance's so-called master whispered through Kallie's memory: *"Man's got horns under all dat dark hair, I just know it. He be too smug and fulla pride. T'inks he knows what be best for all of us—practitioners and switched-off alike. He gonna reawaken the witch-burning days, see if he don't."*

Shoving her hands into the pockets of her robe, Kallie studied the man who had organized magicians, conjurers, and rootworkers into a connected fraternity guided by laws established to keep magic practitioners safe and secret and the switched-off safe, secure, and unaware.

In theory.

He'd also organized an annual carnival for magical society to unwind, share notes, and hook up, a wild and wicked week to celebrate May and each other. And for the last forty years—*huh, man must be older than he looks*—since it had begun, the May Madness Carnival had been the only opportunity for magic users from all parts of the world to meet in peace, no matter their beliefs or the type of magic they practiced.

"Carnival of Fools—dat's what it be. Hoodoos would be wise to keep away. Of all the many t'ings you are, girl, a fool ain't one of dem. Stay home. Carnival ain't de place for you."

Kallie's gut knotted. She was beginning to wish she'd listened to Gabrielle. If Belladonna had it right and the hex *had* been intended for her and not Gage, then the nomad would still be alive if she'd only stayed home.

"Excuse me, Lord Augustine," the hotel manager said, shaking free of her shock and stepping up beside him. "But we need to call the police and report this . . . death."

"Of course," Augustine said, voice low, "and we would

if the young man was actually dead, Mrs. Conti." Withdrawing his hand from his trouser pocket, he reached inside his suit and slipped free a silver cigarette case.

Mrs. Conti and the perplexed paramedics stared at the Brit as he opened the case, selected a brown cigarette, and placed it between his lips.

"He appears to be quite dead, my lord," Mrs. Conti said finally. "His eyes . . . the blood alone . . ."

Augustine sparked up the cigarette with a slim silver lighter. He nodded, then exhaled a plume of pale smoke into the air. The sharp smell of anise-and-vanilla-scented tobacco curled into the room.

"The key word, Mrs. Conti, would be *appears*."

"I'm afraid I don't understand," the hotel manager said, a frown creasing the skin between her eyes.

Kallie had to agree with Maria Conti. She wondered if Augustine believed himself a Jedi master using the Force on hapless bystanders.

These aren't the droids you're looking for.

"But this *is* carnival, and these young people are playing pranks on us, yes?" A pleasant smile crinkled the skin at the corners of the Brit's eyes as he emphasized his words with graceful movements of his hand, the cigarette trailing sweet-scented smoke through the air.

Tracing enchantment sigils. Crafting illusion.

Kallie caught a hint of an earthy undertone in the smoke—frankincense, or myrrh—along with a whisper of gardenia. Power thickened in the air with each twirl of Augustine's hand, streaming into Kallie's lungs with every breath.

"That's why we didn't want you to touch him," Layne said, nodding at the paramedics and wading into the lie with all the ease of a longtime pro. "We knew you'd blow the whole prank otherwise."

Augustine glanced at the nomad, brow arched. "Indeed. The young man is only pretending to be dead. Wine stains the sheets, not blood," he said, his tone a low and soothing singsong. A soft command. "Please look again."

A gray veil created by the perfumed smoke descended over Gage's body, and it seemed even to Kallie that the nomad lifted his head and smiled a *gotcha* grin. Her blood chilled.

Maria Conti studied Gage's body, the pupils of her eyes nearly swallowing the irises. Relief restored rosy color to her cheeks. "Ah," she breathed. "I was completely fooled."

The paramedics, eyes equally dilated, shook their heads, looking unhappy. "Shee-it. Our time's been wasted," one muttered. "Y'all can expect a bill for that time too."

"Of course, and please accept my apologies," Augustine said, his voice and expression sincere. "Trust me, I'm not pleased with this little stunt either. The perpetrators *will* be disciplined."

The hotel manager nodded, and another tendril of auburn hair escaped her fraying bun. "As they should be. And we shall leave you to it, Lord Augustine." Touching one of the paramedics on the forearm and speaking to him in low, sympathetic tones, she followed him and his partner out of the room, closing the door behind her.

"Which one of you bloody idiots called the paramedics?" Augustine asked, stubbing his cigarette out in an empty champagne flute. The illusion of life wisped away from Gage's body along with the snuffed smoke.

"I'm the bloody idiot," Kallie said, not sure who had actually called and not really caring. The Brit's snippy tone stiffened her spine. "And as far as I know, when someone goes into cardiac arrest, doing CPR and calling the paramedics are the right things to do."

Augustine looked at her, his face cold as marble. "Not when you have the body of a man murdered by magic in the room, Ms. Rivière. Just how had you planned on explaining his death to the police?"

Kallie glanced at the bed, at Gage's body. "I don't know," she admitted. She caught a whiff of tobacco and musky incense as Augustine walked around the bed to stand beside her, his gaze on the black-dust hex on the mattress.

"Looks like a hoodoo trick," he murmured. "And you *are* a hoodoo, are you not, Ms. Rivière?"

"So? I ain't the only one here. And I had nothing to do with this."

"So she claims," McKenna interjected.

"She's the intended victim, not the hexer," Belladonna said, hands on her hips, leveling a Class One Belladonna Brown Death Glare at the leprechaun. "And she saved your ex's life, by the way."

"Not just my life. She saved my soul too." Layne eased down into one of the blue cushioned armchairs near the flat-screen TV at the foot of the bed, one arm angled tight against his sternum. He nodded at the bed. "That's a soul-killing spell. And it almost had me." His gaze came to rest on Kallie, direct and intense.

Butterflies winged through Kallie's belly when she met Layne's pine-green eyes. "It could've had us both," she said softly. She glanced down at Gage's body, and her butterflies disappeared beneath a surge of guilt.

"Your *soul*? And how do you know this?" Augustine questioned, slanting a sharp glance from beneath his brows at the nomad.

"I'm a Vessel," Layne said. "And that hex destroyed Gage's soul when it killed him."

Augustine arched an eyebrow. "Ah, so *you're* Layne Valin, the nomad Vessel my assistant told me about. I hope the dead haven't troubled you during your stay?"

"No, not yet."

"Good. Well, I must admit this situation is very intriguing, if true. The kind of power needed for soul-killing is rare." Augustine glanced at Kallie. "Perhaps, Ms. Rivière, if you would start at the beginning?"

Just as Kallie opened her mouth, the phone on the bedside table trilled. Everyone stared at the phone like it was a cotton-candy-sticky child screeching for attention while the adults tried to have a conversation; then everyone looked at her, frowns of various shapes, sizes, and intensities on their faces.

Child needs to learn manners. What kinda mama are you?

One that hands out goddamned cotton candy. Go screw yourselves.

Blowing out her breath in frustration, Kallie hurried to the table and snatched up the receiver. Before she could even say hello, an urgent voice—familiar and unexpected and brimming with the bayou—said, "Hon, you need to be very careful. I see *beaucoup* big trouble on yo' doorstep."

"It's already here, Gabrielle," Kallie said, her pulse picking up speed. "Can you tell me who sent it?"

"I see the King of Spades lying across the Ten of Spades."

Jail, imprisonment. Bad luck caused by a man.

"But dat ain't all, girl. I got a pair of black aces here staring at me."

Kallie's fingers tightened around the receiver. Ace of Spades and Ace of Clubs. *Death.* "It's already happened," she said quietly, wishing she could talk to her *tante* alone. "It was meant for me, but someone else died instead."

"Sweet Jesus. You all right, girl? Who died?"

"Who are you talking to, Ms. Rivière?" Augustine asked. "I'm afraid you can't discuss this matter with anyone at the moment."

"Who de hell be dat? You got one-a dem fools in yo' room? Sounds like a *British* fool."

Kallie waved a just-a-minute hand at Augustine, then said into the phone, "Yeah, a carnival official. No one important."

"Listen to me—the danger ain't over, child. I read de shells along with de cards, and de only pattern de shells revealed was dat of darkness and chaos."

Death. Night. Ancestors. Destiny about to be disrupted. As the meanings for that particular pattern fanned through Kallie's mind, her blood grew colder. "Mama . . . is she . . . I mean, she ain't . . . ?"

"No, hon, no," Gabrielle said, her voice soft and soothing, a tucked-safe-in-your-bed lullaby. "Your mama's still in Saint Dymphna's."

Kallie closed her eyes as relief trickled through her. "So what do I do?"

Gabrielle tsked, the softness vanishing from her voice with all the speed of a yanked-away blanket. "Dat fool carnival's already done rubbed off on you. Do some protection spells, girl, and take a bath—the blessed thistle one—to wash dat crossing away. Psalm 68, too, girl. Don't forget yo' Psalms. Stick close to Belladonna, you shouldn't be alone. And get yo' heinie home as soon as it's safe."

"It was a hoodoo trick, if that makes any difference," Kallie said, deciding just that moment to keep mum about the soul-killing aspect of the hex. No need to add to Gabrielle's worries.

Some one hundred miles and change away, her aunt said, "It might. Is Belladonna dere with you? If she is, let me talk to her."

"Why? I'm a grown woman and a more than capable hoodoo, and I can craft spells and potion up a bath just as good as she can."

"Mmm-hmm. Did you happen to bring any of dem potions or oils or incense or mojo hands with you?"

Oops. Swiveling around, Kallie extended the receiver to Belladonna. "She wants to talk to you."

Surprise flickered in Belladonna's hazel eyes as Kallie handed her the phone. Belladonna held it to her ear and, after a brief pause, started saying, "Yes, ma'am. That's right, ma'am. I do, as a matter of fact, ma'am."

Kallie turned around and met Augustine's cold gray gaze. "My aunt," she explained. "She just did a reading and—"

"I don't care if she just performed handsprings across the Atlantic," the Brit said. "You are *not* to discuss what is going on here with anyone."

"She simply called with information," Kallie said. "What's got your boxers in a twist?"

"Aside from the murdered man lying on the bed right in front of us? *Your* bed?"

Kallie looked at Gage and the sight of his bloodied face jabbed her heart. If she'd just stayed home, he'd be alive, maybe sleeping off a hangover, maybe snuggled up warm against another tipsy May pole dancer, maybe sitting with Layne and laughing.

"I need some air," Kallie whispered. As she rounded the bed, Augustine stopped her with a hand to her biceps. A light touch, but firm. And one that sparked a firestorm inside, one she struggled to control.

One-Mississippi. Two-Mississippi . . .

"Get your goddamned hand off me."

"I'm afraid your quest for fresh air will have to wait, Ms. Rivière," he said. His hand remained right where it was. "You are not to leave the room, not until we get things, including your role in them, sorted out."

Three-Mississippi. Four-Mississippi . . .

"Get your goddamned hand off me."

Something cold and dark and ancient like a primeval forest full of striding giants flashed to life within the gray depths of Augustine's eyes. Kallie's skin goosebumped.

"Or what?" he asked.

Five-Mississippi. Six . . . Aw, to hell with it.

"Or this." Kallie hammered a hard-knuckled fist into Augustine's jaw.

SIX

ROOT DOCTOR

Belladonna Brown, in a red miniskirt and halter top, sashays into Dallas Brûler's dreams and leans a rounded hip against his herb-and-root-cluttered worktable.

"I hear you have potions to fix up anything that might ail a woman," she says.

Dallas sets aside his mortar and pestle and straightens. "Depends on what's ailing you, sugar," he replies, a smile playing across his lips as he allows his gaze to take its own sweet time caressing the luscious curves and pushed-up cleavage on display.

"You, Dallas Brûler, you gorgeous hunk of man, you're *what's ailing me." She hurries around his table, flings herself onto the wood floor at his feet, and wraps her arms around his thigh. He suddenly feels like the centerpiece—albeit a white one—in a '70s blaxploitation movie poster. Not a bad thing.*

She looks up at him with lusting eyes. "I gotta have you. It's the only way to stop this never-ending ache."

Dallas realizes his clothes have vanished and he's standing in boxers, Belladonna's hands warm against his bare thighs.

Nice. Nude woulda been even better, but . . . hey, this works. *"And where is this ache, sweet thing?"*

"Should I show you?" The tip of Belladonna's tongue touches her

deep plum-glossed lips, and Dallas feels his boxers tenting as he imagines her tongue and lips elsewhere. "Should I show you where the ache is?"

"By all means, let's take a look." Dallas bends and helps her up to her feet. "They don't call me Doctor Snake for nothing, darlin'."

"That's my deepest hope." With a coy flutter of her lashes, Belladonna grabs the hem of her skirt and slowly inches it up her dark, bare thighs.

Dallas drops to his knees. His fingers caress her revealed flesh, and he follows the skirt's path up with his hungry lips. As he kisses her through her purple panties, her hoo-hah suddenly jingles and trills. Insistently. He looks up at her. "Darlin', you're ringing."

"I hope you're answering," she purrs. "Please, please, please answer. Now!"

Jingle-jingle-jingle. JINGLE-JINGLE-JINGLE!

Dallas jerked awake. Squinting in the rosy dawn light, he slipped a hand underneath the waistband of his boxers trying to recapture his dream—Belladonna, of all women! But a *nice* Belladonna. *Very* nice—then realized he was still hearing the shrill jingling.

With a groan, he pulled his hand free and fumbled for the ringing phone. He snagged the receiver and dropped it once, earning himself a sharp *ding!* from the phone, before he managed to tuck the receiver against his ear. "You ruined a damned fine dream, podna," he growled, "so this had better be *real* fucking good."

"Be dat how you say hello, Dallas Brûler? I'm sure yo' mama taught you better manners," Gabrielle LaRue said.

Dallas sat up in bed, wide-awake, and suddenly feeling twelve and not thirty-two. And definitely no longer horny. "Gabrielle, I'm sorry, I thought one o' the guys was messing with me." He scrubbed a hand through his hair. His gaze flicked to the empty pint bottle of Wild Turkey on the nightstand. He closed his eyes. "Busy night."

"You need to get yo' heinie out of bed and moving," Gabrielle said. "I just talked to Kallie and she says someone tried to lay a nasty trick on her, but it done ended up killing some other poor soul instead."

Dallas's eyes flew open. "What the fuck? She was fine when I last saw her. She was with some nomad conjurer . . ."

"*Was fine* be right, boy," Gabrielle said. "I t'ought I sent you to watch de girl, not have *busy* nights. You need to find out what's going on. I just did a reading and de cards and de shells showed me a few t'ings I don't much care for."

"What kinda things?"

"I think Kallie's going to be accused of murder by dat foolish Hecatean Alliance and jailed. We can't allow dat."

"Jesus Christ. What happens if she is—jailed, I mean?"

"We can't allow dat," Gabrielle repeated, her hard and flat voice brooking no nonsense or failure. "Now you go make sure it don't happen."

"What if I'm too late?" Dallas asked, then added before Gabrielle could answer him, "and what if the cards were wrong about the danger they warned you about all those years ago?"

"Hush, boy. The *loa* be listening, and dey don't like being called liars. Neither do I."

"I'm sorry, ma'am, I didn't mean to imply anyone was a liar, just that a mistake mighta been made."

"No mistake. You be a root doctor, Dallas Brûler, one *I* trained—so you tell me, how many times de cards been wrong for you?"

Dallas trailed a hand through his hair. He sighed.

"Cards ain't never been wrong," he admitted. "But sometimes I am."

Gabrielle snorted. "Meaning you be human. Me too. But Kallie ain't, not completely, dat is. You need to find out who died and how, and if she be guilty of it or not, den—no matter what—keep her outta Hecatean hands."

"Like I said, what if it's too late?" Dallas bent and scooped his jeans up from the beige carpet. Balancing the phone receiver between his cheek and shoulder, he stood and pulled on his jeans, zipping them up.

"Den you let me know." Gabrielle's voice suddenly sounded weary and wrung out. "And I'll be dere as soon as I can to take care of my girl."

Dallas's fingers paused at his belt buckle. Her unspoken words iced his spine. *For the last time*. "I'll do my best to make sure that ain't necessary, Gabrielle."

"You a good man, Dallas Brûler," Gabrielle said, ending the call.

Dallas plopped the receiver back into its cradle. Yeah, he had a feeling Kallie wouldn't agree with that if she knew the only reason he was in New Orleans attending the carnival was to keep a close eye on her at her aunt's request. And if she learned the reason why . . .

He hurried to the dresser across from the bed and, as he rummaged through his opened suitcase for a clean shirt, his thoughts returned to the long, intense conversation he'd shared with Gabrielle a few weeks ago in the ivy-and-jasmine-draped courtyard of her Circle of Protection botanica in Bayou Cyprès Noir.

"De loa *done revealed a dark secret to me, Dallas. One I been keeping for years."*

Unsettling words, for true. But those words had

nothing on the ones that had followed from his former mentor's lips, each word taut and knotted and rough like hand-twisted rope. A rope leading into a tar-black pit.

"A seed done been planted inside de girl, a seed dat can never be allowed to blossom. If it does, Dallas-boy, den somet'ing more wicked den long-fallen Babylon and crueler den hell will walk de earth once more."

He remembered his own question: *"How will we keep the seed from blossoming?"*

And Gabrielle's answer: *"You keep it away from de t'ings dat make it grow. Dis seed craves darkness and strife and blood. We gotta make sure it don't get dem. Gotta make sure de seed ain't fed."*

Dallas touched his fingers to the red flannel mojo bag hanging on a leather cord around his neck. He pinched it, releasing the pungent and protective scents of sandalwood and five-finger grass into the air.

"Gotta make sure de seed ain't fed."

Sounded like someone else had just tried to do the very opposite.

Dallas buttoned on a teal long-sleeved shirt, his fingers working the pearl buttons with record speed; then, leaving it hanging over his jeans, he tugged on his Durangos.

Dallas nabbed his keycard from the nightstand and headed for the door. He paused, hearing footsteps—quiet and full of purpose—approaching from the other side of the door. The hair prickled on the back of his neck. Somehow he had a feeling it wasn't just the maid with her smooth café-au-lait skin and tight platinum-blonde curls, carrying an armload of fresh towels.

Pulse racing, Dallas inched away from the door and put his back against the wall. He lifted his tight-knuckled fists up against his chest, in prime position to launch a knockout jab or bell-ringing roundhouse swing. He held his breath. Listened.

But the door latch didn't jiggle as someone tried it, or swing open to admit a furtive shape. No one knocked. Dallas only heard the soft sound of steps padding *away*.

Well, hell. Dallas blew out his breath and lowered his fists. Flexed his fingers. Maybe it *had* been the pretty little maid with her cap of bright curls and liquid shadow-dark eyes, after all.

He tried to remember if he'd hung up the DO NOT DISTURB sign when he'd staggered back to his room last night, pint of Wild Turkey in hand. Unlocking the door, he swung it open. Empty hall. No cart full of fresh linen and cleaning supplies. No maid.

Then Dallas glanced down.

A bucket of water stood in front of his door. And at the bucket's bottom Dallas saw a hand-stitched poppet wrapped in chains, its red yarn hair undulating in the water.

Chest suddenly tight, Dallas coughed. He tasted bitter wormwood and ashes as water bubbled up from his lungs and filled his mouth. He tried to kick over the metal bucket, but he fell to his knees instead, choking.

Drowning.

The Brit staggered back a step, his expression shocked blank, and Kallie jerked free of his hold. She raced to the door, threw it open, and dashed down the hall for the elevators.

"Are you outta your mind?" Belladonna asked, her voice coming from right behind Kallie. "You can't go around punching people! Especially not the master of the Hecatean Alliance."

"Why the hell not?"

"Oh, no, you don't. I'm *not* having this conversation with you again."

"Hey, he was the one who asked 'Or what?'" Kallie said, breathless. "All I did was answer his question."

"Girl, you need to learn to use words, *not* your fists, to answer questions. Did you count to ten?"

"Of course," Kallie lied.

"Mmm-hmmm. You'll be lucky if he doesn't outlaw your ass."

"He can outlaw every goddamned inch of me. I don't give a good goddamn."

"Y'know that's what I meant, right? All of you—not just your ass? Though that'd be pretty damned interesting."

Kallie ignored her. Halting at the elevator doors, she slapped her palm against the Down button. The arrow pointing down lit up orange.

"Where we going, by the way?" Belladonna asked, stopping beside her.

"Other than away? Goddamned if I know. I just need to think. You don't need to jump off the cliff with me. Go on back. You ain't in trouble and—"

"Ever heard of guilt by association?" Belladonna cut in. "Besides, I promised Gabrielle. Let's go to my room. Get you calmed down and into something more useful for a walk outside than a pink bathrobe."

Kallie glanced down at herself. "Good idea, but isn't your room the first place they'll look for us?" She nodded a polite good morning at the couple standing on the opposite side of the elevator doors and tugged her bathrobe belt a pull tighter. The couple, dressed casually for breakfast in shorts, pentacle-laced tees, and fanny packs pretending to be hip wallets, cautiously returned the nod.

"Yeah, most likely, that's why you'll be in the Wiccan's room across the hall while I grab clothes." Belladonna tapped the Up button.

"Will the Wiccan be okay with that?"

"Given that I've caught him spying on you with binoculars, I think he'll be more than okay with that. Just be sure to jiggle a bit."

Spying? Binoculars? *Jiggle?*

Before Kallie could untangle a proper retort, a flash of movement down the hall drew her gaze. Basil Augustine stood in the center of the hall's Persian carpet, rubbing his jaw and speaking into a slim cell phone. He turned to face the elevators, but remained where he was. Just watching. And speaking into the cell. Goddamned lovely.

Kallie swiveled around and stabbed the Up button one more time. "C'mon, already," she muttered. Beyond the closed steel doors, cables groaned and creaked.

"Maybe we should take the stairs," Belladonna said. "It's only two flights."

"Another good idea." Kallie hurried over to the door marked EXIT and pushed it open. She raced up the stairs, her bare feet slapping against the concrete, Belladonna just a step behind her. Shoving through the exit door onto the sixth floor, Kallie trotted down the hall, glancing automatically at the gold numbers on the doors as she passed.

"What's the goddamned spying Wiccan's room number?"

"Room 632—just up ahead and to the right."

A woman's shrill scream raked across Kallie's taut

nerves like badger claws. Adrenaline poured like jet fuel through her veins, propelled by years of Gabrielle's teaching: *Never turn yo' back on another in need, honey-girl. Help and heal, always. No matter de cost to yo'self.*

She bolted down the hall, swinging to the right, then came to a dead stop. Magic ripe with a rotten-egg-and-bitter-wormwood stench thickened the air.

Surrounded by scattered bed linen, a man lay sprawled on the hall floor, half in and half out of his room, his hands at his throat. Water gleamed on his face and dampened the carpet around him, soaked his hair. A hotel maid with long, dark ringlets framing her face knelt beside him, her expression uncertain, a wad of towels clutched in her hands. She looked up at Kallie.

"Get away! Don't touch him!" Kallie yelled.

The maid scooted away from the man, her dark eyes shifting from uncertain to fearful. Across the hall and a few doors down, another maid with toffee-colored skin and blond curls stood in an open doorway, her hand on the handle of a vacuum, her eyes wide with shock.

Kallie burned rubber down the hall and dropped to her knees beside the man, then realized with a shock that she knew him. "Dallas?" she said.

Good God, couldn't the man go *anywhere* without someone trying to kill him?

This was the man she'd idolized ever since he'd sat down beside her on Gabrielle's porch steps her first night there and had spoken to her like she was an adult and not a wounded kid who needed to be surrounded with emotional packing peanuts before conversation.

"I hear your mama killed your papa and tried to kill you. That's fucked up, for true. But in no way was it your fault. I don't care if you

were the worst brat on earth or not. Don't make a difference. I'll teach ya how to fix some tricks to keep people from messing with you—if you wanna learn."

And she'd very much wanted to learn. Idolized Dallas, yeah. Crushed on, ditto. But often he deliberately made caring for him difficult. And for the last couple of years, he'd made it damned near impossible as he eased his wounded heart with booze and women. Now she thought of him as more of an older brother or young uncle. One who was always in goddamned trouble.

At the sound of Kallie's voice, Dallas looked at her; tendrils of wet red hair clung to his temples and forehead. Water spilled from his gasping mouth, and panic glimmered deep in his blue eyes.

Belladonna whistled. "Holy . . . Is that who I think it is? Wonder who he pissed off *this* time?"

"No telling. Hold on, Dallas," Kallie said, wrapping her arms around his cold, wet shoulders and trying to lift him up into a sitting position. "Just hold on, *cher*."

"Get him on his side." Belladonna's voice was calm and practical. "He's drowning."

Kallie struggled to roll Dallas onto his side, but he felt as heavy as a pile of steel crossbeams and, without a freaking crane, just as immovable. An alarm triggered inside of her. Sure, Dallas stood over six feet, lean-muscled and athletic, but she should be able to roll him over. This was all wrong.

"Help me, Bell. He's too heavy." With Belladonna's help, Kallie managed to roll Dallas onto his side. But that didn't help. Water still streamed from his mouth and nose. His struggles for air grew weaker.

The maid said, "I'll get help."

"No! No outside help," Kallie insisted.

But, perhaps deciding that Kallie was confused, the maid jumped to her feet, and raced down the hall, so eager to be gone she left behind her cart, the linens she'd dropped, and even her bucket of water. The mingled odors of wormwood and pine drifted up from the bucket's interior.

Wormwood? Not your usual cleanser.

Releasing her hold on Dallas, Kallie leaned over and peered into the water-filled bucket. Her heart hammered against her ribs when she saw the doll with red yarn hair anchored to the bucket's bottom with chains.

Kallie grabbed the bucket and dumped it out on the carpet. "Goddammit, Bell, more black work."

Belladonna glanced over her shoulder. "What do you wanna bet it's a gift from an unhappy husband or boyfriend?"

"Could also be connected with the hex in my room," Kallie said.

"Oh. Well. Could be, yeah."

Dallas choked, then coughed, before sucking in a ragged breath of air. Then he coughed some more, the sound sandpaper raw.

"That's it," Belladonna said. "Just stay on your side. Water out, air in."

Kallie snatched up the doll and unwrapped what looked like a bike chain from around its cloth body. She dropped the chain. It landed on the carpet with a soft squelch. She examined the doll and the expert blanket stitch holding it together. A basic poppet, nothing fancy, but you didn't need fancy to get the job or a nasty trick done.

She picked up one of the towels the maid had dropped and spread it out. "You got scissors on you, Bell?" she asked.

"That I do," Belladonna said. "A *mambo* is always prepared."

"Do y'all get badges and sashes like the Scouts?" Kallie asked, holding out her hand.

Belladonna snorted. "Scouts. Girl, please." She dropped her cuticle scissors into Kallie's waiting palm. "Scouts don't know diddly about being prepared. They think being able to rub two sticks together when they need a fire and knowing how to deal with a rabid squirrel are survival skills, but what would happen if they ran up against a *loa* pissed off about the poor offerings left on a graveyard altar? They'd run and scream like little girls."

"*Boy* Scouts, sure." Kallie used the cuticle scissors to snip open the doll's seams. "What would Girl Scouts do?"

"No doubt they'd stand frozen, mouths hanging open, eyes bugging out. Would *not* be attractive. But at least they'd be quiet."

"Nothing quite like silent terror," Kallie agreed as she opened up the doll and dumped out its contents onto the towel. Spanish moss and ivy root; dirt—most likely from a graveyard; powder smelling of bitter wormwood, sulfur, and pine; a small piece of ribbed white fabric. She'd bet anything it'd been cut or torn from one of Dallas's tees.

And, curled up like a rain-drunk earthworm, a small twist of paper with *Dallas Brûler* written on it in smeared red ink over and over.

Kallie nudged the paper with a bathrobe-protected fingertip. It flipped over, revealing smudged black letters reading: *Compliments of Gabrielle LaRue.*

She stared at the words, pulse pounding in her temples, trying to make sense of them. Whoever was doing this was one sick jackass. No way would Gabrielle try to harm, let alone kill, Dallas. Or her. Someone was playing some very twisted games.

Sure about that?

"Sorry, baby, I ain't got a choice."

Kallie felt sick, lightheaded. She swiveled around on her knees to face Dallas and Belladonna, the intensity of the root doctor's coughing summoning up the image of Gabrielle's pair of black aces. *Death.*

The mojo bag hanging around Dallas's throat hadn't been powerful enough to protect him from the jinxed poppet.

Soul-eating hexes. Poppets more powerful than a strong and *beaucoup* skilled root doctor. Fear sawed along her nerves. What the hell was going on?

"Kallie, go," Dallas rasped, rolling onto his hands and knees. "You gotta—" But whatever he intended to say was lost in another lung-scraping coughing fit.

"Don't talk," she said. "Just breathe."

Dallas shook his head, still coughing, fist against his mouth. Sweat popped up on his forehead, mingling with the water dripping from his hair. Just a rim of cornflower blue encircled his dilated pupils.

Wonder how much wormwood and sulfur and bon Dieu *knows what else he sucked in along with all the water?*

"He's right," Belladonna said. "We gotta get you outta here before Augustine shows up. Go inside and grab some of Dallas's clothes, and let's get your ass gone."

Dallas waved a hand—*go ahead.*

"You seem to have a deadly, if not fatal, effect on males, Ms. Rivière."

Kallie stiffened. Her gaze skipped past Belladonna's

oh-shit! expression, following the posh sound of Augustine's voice to its source.

The Brit, a bluish bruise shadowing his jaw, strode down the hallway, but he wasn't alone, dammit. A man and a woman wearing tailored and expensive-looking black suits and sleek shades flanked him, their strides smooth, their black-gloved hands hanging easy at their sides. But their flowing movement, balanced and sure, whispered to Kallie of hidden and deadly skill.

Not hotel security, no. Hecatean Alliance security. Warriors trained in martial arts and magic. But knowing that still made it hard to keep from laughing at the Hecatean Alliance symbol stitched in red above the right breast pockets of their suits—a pentagram containing the letters *HA* in gothic script. All that was missing was a red-stitched exclamation point.

Kallie rose to her feet as Augustine sauntered to a stop in front of her, the black-suited guards halting behind him. He pointed at the floor with a discreet index finger. *Stay. Good HA(!) warriors.*

Augustine tilted his head at Dallas, a lock of nutmeg hair sliding across his eyes. "So what has happened here, and how did you—of all people, Ms. Rivière—manage to stumble across it?"

"Dallas is a family friend," Kallie said. "And it looks to me like I'm not the only target. Seems like someone is killing hoodoos."

"Trying to, at least," Augustine said. "Or perhaps someone is trying to make it *look* that way, yes? So far only a nomad conjurer has died. No hoodoos."

Kallie's hands knotted into fists. "What are you saying?"

"You're either a very clever murderer, Ms. Rivière, or

an intended victim in need of protection. In either case, I need to take you into custody."

"No!" Grabbing the doorjambs, Dallas hauled himself to his feet and fixed his dilated gaze on Augustine. "Who the . . . hell are . . ." His words trailed off as he swayed, his square-toed Durangos scuffing across the carpet like a drunk surfing a flat floor.

"Uh-oh." Still kneeling beside the doorway, Belladonna reached up a steadying hand and grabbed hold of Dallas's forearm.

Dallas rallied enough to finish his question in a slurred whisper: ". . . you?" Then his eyes rolled up in his head and his hands slipped from the doorjambs. He fell, collapsing onto Belladonna and riding her down to the floor.

Kallie dropped to her knees and grabbed two handfuls of Dallas's shirt. "Bell? You okay?" Despite the unconscious root doctor's deadweight, this time she heaved him off of her friend without any difficulty.

No chained-up poppet anchoring him to the goddamned floor this go-round.

Belladonna blinked at the ceiling. "Caught him," she gasped.

"Lucky you, Ms. Brown," Augustine said, voice dry enough to spark a forest fire. "Congratulations. I shall leave you to tend to your magicked friend while I take Ms. Rivière into custody."

Belladonna sat up and darted a glance at Kallie, distress shadowing her face. "I need to go with her."

"I'm afraid that's not possible," Augustine said, not a single ounce of regret in his polished voice.

"Am I under arrest?" Kallie rose to her feet and swiveled to face the Hecatean master.

Augustine lifted his shoulder in an elegant and very European half-shrug. "If you wish to be technical."

"I wish to be."

"Then yes. You're under arrest."

"She's not guilty of anything," Belladonna insisted, climbing to her feet. "And I promised her aunt I wouldn't leave her alone."

"Ms. Rivière won't *be* alone; myself or someone else will be with her at all times. And, if it's any comfort, I'll be sending someone to debrief you and . . ." Augustine glanced at Dallas and cocked an eyebrow.

"Amazing. Someone's name you *don't* know." Belladonna said, hand on hip. "This is Dallas Brûler, a root doctor outta Chalmette."

"I'm fine with going, Bell. I'd like to get this all straightened out," Kallie said. "I didn't kill Gage, so I ain't got nothing to hide."

"I promised Gabrielle, dammit." Belladonna focused a narrow-eyed gaze on Augustine. "You'd better keep her safe."

Genuine amusement defrosted the winter-ice expression from Augustine's face. "I admire your loyalty to your friend, Ms. Brown. She'll be quite safe."

"Mmm-hmm. You'd better hope so." Belladonna shifted her weight onto one hip, looking unconvinced.

Kallie bent and bundled up the bike chain and the doll's evil innards in the towel. When she straightened, she handed the poppet package to Belladonna. "Take care of that," she said. "And talk to Dallas. Find out if he saw anyone."

"Sure thing, Shug."

"I apologize," Augustine said, again without an ounce

of regret, "but I'm going to need that. Evidence. Magic DNA. I can't allow you to destroy it, Ms. Brown."

A muscle ticked in Belladonna's jaw, but she handed the towel bundle to the Brit.

"I think you just made up the 'magic DNA' bit. Just be sure you let me or Kallie finish unwinding that spell when you're done."

Augustine nodded. "Of course." He looked at Kallie. "Shall we, Ms. Rivière?"

Kallie's gaze flicked from Augustine to the waiting HA(!) warriors. *Like I have a choice.* "Let's get this goddamned show on the road." Spinning on the ball of one bare foot, Kallie marched down the hall, chin lifted. She wondered if her black-uniformed escorts would just glide up beside her as a reminder that she was under arrest and not leading a parade, or if they'd just tackle and cuff her.

Prisoner or protected? At the moment, she didn't give a rat's ass.

The words written on the curl of parchment paper burned molten in her mind: *Compliments of Gabrielle LaRue.*

If they were true, she'd never be safe anywhere. Not unless she fought back with everything she had—magic, muscle, and cold heart.

And lost the only family she had.

SEVEN

BONDALICIOUS

Bracing his arm against his broken ribs, Layne eased up from his chair. "That was one helluva wicked right hook," he said. "Woman knows how to throw a punch."

"Knows how to land one too," McKenna agreed sourly. "I hope ol' Basil can catch up with her before she disappears."

"If he loses her, *we'll* find her. She ain't slipping away from us."

"She'd better not."

Walking to the door, Layne grabbed hold of each side of the threshold and leaned out into the now quiet hall. His breath caught in his throat as the movement skewered red-hot pain through his sternum. *Holy shit, okay, not smart. I'm giving myself permission to kick my own ass if I do that again.*

"Where do you think yer going? Sit yer arse back down in tha' chair."

Once the pain eased off the throttle and he could breathe again, Layne said, "There you go again. Acting like we're still married." The scent of cinnamon and fresh-baked pastry from the kitchens below squeezed a growl from his empty belly.

"An' there *you* go again, acting all knuckle-dragging

man-stupid. I was yer teacher long before I married you and I am *still* yer teacher. It's yer best interests I have in mind."

"I hear you, *shuvani,*" Layne murmured, watching as Basil Augustine, cell phone pressed to his ear, stalked into the elevator at the end of the hall. Calling for reinforcements, most likely, to chase down one pissed-off hoodoo beauty with riveting violet eyes and quick-swinging fists.

And possibly Gage's murderer.

But something deep inside Layne whispered *no, no, no*. Intuition or enchantment? It bugged the ever-loving hell out of him that he couldn't be sure of *anything* at the moment except that he was alive and sucking in painful breaths of air, thanks to Kallie Rivière.

Basil Augustine swiveled around in the elevator's white-and-gold interior, jabbed a long finger against a numbered button, then stepped back. He flipped his cell phone closed. A lock of dark hair swept across his eyes, shadowing his face. His glittering gaze caught Layne's, and his lips thinned into a tight, arrogant smile.

Doesn't think much of nomads. Well, let's just justify that opinion.

Layne released the threshold and sauntered into the hall. He returned Augustine's smile with an upward tilt of his chin, then rubbed his middle finger alongside his nose. Augustine arched one dark eyebrow. But as the elevator's polished-steel doors slid shut, blocking the illusionist from view, Layne caught a glimpse of Augustine's taut smile relaxing into one of genuine amusement.

"Huh. Didn't think he had it in him."

"Didn't think he had what?" McKenna asked.

"Humor."

"Maybe he was just giving you what he thought you needed to see," McKenna said in her calm and neutral teaching voice, switching in an instant from friend to *shuvani*. "Appearances are everything to illusionists."

"I wonder what he'll show Kallie when he catches up to her? I got a feeling it ain't gonna be what *she* wants to see."

"That's fine by me," McKenna said. "Whether she intended it or not—and I'm not convinced that she's *anywhere* near innocent in this—our Gage is dead because of tha' woman."

Layne looked down into McKenna's dark eyes. A storm of furious grief raged in their depths; a storm matching the maelstrom battering him from within. "I know," he said quietly. "Believe me, Kenn, I know."

"Still . . . because of her, yer alive, yer soul intact," McKenna said. She raked her fingers through her short dark hair, and Layne caught a faint whiff of musky amber, her natural perfume. "And that bugs the shite outta me because now—whether any of us like it or not—yer fate is tied to hers."

"The least of my worries, yeah? I'll deal with it later." Layne turned around and red-hot pain spiked through his chest. His vision grayed. "Christ," he whispered.

McKenna's hands locked around his biceps, her strong fingers steadying him until his sight cleared. "That's what I'm talking about," she said. "You need to rest, so sit yer arse back down."

"No." Layne carefully peeled her fingers from his arms. Pink finger-shaped marks branded his skin. "Not until I've tended to Gage."

"Or better yet," McKenna continued, dark brows slashing down, "you should go back to yer room and lie down. I'll take care of things here."

Layne shook his head and strode back to the room, pain twinging against his sternum. *Hurt all you damned want, you ain't stopping me. Nothing's stopping me.*

"Layne, please, there's nae one to tend to anymore," McKenna said, her brogue thickening. "Ain't nothing left o' him. Go lie down."

Layne paused in the room's threshold. The pain knotting around his heart had nothing to do with his broken ribs. "I'm going to get his body ready," he said, voice rough. "He woulda done the same for me. No matter what."

Behind him, McKenna sighed, but said nothing more.

With a tap of his fingers against the door frame, Layne walked into the room and to the bed. Gage lay half on his side, half on his belly near the edge of the bed where Kallie and her friend had pushed him, pillows propped against his back.

"We need to get him off that bed, first of all," McKenna said, eyeing the hex on the mattress. "Probably safe to touch him since he's no longer in contact with the spell."

"You sure about that?" Layne barely suppressed a convulsive shudder as he remembered the feel of the hex's tainted magic rampaging through his body.

"No," McKenna admitted. "I'm not sure. But if you go to me room and fetch me staff— "

"Nuh-uh. You ain't sending me off on some errand and then taking all the risks yourself, woman." Layne held McKenna's dark gaze. "I know you."

She tilted her head. "You *think* you do, anyway. But you only know what I've *allowed* you to know."

Layne glanced up at the ceiling and counted to ten, refusing to take the bait. "I know you think you'd be protecting me because I don't have any real magic skill," he said, returning his gaze to hers, "through no fault of your own. I couldn't have asked for a better *shuvani* because one doesn't exist. But it's just not in me—not the way it is . . . was . . . with Gage."

Was. The word hollowed out Layne's heart.

"Ah, but yer wrong, lad. The two of you worked so well together, completing and enhancing each other's spells," she said, a sad smile brushing her lips. "You were true brothers-in-magic." She looked at Gage's body. The smile vanished from her lips. "I won't lose you too. Now go fetch me staff."

Layne bent and kissed the top of McKenna's head. "Thanks, buttercup, I appreciate it, but I ain't leaving. Fetch your own damned staff." He straightened.

"Man-stupid." McKenna's hand snapped up and caught a fistful of dreads. Yanked. Pain rippled across Layne's scalp. She yanked again. Then once more. His eyes watered. Grip of steel, that woman, but he refused to give her any satisfaction.

"Did you want something?" he asked, pleased at the levelness of his voice.

"I wanna knock some sense into yer head, but since yer head seems to be lacking a brain, there's no point in the knocking." She gave his captured dreads one more eye-stinging yank before releasing them. "So I'll settle fer keeping you alive and on yer path."

Curling his hands into fists in order to keep from rubbing at his scalp, Layne asked, "And what path is that, Kenn? Not many are laid out for a Vessel."

"You've already lived longer than most Vessels and, except for occasional bouts of man-stupidity, yer still sane."

"That's me, breaking records all over the place. Spill—what path?"

McKenna walked away, pacing around to the opposite side of the bed, her fingers smoothing and twisting locks of nearly black hair into points along her temples and cheeks, a rakish and sexy habit that Layne still enjoyed watching. But right now, she was using it to distract him. *Not going to work.*

"What path?" he repeated.

McKenna looked at him, her hand dropping to her side. Her lovely face held a careful neutrality that he recognized as the Teacher, and he knew he wouldn't get his answer. Or he *would*, but his answer would be twisted into a riddle impossible to unwind.

"Answer hazy," she replied. "Try again later."

"Will I need to shake you first?" Layne growled.

"Oh, what a rare pleasure, truly," a female voice with a posh British accent cut in. "I've never met a human Magic 8 Ball before."

Layne spun around, automatically reaching for the gun normally tucked into his jeans, but it wasn't there, and pain rippled hot and liquid through his chest with the movement. Vision peppered with black specks, he stumbled. "Shit."

Hands gripped his arms before he could fall—inquisitive, touchy-feely hands, sliding along his forearms and caressing his biceps—and guided him to a chair.

"My, my, my, aren't we well built and firm?" the British voice murmured. "Here. Please sit down and catch your breath."

Layne half fell, half sat in the chair, then leaned his forearms against his thighs, lowered his head, and closed his eyes. His heart hammered against his aching ribs.

"Who the hell are you?" McKenna asked the woman Layne still felt standing beside him, an energetic, hummingbird-busy presence.

"Felicity Fields. I'm Lord Augustine's assistant. And may I extend my condolences for your loss?"

"You may, but are you kidding me?" McKenna asked, her tone dubious, but Layne heard the humor beneath her words. "Felicity Fields sounds like the name of a Bond babe. You a double-O spy?"

"No, but—my, my, my—what a fascinating possibility. A spy. Me. But no, I'm here because Lord Augustine asked me to tidy up the situation."

Layne opened his eyes at the woman's words and lifted his head. "A man was fucking murdered. That ain't something you can just tidy up."

Felicity Fields—tall and curvaceous in a knee-length rose-colored skirt belted at the waist below a gauzy white sleeveless blouse—met his gaze. A rose-colored Bluetooth cupped her right ear. Strawberry-blonde hair fell sleek to the tops of her shoulders, framing a fair-skinned and freckled face. She regarded Layne with sympathetic hazel eyes. "I'm referring to the physical aftermath, of course," she said. "Not the emotional."

"You ain't taking his body," Layne said, rising to his feet.

"The deceased was nomad," McKenna said. "You can't."

Felicity frowned, a deep crease cutting into her forehead between her eyes. No Botox for this Bond babe. "I'm afraid my instructions say otherwise. We need to perform an autopsy to determine—"

"That fucking hex on the mattress is what killed Gage," Layne said. "No mystery there. Why don'tcha take a look? Perform an autopsy on *that*."

Her eyes brightened, and her smile made an encore performance. "Oh. My." She drew in a shuddery breath. A *happy* shuddery breath.

Now it was Layne's turn to frown. *Wasn't my intention to turn the woman on.*

"We don't need to know how Gage was killed," McKenna said. "Or even why. We just need to know *who* created tha' hex and where to find them."

"Then *we'll* tidy things up," Layne said.

Felicity's smile vanished beneath a rose-glossed frown. She darted over to the dresser on the other side of Layne's chair and drummed her fingers against its lacquered surface, her nails clicking in a staccato rhythm. "My, my, my. A fascinating dilemma," she murmured.

Layne glanced at McKenna, surprised at Felicity's response. Her body practically vibrated as she considered the tin ceiling, mulling over their words, her fingernails click-click-clickety-clicking against the dresser. Layne half expected her to flit away to the nearest flower.

McKenna offered a half-shrug, expression bemused.

"I hope you realize we ain't asking permission," Layne said. "We're telling you how it's gonna be. I'm taking Gage back to our room. What you do here after that, I couldn't care less."

Felicity's vibrations stilled, and she returned her attention to Layne. She nodded. "Given that the victim is nomad, perhaps we can waive the usual rules."

"You have enough murders during carnival to require rules?" McKenna asked.

"The rules—the *laws*—aren't just for carnival, my dear Lady 8 Ball."

The indignation that rippled across McKenna's face at her

new and unwanted title didn't faze Felicity one bit, provided the hummingbird Bond babe had even noticed. But Layne suspected that Felicity counted on being underestimated, suspected that maybe her mannerisms had been created with that goal in mind. Suspected that she missed very little.

"We may be a society of conjurers, illusionists, and diviners," Felicity continued, "a secretive minority bound by a common interest, but we're still quite human. Therefore, Lady 8 Ball, we need laws to keep us safe even from one another."

"Call me 'Lady 8 Ball' again," McKenna muttered, her death-in-a-thousand-different-and-painful-ways glare fixed on Felicity, "an' I'm gonna ring yer skull like a bell at a boxing match."

Excitement kindled in Felicity's eyes. "Really?"

McKenna blinked, but managed to keep her death glare going. "Really."

"My, my, my."

Almost seeing the steam curling out from McKenna's ears, Layne decided to break up the weird staring match by saying, "You know what you can do with your Alliance rules, right?"

"Shove them where the sun doesn't shine, perhaps?" Felicity responded, shifting her attention to him.

Annnnd mission accomplished.

"Exactly."

"Ooooh." All shuddery and breathy again.

Layne walked back to the bed. He grabbed the blankets piled up at its foot and spread them out on the floor to cushion Gage's coming fall.

"What are you doing?" McKenna asked. "Ye'd better no' be doing what I *think* yer doing."

"And that is?" Layne said, picking up the pillows.

"Moving Gage."

"Gotta be done, Kenn."

"Well, then, I'm helping," she muttered, then walked around to his side of the bed. "Yer just gonna hurt yerself."

"My, my, my. Fascinating."

Layne wasn't sure what the Brit found so frigging fascinating—the quibbling nomads, their attempt to move a body, the possibility of more magic carnage—but he decided that if Felicity said *fascinating* or *my, my, my* one more time while they sweated over Gage's body, he would toss her onto the mattress just to see if the hex was all used up or not.

Handing McKenna one of the blood-spattered pillows, Layne said, "On three."

McKenna nodded, her elfin face dead serious. "Your count."

While McKenna climbed onto the bed, kneeling at its head out of hex-touching range, Layne knelt on the mattress at the foot of the bed and pressed his pillow against Gage's lower back.

The fall won't hurt him.

And even though he *knew* nothing remained of Gage, that Gage's body was as empty as a snake's shed skin, tension coiled around Layne's spine, knotting his muscles and radiating pain through his chest. Because his heart refused to believe, refused to let go of a breathing Gage.

He's just out cold. Too much booze. The fall will wake him up. Piss him off.

I've gotcha, Gage.

Glancing at McKenna, Layne counted down. "One. Two. *Three.*" He shoved against the pillow hard at the same time McKenna pushed hers against Gage's shoulders. His clan-brother's body rolled off the bed, hitting the floor with a heartbreaking thud. Layne released the pent-up breath he'd held.

The fall didn't hurt him. Can't hurt him. Gage is gone.

And as bad as that hurt, the death, the loss of his best friend and *draíocht-brúthair,* the knowledge that Gage no longer existed in any shape or form hurt worse.

Dead, body and soul, because someone had intended to kill a dark-haired hoodoo beauty, but missed. He remembered Gage's parting words before he'd left their shared hotel room: *"Her eyes, bro, you should see her eyes. Purple-blue like hyacinths in sunlight. Fuck, man, she dazzles me."*

The pillow fell from Layne's hands onto the blighted mattress. He slid off the bed and knelt beside Gage's sprawled body.

"Well, that was easier than I expected," McKenna said, tossing her pillow onto the blankets, then scooting off the bed.

Throat too tight for words, Layne nodded.

She dropped to her knees beside Gage's head. Her hands hovered above Gage's black curls, yearning stark on her face. Then her hands clenched into fists.

Layne looked away, a lump aching in his throat. He used a blanket to glove his hands, then straightened his clan-brother's body and smoothed out his limbs.

"Fasci—"

"Don't fucking say it," Layne warned. "Or you'll be trying that hex on for size."

Felicity's side of the room fell so silent that Layne imagined he could hear crickets clear from the bayous outside the city. Smart woman.

Layne folded the blankets closed over Gage's face and

nude body, finally able to give him back some dignity.

"Ah, Gage," McKenna mourned, bowing her head.

"I need you to contact the clan and let them know what's happened," Layne said, sitting back on his heels. *Keep busy*. Planning his next moves, thinking ahead, would shift his attention from his grief. "Let them know I ain't returning until I've found Gage's killer and dealt with him or her."

McKenna lifted her head. Her dark eyes glistened with unshed tears. The corners of her mouth quirked up into a fierce smile. She nodded. "Aye. As his *draíocht-brúthair*, ye have the right. But you won't be alone. As his *shuvani*, I have the right too, so I won't be going back either. Together, we'll avenge our Gage's death."

"Or die trying," Layne said.

Blinking hard and fast, refusing tears—as always—McKenna rose to her feet. "I always knew it was more than yer looks and brawn that won me away from Raven clan."

Layne felt a smile curve his lips. "I thought I snuck into your camp, tossed you over my shoulder, and rode off with you."

"At *my* suggestion," McKenna said with a half laugh, half sob. She wiped at her eyes with her knuckles. "I'll contact the clan, let Frost know what's happened here."

Layne nodded. "It's bad enough that Gage is dead, but if his family knew that his soul was gone too, it'd destroy them. Ask her to keep that part secret."

"I'll ask her," McKenna said. "But I'll bet it ain't necessary. Yer mum's a savvy and compassionate chieftain."

"I know. But I just wanna be sure."

"Where will you be?" McKenna asked.

"In my room, preparing Gage for cremation."

"Nomad funeral rites," Felicity said. "My, my—"

Layne looked at her from beneath his lashes. "Hex," he reminded.

Felicity's sentence remained unfinished.

From out in the hall, Layne heard the sound of wheels squeaking along the carpet. He arrowed a look at Felicity. The Bond-babe Brit, vibrating with enough suppressed energy to make the pearl buttons on her blouse shimmy, met his gaze with a curious lift of her eyebrows.

"If that's the maid," Layne said, "you'd better tell her to pass us by. If it's anyone else, you'd better tell them to fuck off."

"Ah, nomads. So deliciously feral," Felicity murmured. She tilted her head, strawberry-blonde locks curving against her face. Freckles were sprinkled across the bridge of her nose and across her cheeks. "I'd think that in your present condition, a gurney should come in handy. It should make transporting the deceased back to your room just a tad easier."

"She's got a point there, lad."

Now that the adrenaline fueling him since he'd walked into Kallie's room had burned off, weariness morphed Layne's muscles into lead while pain crackled like lightning along his nerves. He wasn't sure he could even get back onto his feet, let alone find a way to carry Gage back to their room.

"Okay, fine, a gurney it is," Layne said.

As if summoned by his words, the metallic front end of a gurney poked in through the doorway. Felicity smoothed her hair back into place, then flitted over to greet the black-uniformed medic maneuvering the gurney into the room.

McKenna walked around behind Layne, then knelt.

He felt her pull some of his dreads back and knot them around the rest, to keep them all out of his face. Knowing he'd need them out of the way while he cared for Gage, and knowing the pain tying them back himself would cost at the moment, gratitude poured through him.

"Thanks, buttercup," he whispered.

"No problem." She leaned in and planted a warm kiss on his cheek. "How are you planning to start yer search for the killer?"

"By staying close to Kallie Rivière. Whoever wanted her dead bad enough to kill her soul too ain't gonna give up after just one try."

"Who says it was the first try?" McKenna said, rising to her feet. "I'll see if Basil-boy detained her and ferret out the situation. In the meantime you bc careful and wait for me."

"I will," Layne promised. McKenna's words rang in his mind long after she'd walked out of the room. *"Who says it was the first try?"* An even darker thought of his own nipped at its heels: *What if she deserves to die?*

EIGHT

THE COLD ALTAR OF REVENGE

Rosette St. Cyr's fingers white-knuckled around the handle of her vacuum cleaner. She couldn't believe her eyes. Didn't *want* to believe her eyes.

Flanked by black-suited Hecatean security, Kallie Rivière stalked down the hall in pink bathrobe and bare feet, chin up, her long hair a lustrous coffee-black stream down her back, her hands clenched into fists.

Very much alive. And accused of murder.

Lord Augustine paused long enough to help Rivière's friend haul the unconscious Brûler back inside his room. Then, with a two-fingered salute, he strolled after the hoodoo student and her guards, the towel containing Rosette's poppet clutched tight in his long-fingered hand and held out at a safe distance.

The chilling conversation Rosette had overheard only a few moments before looped and twisted through her thoughts.

"Seems like someone is killing hoodoos."

"Trying to, at least. Or perhaps someone is trying to make it look *that way, yes? So far only a nomad conjurer has died. No hoodoos."*

Rosette's heart drummed a ferocious rhythm of denial

against her ribs. Had Papa's hex killed an innocent? And worse—an innocent's *soul*?

Icy bricks of dread plummeted to the pit of Rosette's belly. If someone else had truly been killed . . .

Rosette shoved the vacuum inside the room she'd been cleaning when that silly Francesca had started screaming, then scooped up an armload of folded white towels from her cart and followed after Kallie Rivière and her forced entourage.

Given that Lord Augustine had mentioned taking the hoodoo apprentice into custody, Rosette felt reasonably certain that he intended to take Rivière to the Hecatean Alliance offices on the fifteenth floor and secure her in one of their magic-warded rooms.

She hurried down the hall, her rubber-soled shoes silent against the burnt-umber-and-scarlet-patterned Persian carpet, the stink of the spilled bucket's sulfur-and-wormwood-tainted contents fading behind her.

She needed to learn the truth; then she needed to call Papa. Because—for whatever reason—she and Papa had failed. Not only was Rivière alive, but they hadn't even managed to kill Brûler, the root doctor from Chalmette.

"So far only a nomad conjurer has died."

But from the sound of things, she and Papa might've murdered an innocent man, a completely unintended target.

Innocent. Murdered. Not good to think in those terms. Because, if you wanted to get fussy about it, Kallie Rivière and Dallas Brûler were also innocents about to be sacrificed upon the cold altar of revenge.

Just like her mama had been.

A cold hand tightened around Rosette's heart. Tit for

tat. This was a war—undeclared, maybe, but a war all the same. But their first bold strikes had failed.

And Papa would be far from pleased to hear the news. He would blame her, at least for Dallas Brûler's survival.

How in *bon Dieu*'s name had Kallie Rivière known about the attack on Brûler? And she *must've* known somehow, because Rosette couldn't think of another explanation for the hoodoo apprentice's presence on the sixth floor just in time to save Brûler's life.

Unless one figured in chance. Or divine guidance. But perhaps another message lurked in their failure—the *loa* disapproved of her and Papa's actions.

To kill a person was one thing. To murder a soul . . .

Rivière and her black-clad escorts reached the polished steel elevators. She folded her arms over her chest and shifted her weight onto one hip, waiting. The female guard leaned past her and poked the Up button with a black-gloved finger.

A cool twist of relief uncorked some of the tension from Rosette's muscles, and she slowed her pace. Up was good. While they headed up, she'd head down to Rivière's room to see what had gone wrong and who had died in her place.

Maybe there would be some way to rectify the situation. She sure as hell didn't want to tell Papa that *both* tricks had failed. That Gabrielle LaRue was still laughing at him even after all these years. Papa's voice, deep and musical and burning with a fire banked deep within his soul, sounded through Rosette's memory.

"I lost twenty-five years in prison to that woman. I lost your mama, my beautiful Babette. I lost my future. I intend to return the favor to Gabrielle threefold. She will lose all she loves, chérie, *just like we did. An eye for an eye is never enough. Never, never, never."*

"Might I have one of those?"

Blinking the memory away, Rosette looked up into Lord Augustine's gray eyes. She stumbled to a stop, barely avoiding plowing into the man. He studied her, head tilted, one lock of dark brown hair sliding down his forehead.

"A woman deep in thought," he murmured. "I apologize. I didn't mean to startle you." He held up his towel-wrapped bundle. A faint rotten-egg stench wafted from it. "It's leaking, so I wondered if I might have one of those?" He nodded at the towels Rosette clutched to her chest.

"Oh," Rosette squeaked in relief. "*Oui*. Of course." She grabbed a towel from the top of the stack and handed it to him.

Augustine accepted the towel with a cool smile. "Thank you. Given your French, you must be a New Orleans native," he said, rolling the fresh towel around the one cradling the dismembered poppet.

"Actually, I'm Haitian, *m'sieu*," Rosette lied. "But I've lived in New Orleans for several years."

"Your English is excellent," he commented. "Not even an accent."

"*Merci*. Your English is also excellent, *m'sieu*, even *with* the accent."

Augustine chuckled. "Touché." The amusement faded from his eyes. "Did you by chance notice anyone—aside from your fellow maid—near room 623 this morning? Did you see or hear anything unusual?"

"No. I was cleaning when I heard Francesca's scream," Rosette replied. "When I looked out, I saw the man on the floor." Nodding at Rivière, she added, "Then I saw her and another woman racing down the hall."

"Ah, thank you, *mademoiselle* . . . ?" Augustine arched a dark brow.

"Rosette St. Cyr."

"If you should think of anything pertaining to this morning's incident, *mademoiselle* St. Cyr, please contact the Hecatean Alliance offices."

Rosette nodded. "Of course, Lord Augustine."

"*Bonjour*, then." Swiveling around, the Hecatean master sauntered the remaining short distance to the elevator, joining the black-pink-black trio waiting in various postures of pretended ease and, in Kallie Rivière's case, impatience.

The hoodoo apprentice stabbed a finger against the already glowing Up button. A musical *ding!* chimed down the hall; then the elevator doors slid apart. Flashing her escort a triumphant look, Kallie stepped inside, followed by Lord Augustine and the guards.

The black-uniformed and -shaded guards turned around in a graceful, almost synchronized movement to face the front of the elevator. The male guard motioned with his brush-cut head for Rosette to take the next elevator. She nodded, smiling. The doors *thunk*ed shut.

Rosette thumbed the Down button; then, sagging with relief, she leaned a shoulder against the cream-colored wall. "*A woman deep in thought.*" More like a woman who happened to be an idiot. Daydreaming when she needed to remained focused. If she was careless, Papa would go back to prison. But not alone, no. She'd go as well.

When the elevator arrived, Rosette hurried inside and punched the fourth-floor button. Her nose wrinkled. A previous occupant's white musk cologne haunted the air, the smell almost thick enough to be visible.

Slipping a hand into her pocket, she brushed her fingers against her universal keycard. A quick visit to Kallie Rivière's room to assess the situation and figure out their next move, then she'd call Papa.

Towels hugged against her chest, Rosette marched down the hall toward the hoodoo apprentice's room. When she was only a door away, a tall man in jeans, a sage-green tank, and boots with painted flames on the sides pushed a gurney out into the hall. Blue-inked tattoos curled in concentric designs from his shoulders to his biceps. Long, honey-blond dreads snaked almost to his waist.

The gurney held a comforter-draped burden. A *body-sized* burden.

Rosette slowed to a halt, her blood chilling in her veins.

"Are you quite sure you don't need help?" a female and British-accented voice said from inside the room—a voice Rosette recognized. A woman in a rose skirt and white blouse followed the words into the hall, her strawberry-blonde hair glimmering beneath the lights. Lord Augustine's bouncy assistant, Felicity Fields.

"Nope. Don't need help. Thanks."

"Will you want your friend's clothing and any other belongings we might find in Ms. Rivière's room brought to you, or would you prefer to pick them up in our offices?"

The gurney stopped. The muscles along the man's shoulders bunched and rippled beneath his tank. He turned around carefully, one arm slanted and braced across his chest—injured?—his dreads swinging against his back. A gorgeous man, tall and lean-muscled, his whisker-shadowed face in need of a shave. Dried blood smudged the skin beneath his nose, streaked a dark line from his ears down along his neck.

Rosette frowned. What had happened to him? A fight? Then an ice-slivered possibility skewered her thoughts. The aftermath of the hex's cold and poisonous kiss?

Not possible. He'd be dead. Not standing in a hall talking to Felicity Fields.

"Just leave a message and I'll come get 'em," he replied. A small tattoo Rosette wasn't close enough to make out curved beneath his right eye. Nomad.

"So far only a nomad conjurer has died."

Rosette's gaze shifted back to the gurney and its burden, and all her rationalizations about the cost of war unraveled. She felt sick.

"Cheerio, then," Felicity chirped. "We'll be in touch."

Without another word, the tall nomad turned around one more time and resumed pushing the gurney toward the elevator. Rosette stepped aside, putting her back against the wall to give the nomad and his burden room to pass.

His gaze cut to her as he pushed the squeaky-wheeled gurney past, his green eyes brushing over her and drinking in details as if by habit. Then he looked away, his attention once more fixed on the elevator at the end of the hall.

Rosette stared after him, pulse pounding in her temples, haunted by what she'd glimpsed in his eyes.

A stone-hard and bone-deep resolve. Unshakable.

A look she recognized, since she'd seen it before—in her own mirrored reflection.

A mysterious wasting disease whittles her mama away a pound at a time, dulls the color of Mama's dark chocolate eyes into a filmy mud.

Rosette watches as hoodoo root doctors and voodoo mambos *and* houngans *drape Mama with fragrant charms, bathe her in potions smelling of frankincense and sharp sage, sprinkle her body and bed with magic powders, and oil her up with herbs and flowers and salts. She watches as they wash and ward the house inside and out. But nothing helps.*

No one can find the trick that's killing Mama or discover who laid it. One by one, they shake their heads, trudge down the porch steps, and never come back.

And so, all alone and in a silent house, fifteen-year-old Rosette watches Mama die. But she knows who jinxed Mama even if the root doctors don't—or claim they don't: Gabrielle LaRue. The evil sorceress who also stole her papa away from her.

Rosette knew that the nomad would never give up. Whoever lay beneath the carefully wrapped comforter-shroud on the gurney—brother, sister, wife, friend—the nomad would hunt until he'd found and killed the person responsible for their death. The fierce resolve Rosette had witnessed in his eyes, a hard and steady flame fueled by rage and grief, told the complete story—grim ending and all.

"An eye for an eye is never enough. Never, never, never."

And, one day, he'd find Papa—her too, no doubt. And then Gabrielle LaRue would win the war without lifting a hand. The crafty old spider would laugh long and hard.

Not if I can help it. But time is ticking away.

Unlike the night Mama had died. *That* night, time had simply stopped.

Rosette shoved away from the wall and continued down the hall, her shoe soles padding against the carpet in perfect rhythm with each hard thump of her heart. As she walked past Kallie Rivière's room, she saw Felicity Fields close and lock the door.

With graceful swirls of the thumb and the index and middle fingers of her right hand, Lord Augustine's assistant traced sigils in the air in front of the door. Rosette caught a flash of brilliant white from the corner of her eye as Felicity's seal activated. A pungent wisp of myrrh tickled Rosette's nostrils.

Felicity swiveled around in her rose-tinted pumps. A sunny smile curved her lips as her gaze landed on Rosette. "Off limits," she said. "*Oui?*"

"*Oui, madame,*" Rosette replied.

With an approving nod, Felicity Fields turned and walked down the hallway, well-rounded hips swaying beneath her tight rose skirt, following the nomad's path to the elevator.

Rosette pulled her keycard from her pocket and stopped at the first door with a PLEASE CLEAN tag, which happened to be the room across and one up from Rivière's. Unlocking it, she stepped inside. She stood for a moment, mind blank, staring at a wedge of sunlight slanting across the carpet.

With Kallie Rivière in Lord Augustine's custody and soon, no doubt, Dallas Brûler as well, she needed to find a way to get them both away from the Hecatean master before the nomad started his hunt. Walking across the room, Rosette swung open the slender French doors and stepped out onto the black wrought-iron-bordered terrace.

The early-morning air smelled fresh, laced with the sweet perfume of the jasmine and carnations growing in baskets along the lips of the railing and the moss-and-fish odor of the Mississippi. The diesel roar of buses and constant honk of horns told a tale of frantic morning-rush-hour traffic on the streets below.

Once she'd loved New Orleans. But now it only reminded her of dimming chocolate-dark eyes, of the vinegar and garlic stink of protective floor washes, of the murmur of useless prayers.

She'd grown up listening to Mama's stories about the tall and handsome Creole she'd loved and married, the papa Rosette had never known, each word woven into the fabric of her being by Mama's smooth and nimble voice.

"Oh, baby-girl, people came from all around the country to seek your daddy's counsel and potions. They called him Doctor Heron because he could find and solve any problem, any jinx, just like a long-beaked heron spearing a fish. No better root doctor existed anywhere on earth.

"But one dark, dark day, a jealous and wicked witch named Gabrielle LaRue fixed her evil eye on your daddy and worked morning, noon, and night to destroy him."

And had succeeded.

But Mama would've been appalled to know what they'd done—Rosette and Papa—in their efforts to settle the score. They had murdered an innocent man—a civilian and not a part of their war—body and soul. How could they ever atone for that?

"An eye for an eye is never enough."

Remembering the tight-jawed grief on the nomad's blood-streaked face, the unshifting granite of his eyes, green and hard, as cold as a winter-frosted tomb—Rosette had a feeling that, for him, no atonement would be possible except through shed blood and stilled hearts and dead souls.

It was a sentiment she understood. One she shared.

And even though Papa had laid the trick, Rosette had been just as culpable. She'd traded floors with another maid and had sneaked Papa into the hoodoo apprentice's room. Then she'd stood watch as he'd stripped the bed and shaped the hex on the mattress.

Rosette knew she had to keep the nomad away from Papa, put an end to his hunt before it even began. Her pulse slowed as a clear light poured through her like molten sunshine, wisping away all shadows, all doubts.

She knew what she needed to do.

Rosette drew in a deep breath, then pulled her cell phone from her dress pocket and hit the speed dial. Papa answered on the first ring.

"Everything went wrong," Rosette said. "The root doctor's still alive, and someone else died in Kallie Rivière's place."

" 'Went wrong,' *chère*? Sounds like it musta gone to hell in a huge goddamned handbasket if both still be breathing. Sounds like you screwed up. Were you spotted?"

Not one question about who had died, not one word of regret. "No, Papa. But Lord Augustine's got possession of my poppet."

"Damned handbasket keeps getting bigger, Rosie," Papa grumbled. "So where's the Rivière girl now?"

Rosette paused, wondering if she should tell Papa about the nomad and what she'd seen in his eyes. Wondered if she should tell Papa what she'd seen in her own eyes the night Mama had died. Wondered if Papa had stared into his own mirrored reflection and had glimpsed the darkness dwelling within his heart, the monster deforming his soul.

"Rosette?"

"She's in Augustine's custody," Rosette replied. "But I know how to fix that *and* how to keep Augustine from sending out the hounds."

A moment of silence, then, "Keep talking, *chère*," Papa replied.

NINE

TRAPPED MAGIC

Perched on the edge of a high-backed, sigil-carved chair, Kallie recounted her discovery of Gage's body and the events that had followed in a low, calm voice as she watched Basil Augustine place the soggy, sulfur-reeking towel on a polished oak examination table.

Hand-carved sigils, ancient and powerful, swirled around the table's rim. She suspected that the sigils acted like an electric fence, trapping all magicked items placed upon its surface until they were either removed by authorized individuals or their magic was dispelled.

Augustine spread the towel open, revealing the disemboweled poppet.

"And then you walked into the room," she finished.

"Yes. A good thing, too. Otherwise Mrs. Conti would've called the police."

Kallie sighed. "Yeah."

Augustine reached inside his suit jacket and pulled out a handkerchief-wrapped object. He unrolled the plain white cloth, revealing a slender steel pick that he used to poke at the poppet's guts—sticks, torn cloth, red yarn, and a foul little knot composed mainly of what looked like Spanish moss, the other ingredients too wet to differentiate—except for that goddamned strip of paper.

"Squeamish much?" Kallie asked, unable to keep the amusement out of her voice. She'd bet anything that the Brit carried the pick for the express purpose of poking at things he deemed icky.

"Cautious when it comes to things of a dubious nature, Ms. Rivière." Augustine's gaze flicked across the smeared ink letters on the strip of paper. "Who is Gabrielle LaRue?"

"My aunt. The woman who raised me and my cousin."

Augustine glanced at Kallie. "Ah. So your aunt is also a hoodoo. I imagine she taught you."

"Conjuring runs in the family," Kallie said. Then, thinking of her cousin, Jackson, she added, "For the most part."

"You mentioned that Mr. Brûler was a family friend," Augustine said, flipping the towel back over the disassembled doll. The bitter smell of wormwood twisted into the air. "Why would your aunt want him dead?"

"She doesn't. She thinks the world of Dallas." Kallie bit back the words *"but dozens of cuckolded men do* not *share those sentiments."* "She taught him everything she knows about conjure." Kallie shook her head. "She's being set up."

"Like you? Does being falsely accused of crimes run in the family also?"

Kallie stared at the Brit, her gaze icing over. "Y'know, you're an asshole, and I wish I'd broken your goddamned jaw. Next time I will. Then I won't hafta listen to your bullshit."

Augustine touched his bruised jaw, and a rueful smile played across his lips. "I have no intention of giving you another opportunity to catch me off guard, Ms. Rivière. I've learned my lesson."

"Doesn't much sound like it," Kallie muttered.

Augustine slid the pick, sheathed in its handkerchief once more, back into his pocket. He strolled around the table, grabbed the only sigil-free chair in the room, and placed it in front of Kallie's. He sat down. "So tell me why you don't think your aunt is responsible for that doll or for the attempt on Mr. Brûler's life."

Kallie regarded the Brit for a moment, taking his measure. His gaze was level, open, his expression attentive and intelligent. Might be an asshole, but at least he wasn't an idiot. "For one thing, Gabrielle isn't even here."

"She could've hired someone to deliver the . . . poppet."

"True, but Gabrielle is *beaucoup* skilled and one helluva rootworker. She never woulda put her name inside that poppet. She woulda written Dallas's name a bunch of times on that piece of paper, along with what she wanted to happen to him—"

"Like drowning."

"Yeah, that's right. But to name herself like that and include it inside the trick? Nah, ain't done. Ain't like her, either. She's a healer for the most part." Kallie gathered her hair in her hands and tossed it behind her shoulders.

Augustine's gaze lit like a fly on the thin, time-whitened scar an inch or so above her left eyebrow and slanting away into the hairline at her temple. "What happened there?" he asked, touching a finger to his own left eyebrow.

Kallie tried to remain casual. She shrugged. "Fell out of a swing when I was little."

"Ah. I see." Pursed lips. Dubious tone. "Well, then, do you and your aunt get along?" he asked, brushing wrinkles from his slacks and watching Kallie from beneath his lashes.

"Sure," Kallie replied, relieved he'd dropped the subject

of her scar. "Well, y'know, as good as any niece and aunt."

"You said she raised you and your cousin. That's quite a burden. Did she do it alone? What happened to your parents?"

A muscle played along Kallie's jaw. "Yeah, she did it alone. She's *beaucoup* strong, Gabrielle. And not that it's any of your business, but my folks are dead."

"My condolences, Ms. Rivière," Augustine murmured. "That must've been hard on you and your aunt. Forced parenthood can take a toll, I'm afraid."

Kallie straightened in her chair. "Take a toll? What the hell you mean by that?"

"You read about it in the papers all the time," Augustine said, spreading his hands out. "Boyfriend shakes girlfriend's baby to death. Woman drowns children in bathtub. Perhaps your aunt has had a hard time adjusting to being a parent."

"You've got your goddamned head up your goddamned ass," Kallie said, voice flat. Old emotions she thought she'd laid to rest long ago flickered to life. "Gabrielle's *never* laid a hand on me or my cousin, Jackson. And even if she had, what would that have to do with anything?"

Holding up a placating hand, Augustine said, "All right, then, does your aunt hold any grudges against you?"

"No, dammit. Are you trying to say that my *aunt* laid that goddamned hex on my bed? Are you loco?"

"Given the timing of the attacks on you and Mr. Brûler, I'm simply considering all angles, Ms. Rivière. I suggest you do the same."

"Listen. There's no way my aunt is behind any of this. But given the power behind the hex and the poppet, whoever's doing this is another hoodoo. Not just someone playing at it."

"But that's what I don't understand. Since your aunt isn't even in New Orleans, why would this mythical, rogue hoodoo bother to set her up for crimes here and not wherever you live?"

"Bayou Cyprès Noir," Kallie supplied. Blowing out a breath, she trailed a hand through her hair, then shook her head. "I got nothin'. I don't know of any feuds over clients or mojo or who's been giving love potions to who or anything. None of this makes sense."

"I certainly agree with that," Augustine said. "A few possibilities come to mind, however." He lifted his right hand and held up the index finger. "First possibility: you and Brûler are working together to frame your aunt for crimes committed by you, perhaps by both of you."

"Why the hell would—"

"Ah-ah. Let me finish, please."

Kallie snorted. "Fine." She leaned back into her chair and folded her arms across her chest.

Augustine held up a second finger. "Second possibility: you decided to eliminate a few hoodoo rivals, including Brûler."

Then why did I save him, asshole? But, with effort, Kallie managed to keep the words unspoken and just arched a *go on* eyebrow instead.

A third finger popped up beside the first two. "Aunt Gabrielle sees a chance to finally be rid of the niece—and rival—she's been burdened with and finds wicked New Orleans not only the perfect place, but a simply lovely alibi as well," Augustine said; then he frowned. "Although one would think that a nice, quiet murder back home, the body dumped into a swamp to be devoured by crocodiles or alligators or what-have-you, would be much easier."

Kallie nodded. "You'd think."

Augustine's pinkie lifted into the air. "And my current favorite possibility: you truly were the intended victim, your nomad lover killed by mistake. But given Brûler's near death by poppet-drowning, you aren't the only target."

"Duh."

Augustine lowered his hand and rested it against his thigh. "Now the question is, who hates you enough to want you dead—body *and* soul? Have you argued with anyone since your arrival in New Orleans?"

"Aside from the usual with Belladonna, no."

"And Mr. Brûler? Did he also travel with you and Ms. Brown?"

"Nope. Me and Bell live, like, two hours away and he lives real close, in Chalmette, so he came by himself." And that was another thing. Given that his place was only ten miles away, why was Dallas spending good money on a hotel room? "But I'm surprised he even wanted to attend."

"Why is that?"

"Dallas thinks the carnival is for fools. We argued about it—"

Augustine perked up. His gaze intensified. "Argued?"

Kallie flapped a hand at him. "We just squabbled, y'know? Gave each other shit. Nothing like a you-suck-and-I-hate-your-guts screamfest or knockdown brawl. I thought he was just parroting Gabrielle's beliefs, since she feels the same way."

"Does she?" Augustine murmured. "A shame. So answer me this, Ms. Rivière, if Mr. Brûler believes the carnival to be a landlocked ship of fools, why is he here?"

"I don't know, and I intend to ask him, but Dallas ain't a part of this. He damn near died."

"True, and I find that 'damn near' part intriguing," Augustine replied. Leaning forward in his chair, he braced his arms against his knees.

A faint, alluring scent curled into Kallie's nostrils, tobacco and vanilla. "Intriguing how?" she asked.

"You've heard of cases where a person hires someone to murder their spouse, then makes sure their hired thug also—but very carefully and with pre-determined precision—shoots or knifes or bludgeons them, as well, in a non-lethal manner, of course, to underscore their innocence."

Kallie frowned. "Yeah, but what does that—" Then it hit her. She shook her head. "No, you're wrong."

"Possibly," Augustine admitted, "but perhaps the relationship between Mr. Brûler and your aunt has changed. Perhaps they are now rivals."

"Even if that was true, why would he try to kill *me*?" Kallie shook her head again. "'Sides, Dallas doesn't have the kinda power it'd take to lay down a soul-eating trick."

"*If* Mr. Valin is correct in his assessment."

Kallie tilted her head, studying Augustine. "Why wouldn't he be correct?"

Sighing, Augustine sat back in his chair, and trailed a hand through his hair. "Vessels tend to be a tad wobbly when it comes to sanity."

"I hear that being worn like a cheap costume and used as a mouthpiece by the dead can do that to a person," Kallie replied, her voice dry. "But Layne seems okay. I mean, aside from losing his clan-brother." She looked down, grief and guilt tightening her throat.

"I'm sure he'll be fine, Ms. Rivière. He's not alone, after all."

She lifted her gaze, all emotion tucked away again. "You've never lost anyone, have you?"

Something flickered in the depths of the Brit's gray eyes, something as hollow and fragile as an empty bird's nest revealed on a winter-stark tree, something that suggested she might be wrong about that statement. It vanished so quickly Kallie couldn't be sure she hadn't imagined it.

"So tell me, Ms. Rivière," Augustine said, refusing to answer her question, "what do *you* think is going on?"

Kallie gathered her hair and pulled it over one shoulder as she considered. Separating the heavy mass into three sections, she started braiding it. "Someone's hunting hoodoos," she said finally.

"I don't think so," Augustine said. "I think it's more personal than that. You, your aunt's former protégé, an attempt to frame your aunt for murder. In truth, your aunt Gabrielle seems to be the connecting factor."

Kallie went still, her fingers caught in her dark tresses. "*I'm sorry, baby. I ain't got a choice.*" She shoved the memory away and resumed braiding her hair. "Sorry, I can't think of anyone who'd want to get even with Gabrielle. I mean, at least, not beyond a small bad-luck trick or a bit of ill-health juju."

"Are you certain of that? Your life and—if Valin's correct—your soul depend upon it."

"No, I'm not certain of anything," Kallie said softly. Her fingers dropped away from her hair. "Look, I'm too tired, too rattled, and too goddamned hungover to think. I'd like to get a few of my things, then go to Belladonna's room. Try to sleep."

"Whoever tried to kill you won't stop just because their first attempt failed," Augustine pointed out. "You'll be safest in here. The room is warded inside and out. I shall have your friend, a bed, and food brought in."

"And assign some HA muscle to escort me to and from

the bathroom?" Kallie shook her head, the plait in her hair unraveling in a slow twist. "I ain't gonna be a prisoner. Me and Bell can throw some protection into place in her room. Hell, we'll keep Dallas with us too."

"Enough to keep you safe from the kind of power that can kill a soul?"

"I sure as hell hope so," Kallie said, a wry smile brushing her lips. "I'm kinda counting on it. The only way we're gonna find this bastard is to let him find me."

"That didn't work out very well for Gage Buckland."

Kallie glared at the Brit. "You can go fuck yourself," she said, voice low and strained.

"Whether you like it or not, you're in danger, and anyone near you gets to join in on the fun—blood, death, and all—even if they'd rather not," Augustine replied. "I plan to question each hoodoo registered at the carnival and check hotel employee records for anyone with connections to hoodoo or voodoo. But if someone else dies because the killer's spell missed *you*—their death falls on your head, Ms. Rivière."

Kallie stared at him, a muscle playing along her jaw. Her fingers curled around the sigil-embellished arms of the chair. "All right, goddammit, I'll stay here. For now."

Augustine smiled, then rose to his feet. "'For now' is a good start, Ms. Rivière. I shall send someone to fetch your friend, and I'll make protective arrangements for Mr. Brûler as well. If you're hungry, I shall have the kitchen send breakfast and coffee."

Kallie's stomach clenched at the mention of food, and she shook her head. "Ugh. No food, but some black coffee would be welcome." Her parched throat made another request. "And water."

"Black coffee and water it is," Augustine said before

turning around and tugging his cell phone from an inside pocket in his suit jacket.

Kallie listened as he called someone named Mrs. Fields and asked her to bring Belladonna and Dallas to quarantine station 1. Her gaze dropped to her hands. All the muscles in her chest knotted when she saw Gage's blood staining her fingers.

"Is there some place I can wash my hands?" she asked, her voice small.

"Just a moment," the Brit replied as he dialed the kitchen, then placed an order for bruschetta, coffee, and water.

Hands still gripping the chair arms, Kallie pushed herself to her feet. Or tried to, at least. Electricity prickled against her skin, weaving invisible straps of nettled barbs around her torso and her arms and legs, effectively buckling her into the sigil-bordered chair like a death row inmate into Ol' Sparky. No matter how hard she twisted or tugged, she couldn't pull free or gain her feet.

Panic blazed a path down her spine. "Hey, you goddamned sonuvabitch! What kind of a stunt you pulling?"

"The bruschetta will help settle your stomach, Ms. Rivière. There's absolutely no reason for hostility." Augustine swiveled around to face her, dark brows knitted, expression stern.

"I'm not talking about the goddamned bruschetta." Kallie glared at him, serving him up dead a thousand different ways as she continued her struggle to free herself from the chair.

Augustine's expression went blank. "Are you actually unable to get out of that chair?"

"As if you don't know, you goddamned bastard," she snarled. "Let me go!"

"What an intriguing impossibility," Augustine said, his voice a near whisper. "Those sigils are meant to trap and hold magic, spells, potions, items." His gaze locked with Kallie's. "Not people."

"Yeah, well, clearly you're goddamned wrong." The electric tingling intensified the more she struggled. Her fingers went numb. "Let. Me. Go."

"No, I am *not* wrong," the Brit said. "I carved those sigils myself. To trap magic. People *perform* magic, Ms. Rivière; they *craft* it and *shape* it. *Command* it. But human bodies don't harbor magic. Don't carry it pooled inside the deep wells of their hearts. Nor does it snap along the synapses of their brains or pulse through their veins. At least, that's the case with *human* bodies."

Kallie went still, her heart hammering against her ribs. "What are you saying?"

Tilting his head, Augustine stared at her. "What *are* you?" he asked.

TEN

WITH NONE TO GIVE

Layne stood beside the gurney he'd parked in the spacious bathroom and washed the blood from Gage's face and body with warm soapy water. He drew his washcloth along his clan-brother's stiffening limbs in gentle swipes. He cleaned Gage's blue-ink-tattooed dark skin until it glistened beneath the room's overhead lights.

But despite the soap's clean scent, he still caught the faint, nostril-pinching stink of decay. Scrub all he wanted, he'd never be able to wash *that* away. Just like he couldn't scrub, bargain, or magic away Gage's death.

Nor could he turn back time. Or stop the fucking endless litany of what-ifs.

If only the nightmare had awakened him sooner.

If only he'd run his breathless dash through the hotel halls to Kallie Rivière's room faster.

If only he'd talked Gage out of the trip to New Orleans in the first place.

Layne whirled and, ignoring the molten pain the movement cost him, hurled the wadded-up washcloth across the room with all he had, a fastball with heat. It hit the wall with a splat, then slid down to the slate floor.

Why the hell had he had the nightmare anyway—a warning of what was to come—if it made no difference? What the *fuck?*

Gage runs in a full-steam-ahead lope past a statue of a man on a rearing horse, his breath rasping in his throat, sweat beading his forehead. Manicured grass cushions his footfalls as he races through the black-iron-fenced square, the spires of a white cathedral looming ahead of him. He tosses a look over his shoulder, panic gleaming in his eyes.

But Gage needs to look up. *The sky bursts into flame, rippling fiery shadows across the statue and the cathedral. Gage slows to a stop and looks up just as a fireball comets through what remains of the night and slams into the earth with a ground-shaking* whoomph.

The statue, the cathedral, and Gage cease to exist. And New Orleans burns.

Even with dreams brimming with omens and warnings, he'd been unable to save Gage. Just like he'd been unable to save his sister.

"Hold that thieving. lying nomad bitch down, boys. Got a few lessons to teach her after we finish stomping her thieving nomad buddy."

Layne's breath caught roughly in his throat as pain shivved his heart, the tip scraping against his soul. *Not now. This won't help anything. Take care of Gage.*

Drawing in a careful breath, Layne pushed away his last memories of Poesy and the shit-kicking, mouth-breathing squatters who'd murdered her in a Winn-Dixie parking lot. He walked over to the washcloth and picked it up with shaking hands. Then he stood there for several long moments, eyes burning, waiting for his hard-pounding pulse to slow and quiet. Once it had, he turned around and walked back to the gurney.

Walked back to all that remained of his best friend and

drinking buddy, his *draíocht-brúthair,* the man who'd saved him and his sanity after he'd handed himself over to his dead sister as her Vessel.

Gage kisses Layne's lips, tender and slow, his own salty with tears. Kisses Poesy good-bye. Poesy kisses him back.

Layne swung the gurney around so he could angle the head of it toward the bowl of the sink, gritting his teeth against the pain in his chest—a distracting physical ache he welcomed. The sweet scent of peaches filled the air as he shampooed Gage's curls.

"You were right about Kallie's eyes, bro," Layne murmured. "Just like you said—hyacinths in sunlight. You were right about a few of her other attributes too." He laughed, the sound just a little rough. "Woman don't take shit, and, bro, those curves. Man." He shook his head, the weight of his tied-back dreads sweeping against his back. Filling the bathroom cup with warm water, he rinsed the shampoo from Gage's hair.

But if she's a murderer...

He used soft white towels to dry the last of the water from Gage's body; then he dried his clan-brother's hair with the bathroom's built-in blow-dryer, finger-combing the blue-black curls as he went. But even clean and groomed, the usual lustrous gleam in Gage's hair was missing—drained away with his blood and his life. And his soul.

Layne pushed the gurney and its burden out of the bathroom and back into the room proper. He walked over to the dresser, his gaze falling on the brochure for the French Quarter ghost tour that Gage had picked up a day or so ago.

"Come with, bro?"

"Sure, what the hell. When in Rome or wherever . . ."

Layne's throat closed. A muscle flexed in his jaw. He yanked open the top drawer and dug through the clothes inside.

"When my time comes, I wanna be cremated. Spread my ashes on the dawn, bro."

"Poetic. But you're talking like I'm gonna outlive you, man. Hello, Vessel here."

"Good point, bro. So how do you wanna be sent off?"

"Hmmm. How about firing me into the night sky from a catapult?"

"You wanna be wearing anything during that catapult flight?"

"Buck naked. Fireworks up my ass."

"You got it, bro. I wanna be wearing my TOLDJA! *T-shirt and my greasiest jeans. Should make me burn like a fucking torch."*

"You got it, man. Wan' another beer?"

Layne tossed shirt after shirt onto the floor until he'd emptied the drawer. Gage hadn't packed his TOLDJA! shirt, or maybe he'd already worn it. Layne went to the dirty-clothes trash bag and dumped out the contents. Crouching, he pawed through wrinkled tees, jeans, boxers, and smelly socks. Not there.

"Fuck," he muttered. Rubbing his jaw with one hand as though he could coax an idea from deep within the bone, he looked around the room. Gage's sketch pad and several Sharpies lay on the table beside Layne's laptop.

Arm braced against his ribs, he stood, and returned to the dresser. Fetching a white tee from his drawer, he took it over to the table and scrawled TOLDJA! on it with a black Sharpie. Good enough.

And as for a pair of greasy jeans, Layne scooped up from the dirty-clothes pile the ones that Gage had been wearing when they'd ridden in from Florida. Again, good enough.

Dressing Gage—black boxers, socks, jeans, and new TOLDJA! tee—took the better part of an hour and left Layne drenched in sweat. Pain sawed at his sternum like a broken-toothed chainsaw. Exhaustion burned through his muscles. A part of him was tempted to call it a morning and crawl back into bed. But just part. And only tempted.

Layne leaned over Gage and kissed his cold forehead, stroking his thumb along Gage's clean curls. Then, straightening, he went to the bed and yanked off the bedspread. He draped it over Gage's body.

Layne stripped and hit the shower, scrubbing his exhaustion and sweat away with the hotel's tiny bar of perfumed soap, shaving his face, the hot water doing little to ease the kinks from his muscles. Once he was dressed again in jeans and a black Inferno tee, he sat at the table and strapped on his scuffed and flame-painted scooter boots.

Hopefully, McKenna had learned where Kallie Rivière had gone or where she'd been taken if Augustine had caught and detained her. If not, Layne's course of action would be straightforward—he planned to ask Basil Augustine for her whereabouts. His gut told him that Kallie was innocent of Gage's murder. But someone wanted her dead—*more* than dead—and if he could figure out why, then he'd have Gage's killer.

Boots on, Layne rose and walked to the closet. He slipped his leather jacket free of its hanger and eased it on, wincing at the pain the movement jabbed through his broken ribs. Kinda warm for leather, but he wanted the Glock and the knives concealed in its pockets and attached to its lining. The knives, most of all.

Once he'd found the bastard who'd killed Gage, he'd finish things like he had in Mississippi after he'd healed enough from his beating to walk out of the hospital. He'd hunted, pounding the pavement and turning over every moss- and lichen-furred stone, until he'd found the shit-kicking mouth-breathing squatters. Every last fucking one of them.

Each had died hard and slow and messy, drenched in their own steaming blood and weeping for mercy from a man who had none to give. That part of Layne had died with Poesy.

After checking the magazine in his Glock and chambering a round, Layne flipped on the safety, then tucked the gun into the front of his jeans near the left hip and underneath his Inferno tee. He'd meet up with McKenna and find out how her talk with Frost had gone; then he'd start his search for Gage's killer and the hoodoo beauty's would-be killer. First stop—Basil Augustine's office.

On his way to the door, Layne paused beside the gurney and squeezed Gage's comforter-draped shoulder. "Be seeing you, man," he whispered, knowing he wouldn't—his best friend was well and truly gone.

Layne reached inside his jacket, the well-worn leather creaking, and drew a finger along the smooth hilt of one of the knives buckled against the lining. He felt a measure of razor-edged calm steal in through his fingertip. A promise to himself.

For Gage.

Layne strode from the room.

ELEVEN

A SHOWER OF WHITE SPARKS

"What the hell do you *mean* 'what am I'?" Blowing hair out of her face, Kallie glared at Augustine, wishing she could slap his perplexed but oh-so-curious expression from his goddamned aristocratic face. "At least I know what *you* are—a goddamned lying sonuvabitch. Let. Me. Go."

"That's what I'm endeavoring to do. But I need you to calm down and hold still."

"*You* calm down and hold still."

Augustine rolled his eyes. "Really, Ms. Rivière, that's not helping the situation."

"Meaning I'm making too big of a fuss for your taste, you lying bastard?"

Augustine pinched the bridge of his nose and sighed. "Fuss away, then. When you've tired of it, then perhaps we can work to get you free."

Stupid Brit. He sounded almost reasonable. Of course, *he* could afford to sound reasonable. He wasn't trapped in a goddamned chair, now was he?

Kallie squirmed and twisted and strained, but remained right where she was. The electric prickling had shifted into a deep-bone thrumming. Pain pounded at her temples like fists against shutters. White light flared through her mind.

She stands beside the bayou's cypress-shadowed waters, a gleaming knife clenched in one hand, a red candle cupped in the other. The mingled scents of roses and cinnamon curl into the air as the anointed wax melts, trickling hot over her fingers. In the darkness behind her, the rhythmic and steady throb of palm-slapped drums echoes through the night.

Ripples arrow along the bayou's green surface as a gator glides toward the bank. But her gaze seeks the shadow flitting among the live oaks and cypress on the bayou's other side, a man-shaped shadow that drops from upright to all fours. A shadow that lopes in easy, four-pawed grace across the sawgrass, moonlight pooled in its gleaming silver eyes.

The vision vanished in a shower of white sparks. Blinking, pulse racing, Kallie looked down at her hands, half expecting to see red wax hardening on her fingers.

Cold fear corkscrewed around Kallie's heart. *What the hell was that?*

"Ms. Rivière? Did you hear me?"

Kallie shifted her gaze to Augustine. "What?"

The illusionist folded his arms over his chest and arched an eyebrow. "I asked if you were wearing any charms or talismans. Any magically inked tattoos?"

"Oh." Kallie quit struggling long enough to look down at her bathrobe-covered chest and realized that, even though her pendants were still in place, her red flannel mojo bag was missing—most likely it had fallen off during all the enthusiastic getting-to-know-you tumbling she and Gage had done the night before. She also noticed that she'd managed to flail around enough in her attempts to wrench free of the chair to loosen up and part her bathrobe. At the moment, Augustine was not only getting an eyeful of her thighs and the vee of red lace panties between them, but of her red lace bra and the pushed-up cleavage it created.

Kallie tried to pull her hands free of the chair arms so she could close her robe, but nada. Still stuck. "Stupid robe," she muttered. "Maybe my pendants are the problem. They're for protection—gifts from my aunt."

"Well, that would qualify as magicked, but mild magic," Augustine murmured, studying the chair. "Let's remove them, shall we?"

"Okay." Kallie bowed her head to give Augustine better access to the clasps. He leaned over her, brushed her hair aside, and then unhooked and removed her pendants.

"Try to get up now," he said, stepping back.

But the thrumming still vibrated through Kallie's bones and veins, buzzed her thoughts. She attempted to lift her hands. Nothing. She blew her breath out in frustration. "Goddammit."

"Very intriguing. You should be able to get up," Augustine said, eyeing the chair.

Kallie realized that the Brit actually *was* perplexed, and that unnerved her. "You really don't have anything to do with this, do you?" she asked.

"Ah, the light finally dawns," he replied, gray eyes glinting. "Have you finished with your tantrum?"

"I can always start another just for you, asshole," Kallie said, wishing she could flip him off and/or knuckle another right hook into his jaw.

A smirk angled across Augustine's lips. "I have no doubt of that, Ms. Rivière. But it won't be necessary." One arm braced against the other, he stroked his chin thoughtfully as he studied her or the chair or both.

"Okay, so now what? How are you going to get me out of this chair?"

"I'm going to search you to make certain you don't have any other charms. Well, you *do* possess ample charms, Ms. Rivière—physical ones, at least, and certain to delight most males—but I'm referring to—"

Most males? Hmmm. "The magical ones, yeah, yeah."

"I'm hoping you won't force me to muzzle you à la Hannibal Lecter?"

Kallie rolled her eyes. "Just search me already. Christ."

Augustine's hands slid along her bathrobe-blanketed sides, his fingers probing the material. She caught a whiff of vanilla and frankincense from his oil-anointed cigarettes. His hand dipped into her left hip pocket, then into her right. "Aha."

He pulled a blue chamois bag from the pocket's depths. A *gris-gris* bag. He held it up for Kallie to see. "Intriguing sigil, but not one I'm familiar with."

"It's a *vévé*," Kallie said. Stitched into the bag was a heart framed by coiled snakes on either side and decorated with various symbols of the *loa*. "Marie Laveau's talisman for protection." And one of Belladonna's favorites.

She must've slipped it into the pocket when she handed me my robe.

Kallie tried to stand, hoping against hope that, despite the still-present thrumming, the *gris-gris* bag had been the problem. But she remained right where she was—stuck in the goddamned fricking chair. She looked at Augustine. "Now what?"

"We resort to desperate experimentation."

Augustine leaned forward and grasped Kallie's upper arms with strong fingers. The deep-bone thrumming quieted, returned to a skin-prickling tingle. The Brit murmured a phrase in what sounded like Latin or Greek.

"What are you say—" Her words trailed off as another shower of white sparks filled her vision; then the invisible straps binding her fell away, vanishing along with the electric prickling against her skin. She bolted to her feet and practically teleported across the room.

Augustine stepped back from the now-empty chair and turned around. He regarded Kallie with a speculative expression. "Why is it, I wonder, that my spell to release magicked *items* from the nullifying power of the sigils released *you*?"

"Because you trapped me there and only fooled me into thinking you hadn't," Kallie said, rearranging and rebelting her robe. She smoothed the pink terry cloth into place. "Or maybe it took a moment for the *gris-gris* mojo to wear off."

Augustine looked unconvinced. "Must be quite a powerful talisman to have kept you in that chair. Normally, the chair would've rendered the bag useless, not trapped its wearer."

Kallie shrugged. "Belladonna knows her shit."

"I have no doubt, but I can't help but wonder what would happen if you sat down in the chair again *without* the bag."

White-hot pain pounded at Kallie's temples and uneasiness twisted through her guts. Damned hangover. "Wonder all you want. I'm still not convinced you ain't playing games." She held out her hand for her pendants.

"I assure you that I'm not, Ms. Rivière." Augustine

gave her back the *gris-gris* bag, then coiled the pendants and their chains into the palm of her hand. "Perhaps you might indulge me? For curiosity's sake?"

"If you're so goddamned curious, plant your own ass in that chair. I'm not going anywhere near it again." Kallie put her pendants back on, fastening the clasps with practiced ease.

"Excuse me? Are you saying you won't go anywhere near my *ass* again?"

"No! The goddamned chair."

An amused smile quirked up the corners of Augustine's mouth. "Ah."

A polite knock sounded at the door. "Room service."

"My bruschetta and coffee," Kallie said, pleased with the interruption. She tucked the *gris-gris* bag back into her pocket.

Augustine looked at her for a moment, as if he was considering tossing her into the chair again; then he nodded. "Indeed. Let's get you fed and settled then, shall we?"

"Let's."

Augustine strode to the door, unlocked it, and swung it open. A young woman with café-au-lait skin and platinum-blonde curls walked into the room, a plastic dome-covered tray in her hands. She looked familiar and Kallie figured she'd probably delivered food to her and Gage the night before; the fruit, cheese, and bread platter that had turned out to be his final meal. Kallie blinked, eyes burning.

Still holding the doorknob, Augustine looked at the woman from over his shoulder. "Rosette," he said, his voice mystified. "You also work in the kitchens?"

"Only today, *m'sieu*," she—Rosette—replied. She

stopped beside Kallie and placed the tray on the table. She grasped the dome's knob.

Kallie's nose wrinkled. Beneath the garlic and tomato and fresh coffee scents, she caught a faint whiff of something off—rotten eggs—maybe from the hall, maybe from Rosette's pockets. Something that smelled like sulfur.

Alarm prickling along her nerves, Kallie glanced out the partially open door into the hall and spotted boot soles. Her heart springboarded into her throat. Someone was down. Sprawled on the carpet. Her gaze whipped back to Rosette.

Black dust. The HA guards. And facing her—the bitch who'd laid the deadly trick in her bed and killed Gage.

Memory clicked into place and Kallie knew where she'd seen Rosette before: the maid from upstairs, the one holding a vacuum's handle and staring wide-eyed as she and Belladonna had raced down the hall to Dallas's prone body.

"Shit! Augustine!"

Rosette tossed aside the plastic dome and scooped up the gun lying beside the plate of bruschetta—a gun Kallie suspected the maid had lifted from one of the drugged and fallen guards. Lips thinned with determination, face pale and beaded with sweat, the maid aimed the gun at Kallie's forehead with locked and trembling hands.

"Sorry," she whispered, "but an eye for an eye is never enough."

Mama turns and faces her, aims the gun carefully between her shaking hands. Her hands shake, but her face is still, resigned.

"Sorry, baby. I ain't got a choice."

Blood roaring in her ears, Kallie hooked a hard left into the maid's nose. Bone crunched beneath her fist.

Blood slicked her knuckles. The maid staggered, the gun wavering in the air, then quickly leveling. Her finger flexed against the trigger.

Time pulsed to a stop.

Rough hands latched onto Kallie's shoulders, and spun her away. Augustine's suit jacket whispered against her robe as he twisted his body past hers. Thunder cracked through the room, spiking pain through Kallie's ears.

Mama pulls the gun's trigger and the side of Papa's head explodes in a spray of blood and bone. He slumps down in his chair, a bottle of Abita still in his hand.

"No!" the woman cried.

Augustine grunted. He stumbled against Kallie, slamming her into the wall as he toppled into a boneless heap on the slate floor. The back of Kallie's skull thumped against the plaster and *into* it. A kaleidoscopic burst of fireworks detonated behind her eyes in a dazzling and dizzying array of color.

Kallie blinked the nauseating sparkles from her vision in time to see the murdering bitch again aim the gun at her forehead.

Mama pulls the trigger again.

Kallie moved without thinking, shoving away from the wall, her adrenaline-amped muscles straining forward with everything she had. She tackled Rosette, and they both hit the floor with a bone-rattling thud. The maid's breath whoofed out of her lungs. A second round of fireworks dazzled Kallie's vision. Then another ear-piercing peal of thunder exploded through the room.

McKenna slapped the button for the fifteenth floor, the three-inch-long pile of silver bracelets encircling her wrist clinking musically. Muzak—a fast-paced zydeco that sounded like a kissing cousin to an Irish reel—spilled from ceiling speakers as the elevator doors *schunk*ed shut.

"So the whole clan is coming to see Gage off?" Layne asked. He leaned against the mirrored back wall, hands shoved into the pockets of his leather jacket. A button she'd given him reading RAISED BY WOLVES was pinned to its right lapel, and a button underneath it asked: NO STRAIT-JACKETS?? WHAT KIND OF PLACE IS THIS??

"Aye. Yer mum figures fifteen hours, give or take, fer travel. They'll be here in the wee hours."

Layne nodded, and McKenna caught a heart-tugging whiff of sweet orange and musky sandalwood from his unknotted dreads. An intimate scent that reminded her of sleeping tucked into the hollow of his arm, her head on his chest.

"And Frost understood the situation?" he asked.

"Aye. Yer mum said nothing of Gage's soul."

"Good."

Layne seemed to study the red digital numbers ticking away each floor they passed, the skin beneath his eyes smudged with shadows, his jaw tight. Despite his casual posture, his cable-tight body almost seemed to thrum with coiled tension.

Her heart ached just looking at him. She'd seen him like this before. Ignoring his body's pain and hiding the anguish tearing him apart inside.

Poesy's gone, Layne. She died on the way to hospital. There was nocht anyone could do, luv.

He'd survived a beating that, by all rights, he shouldn't have. He'd survived the murder of his big sister, the sister who'd taught him everything she knew about running cons for quick cash from squatters.

Until one night, the con had failed and they were caught.

Nearly lost him that night. Almost lost him this morning too.

He'd even survived Poesy's ghost, her uncrossed-over spirit, climbing inside of him, pressing cold against his soul and mind, and wearing his body like a costume, using him to say her good-byes and vent her despair.

Survived, aye, but all the laughter and tenderness had been stomped out of him. His wild and poetic heart now caged and voiceless.

"Hey," she said softly. Layne glanced at her, his forest-green gaze steady. "How are you holding up?" she asked.

"I'm fine, woman. Holding up as well as you are."

McKenna snorted. "Then we're both doomed, lad."

A smile brushed his lips. He nodded. "That we are, buttercup."

The elevator slowed to a stop with a solid thunk. The doors slid open, revealing a busy administrative office. A male receptionist wearing a navy blue suit and tie sat behind a sleek mahogany desk beneath a sign proclaiming in a flowing and elegant script: *HECATEAN ALLIANCE, INC.* The sharp, clean scent of sage drifted into the air from a charcoal-burning brazier.

To the right of the desk, comfortable-looking chairs clustered around end tables piled with slick magazines; cubicles occupied the left side of the room. Voices in warm, fluid French and crisp, cheery English floated from the cubicles as employees chatted up clients, the sound filling the air like the busy hum of bees.

McKenna took note of the double steel doors marked

HOLDING barricading a hallway running past the receptionist's desk. Round signs containing a wizard's pointy hat with a red slash through it were emblazoned on both doors: no magic allowed.

Must be the detention facilities.

And most likely where Little Miss Striptease was being held.

Just as McKenna stepped from the elevator and into the foyer, a gunshot silenced the hum of voices from the cubicles. A second sharp *crack* followed a split second later. The receptionist dove under his desk.

McKenna leaped back inside the elevator and dropped down into a crouch to make herself a smaller target. Gunfight Survival 101. And apparently a course Layne had skipped somewhere along the line, since the bloody idiot rushed out of the elevator, his hand disappearing inside his jacket.

"Dammit, Layne, no!" McKenna cried.

But his long legs and adrenaline-spiked pulse had already carried him across the foyer. He slammed through the steel doors shoulder first, honey-blond dreads dancing against his leather-jacketed back.

The gleaming doors swung wide, and McKenna's heart pogoed up into her throat. The hall beyond swarmed with grim-faced guards in black, guns gripped with a deadly purpose in their gloved hands. Guards who now seemed to be zeroing in on the nomad who'd just barreled through the door.

"Holy Mother," McKenna muttered, jumping to her feet and joining the madness.

TWELVE

A MAN WHO SPEAKS HIS MIND

Men. Great for knocking boots together. Worthless in a pinch.

One hand on her hip, a damp, wrung-out rag smelling of sandalwood, patchouli, and gardenia petals in her other hand, Belladonna regarded Dallas Brûler. Considering that Kallie had saved the root doctor's messed-up life, you'd think the very least he could do would be to chase after Basil Augustine and demand Kallie's freedom.

But no.

Dallas Brûler allowed a little thing like unconsciousness to stand in the way. You'd think he'd chugged the actual contents of the potioned-up bucket, the way he'd dropped to the floor like an air-gunned steer. Belladonna snorted. Men. A little juju, a little wormwood, a near death, and they curled up like salted slugs.

So now Kallie had been hauled away by Basil Augustine and his black-suited guards, suspected of Gage's murder and facing an inquisition Hecatean Alliance style.

And what was Dallas doing? Standing beside Kallie—his rescuer—his strong hand on her shoulder, his steady gaze on her accuser? Murmuring encouragement and reminding her that the truth always shines and that the radiant truth of her innocence would sear the sight from Basil Augustine's eyes?

Oh, hell, no. Dallas was *snoring*. Sprawled on *her* bed, thank you, his head with its cap of damp red hair pillowed on his arms, his mouth open, his beard-shadowed face relaxed. Snoring. And reeking to high heaven of wormwood and cheap whiskey.

And she'd promised to take care of the sonuvabitch until he was conscious enough to do it himself. Not that he'd been doing such a bang-up job of that so far . . .

Not very nice. Not very fair. It's not Dallas's fault someone tried to kill him. Oh. Wait. Yes, it probably is.

Now Kallie, on the other hand . . .

Sighing, Belladonna walked into the bathroom and tossed the rag into the milky-green granite sink. Leaning against the threshold, she closed her eyes. Poor Kallie. All she'd wanted for the last nine years was to forget her dark and ugly past. She'd yearned to forget her papa's murder and her own miraculous survival . . . pounded a heavy-duty punching bag every day with taped-up fists, throwing heart, mind, and taut muscle into each knuckle-bruising blow.

Strived to understand why.

But Kallie's search for why would shackle her to the past forever. Sometimes *why* had no answer. Until she accepted the fact that her mother had been bat-shit insane and had access to a gun, she'd never let go of the past. Never accept her future.

She'd always be looking behind her.

Belladonna opened her eyes and rubbed her face. She wished she could be with Kallie, just so Kallie wouldn't be alone. To offer a little moral support. To keep her from blaming herself.

Kallie drops the sheet back over the hex, then sinks to her knees on the carpet. She closes her eyes.

Probably way too late for that. With another sigh, Belladonna pushed away from the bathroom threshold and walked back over to the table. Scooping up the small bottle of golden protection oil from beside her purse, she returned to the bed.

Belladonna plopped down onto the mattress beside Dallas. She uncapped the bottle and tipped it against her index finger as she studied the root doctor. A fine-looking man, Dallas Brûler—tall, lean-muscled, his looks more Texas-rugged than movie star–classical with his dark red hair and belly-fluttering deep blue eyes.

How many relationships had he busted up just to see if he could?

"No one stays true, Bell. Fidelity simply ain't a part of human nature."

"Excuse me, Dal, but your bitterness is showing. Not everyone is like Lucinda."

Still, if Belladonna ever found herself stuck with a flat tire on a dark and lonely stretch of road, the first person she'd call (provided she couldn't reach Kallie)—and the one who'd show up quicker than spit, no questions asked—would be Dallas Brûler.

Belladonna touched her oil-slick finger against the snoring root doctor's forehead, anointing him with the same sandalwood, patchouli, frankincense, sage, and gardenia mix she'd used to protect the room's doorway and windows.

Murmuring the sixty-eighth psalm, "'Let God arise, let his enemies be scattered,'" she touched her oiled and fragrant finger to the base of Dallas's throat, then the center of his sternum. "'As smoke is driven away, so drive them away—'"

A sharp knock on the door ended Belladonna's prayer. Her pulse leapfrogged through her veins. Dallas never even twitched, snorted, or stirred. Just kept snoring.

"Ms. Brown?" a female and oh-so-British voice inquired. "Lord Augustine requested that you and Mr. Brûler be taken into protective custody."

Protective custody? Not sure I care for the sound of that.

Belladonna twisted the cap back onto the bottle of protection oil, then dropped the bottle into a pocket of her tunic. Rising to her feet, she tiptoed across the carpet to the door, as silent in her two-inch-heeled half-boots as a barefoot ninja on grass.

Sidling up against the door, Belladonna peered through the spyhole. A smiling woman with sleek and curving strawberry-blonde hair met her gaze, the woman's happy hazel eyes level with Belladonna's.

Hmmm. Must be five-nine, five-ten, like me. Wonder if she's wearing heels?

Two tall and expressionless male guards—no doubt they'd left *their* heels at home—in neat black suits with the embroidered red HA insignia flanked the woman.

"And you are?" Belladonna challenged.

"Felicity Fields, Lord Augustine's assistant."

Belladonna snorted. "Felicity Fields? You kidding me?"

"I could ask you the same, Belladonna Brown."

"Touché." Belladonna unlocked and opened the door.

The guards, their eyes hidden behind stylish shades, broad-shouldered their way into the room and took up positions on either side of the door.

Felicity Fields, smile bright enough to inflict permanent damage to the retinas, bounced into the room, a May vision in white and rose, a small overnight bag in one hand—a black bag decorated with neon-green tree frogs.

Belladonna frowned. "That looks like Kallie's bag."

Felicity glanced at the bag, then returned her gaze to Belladonna. "Yes, it *is* your friend's overnighter. I was asked to bring her some clothing. Please do the same for yourself." She eyed Dallas. "My, my, my. Sleeping like the proverbial baby, is he?"

"Mmm-hmmm. Least he isn't crying like one," Belladonna replied. "Not yet, anyway. He's not used to being on the receiving end of a hex."

Dallas's snoring cut through the air like a buzz saw.

Felicity laughed, a throaty and intimate sound. "Men."

Belladonna found herself smiling. "Exactly."

Felicity dropped the overnight bag onto the carpet, then leaned over the bed and squeezed Dallas's biceps. "Oh," she chirped happily.

"Y'know, I'm none too happy with how your boss has been treating Kallie," Belladonna said, crossing to the closet and pulling out her ugly-ass Pepto Bismol–pink, but easily spotted, overnight bag. "Someone tried to kill her, then they tried to murder Dallas." She slipped a blouse and a pair of slacks from the closet's wood hangers, then folded them into the bag.

"It's my understanding that the situation has changed," Felicity said.

"Well, I should hope so, because the whole thing's stupid," Belladonna groused. Striding to the dresser, she yanked open the drawers, grabbed a handful of undies and stockings, and stuffed them into the ugly-ass overnighter.

"Instead of searching for the coldhearted bastard responsible, your boss decided to follow the time-honored tradition of accusing the victim. Something I bet the *real* killer is happy as hell about, by the way. As a detective and as a human being, Lord Augustine sucks."

"My, my, my. Please tell me how you *really* feel," Felicity murmured. "Well, then, it should make you happy to learn that Lord Augustine's opinion has changed and he now believes your friend innocent of Mr. Buckland's murder."

Belladonna glanced over her shoulder. "Seriously?"

Felicity nodded, her sleek and shining hair swinging with the movement. "Yes. Please finish packing, and I'll awaken Mr. Brûler." A smile blazed across her lips as she grasped Dallas's shoulder with one pink-nailed hand.

"Good luck with that," Belladonna said, stepping into the bathroom to fetch her toiletries. Given the way Felicity had been feeling up the root doctor's muscles, Belladonna wondered if the woman intended to kiss Dallas awake like he was an enchanted prince instead of an unconscious and drooling hoodoo.

Sauntering out of the bathroom, shampoo and cosmetic bag in hand, Belladonna glanced at the bed. What she saw iced her blood and froze her to the floor like a water fountain caught in a flash freeze.

Felicity pressed a glinting silver stiletto against Dallas's throat. A bead of dark blood trickled down his skin to the oil-anointed spot in the hollow of his throat. "Wake up, Mr. Brûler," she said. "You have some explaining to do."

Dallas's eyes snapped open, midsnore.

Dallas stared into cold hazel eyes—pale green flecked with brown—set in a lovely freckled face framed with shining strawberry-blonde hair. A face he couldn't recall—but, given his booze-blurred nights, not an unusual situation. Neither was a pissed-off husband, fiancé, or boyfriend shoving a gun in his face or swinging a tire iron in a whistling arc toward his head and/or balls.

But a knife pricking the vulnerable skin of his throat—*that* was a unique situation, for true. And given the stinging pain and the hot trickle along his neck, he was pretty damned sure that it *was* a knife the luscious babe was pressing against his throat and not, say, a salad spoon or metal tongs.

Dallas couldn't help but wonder if she was the one who'd tried to drown him via bucket-chained poppet.

Belladonna stood behind the woman, her eyes wide enough to send her eyebrows crawling for her blue-and-black-curled hairline, her mouth hanging open. As motionless as a wax figure. And just as useful. Great. The day kept getting better and better.

Not seeing Kallie, he felt panic ripple through him like a gator through a sunlit swamp—fast and ugly. Had she been arrested? "Where's Kallie?" he asked.

"Safe, Mr. Brûler," the babe with the knife said. "Now if you would be so kind as to answer in turn."

Dallas said, "Sorry, sugar, but I missed whatever it was you asked."

The knife-wielding babe's eyes warmed to golden brown. "I said you had some explaining to do."

"Sugar-doll, I'll be happy to explain to your little heart's content," Dallas reassured her, keeping his voice low and light. "Once you've told me where Kallie is, and once you've put that knife away."

"My, my, my. Smooth as silk you are, Mr. Brûler. But

the knife stays. For now. And Ms. Rivière is quite safe."

"I'm afraid you've got me at a disadvantage, darlin', knife-wise *and* name-wise."

"Felicity Fields, Lord Augustine's assistant. And he's a tad concerned about your presence here given that you believe the carnival is for fools only."

Belladonna blinked. "And the biggest one of all is lying on my bed."

"And she's back," Dallas muttered. "Thanks for the heads-up, Brown."

Belladonna perched her hands on her hips. "Oh no you don't. I am *not* to blame here, Dallas Brûler." She shifted her attention to Lord Augustine's assistant. Narrowed her eyes. "Besides, she neglected to mention the whole knife-to-the-throat thing."

"True, but I couldn't be sure that Mr. Brûler wasn't faking being asleep," Felicity Fields chirped, "and I really didn't want to give up the element of surprise."

"What, with all the damned snoring and drooling? You can't fake buzz-saw shit like that," Belladonna declared.

"Wait. Hold on. *Who* snores?" Dallas asked.

"*You* do, loud enough to bring the levees a-tumbling down."

"Bullshit, Bell. I only snore when I'm drunk."

Belladonna rolled her eyes. "Then no wonder you always snore."

Dallas glared at her and found himself wishing for the compliant and adoring Belladonna from his dreams. Felicity leaned in close enough to kiss, blocking his view of Belladonna, her heady, heated, sexy/intimate perfume teasing his nostrils.

"You snore in a robust and manly manner, Mr. Brûler,"

she whispered, her succulent, rosy lips drawing his gaze. "But I really think we should return to the matter at hand. Why are you here? And the truth would be in your best interests."

More blood trickled hot along Dallas's throat as Felicity gave the knife a little nudge. He managed a smile, despite the icy fingers of fear trailing along his spine. "Not a problem, darlin'. The truth it is." He wracked his brain for a reasonable lie, one that wouldn't earn him a deeper taste of the knife's edge, but his brain curled up into a ball on the far side of his skull and left him with only one choice.

The truth. Or part of it, anyway.

Dallas sighed. "Gabrielle asked me to keep an eye on Kallie, this being her first Hecatean carnival and all."

"Hellfire, and you *agreed* to play spy?" Belladonna muttered, shaking her head. "I know Gabrielle's protective, and that's understandable and all, given the circumstances, but Kallie's a grown woman."

Felicity studied him, her autumn-dappled gaze penetrating and steady, and for the first time in more years than he cared to number, Dallas felt stripped naked, but not in a good way.

"That's not all, is it?" she said. She flicked the knife.

Dallas felt another hot trickle of blood ooze down his throat and into the collar of his shirt. "Can't tell you nothing, sugar, if I bleed to death," he said.

"Then speak fast," Felicity advised. The knife didn't budge.

"All right, since it ain't no secret that Gabrielle thinks this stupid May Madness Carnival is for fools, she was worried that y'all would brainwash Kallie," he lied, wondering how Felicity's lips tasted.

"Jesus Christ," Belladonna groaned. "Are you kidding me?"

"'Fraid not, Bell."

"And you share those views, Mr. Brûler?" Felicity asked. "The carnival is for fools waiting to be brainwashed?"

Cherries. Dallas would bet anything that her lips tasted like sweet black cherries. "Yeah, it's definitely for fools. But no on the brainwashing, since most fools tend to lack brains."

"My, my, my," Felicity murmured, her bright gaze flicking down to Dallas's mouth as if she was making a flavor wager of her own. "A man who speaks his mind even with a knife at his throat."

"How about getting rid of the knife and letting me up?"

Felicity chuckled, a warm and throaty sound that slid like hot liquid velvet along Dallas's spine. "I suppose I shall. It's time we got you and Ms. Brown safely to new rooms." She sat up, and the steel-edged pressure vanished from Dallas's throat.

For a moment, Dallas didn't know whether to feel relieved or disappointed. He sat up and tried to finger-comb his hair—still damp and stinking of bitter herbs—into some kind of order and failing. He eyed the black-suited guards standing motionless at either side of the door.

Doesn't bode well, podna.

Face scrunched up as though she smelled a dead rat under the floorboards, Belladonna fanned her nose. "Whew! You smell strong enough to stun a bushel of skunks, Dallas Brûler. Booze and man-sweat and sulfur, and the devil knows what else. You need a shower in the worst way."

"Thank you, darlin'," he drawled as he flipped her off.

"Tell me something I don't know, like why we need new rooms. What the hell is going on, anyway?"

"Someone tried to kill both you and Ms. Rivière," Felicity replied, "but managed to kill Ms. Rivière's paramour instead." Untucking a rose lace handkerchief from her belt, she wiped Dallas's blood from her knife blade with a quick and expert twist of the cloth. "So Lord Augustine has arranged protective custody for all of you."

Dallas frowned. "Kallie's paramour?"

"No, not for him, I'm afraid. He's beyond the need for protective custody."

"No, I meant . . ."

Felicity glanced at him from beneath her long, blackened lashes. A coy and knowing flash of eyes. "I know what you meant," she murmured. "Given the tragedy Ms. Rivière just endured, perhaps it was good that you spent the night alone, Mr. Brûler."

Dallas winked. "Who says I did?"

"I do." A smile dimpled Felicity's cheeks. She slid her knife into a sheath tailored into her belt. "The one thing you *don't* smell of, Mr. Brûler, is a woman."

Dallas opened his mouth, closed it, mulled over a few possible retorts, then decided to change the subject. "You think Bell's life is in danger too?"

"No attempt has yet been made on Ms. Brown's life, but given her association with you and Ms. Rivière, best not to risk it, wouldn't you agree?"

"Oh, I definitely agree," Belladonna said. "Let's get our asses moving."

"Fine by me," Dallas said, standing. "Do y'all know if some wacko is just targeting hoodoos in general, or is it personal?"

"It's personal, all right," Belladonna said, her voice low. "The hex on Kallie's bed was a soul-killer."

Dallas stared at Belladonna. The grim steadiness of her gaze told him she wasn't kidding. Ice coiled cold through his guts. "Holy shit," he whispered.

"Did anyone besides Gabrielle LaRue know you'd be attending carnival?" Felicity asked.

Wrenching his gaze away from Belladonna, Dallas said, "No. Look, if you're implying that Gabrielle had something to do with all this, you're wrong. She's the one who called me—"

"And did Ms. LaRue's call lead you to your door and the bucket beyond? . . ." Felicity's words trailed off. She held up a *just a moment* finger before touching the Bluetooth curving against her ear. "Yes?" she inquired.

Dallas noticed that the guards had tilted their heads just slightly, as though listening to their own Comsats.

Once again, podna, this doesn't bode well.

Felicity's breath caught in her throat. She jumped to her feet, disbelief flickering across her freckled face. "Bloody *'ell*," she exclaimed, all the posh and polish in her voice scrubbed away in a Cockney-accented flare of emotion.

"Summon the healers and get the medical facilities operational," Felicity said into the rose-skinned Bluetooth, the polish once more glossing her words. But Dallas saw worry lines crinkling her forehead. "I'm on my way."

The guards shoved away from the wall, bodies tensed. One spun on the balls of his black-sneaker-clad feet, unlatched the door, then disappeared down the hall as swift and silent as a hunting wolf, his partner dogging his heels.

"Is it Kallie? Is she all right?" Belladonna asked. Her fingers locked around the handle of her pink overnight bag.

Felicity looked from Belladonna to Dallas, her face composed once more. "You and Ms. Brown shall stay here and wait for word from me. You should be perfectly safe in the meantime."

"All of a sudden we're safe? What's going on?" Dallas asked.

"We've found the killer," Felicity replied, a feral light glinting in her eyes. "Or rather, she found us."

"Hellfire," Belladonna breathed. "Then it's over?"

"You'll be among the first to know," Felicity replied, striding out into the hall. "But until then, both of you remain here. Keep the door locked and warded."

Dallas exchanged a quick look with Belladonna, cocked an eyebrow. She nodded, her hair a bobbing blue-black field of curls, and grabbed her purse from the table.

"We ain't the sit-and-bite-our-fingernails types, sugar," Dallas said, following Felicity into the hall. The woman was already halfway to the elevator, walking in brisk but still hip-swinging strides. "We're coming with you, like it or not."

"I choose the '*or not*' option," Felicity called. She never looked back or slowed her pace.

"Better run," Belladonna muttered, brushing past him and sprinting down the hall.

Dallas knew a good piece of advice when he heard one. He ran.

THIRTEEN

SHANGHAIED

Nausea spun like a Ferris wheel through Kallie's guts. The sharp and crackling scent of cordite smoked the air, intensifying the roiling in her belly. She swallowed hard and closed her eyes, concentrating on not puking. At least the killer slumped underneath her wasn't moving. A big ol' blessing, that.

Better get up, Kallie-girl, and find that goddamned gun before she wakes up.

Opening her eyes and disentangling herself from the maid's lax body, Kallie rose to her knees. Blood smeared Rosette's face, flowing from her rapidly swelling and now-canted-to-the-left nose. Out cold.

She hoped the platinum-blonde murderer's skull had bounced as hard against the floor as her own had against the wall when Augustine had shoved her.

Augustine . . .

Spotting the maid's gun underneath the table, Kallie stretched and snagged it. She slipped it into her bathrobe pocket, then swiveled around on her knees. She crawled over to Augustine, pain throbbing at her temples and at the back of her head. Another bout of nausea bounced through her belly.

The Brit lay on his back, face ashen and slicked with sweat, eyes closed. A dark and glistening patch of blood spread chest level across the front of his white dress shirt.

The man who'd stepped in front of Mama's gun.

No, not Mama's gun. The crazy-ass murdering maid's gun.

She needed to stop the bleeding. Not seeing anything else she could use to staunch the blood soaking into Augustine's shirt, she unknotted her belt and yanked off her robe. Just as she pressed the pink wad of terry cloth against his wound, the door flew open, slamming into the opposite wall. An avalanche of plaster flaked to the carpet in a creamy snowfall.

Kallie felt the action's violent vibrations more than heard it, since her ears were still ringing from the gunshots.

A handful of HA warriors slipped into the room, one after another, with SWAT team speed and efficiency, faces expressionless enough to win poker games, their huge black guns aimed at her.

Keeping pressure on the bathrobe/towel, Kallie nodded at the unconscious murdering bitch sprawled on the floor. "She was trying to shoot me, but got him instead." Her voice sounded distant and muffled, lost in a thick bank of fog. Pain ricocheted against the inside of her skull.

Two guards stepped past Kallie and Augustine to deal with the maid, while another knelt on the floor beside Augustine and across from Kallie. The guard pushed his shades up to the top of his brush-cut blond head as he thumped a black medic's case onto the floor. "Your head's bleeding," he said, unlatching the case. "You sure you didn't take a bullet?"

"I'm sure. Just got knocked into a wall," Kallie replied. "What can I do to help?"

The guard looked at her from beneath his pale brows, a faint smile pulling at one corner of his mouth. Kallie realized that she'd probably shouted her reply. Pointing to her ears, she shrugged.

The guard snapped on latex gloves, his ice-blue eyes sweeping over her and lingering for a split second on her red-lace-framed cleavage. "Just what you're doing. Keep applying pressure. I'm gonna get an IV line going."

Kallie blinked. Warriors, magicians, and . . . medics? "Got it." She pressed down with both hands, but dread curled cold along her spine when she saw blood darkening her bathrobe compress.

From out in the hall, Kallie heard strained shouts, some desperate—*is that the leprechaun?*—some frost-edged and insistent—*and Layne?*—while others barked commands, but she couldn't make out any words.

If it is *the nomads, what the hell are they doing here?*

Augustine groaned as the guard/medic slipped a needle into a large vein on the back of his right hand. His eyelashes fluttered.

Deciding to whisper in hopes of keeping her decibel level down, Kallie said, "Augustine, hey, hang on. You're safe now. Just hold on, okay?"

The Brit's eyes shuttered open, revealing dilated eyes rimmed with thunderhead gray. "Yes, by all means," he gasped, his voice bubbling and liquid. He blinked. "Where is your bathrobe, Ms. Rivière?"

"You're wearing it. And it looks like I owe you big-time.

Since I don't like owing anyone, you're just gonna hafta to put all of your effort into pulling through this so I can pay my debt."

Augustine crooked an unsteady finger. Kallie lowered her head, angling her ear against his bloodstained lips. "Naturally, the last thing *I* want is for my death to inconvenience *you*, Ms. Rivière," he whispered.

Kallie lifted her head and smiled. "You give good sass. That's a fine quality in a man. But you ain't dying. Now shut up and save your breath."

"You know, you really need . . . to stop punching . . . people," he bubbled.

"Shut up, I said."

"Your bedside manner must draw . . . admiring students from all . . . around the globe."

"Hush, you, or I'm gonna fetch the duct tape."

Closing her eyes, Kallie tried to draw white light into her, tried to visualize it flowing smooth and bright as sunlit chalk through her fingertips, tried to filter it through the bathrobe and into the Brit's gun-shot chest, but the light—thin as a ghost and twice as pale—wisped away whenever she reached for it.

Pain drummed a fierce rhythm behind her eyes, shattered her focus. For one dizzying moment she felt just like she had while trapped in the goddamned chair—bound with tight straps of prickling energy while pain pummeled her from the inside, as if someone was trying to batter their way free. Then the uncomfortable and alien—*Alien? Really? Sure you didn't feel something like this after you saw Mama put a bullet in Papa's skull?*—sensation vanished. Uneasiness coiled around her spine.

Gotta be this sigiled-up room, that's all. Now focus.

Kallie reeled in her fragmented thoughts and tried to hook them together again. Centering herself, she chanted, "Seal the wound to keep the blood where it belongs . . ." But her aching mind refused to cough up a rhyme and refused to guide the incantation's flow.

Despite the fuzziness blurring her thoughts, Kallie reached again for the white light. But it wisped away once more and her concentration dissolved like sugar in hot tea.

"I knew it."

Kallie opened her eyes and met Augustine's victorious gaze. "You're supposed to keep quiet," she reminded him. "So you can, y'know, keep breathing."

A faint smirk tugged at his lips. "I *knew* it wasn't just that charm—" His eyes widened as his words ended in a long, low sigh. The triumphant light in his eyes vanished like a flame snuffed by a yanked-open door. His head lolled to one side, a dark wing of hair sweeping across his forehead.

Fear spiked through Kallie. "No, no, don't do this. Stay here!" She grasped his chin with one shaking hand, turning his face back to her. His half-lidded and unfocused eyes looked through her. Empty as Gage's.

The monitor the HA guard/medic had just hooked up to Augustine emitted a long and steady *beeeeeeep*. "Shit! He's crashed!"

Someone grabbed Kallie by the shoulders, shoving her back as another guard dropped beside Augustine's body to help with the resuscitation efforts. Her bloodied bathrobe was tossed aside and Augustine's shirt torn open. Muffled voices swirled around her, shouting instructions. Kallie sat back on her heels, numb to the heart, knowing it was too late, their efforts futile.

Basil Augustine was dead.

Multiple *ka-chunks* ricocheted through the hall as gun slides were pulled back and rounds were chambered. Multiple pairs of sunglass-shaded gazes targeted Layne. Aimed big-ass gun barrels.

Layne released his fingers from the grip of the Glock still tucked into the front of his jeans and lifted both hands palms out into the air. "I came up here to talk to Augustine," he said, keeping his voice level. "Then I heard the gunfire. Just here to help."

"Gun on the floor and move slow if you plan on remaining lead-free."

Keeping his empty hand in the air, Layne slipped his Glock free of his jeans. He bent, jacket creaking, and placed it on the scarlet-flowered Persian carpet. Slid it toward the guards fanned out along the hall. Each and every gun barrel seemed to be aimed at the center of his forehead. He straightened slowly, pain radiating out from his sternum. He kept both hands lifted.

A strange odor floated in the air—the stink of rotten eggs and brimstone mingled with sweet black licorice. The brimstone spoke of discharged magic and explained the pair of crumpled bodies in black stretched out along the carpet in front of one of the rooms marked with a Q.

A hard fist knuckled into Layne's shoulder blade—a punch quickly followed by an eye-watering yank on his dreads.

"Dammit, Valin," McKenna spat, "yer—"

"Man-stupid," he finished. "Yeah, yeah. I know." And

at the moment, he agreed, even if he had no intention of saying so out loud.

"Freeze! Hands in the air!" one of the guards shouted.

"Maybe *I* should just kill you and save myself further grief," McKenna said, releasing his dreads so she could knuckle another blow into his biceps before complying with the guard's demand. "Ye planning on following Gage into the grave? Is tha' it?"

Startled, Layne looked at her. Standing beside him, her hands in the air, McKenna regarded him with cold dark eyes, her face a shaman's unreadable mask. "No, *shuvani*, no. That ain't it."

"Running *toward* gunfire? You coulda fooled me."

Layne held her icy gaze for a moment before shaking his head. He couldn't explain to her what he himself didn't understand—the feelings burning through his heart—not without sounding like an even bigger man-stupid idiot.

Gage died in Kallie Rivière's place and paid for her life with his own, and now it's my duty to make sure she stays alive, to make sure that no one succeeds in closing her violet eyes forever. It's the only way I can give his death some kind of meaning.

"It was all adrenaline, *shuvani*," Layne murmured.

"Both of you—hands against the wall, legs apart," one of the guards barked, waving toward the other side of the hall with his big-ass-barreled gun.

With a sigh, Layne turned around and splayed his hands against the cream-colored damask walls and spread his feet apart. The cold barrel of a gun slid between his dreads and nuzzled the back of his neck.

"Take your jacket off and drop it on the floor," a female voice said.

Keeping his movements slow and deliberate, Layne shrugged off his jacket, then dropped it as instructed. The round metal studs decorating the leather jacket's bottom half jingled as it hit the carpet.

"Hands back on the wall," the guard said. "And keep very still."

"Like a stone," Layne said. "Can you tell me what's happened? Does it have anything to do with the murder that happened a coupla hours ago?"

"By 'keep very still,' I meant your mouth too, road-rider."

"Ain't you just fulla sunshine?"

"Don't make me Tase you."

"Wouldn't want that, no." After a hard poke against the back of Layne's neck, the gun barrel vanished and he breathed a little easier. Easy for a finger to slip on a trigger—sometimes even accidentally.

From beside him, Layne heard McKenna tell whoever was searching her, "You put those hands anywhere they don't belong an' ye'll be getting yer face panned in."

"I think I'd have to find you a stepladder first, ma'am."

"Aye, most likely," she grumbled.

Layne snorted in amusement. "I wouldn't advise it. She'll tear you up."

"One more peep outta you," Layne's guard advised, "and you'll make me do something you'll regret and I'll enjoy."

Layne had a feeling she wasn't bluffing. He nodded. She patted him down with quick but thorough movements, then ordered him to put his hands behind his back.

Shit. Figuring it'd only earn him a Tasing if he protested or resisted, Layne slid his hands from the wall and swung them behind him. The guard looped flex-cuffs around his wrists, pulling them tight enough to make his fingers tingle.

"Turn around," she said.

Layne swiveled around and his guard—tall and slim, her ink-black hair pulled back into a tight, sleek ponytail—hooked a hard-fingered hand around his biceps. Her name, stitched in red above the HA logo on her uniform, read: BECKHAM.

"Can I speak now?" Layne asked.

"Fine," she sighed.

"This ain't necessary. I ain't the threat here."

"Says the man who barged into a restricted area with a gun tucked into his jeans," Beckham retorted. She led him down the hall to a black steel-mesh bench. "Sit your nomad ass down."

Layne sat his nomad ass down, his gaze fixed on the open doorway across the hall that guards bustled in and out of—a room marked Q1. He had no doubt that was where the shooting had taken place. His guard planted herself beside the bench, her posture tense, her gun clenched in her right hand.

"So *now* can you tell me what happened?" he asked. "Who got shot, and who did the shooting?"

"The scene is still being secured," she replied. "And that's all I'm going to say."

"Yup, just an illuminating little ray of sunshine," Layne muttered.

McKenna's guard, his red-stitched name proclaiming him to be Jennings, walked her to the bench to wait with Layne. McKenna lifted her uncuffed hands and twirled them through the air. Arched a dark eyebrow.

"Yeah, yeah," Layne muttered.

McKenna graced him with a withering look and folded her bracelet-ringed arms with their curling blue-ink tattoos underneath the curve of her breasts. She sat down beside him, chin lifted, nearly regal despite her gauzy sleeveless royal-blue blouse and her hip-hugging jeans—so faded they looked nearly white, her feet laced up in Roman sandals.

Looking at her, Layne couldn't help thinking that, even angrier than a stirred-up hill of fire ants, she was beautiful. Even after their divorce, she'd always had his back. He knew he should apologize, or offer an explanation, or say something, *anything,* but just as he opened his mouth, a low, monotonous *beep* sliced into the hall from the room across the hall.

Flatline. Was it Kallie? Would he fail Gage all over again?

Heart kicking against his ribs and spiking pain through his chest, Layne jumped to his feet, his gaze on the open doorway across the hall.

A hand clamped onto his shoulder and practically shoved him back down onto the bench. "You get up again—"

"You'll Tase me, I know," Layne growled, looking up at Beckham. He noted beads of sweat at her hairline. *She's worried.* And he relaxed a little, thinking a Hecatean Alliance guard wouldn't get worked up over a stranger like Kallie. So maybe it had been another member of the security force who'd taken two bullets.

And maybe, just maybe, Kallie hadn't even been involved.

A guard pushing what looked like a medical crash cart raced down the hall. The cart nearly popped a wheelie as he took the turn into the room.

"Can you see anything?" McKenna asked in a near whisper, her voice still bristling with ice.

Layne shook his head. "Nope."

Basil Augustine backed out of the room, a bemused expression on his face. He smoothed a hand down the front of his pristine suit jacket.

A shout of "Clear!" echoed from the Q1 room, followed by a sharp *ker-thap.*

<Looks dreadfully painful,> Augustine murmured. *<I must admit I never saw* this *coming.>* He turned around and relief flashed across his face when he spotted Layne. *<Valin. How very fortuitous.>*

"Shit," Layne breathed, staring at the Brit. An electric prickle stood the hair up along the back of his neck and goosebumped his skin—a familiar and blood-chilling sensation, one he'd experienced more times than he cared to remember.

"Again! Clear!" *Ker-thap.*

Not only was Basil Augustine dead, but he hadn't crossed over. And given the intensity of his gaze, it looked like he had no intention of doing so any time soon.

"Shit," Layne repeated. The last thing he needed at the moment was a passenger—not when he had Gage and his family to tend to, a killer to hunt, and a blood price to collect.

<Truly a relief, Valin. There is so much I need to finish and instructions to pass along, et cetera, et cetera.>

"Hey, that's what everyone thinks," Layne said, "and that's understandable, but you're done. I'm sorry about that, I truly am, but you don't get to finish stuff. You need to move on."

"Who you talking to?" McKenna whispered. "Who died?"

"Augustine, and he's looking for a body."

"Holy Mother. Where is he?"

"Right in front of us."

Augustine sauntered across the hall, moving just as he had in life. Newly dead and possibly in shock after a violent death, he was unaware that the laws of the physical world and of his own cooling body no longer applied.

But he'd learn soon enough. They always did.

"Clear!" *Ker-thap.*

Augustine stopped at the bench, his attention fixed on Layne. Layne smelled ozone crackling through the air—the thunderstorm scent of ghosts.

<This is all quite bizarre and a bit of a shock, I admit. I never anticipated an attempt on Ms. Rivière's life in here. *And certainly not in such a mundane manner.>*

Layne's heart skipped a beat. "Is she all right? Was the killer caught?"

Augustine nodded. *<Yes, on both counts.>*

"Who was the sonuvabitch who killed Gage?"

McKenna stiffened beside Layne. "They caught Gage's killer?"

<We caught a *killer, but I have my doubts about it being Mr. Buckland's killer.>*

"Why do you think that?"

<I have my reasons. And I shall require a body in order to fully explore those reasons.>

"Uh-huh. And this is in addition to all the things you have to finish and all the instructions you need to pass along?" Layne asked. "Ain't buying it."

<Then tell me, Valin, how does one go from laying a soul-killing hex to being content with just a physical kill?>

"Desperation. Lack of time. Who knows?"

<Perhaps. Perhaps not. But it's worth exploring.> Curiosity gleaming in his eyes, Augustine bent and touched a hand to McKenna's gelled and anime-angled dark hair.

Goosebumps prickled along her bare arms, and she hugged herself, shivering convulsively. "Did that bloody bastard just touch me?" she asked, eyeing the empty air in front of the bench.

"Yup."

"Wanker."

"Who's a wanker? Me or him?" Layne asked.

"He is. You're just man-stupid."

Chuckling, Augustine lifted his hand. *<She has a point on both counts.>* He returned his gaze to Layne. *<So let's see how this works, shall we?>* he said, grasping Layne's shoulder.

Electricity thrummed into Layne as the Brit's hand disappeared into his flesh. Twisting away from Augustine's grip, Layne bolted to his feet. Pain jabbed into his ribs with each panicked thump of his heart. "Get the fuck away from me!"

Augustine straightened and looked at his hand, wriggling his fingers. *<How utterly intriguing. Touching you is like slipping into a crisp new shirt.>* He raised his shining gaze to Layne. *<It's like returning home.>*

"*My* home, and you ain't getting in."

Frowning, Augustine flipped his hair out of his eyes with a flick of his fingers. *<Permission isn't required, and Vessels aren't supposed to be capable of resisting. At least that's always been my understanding.>*

"Most can't. But I've learned how, and you ain't getting in."

<I believe you're bluffing. You are a Vessel for a reason, Valin. You are a natural and needed resource. And, since I don't believe in

coincidences, your arrival here when you were needed most shouldn't be wasted.>

Layne backed up a few paces as Augustine stepped toward him.

"Freeze, asshole! Or her brains will decorate the wallpaper."

Layne heard the click of a trigger being pulled back. He turned around. Beckham pressed the muzzle of her gun against the back of McKenna's head. Fear trailed cold fingers down his spine. The other guard, Jennings, stood against the wall, fingers touching the mouth of his gun holster, looking both startled and uncertain. But Layne had no doubt he'd back his partner's play—whether he agreed with it or not.

"You, me, and my gun are gonna sit your nomad ass back down," Beckham said. "You said that Lord Augustine was dead and looking for a body. You must be a Vessel."

"No, I'm just bored and spouting bullshit," Layne replied.

"He *does* spout bullshit fer the sake of it," McKenna affirmed. "I wouldn't pay him any mind. Men, y'know?"

"You both need to shut the hell up," Beckham said. "If Lord Augustine needs a Vessel, then I guess you're his man. If you're not a Vessel, then you have nothing to worry about, do you?"

<*Note the name—Beckham. Remind me to give her a much-deserved raise.*>

"Screw yourself, Basil."

"Do you know what yer askin' of him?" McKenna pleaded. "Do you know what it's like to carry the dead inside of you? To take a backseat in yer own body?"

"Don't know," Beckham replied, her voice taut, "and really don't care. Now shut up before I have you Tased."

"In addition to being shot? Sounds like someone needs tha' Taser shoved up her tight little arse," McKenna muttered. "Along with her gun."

"Bring it, baby." Amusement curled through Beckham's voice.

A dark smile curved McKenna's lips. A smile Layne knew well. She'd never leave New Orleans without answering the guard's challenge. Beckham might as well save herself extra pain, bruises, and humiliation by bending over, inserting said item into said arse, and being done with it.

"Put the damned gun away. Christ!" Layne sat back down on the bench. "It ain't necessary. I won't resist the bastard."

Beckham snorted. "Like I'm going to take your word for it. The gun stays put."

"It's all right, lad," McKenna said, offering him a smile. "Don't worry about me. Just keep yourself safe and intact, yeah? I'll be waiting for you."

Layne nodded. "You watch your ass too, buttercup."

Augustine eased onto the bench beside Layne. *<I hate to force you, Valin, honestly, I do. But necessity requires it. I promise to vacate as soon as I've finished the task at hand.>*

"Whatever. Shut the fuck up and just get in already." Layne closed his eyes and exhaled. He tried to force his tensed and knotted muscles to relax, but only managed to twist them up even tighter.

Augustine sieved into Layne, cell by cell, pouring into him in a cold, numbing flood of charged and ozone-drenched energy, short-circuiting Layne's control over his own body. Alien memories, sensations, and thoughts swept him up like a canyon hiker caught in a raging flash flood.

As crackling static filled Layne's mind with white noise and he felt his sense of self slipping, the first flutterings of panic winged through him. A violent storm of electricity thrummed into him. Isolating and caging him in a pit of noisy white light—voiceless, blind, and deaf.

A vessel filled once more.

FOURTEEN

DEADLY TO THE MALE OF THE SPECIES

"You all right, Shug?"

Kallie lifted her chin from her knees and looked up, following the voice to its source. Belladonna stood in the doorway, black leather bag slung across one shoulder of her tunic, sympathy and worry battling for dominance in her hazel eyes.

"Hey, Bell." Unwrapping her arms from around her legs, Kallie pushed her hair back from her face. Her head ached and throbbed. "Actually, it's been a really sucky day." The smell of rubbing alcohol and coppery blood stung her nostrils.

Belladonna's gaze flicked over to Augustine's body. Torn packaging from medical supplies haloed him in shredded plastic and paper. Useless leads trailed away to silent monitors. "No shit," she murmured, walking into the room. "I think that's a monster understatement, Shug."

Belladonna's movement caught the eye of the guard/medic who'd struggled so hard to resuscitate Augustine. He looked up from where he knelt beside the Brit's body packing up equipment. He opened his mouth as though he was about to order Belladonna out, then he glanced at

Kallie. Shaking his head, he resumed what he was doing without a single word spoken.

"You did everything possible," Kallie said to him. "It ain't your fault." But guilt burned the back of her throat. Not his fault, no. But if not for her, Augustine—just like Gage—wouldn't be dead.

A muscle jumped in the guard's jaw. He kept packing.

Belladonna crouched down beside Kallie. A heated whiff of patchouli curled out from the neck of her tunic. Frowning, she pushed Kallie's hair aside and pressed gentle fingers to the back of her skull. Pain flared at Belladonna's touch, merging with the red-hot knot of hurt pounding against Kallie's mind. She pulled away from her friend's probing hand.

"*Ow.*"

"You're hurt," Belladonna said, her voice indignant. "Has anyone taken the time to look at you?"

"They're pretty busy, and it's nothing serious. I hit my head, that's all. Looks worse than it is, yada yada."

"Girl, how would you know? You could have a concussion or a brain injury that's swelling this very minute. You could be in a coma soon."

"You promise?" Kallie rested her forehead on her knees again. "You've *got* to stop looking at those goddamned medical sites. Besides, a coma sounds damned good right now. I just want a bottle of aspirin and years of sleep."

"If you've got a concussion, then sleep's the *last* thing you should have."

"Don't even *think* about trying to keep me from sleeping, Belladonna Brown. I don't give a rat's ass what WebMD says."

"Mmm-hmmm. You're gonna regret those words one day."

"Not likely."

"Well, then, let's get you to my room so you can lapse into a death-coma in comfort at least," Belladonna said. "Since your bathrobe's ruined, I'm gonna see if I can rustle up a blanket or a sheet to cover you with. You can't go prancing down the halls in your undies—pretty as they are."

"Prancing ain't on my to-do list," Kallie muttered.

Belladonna slipped an arm around Kallie's shoulders and gave her a quick squeeze, murmuring, "I know, Shug." The comforting warmth of Belladonna's arm vanished when she rose to her feet and padded away.

Kallie raised her head and the room twirled around her in a slow pirouette. Her belly clenched. She swallowed hard, waiting the nausea out. Once it had eased, she peeked under the table. At the far end of the room, beneath the sunlight-filled windows, she caught a glimpse of Rosette's rubber-soled shoes and the black-clad knees of two more guards.

"Sorry, but an eye for an eye is never enough."

What had the murdering maid meant by that—aside from implying that she was one-upping the standard biblical thou-shalt-reap-bloody-revenge permission slip? Kallie had never seen the woman before, didn't know her, so how could she have wronged her?

And why had the bitch gone after Dallas too?

Augustine's words, spoken maybe only thirty or forty minutes ago, circled through Kallie's thoughts.

"I think it's more personal than that. You, your aunt's former protégé, an attempt to frame your aunt for murder. In truth, your aunt Gabrielle seems to be the connecting factor."

Maybe he'd been right about that. Only one way to find out.

Kallie eased to her feet. Pain pulsed behind her eyes. A cold sweat beaded her forehead. She waited a moment to make sure she wasn't going to puke or drop to the floor in a dead faint, then padded around the sigil-etched table—careful not to brush against it, just in case. She stopped behind the HA guards as they hauled the now-conscious maid into a sitting position against the wall.

Hands cuffed behind her back, Rosette looked a little the worse for wear with her nose swollen and slanted, her face blood-smeared. Black bruises were just beginning to wing out from the bridge of her nose and underneath her dazed eyes.

One of the guards glanced over his shoulder at Kallie. "Keep your distance."

"Ain't gotta tell me twice." Kallie said. "I just have a few questions for her."

Rosette looked up at the sound of Kallie's voice, and her gaze latched onto Kallie, no longer dazed or unfocused. An expression Kallie couldn't name—resignation, despair, hatred, maybe all three—rippled across her bruised face.

"And I have one for you, Kallie Rivière," she said. "How many people are you going to allow to die in your place before you accept your fate?"

Allow to die?

Mama turns and faces her, aims the gun carefully between her shaking hands.

Uneasiness iced Kallie's guts. "What fate? And who the hell *are* you?"

"An eye for an eye is never enough. Never, never, never."

Kallie added madness to that list of emotions she couldn't name. She took a step closer, but the guard swiveled to face her, one hand out at chest height. His gaze swept over her, pausing at her breasts, lingering at her thighs, before returning to her face, a happy little smile on his lips.

Kallie lifted her chin, cheeks burning. Well, what had she expected? She *was* in her goddamned undies, after all, and the guard *was* a breathing male with eyes.

Looking past him to Rosette, Kallie said, "You murdered two men who never did you any harm, and for what? Why? You even killed Gage's soul, you goddamned *chienne*!"

Guilt pooled deep in the maid's dark and dilated eyes, guilt she tried, but failed, to blink away. Kallie saw it as the maid looked away and down, a translucent ghost of shame and regret haunting her eyes.

So *that* had bothered her, at least. Small comfort. Gage had been more than murdered; he'd been destroyed. And maybe that was why she'd come with a gun this time instead of waiting for Kallie in a magic-allowed zone with another soul-shredding hex.

"That wasn't supposed to happen," the maid said. "How did you know?"

"That doesn't matter. What *does* matter is why."

Rosette lifted her gaze, sunlight shimmering in her cropped platinum-blonde curls. The vulnerability Kallie had seen before was gone. Now a cold, hard light glinted in her eyes. "Your fate comes compliments of Gabrielle LaRue, and you can thank her for it," she said. "You want answers? Ask her."

Kallie had half expected those words or others like

them, given the wet curl of paper she'd dumped from the eviscerated poppet, but to hear the lie spoken aloud hit as hard as a low-hanging tree branch snapped back by a grinning and obnoxious cousin.

"Who *are* you?" Kallie repeated. Her pulse pounded in her temples.

"Check my employee file," the maid said, her voice flat.

"That's it for the Q-and-A session," the guard said, swinging his other hand up. "You need to vacate the room so we can move her to a secure location."

"A secure location? Y'all got such a thing?" Kallie asked, glancing across the room at Augustine. A sheet now draped his bloodied form. A pang pierced her. "I thought *this* was a secure location. So did he." She gave her gaze back to the guard.

His jaw tightened and he shifted, his boot soles scuffing the slate. "A *more* secure location," he replied. "You need to leave, miss."

"Not a problem, sir," Belladonna said, handing Kallie a beige blanket. "We'll get our butts in gear."

Kallie twirled the blanket up over her shoulders and clasped it closed in front of her. No longer feeling quite as exposed, vulnerable, some of the tension leaked from her muscles. "Thanks, Bell."

"Hellfire. There's that word again," Belladonna said. "Twice in one day. Either you've got a concussion or you've been replaced by a pod person."

"Maybe a thump to the skull will convince you otherwise."

"I think I'd prefer the polite pod-Kallie to the skull-thumping non-pod version."

"And I bet the pod-Belladonna would be quiet. As quiet as a mouse in a library."

Belladonna snorted. "Now you're just delirious."

The guard sighed. "Time to go, ladies."

As Kallie started for the door, Rosette called, "All of this and anything else that's coming can be laid upon the doorstep of Gabrielle LaRue. Remember that."

Kallie paused. "The only doorstep Gage and Augustine's deaths can be laid upon is yours. And yours alone." She resumed walking as guilt shifted inside of her, restless and cold, a snake seeking the sun.

Dunno, Kallie-girl. Maybe the blame ain't hers alone.

"Do you know what the crazy bitch is talking about?" Belladonna asked.

Kallie shook her head. "Not really. She claims to have some kinda grudge against Gabrielle." Stopping in the doorway, she turned and looked at Augustine's body one last time.

Blood had soaked through the sheet in a couple of quarter-sized spots. She tried to think of something to say, something meaningful, a good-bye and thank-you to the man who had taken a bullet for her, had died in her place, but—once again—her aching mind only tossed out clichéd and trite crumbs.

Wish I could turn back time. . . .

I can never repay you. . . .

I'm so sorry. . . .

Thank you. . . .

"Eternal rest grant unto him, O *bon Dieu*," she whispered, but the rest of the prayer wisped away like smoke beneath a ceiling fan, the words beyond her recall. "Good journey," she wished him. Turning away, she walked out of the room, Belladonna a patchouli-scented pace behind her.

Kallie was surprised to see Dallas sitting on a black metal bench against the opposite wall, his jeans-clad legs stretched out in front of him. His red hair stuck up in various odd places on his skull and was flattened down in others; his good-looking face bristled with reddish whiskers. But at least he looked a damned sight better than when she'd last seen him. He was conscious, for one thing.

Relief flashed across Dallas's face when he saw her. Jumping to his feet, he said, "Hey, darlin'. You okay? You're looking a little rough."

"There's the pot calling the kettle black," she drawled. "Take a look in the mirror lately?"

A rueful grin tugged at Dallas's lips. "Afraid it'd crack if I did, and I don't wanna add to my sudden run of bad luck." He raked the fingers of both hands through his hair—for all the good it did. His hair remained spiked and flattened. "But you ain't answered me. You okay, hon?"

"Yeah, I'm okay. Compared to the condition Basil Augustine and Gage Buckland are in, a little rough ain't nothing to complain about."

Dallas nodded, sympathy in his summer-evening-blue eyes. "True enough. Let's head on outta here then. Maybe you should forget the rest of the carnival and head on home."

"Maybe. But that's for me to decide, Mr. Bossy. By the way, why are you spending money on a hotel room when you live so close?"

"Yes, Dallas, why, oh, why, pray tell?" Belladonna said, tone gleeful.

Dallas glowered at Belladonna from underneath his ginger brows and Kallie saw the accusation in his eyes: *Did you blab?*

"Nope," Belladonna said, apparently seeing the same question in his eyes. "But if you don't fess up, Dallas Brûler, I *will* tell her."

Kallie groaned. "No confessions until after I've had some sleep."

"Fair enough," Dallas agreed, relief in his voice.

"I'll make sure you don't forget," Belladonna said, patting his shoulder.

The root doctor aimed a sour look at her. "Thanks."

Kallie saw Layne a couple of yards to her left, standing in a little knot of people composed of a pair of HA(!) guards, a tight-jawed McKenna-pixie, and a strawberry blonde in a rose skirt.

So I did *hear the nomads. Wonder what brought them here? And why the hell is Layne cuffed?*

One of the guards slipped a pair of needle-nosed pliers from inside his suit jacket and snipped off the flex-cuffs binding Layne's wrists. The nomad swung his arms around, then winced. Touching a hand to his sternum, he said, "I had no idea he was injured. This is most inconvenient."

Kallie stared at Layne, cold beneath her blanket. Between the gunshots, Augustine's death, the guilt coiled in the pit of her belly, and her weariness, she *had* to be hearing things, because she could've sworn the nomad had just spoken in a posh British accent.

"What the hell?" Belladonna asked. "Is Layne mocking Felicity?"

"Dunno. Who's Felicity?"

"Lord Augustine's assistant. The Bondalicious chick

with the Bluetooth and the gorgeous rose-colored pumps."

Leave it to Belladonna with her budding *America's Next Top Model* fashion sense to notice the color of someone's shoes. But . . .

"*Bondalicious*? Seriously?" Kallie slid Belladonna a sidelong glance.

"Seriously. Look at the woman."

"You forgot to mention the knife in her belt," Dallas grumbled.

"Knife?" Kallie zipped her gaze back over to the tall, curvy—okay, all right, Bondalicious—strawberry blonde.

"Long but amusing story," Belladonna whispered. "I'll tell you later."

"Yeah," Dallas muttered. "Another one I come off well in."

"I'll make arrangements for a healer to meet with you, my lord," Bondalicious Felicity said in efficient and cheery tones. She touched a finger to the Bluetooth curving from her ear.

My lord? A dark suspicion sparked in Kallie's pain-pricked mind.

"Thank you, Mrs. Fields. Also, please see to it that Beckham receives a promotion to sergeant," Layne said, continuing in a very definite British accent.

A pleased smile touched the lips of the female member of the guard pair standing beside him. "Thank you, my lord."

When Layne spotted Kallie, a smirk played across his lips. An oddly *familiar* smirk. "Well, well, well, you proved me right, Ms. Rivière, but not in a manner I'd anticipated."

"Right?" Kallie repeated, pulse racing. "About what?"

Rubbing his wrists one after the other, the nomad sauntered over to where she stood in front of the bench. She smelled sandalwood, sweet orange, and soap as he stopped in front of her.

Layne's gaze seemed wrong somehow, different, like a stranger looked out of his pine-green eyes—an aloof and coolly amused stranger lacking Layne's deeply felt and open emotions, his passion.

Or maybe not a stranger at all.

"You seem to have a deadly, if not fatal, effect on males," he said. "Myself obviously included."

Kallie's skin prickled underneath her blanket. "Augustine," she breathed.

FIFTEEN

ON THE WINGS OF THE PAST

"Shit and hellfire," Belladonna said. "The nomad told the truth. He *is* a Vessel."

"Indeed," Layne-Augustine agreed. "A fact I'm quite grateful for." His gaze slipped past Kallie, and she wondered if he was looking at the room he had died in, the room containing his cooling body. "I want you to know, Ms. Rivière, I appreciate all the effort you made on my behalf in there."

Kallie frowned, not sure she'd heard right since her ears were still ringing. "Appreciate? You got shot because of me. You *died* because of me."

Layne-Augustine waved a dismissive hand. "Hardly, Ms. Rivière. I got shot because I wound up in front of a gun barrel, and the bullet in my chest is the reason I died. Not you."

"What a bloody lovely reunion this is." McKenna stalked over, her dark brows slashing down, cold fury icing her eyes. "Do whatever it is you need to do, Basil, then get the hell outta Layne's body. Ye've no idea how much this costs him."

"That is what I intend to do, Ms. Blue," Layne-Augustine replied, trailing a finger along one thick dread.

Glancing down at the nearly waist-length, honey-brown tendrils, he murmured, "Do you think he'd mind a haircut? And perhaps clothing that didn't come out of the Salvation Army or wherever it is you nomads gather your rags?"

A deadly smile tilted the pixie's lips. "Try it, ye bloody blighter, and see what happens if you change a single thing about him."

Layne-Augustine arched an eyebrow, an expression that gave Layne's handsome face a naughty-wicked edge. "That's an empty threat, Ms. Blue, since we both know you won't do anything that might harm Valin or his body."

"Trust me," McKenna said. "I know ways to make you suffer without causing Layne one wee lick of pain. You forced him into this; you'd goddamned better treat him with respect."

Kallie started. "You *forced* Layne? Why would you do that?"

A faint scent of sweet and minty wintergreen drifted up from Belladonna's black leather bag as she leaned into Kallie and whispered into her ear, "Ghost ships are *always* shanghaied, Shug. It's one of the reasons Vessels lose their minds."

"Ol' Basil here refused to cross over," McKenna said, her voice bitter and barbed. "Maybe he's claiming unfinished business or the shock of a violent and unexpected death, but I'd bet my life that he never even attempted to cross."

"Is that true?" Kallie asked.

"My reasons and my business are my own, Ms. Rivière." Layne-Augustine's gaze shifted inward, distant and icy. "Valin was here when he was needed most, and I made use of him. But I assure you both, Valin will be well treated. I—" His gaze lanced past Kallie, and his words broke off.

She turned around in time to see two guards escorting the cuffed and shackled Rosette into the hall. Rosette looked at Kallie, a fierce and unrepentant light burning in her dark eyes. A smile curved her lips.

"My, my, my," a woman's British-accented voice said. "Her nose appears to be a tad out of joint."

"Well said, Mrs. Fields," Layne-Augustine said. "It turns out that Ms. Rivière is quick with her fists."

Guilt squeezed Kallie's heart. Not quick enough to keep Augustine from getting killed and being in need of someone else's body. Or to keep Layne in charge of his own.

"A pugilist, then. How fascinating. Do you accept challenges?"

"No, I ain't a prizefighter," Kallie replied. "I just work off steam."

"Ah." An oddly disappointed sound.

Kallie lost sight of Rosette's bruised and luminous face—Joan of Arc marching toward the stake—when the woman's guards seized her by the biceps and propelled her down the hall toward another pair of polished-steel doors.

A niggling doubt cavorted at the back of Kallie's aching mind. The maid hadn't looked like someone who had just failed and been caught. Of course, she wouldn't if she was insane. . . .

The squeak of wheels drew Kallie's gaze back to the assassination room. A gurney rolled out and into the hall, the thick carpet muffling the squeaks. The bloodstains on the sheet draped over Augustine's body had grown and spread, twisting into a dark and unfathomable Rorschach design.

"An intriguing and extremely rare moment," Layne-Augustine murmured.

Kallie couldn't imagine what it must feel like to watch your own dead body headed for the morgue.

She swiveled back around in time to catch the look on the freckled face of Augustine's assistant as she watched the gurney that held Augustine's remains glide away. Something in her expression crumpled. Grief, stark and barren, stripped all the vibrancy from her hazel eyes. She lowered her gaze and stood still and silent, her hands clasped in front of her.

"Are you all right, Mrs. Fields?" Layne-Augustine asked gently.

The muscles in her slim neck corded. "Quite, my lord," she replied. She looked up, her eyes once again clear and composed. "The healer shall meet you in your rooms to tend to the nomad's ribs."

"Excellent, thank you." Shifting his attention to McKenna, Layne-Augustine said, "You needn't worry about Valin. I promise to take good care of him and return him to you in even better condition than when I entered him."

Both Dallas and Belladonna snorted, and Kallie bit her lower lip to keep from snickering with them like a nine-year-old.

A faint smile tugged at Layne-Augustine's lips and one knowing eyebrow lifted.

"Gage's family and our clan will be arriving before dawn," McKenna said. "Layne needs to be here for Gage's wake and cremation tomorrow."

Layne-Augustine frowned. "That doesn't give me much time."

"Ye'd better hurry, then," the fierce little pixie growled. "Because yer ghostly arse had better be out of him before then."

Sighing, Layne-Augustine nodded. "Fair enough." Turning to Felicity, he said, "Shall we, Mrs. Fields? I have much to do and little time remaining."

"Of course, my lord."

"Wait, there's one more thing," McKenna said. "The bitch who killed Gage—she's ours. I know you ain't gonna hand her over to local law, given the circumstances, so I'm invoking *Daoine shena liri*."

Kallie knew that nomads referred to themselves as the *Daoine*—the People—but she had no idea what the words that'd followed McKenna's proclamation meant.

Layne-Augustine rubbed the bridge of his nose. "I hope you won't also be invoking the Blood Hunt as a method of dispensing justice, Ms. Blue."

"How we dispense justice to the soul-murdering bitch is none of yer concern."

"Given that I am another of her victims, I believe it is."

"Holy Mother," McKenna muttered, and she jabbed a hand through her black hair, her bracelets clinking. "You saying you wanna participate?"

"Perhaps, perhaps not. We'll discuss the details later, yes?"

"Later, aye," McKenna replied, voice low and hard. "I'll drop in on ye tomorrow morning."

"Then we're finished here. Ladies, gentleman . . ." Layne-Augustine paused, eyeing Dallas, then leaned his head toward Felicity's. Shielding his face with the edge of one hand, he stage-whispered, "And have we determined Brûler's status?"

"We have. His status is flirtatious and in need of a shower. But not a threat."

"So *that's* what I smell," Kallie teased, pulling an edge of her blanket up over her nose.

"Well and good, then. Ladies, gentleman, good day. Enjoy the carnival." Shoving his dreads behind his shoulders, Layne-Augustine strode toward the steel doors and the foyer and cubicles beyond them, Felicity marching briskly at his side.

Once Layne-Augustine and his Bondalicious assistant had pushed through the doors and out of sight, McKenna twisted around and scooped up a leather jacket lying on the carpet beside the wall—one too large to be her own.

Must be Layne's, then.

The pixie nomad straightened and tossed the jingling jacket over her shoulder. Kallie caught a glimpse of a fox's red tail painted on the jacket's back.

"Will Layne be all right?" Kallie asked.

McKenna swiveled around to face her, and the mingled fury and contempt blazing in her dark eyes hammered into Kallie with all the force of a lead-loaded boxing glove to the sternum. She sucked in a sharp breath.

"*You* dinnae get to ask about Layne," the leprechaun snapped. "All of this is yer fault. Gage is dead because of you, and so is bloody Basil Augustine, and because he's dead—many thanks to you—he made use of Layne when Layne could least afford it."

"When he's grieving over Gage," Kallie said. Guilt looped another cold coil around her heart. "I know, and I wish I could change everything that's hap—"

"Spare me," McKenna spat. "I don't give a flying fook what ye know or what ye wish. It changes nothing." She stabbed a finger at Kallie. "Don't come near me or Layne ever again. Ye do, and yer a dead woman—I promise you." The nomad spun and stormed away down the hall, slamming through the double steel doors at its end.

"Y'all have *got* to tell me what the hell is going on," Dallas muttered.

"Hellfire. What a bitch!" Belladonna said.

"Me or her?" Dallas asked.

Belladonna snorted. "Her. I've called you a lot of things over the years, Dallas Brûler, but never a bitch."

"That's a relief, darlin'."

"Maybe she's a bitch," Kallie said, "but she's right. Two people are dead because of me. I can't blame her for wanting to protect Layne or herself."

"Sure you can. *I* do. Give it a try, Shug," Belladonna said. "Feels good."

"You're pure down-home evil, Bell," Kallie said, a smile brushing her lips—a smile she felt fade almost immediately. A dark tide of exhaustion poured through her, sweeping away the last of her strength and merging with the pulsating pain in her head. She locked her knees to keep from tumbling to the floor.

She would give anything to curl up somewhere dark and quiet. To transform this heartbreaking morning into a nightmare from which she would actually awaken.

Just like on that other morning nine years ago.

"Let's get out of here," she said, and started walking.

Her mind had been stuffed inside an iron maiden bristling with white-hot spikes. Correction: a *spinning* iron maiden bristling with white-hot spikes. Acid burned its way up her throat as her stomach lurched. She swallowed hard. She almost reached for the trash can Belladonna had placed beside the bed, but decided the movement would tip her stomach over the edge.

C'mon, coma, let's go. Of course, that would mean that Belladonna's WebMD prophecies would be proven right, but, ah, hell, who cared? *C'mon, coma!*

Kallie heard the door click open, then ease shut again. Heard the tread of cowboy boots. Smelled the stink of valerian underneath the sweet aroma of allspice, cinnamon, and poppies, and something sharp and prickly that she couldn't name. Caught a whiff of Dallas, wormwood and stale whiskey, as he knelt beside the bed where she lay curled on her side. Her stomach lurched.

"Get your ass into the shower, Brûler," she muttered.

"Why, thank you ever so much for the potion, Doctor Snake," he said in a falsetto. "What in heaven's name would I do without you, Doctor Snake? Why, no thanks are necessary, darlin', and you're ever so welcome."

Kallie lifted the cold cloth off her eyes. Dallas was hunkered down in front of her, a coffee mug in his hand, shadows clinging to him like a second skin. Belladonna had closed all the blinds, and a deep gray gloom fell thick throughout the room.

Even though a smile curved his lips, Dallas's expression was somber. "Drink up," he said, nodding at the mug.

Easing up on one elbow, temples throbbing, Kallie wrapped her fingers around the handle he'd turned to face her and lifted the mug to her lips. She sniffed at the steam curling up from the white tea-based potion. "You got booze in here?"

"Yup, just a splash of Wild Turkey to help everything go down smooth."

"Where'd you get Wild Turkey?"

"From the hotel bar; the herbs and roots I got from the carnival dealer's room, since mine are at home. Now quit stalling and drink."

Holding her breath against the nose-pinching odor of the valerian, Kallie chugged the potion. It poured as smooth and warm as heated honey down her throat.

"Medicine in, let the healing begin," Dallas chanted, his voice a cool hand against her fevered forehead. "Down in the dreaming deep, pain-free you sleep. Medicine in . . ."

Kallie breathlessly handed back the empty mug. The taste of cinnamon lingered on her tongue while the whiskey burned like a coal in her belly. "Thanks," she said, lying back down and flipping the cloth back over her eyes.

"Did you just say . . . ? Bell, did she just say . . . *thanks*?"

"Mmm-hmmm."

"Okay. *Now* I'm worried."

Kallie couldn't find the energy to think of a retort, or even to lift her hand so she could flip both smartasses off. Maybe later. Dallas's potion tingled through her veins, warm and soothing. Her muscles relaxed one by one. The iron maiden's wild spinning slowed and the white-hot spikes cooled, retracted from her mind—courtesy of the poppies in the potion.

Whispers threaded through Kallie's mind in streamers of purple and blue light.

I knew it wasn't just the charm . . .

"Sorry, baby, but I ain't got a choice."

Bullshit, Mama. There's always a choice.

Warm lips pressed against her cheek. "Sleep, Kallie," Dallas murmured. "And thanks for saving my life."

Following the rhythmic pulse of drums from deep within, Kallie kited into darkness on the wings of the past and a dying man's words.

SIXTEEN

IN THE DREAMING DEEP

The healer left Augustine's private suite, the door clicking shut behind him. With a soft sigh, Augustine, shirtless and feeling more than a little relaxed after the healer's ministrations, stretched out on the sofa, its leather upholstery squeaking beneath his shoulder blades.

He closed his eyes, grateful for the healer who had so skillfully knitted Valin's broken ribs whole again. Still tender, yes, and aching, but connected once more to his—well, the nomad's—sternum.

Hard to believe he had roughly twenty-four hours to wrap up an existence centuries old. Even harder to believe he was dead. He certainly didn't *feel* dead.

Augustine traced a finger along one slim, sharp sideburn on Valin's face. Slid a finger along the curved lower lip. Sexy. Easy to imagine kissing those lips. Or being kissed by them. Easy to imagine those lips doing all manner of pleasant things. Augustine felt himself stir.

Mmm. So responsive.

Augustine opened his eyes and eased up into a sitting position, the weight of Valin's dreads at his back since Felicity had tied the annoying things back to keep them from swinging into his face. He glanced down at his—Valin's—bared, but tattooed, torso. Defined chest and pecs, six-pack abs, a wonderful body, strong and lean-muscled and *young*.

Mmm. So lovely.

He trailed his fingers over a few intriguing scars, some puckered like old bullet wounds, some straight and ridged like knife cuts. His breath caught in his throat at the dizzying double sensation of being both touched by unfamiliar fingers and stroking a stranger's heated flesh. He stiffened.

Mmm. So hot-blooded.

Augustine's pulse picked up speed as he slid a hand down across that flat, muscled belly to the trail of dark blond down beneath the nomad's belly button and followed it down into his jeans. His fingers wrapped around Valin's hot, hard, satin-smooth length. Pleasure pulsed through Augustine and he uttered a small, ecstatic gasp.

Dear God.

Augustine fumbled at Valin's belt with his other hand and unfastened the jeans. He lifted his hips as he worked both jeans and boxers down to free the magnificent package he'd discovered.

It bears repeating: Dear God. Thank you.

Augustine's eyes fluttered shut again and, as he explored the nomad's hard body, a fantasy smoldered into shape in the darkness behind his eyes.

Valin buckles the last sheepskin-padded leather restraint around Augustine's ankle. "All strapped down," he says, looking at Augustine from beneath his lashes, a mischievous, yet deliciously dangerous glint in his green eyes. "As requested."

Augustine manages a nod, his mouth too dry for speech as the nomad climbs fully clothed onto the bed and, on his knees, straddles Augustine's nude body. He peels off his T-shirt and tosses it on the floor. His dreads coil nearly to his lean waist. He looks Augustine over from head to groin, his simmering gaze trailing heat across Augustine's skin. His hand drops to his belt buckle. He unfastens it, then unsnaps his jeans.

"You sure you don't wanna do this for me?" the nomad asks, his hand pausing at the zipper.

"I do," Augustine replies. "But not this time. Keep undressing, road-rider."

"And after that?"

"Show me how you'd like to be touched."

A wicked smile curves Valin's lips. "And after that?"

Augustine offers a lustful grin. "Then you'll release me."

"You hope." The nomad laughs and the sound of it, low and warm, wraps around Augustine like sun-soaked silk.

Valin eases the zipper on his jeans down; then his hand slips underneath the waistband of his navy-blue boxers. His eyes close, and he sucks in a breath as he touches himself.

Every cell in Augustine's body feels erect. Quivering. All the blood in his body rushes to points elsewhere.

The nomad shoves his jeans and boxers down to give Augustine a better view as he demonstrates just how he likes to be touched. He reaches up with his free hand to pinch first one stiffened nipple, then the other, a soft moan escaping his lips. Then he scrapes his fingernails down across his flat belly, slides his hand lower, lower, down to cup his tight balls.

Shuddering with strapped-down lust, Augustine memorizes every move of Valin's hands so he can do the same and more once he's freed. He plans to make sure he leaves the untamed nomad moaning for more.

Valin's scent of musk and sweat and sandalwood, sexy and masculine, triple-times Augustine's pulse. His breath rasps in his throat. And pleasure loops and coils through him in heated twists as he watches the nomad, muscles rippling, bring himself off.

Augustine came in a molten rush that stole his breath and filled his vision with black specks. He fell back onto the sofa in a half-swoon, panting for air.

Once again: Oh. Dear. God.

As he lay there waiting for his breathing to drop back into a normal rhythm, he wondered if Valin was aware of his explorations—*more like a one-nighter, really*—or if he'd even felt the orgasm.

I suppose at the very least, I owe him an expensive dinner and a movie.

Augustine felt no trace of Valin. Hadn't from the first moment he'd flooded into the nomad's body. And that worried him—a little. He supposed he'd be more worried if he had fewer pressing matters on his mind.

Like the one in your hand?

Just a much-deserved break. These are my final hours on this earth, after all.

Much deserved, yes, but now it was time to get back to work. Augustine also needed to do a little inner reconnaissance. He had a proposal for Layne Valin, one he hoped would buy himself a little more time. But first he had to find the nomad.

Augustine closed his eyes and dove into darkness.

Silence greeted Augustine. A chilling silence, save for the crackle of energy flaring along nerves. No phantom snippets of the nomad's memories roamed loose, no ethereal or profane whispers haunted the airwaves, no sudden yearning to straddle a Harley and gun it down a long and lonely stretch of highway.

A distinct disappointment.

Layne Valin seemed to be missing in action. But given

that Augustine's situation—dead and commandeering a living man's body—was new, he wasn't sure what to expect. Perhaps Valin was *supposed* to be missing in action.

<*Valin?*> More crackling and empty silence.

Augustine's internal balance shifted and for a moment he felt like he stood on the deck of an old-fashioned timber-and-tar ship rolling upon storm-heaved waves, the tang of brine and ozone heavy in his nostrils.

Ghost ship—one passenger, one crew, no lifeboat.

Technically speaking, Valin *was* a lifeboat.

Augustine imagined rigging for his hand to grab hold of as he reached out . . . and curled his fingers around rough, braided hemp. Orange, gold, and white balls of light flashed through the darkness, the lightning strobe of neuron pulses. And all zipped in the same direction.

A path to the nomad?

Let's see, shall we?

Visualizing a large ship's wheel, Augustine grasped its smooth wooden steering knobs and spun the wheel until the ship faced the neuron brick path. In the distance a large luminescent sphere hovered in the darkness.

<*Valin?*>

This time Augustine detected a faint buzz of static. And experienced a sudden craving for a French dip sandwich piled high on fresh sourdough bread—the layered beef tender and garlicky and hinting of black pepper and enhanced by the salty *jus* dripping from it.

Excitement pulsed through Augustine. He despised French dip sandwiches. But he would bet anything that Layne Valin felt quite the opposite way about the loathsome things.

Guided by the leaping dolphin dance of flashing

neurons, Augustine steered the ship through the restless and swelling dark toward the gleaming sphere of white light.

Since it's a time-worn classic passed down through generations, the con should go like clockwork. It always has before. All that's required is an eavesdropper and greed. Well, that and bait.

It starts out fine. . . .

Layne, cheap-ass guitar slung over his shoulder, saunters to the restaurant's cash register to pay for the overpriced French dip sandwich, tossed green salad, and spicy Cajun fries he's just eaten. As he flirts with the cute but way-too-skinny cashier, confiding that he's a street musician who's had a helluva good morning, he discovers that his wallet is missing.

After searching his booth to make sure the wallet hasn't slipped from his jeans pocket, Layne slaps his forehead and groans. It's probably in his jacket—which is in his sleazy motel room down the street.

Layne offers to leave his guitar—the source of his livelihood—as collateral while he runs back to get his wallet.

The cashier hesitates, chewing on her lower lip. Behind her the cook bellows for order pickups. Layne promises it'll just take a minute. She nods, and he slips off the guitar and hands it to her. Thanking her, he hurries out the door and down the street.

A moment later, Poesy, in a professional-looking black skirt suit, her long, wheat-blond hair pinned up into an artfully loose twist, pale tendrils curling alongside her face, finishes her lunch and strides, briefcase in hand, to the cashier. She spots Layne's guitar behind the counter and launches into her oh-my-God-is-that-a-rare-Craig-Smallman-guitar spiel.

Long story short, cashier allows businesswoman a look at said guitar. Businesswoman raves about the guitar loud enough for everyone nearby to hear. She declares the guitar a rare and valuable 1984 Craig

Smallman worth $25K that she would love to buy for her collector husband, but since she has a meeting to hurry off to, she leaves her business card with the cashier to give to the musician.

But before the musician returns, a small group of squatters drinking beer and devouring burgers at the booth closest to the cashier send a delegate to chat the cashier up in order to convince her not *to give the musician the businesswoman's card.*

The delegate explains how they all stand to make some money if the musician remains in the dark and they buy the guitar from him on the cheap, then sell it to the businesswoman for her husband's collection for $25K—which they generously promise to share with the cashier.

Musician returns with missing wallet and pays his tab. The cashier tosses a defiant glance at the beer drinkers, then hands the musician the businesswoman's card along with his guitar and shyly informs him of the good news.

"Did you know your guitar's worth twenty-five thousand?"

And, just like that, the con fizzles out—due to the cute, but skinny, cashier's honesty.

Layne shakes his head, feigning surprise, but offers her a genuine smile. Thanking her, he splits the restaurant. He meets up with Poesy and, laughing, tells her how things have gone south.

Poesy laughs too. "Well, hell, that's gotta be a first."

"Yup."

And another first? The marks have followed Layne.

A bell's sharp *clang, clang, clang,* insistent and clear, summoned Layne from the past and his chain-saw-toothed memories, memories triggered by the loss of Gage. The bell continued to toll—three pealing *clangs*, a pause, then three more.

Alarm prickled through him. He shouldn't be able to hear *anything* past the white-noise safety zone he'd constructed to keep his identity from bleeding into Augustine's while the Brit wore him like a soul suit.

To keep his mind, his thoughts, and his history his own.

The bell tolled three more times, the sound both ominous and forlorn, resonating against and through the static. *Clang-clang-clanging* against his consciousness. Cracking his concentration.

The briny smell of salt water filtered into his awareness, and Layne's alarm escalated, hovering between orange and red alert. A breach? Or the first stirrings of the madness he'd managed so far to skate past, possession after possession?

Clang. Clang. Clang.

Or maybe McKenna was trying to reach him.

Layne stilled his thoughts and dialed down the static's comforting noise.

<Valin? You in there?>

Shock rippled through Layne, widening the cracks in his concentration. The wet tang of ocean air intensified. What the hell? Even Augustine's *thoughts* carried a British accent.

<*You* must *be in there. You've certainly been nowhere else. Valin?*>

Layne's shock vanished beneath an icy blast of fury. Fucking bastard had a lot of nerve. Glacial slabs of ice sealed off the gaps in Layne's concentration. The ocean scent vanished.

Clang. Cla—

<Stop ringing that fucking bell. You've got a lot of fucking nerve, y'know that?>

<You are *in there. Marvelous! May I come in? We need to talk.*>

<You holding a gun to anyone's head?>

<A gun? No, of course not.>

<Then you can go fuck yourself real quick, cuz you're all outta time.>

Layne tightened the bubble of energy surrounding him—his personal Fortress of Fucking Solitude—and spun the static noise up to full blast, drowning Augustine out.

Clang! Clang! Clang!

Asshole. What the hell was there to talk about, anyway? Was Augustine planning to scrapbook his experience? Hoping for a possession performance review? Bastard needed to finish up his business, then split—as promised.

Yet, as McKenna had once explained to him, the separation of dead passenger from living Vessel often led to a possession's most deadly moment, when the departing dead, accidentally or otherwise, ran the highest risk of hooking into the Vessel's mind and unthreading memories like satin ribbon from a wood spool.

McKenna didn't know how it happened or why, and Layne couldn't supply an answer for her either, since he never remembered any of the ghost disembarkations after they'd occurred.

But Layne knew, thanks to Gage, that he hadn't always returned unscathed or with all memories intact.

"No one wants to tell you, because they love you, bro, and don't want to see you hurt, but it's happened again."

"Shit. What did I lose this time?"

"See that woman over there? The yummy little brunette?"

"Yeah, man. You kidding? That's McKenna, our gorgeous shuvani.*"*

"Yeeaahh. And she's your wife too, bro."

"Fuck me. My wife?*"*

Once Layne had recovered from the shock that he no

longer remembered the time he and McKenna had spent together as a couple, he'd begun the process of getting to know her as a woman and partner all over again. His body had remembered hers well, with a heated and natural ease, and that had comforted them both for a time.

And despite the hurt and grief she had tried to hide from him, McKenna had patiently taught him about their relationship, showing him photos and poems and trinkets from their time together, not understanding that she couldn't awaken memories that had been stolen and were no longer there.

It had been a loss he and McKenna had never really recovered from, and the last thing he'd wanted was to put her through another nightmare like that, so he'd divorced her—even though he'd learned to love her again.

CLANG! CLANG! CLANG!

Sounded like Augustine had no intention of giving up or going away. If Layne had any hope of keeping his concentration intact enough to keep himself whole, he needed to persuade the Brit to keep as far away from him as possible.

And to keep the idiot from ringing that freaking bell.

Damping down the static buzz, Layne sent, <*Go the fuck away.*> Okay, maybe not smooth and persuasive, but at least it was to the goddamned point.

<*I can't. We need to talk, Valin.*>

<*No, we don't. In fact, we need to keep apart so we don't mesh.*>

<*Are you certain? Has it happened to you before?*>

<*Would we be speaking if it had?*>

<*Ah. Excellent point. And it's my thought that if you're strong enough to withstand possession by the dead, you're strong enough to withstand pretty much anything.*>

Uneasiness curled though Layne. <*Just how much time has passed?*>

<*Only a handful of hours at this point. I owe you dinner and a movie, by the way. I hope you realize that you have an incredible body.*>

<*Huh? Dinner and a movie? What the hell have you been* doing *with me?*>

<*Nothing you didn't enjoy.*>

<*Christ! You'd better finish up your* business *soon, and get out.*>

<*That's what I'd like to speak to you about. May I come inside?*>

<*Nope. And if you're planning on asking for more time, forget it.*>

<*I don't believe you can force me out, Valin. Am I correct?*>

Fury whipped through Layne like a downed and writhing power line. Sounded like the asshole was planning on sticking around. <*Depends on how much of myself I want to lose in the attempt. But I could, and so can McKenna.*>

A low and amused chuckle. <*I do believe you're lying, Valin. Trust me, if your ex-wife was capable of expelling me, she would've done so already.*>

<*Nope, only as a last resort. An eviction-exorcism spell runs the risk of casting me out too. But if you don't leave like you promised, she'll view it as a last-resort kind of situation. Do us both a favor and go.*>

<*Hmm. That* would *be problematic. I have a proposal for you, and I need you to hear me out, if you would.*> A cough. <*Please.*>

Christ on a taco shell. Had Augustine just said <*Please*>?

<*Fine, I'll fucking listen to your proposal. But nothing you say is gonna give me the warm-and-fuzzies.*>

<*No warm-and-fuzzies. Duly noted. Your lovely ex-wife invoked* Daoine shena liri, *which I, of course, granted. And since the maid, Rosette, was also responsible for my death, I believe I would like to witness justice being rendered or even to participate in her punishment.*>

Surprise pulsed through Layne. A *woman* had

murdered Gage, body and soul. For some reason, he'd imagined a man had been responsible.

<I can understand that, yeah. But I plan to help Gage's murderer get what's coming to her, so sorry, but you gotta get out and soon.>

<I believe we can both *be there, Valin.>*

<I'm beginning to think that you're the crazy one, man.>

<I believe that it's possible for us to share your body, for us to take turns at the controls.>

<And I *believe you're stalling. Still avoiding the fact that you're dead. I'm sorry, I am, but you need to let go. I'll make sure the cold-hearted bitch pays for you too.>*

<Perhaps I am *stalling, avoiding the inevitable. You might be right about that. But if we can work together long enough for us* both *to see justice rendered, and to ensure that Ms. Rivière is truly out of danger, then why not do it?>*

<You have the killer. Why would Kallie still be in danger?>

<My intuition leads me to believe the woman wasn't acting alone.>

<Your intuition? Is this another stalling tactic? Why the hell should I believe you?>

<I've discovered some disturbing discrepancies. Perhaps they mean nothing. Perhaps they mean the difference between life and death for Ms. Rivière. I don't know, but we could find out together.>

<Why the hell do you care what happens to Kallie?>

<And why do you *care what happens to her?>* Augustine challenged. *<Your clan-brother died in her bed, after all.>*

Images filled Layne's mind, all his reasons why.

"That's it, Layne, keep fighting, damn you," Kallie says. "Don't you give up."

*"*I am *fighting, woman. Quit pummeling me."*

The dark-haired swamp beauty in her red undies—filled out well enough to stop his heart again—quits pounding against Layne's chest and opens her eyes. Just mere pinpricks, her pupils, as though she's been staring into the sun, her violet eyes gleaming with light and heat—a heat Layne feels inside of him with each renewed pulse of his heart.

<I owe her my life and soul.>

<I understand, Valin. Ms. Rivière stayed beside me as I was dying, as well. Tried to offer comfort and fought to keep me alive—even though she no doubt considered me a pain in her lovely behind.>

<No doubt.>

If Augustine was telling the truth and a possibility existed that Kallie remained in danger, Layne couldn't leave her well-being to chance. He couldn't let Gage's death have been for nothing.

Hoping he wouldn't regret it, Layne hushed the static and thinned his shield. The white walls encircling him faded to translucency. What he saw stunned him into silence.

Augustine—or a self-projected image of him—stood at the bow of an old-fashioned three-masted ship, dressed in what Layne could only think of as pirate high fashion—feather-plumed hat; swashbuckler's boots stretching above the knees of black breeches; red sash; a white shirt unlaced at the throat, its billowing sleeves fluttering in a breeze that didn't extend to Layne. The thick smell of the sea filled Layne's senses.

<What the hell?>

<It just sort of flowed from the situation. Rather fun, actually.>

<Christ. Whatever. So let's hear it. How's this going to work?>

Augustine winked, a smug smile curving his lips. *<Have you ever ridden a tandem bicycle?>*

SEVENTEEN

SOMETHING MORE THAN A DEATH SENTENCE

Layne followed a gaggle of pudgy sightseers clad in tourist regulation wear—shorts, sun visors, baseball caps, shades, and pungent sunscreen—through the black-iron gates of St. Louis Cemetery No. 1. He paused on the gravel and seashell path, looking for McKenna in the city of the dead, among all the stone monuments to loss.

"Did she say why she chose to visit the cemetery?" Felicity asked.

"No," Layne replied. "But I imagine it suited her mood." Sunlight glinted on the white tombs and crumbling brick, and Layne shaded his eyes with the edge of his hand.

A melancholy air permeated the cemetery, sieving into the crypts, black-iron railings, and the living like a ghost into a Vessel. But since the uncrossed-over usually lingered at places they'd known in life, or in the spots where they'd died, Layne found cemeteries peaceful and relaxing—ghost-free.

The sorrow he felt emanating from the crypts and well-trod paths belonged to all of those left behind over the centuries.

Felicity shifted beside him, and he caught a whiff of her body-warmed perfume—fresh-cut roses, a welcome distraction from the odd sensation in his head of Augustine's presence.

The ghost in the cargo hold.

As a safeguard against personality and essence meshing, they'd decided that whoever wasn't in charge—the one not steering the tandem bicycle—would stay out of the way, tucked behind a shield of static, a shield Layne taught the Brit how to create and shape.

The transition had been as easy as the riders of that mythical tandem bicycle switching seats while pedaling, and doing so without touching each other. Once during the shift, Layne's mind had grazed against Augustine's like a ship scraping along the rough face of a glacier. Images and sensations not his own had bled into Layne's consciousness.

He finds himself standing beneath an old-fashioned big-top circus tent, a deck of slick new cards in one hand and a black top hat in the other—hands less scarred than his own—the gaslight-heated air pungent with sweat, fresh sawdust, and animal shit. He feels the burn of booze in his belly and tastes the oak bite of good whiskey on his tongue. The loud and cheerful whistles of a calliope accompany the trumpet of elephants and the raucous roar of an entertainment-hungry crowd.

But what holds his attention is a man in a dust-grimed tuxedo hurling knives at a woman strapped to a huge spinning wheel. . . .

She never, ever flinches, that one. She revels in the danger. God, but she's beautiful. She'd make one hell of a magician's assistant, with her nerve and long legs.

Pain skewers Layne's thoughts—no, Augustine's *thoughts—and the images disintegrate, a painting scrubbed clean from its canvas.*

Layne had no idea what Augustine had experienced

from *his* memories, if anything, but planned to ask him later.

They'd agreed to signal each other whenever they needed to switch places. Augustine had chosen his fricking clanging bell as his signal and, just to get back at him, Layne had selected the sound of a revving and unmuffled Harley.

"Did Ms. Blue agree to meet you at a specific spot?" Felicity asked.

Listening to a tour guide's spiel about Marie Laveau's tomb—*"Visitors often chalk X's or crosses on her tomb for luck. . . ."*—Layne shook his head. "Nah. I'll find her. Place ain't that big."

Gravel crunched beneath Layne's boots as he headed up the narrow path, past a wall of small pizza-oven-like tombs, the stones sealing their arched mouths painted a clean, fresh white. He caught peripheral flashes from cameras as the tourists immortalized their visit.

"Hardly the proper place to hold a private discussion," Felicity commented.

"No choice. McKenna's here and I need to speak to her. Augustine's gonna be busy later and not so willing to switch places."

"Of course," Felicity murmured.

He spotted McKenna standing in front of a wall tomb painted a vivid cornflower blue. Stones, flowers—yellow marigolds and pink roses—and pictures surrounded it. Despite the May heat and humidity, she wore her leather jacket and jeans.

She studied the pictures taped beside the gaily painted tomb, her hands jammed into her jacket pockets, her eyes hidden behind sunglasses. But grief tightened the line of her jaw, her throat.

Layne sauntered to a stop beside her. "Hey, buttercup."

McKenna swiveled around, lifting her shades to the top of her head as she did. Her joyous gaze darted from his face to Felicity's, then back, before morphing into one of wariness.

"What's she doing here?"

"Protecting Augustine's interests," Layne replied.

"Interests? You *sound* like Layne, but I need you to tell me something only Layne would know. Nothing tha' fooking Augustine or his Bond assistant could look up."

"But what if Lord Augustine had delved through Mr. Valin's memories?" Felicity asked. "Then he'd know practically everything about Mr. Valin—including things we couldn't look up."

"Yeah, *that's* helping the situation," Layne muttered.

"Trust me, I'll know the difference," McKenna said.

Rising up on her tiptoes to meet him halfway, she grabbed a handful of dreads and gently tugged Layne down into a soft-lipped kiss, her warm tongue darting between his lips. She tasted of wintergreen toothpaste, cool and clean.

Layne kissed her back, the old, familiar heat burning through his veins, coiling in his belly. Even as he slipped an arm around her waist and pulled her closer, he knew he shouldn't. Knew he was plucking at the half-healed scars of old wounds on both of them. Knew he needed to let her go before their affection decayed into something bitter and they started hating each other.

But all the knowing in the world couldn't seem to make him release her—not after spending time locked away from his own body—couldn't stop him from drinking in her clean scent of soap and wildflower shampoo.

"Why did you divorce me?" she murmured against his lips.

"You know why," he whispered back.

"No, ye choob—this is yer prove-yerself question." She pulled back and studied his face.

Layne noticed she kept her grip on his dreads. His scalp prickled. He met her clear gaze and held it. "You could've picked a different question."

"Aye, I coulda. But I didn't, so answer it."

A muscle jumped in Layne's jaw. "Because you deserve to be with a man who will always remember you."

McKenna's gaze softened. "It *is* you, then, luv." She gave his dreads one hard and painful jerk before releasing them. "And yer still an arsehole."

"Virgin Mary in a sidewalk stain, woman! *Quit* yanking at my hair." Layne pulled his arm back, ending their half-embrace without a problem this time.

"I will—when you quit being an arsehole."

"Fascinating. Nomad mating ritual."

"No, it ain't," Layne and McKenna denied in unison.

"Ah. I see," Felicity murmured, her tone saying the opposite. "In that case, might we get to the business at hand?"

"What business is that?" McKenna asked, suspicion edging her voice again.

Layne half turned to face Augustine's assistant. "Look, you need to back off and let me handle this."

Felicity tilted her head, her sleek hair swinging against her face like a strawberry-blonde silk curtain, her hazel-eyed gaze probing him. "Will there be violence if I don't?" Excitement danced in her voice.

"Nope."

"Will there be violence with Ms. Blue?"

"Make that another nope." At least, he hoped not.

Felicity sighed. "A pity." She turned around and walked back up the path.

Layne swiveled to face McKenna. "Let's walk."

"Why do I get the feeling I'm not going to like this?" she muttered.

"Cuz you're not," Layne replied.

McKenna held his gaze for a moment, her dark eyes scanning him deep. A crease appeared between her eyes. "All right, let's walk, then."

As they strolled along the path, easing past chattering tourists, she said, "I'm surprised Augustine split yer body so soon. I honestly thought I'd hafta wrestle him out of there."

Layne drew in a deep breath. He glanced at McKenna. "Augustine didn't split. He's still inside."

McKenna stopped and stared at him as if he'd suddenly sprouted wings or a unicorn's horn or maybe a huge honking eye in the center of his forehead. "But that isn't even bloody possible," she said, her tone bewildered. She wriggled a finger first in one ear, then the other. "Would ye repeat that?"

"You heard right, Kenn. I'm still carrying Augustine. We've worked out a system that allows us to switch—"

"A system? A bloody *system*?" Fury torched the uncertainty from McKenna's voice. "He was supposed to get out of yer body and go into the bleeding light or whatever it is ghosts do when they leave a Vessel. Not create a *system* so he could stay longer!" She knuckled a fist into Layne's biceps. "And you *let* him?"

Layne rubbed his arm. Woman had pointy damned knuckles. "Yeah, I did."

"Why the hell would ye *do* tha'?"

"Because he's got a right to see justice done to the woman who murdered him." Layne grasped McKenna's shoulders. "Once I realized we could do it without losing ourselves, I felt this was business he needed to see through to the end—if he's ever to cross over."

"But that's not your concern!"

"Ain't it? What's the purpose of a Vessel, then? I gotta believe we're this way for a reason, that we can do some good, something useful, otherwise . . ." He shrugged. "We're just fucked."

Sympathy glistened in McKenna's dark eyes. "But the risk is too high. The loss of self and sanity." She shook her head. "You've held on better and longer than any Vessel I've ever heard of, but that could change if you interact with the dead inside of you, if you try to guide them."

"I can do this, Kenn. I've got to do it. Hell, I *am* doing it." Layne rubbed his thumbs back and forth across McKenna's jacketed shoulders, the leather sun-warmed and smooth as butter. "Augustine gets his justice, then he leaves."

"You sure about that?"

"Yeah. I'm sure."

"And then?"

"I dunno. Maybe I'll try to turn this—what I am, and others too—into something more than a death sentence."

McKenna reached up with one hand and trailed the backs of her fingers against Layne's cheek, her touch warm. Something sad and wistful flashed in her eyes. "Ah, such a fool you are."

Layne bent and pressed his lips to her forehead, tasted

a hint of sweat and salt. "I know, buttercup," he whispered. "And I'm lucky to have you bringing it to my attention."

"Very lucky. And don't worry, luv, I'll make sure the bloody wanker leaves when he's supposed to."

"I don't think that's going to be a problem," Layne said, straightening. He released his hold on her shoulders. "Once he sees Rosette get what's coming to her, he'll go. But, in the meantime, he's got work to finish."

And so do I. Making sure no one else is trying to kill Kallie Rivière.

"Keep yourself safe," McKenna said, her dark eyes somber.

"I will, buttercup," Layne promised, then turned and walked up the path to the black-iron gate.

EIGHTEEN

SUMMONING

She stands beside the bayou's cypress-shadowed waters, a gleaming knife clenched in one hand, a red candle cupped in the other. The mingled scents of roses and cinnamon curl into the air as the anointed wax melts, trickling hot over her fingers. In the darkness behind her, the rhythmic and steady throb of palm-slapped drums echoes through the night.

Ripples arrow along the bayou's green surface as a gator glides toward the bank. But her gaze seeks the shadow flitting among the live oaks and cypress on the bayou's other side, a man-shaped shadow that drops from upright to all fours. A shadow that lopes in easy, four-pawed grace across the sawgrass, moonlight pooled in its gleaming silver eyes.

A long, rising howl slashes into the night, a howl answered by others, merging into a wild, multitoned song, raw and wild and fierce. The hair rises on her arms, the back of her neck. Hands thump faster against the drums.

She lifts the candle, its flame flickering with the movement. Her heart pounds in time with the drums, and her courage flares and dims like the flame.

"He comes," *a woman's voice says—an unknown, but strangely familiar bayou-spiced voice. "And the others too. I hope you know what you be doing,* p'tite doux."

She hopes so too. What she's doing scares her spitless.

She summons the loup-garou *to offer him a traitor's still-beating heart.*

Her own.

Kallie jerked awake, the eerie howls of hunting wolves still echoing in her head. Like a line-drying sheet caught in a hurricane, her dream and its images vanished. And even though she tried to recapture it, her dream eluded her, beyond all recall. Instead, Layne Valin's image filled her mind's eye, tall, lean, and yummy, his pine-green eyes locked on hers.

For a second, everything quiets inside of her as though he presses a soothing finger against her lips and whispers, Shhh. *His eyes widen a little as though he feels the strange connection too; then Kallie notices the small black fox inked beneath his right eye, and her heart sinks. . . .*

Gage.

A nightmarish flood of images rushed through her mind: Gage's bloodied body in her bed, Layne's stark and grief-stricken face, the black-dust hex on the mattress, Dallas sprawled on the floor, the maid and her gun, Augustine's death.

"*Your fate comes compliments of Gabrielle LaRue, and you can thank her for it. You want answers? Ask her.*"

"Shit," Kallie whispered.

"Hey, Shug. You're alive."

Still curled on her side, Kallie looked in the direction of Belladonna's voice. Her friend sat beside the open French windows, a paperback in her hands. Beyond her, twilight smudged the sky purple and deepest blue.

"Hey, Bell," Kallie croaked. "What time is it?"

"Seven-thirty, a quarter to eight. You've been out about ten hours, girl. How you feeling?"

Kallie considered. The headache seemed to be gone, and she felt clear-headed. Physically she was okay. But emotionally? She had a little work to do—like figuring this whole mess out.

The spicy smells of fried chicken and grilled shrimp filtered into the room from outside. Her stomach rumbled. "I'd kill for a beignet and a café au lait," she said.

"Mmm. Maybe even maim," Belladonna agreed, tossing her book—a historical romance, judging by the buff, bare-chested, kilt-wearing man on the cover—onto the table. "Let's grab Dallas—boy's got a story to tell you—and get our butts over to Café Du Monde."

"Sounds good," Kallie said. "But first, can I borrow your cell? I have a call to make."

"I don't know where she is, Kal," Jackson Bonaparte said, shoving his chair back from the kitchen table. "I got in from Grand Isle this mornin', and she was *beaucoup* worked up about somethin'." Finished with his supper of Trix (mixing bowl-sized serving), he placed the purple glass bowl on the floor in front of Cielo's front paws. The Siberian husky eagerly shoved her muzzle into the bowl and lapped up the pink-tinted milk, her name tag clinking against the glass rim. "Gabrielle put a mojo bag around my neck and made me promise to stay home until she got back."

"Did she say why?" Kallie asked.

Jackson rose to his feet, crossed the kitchen to the back door, and leaned against the frame. "Somethin' about a storm comin'. But I'm pretty damned sure she didn't mean an actual storm, y'know?" He watched the deepening night through the screen door's mesh. Katydids buzzed in humid air thick with the smell of his aunt's roses.

"Did someone pick her up?"

"Nope, she headed off on foot. But . . . is somethin' goin' on between you two? Cuz I saw a poppet on her table. One that freaked me out a little."

"*You?* Freaked? Why's that, Jacks? You've seen tons of poppets."

"Yeah, but this one's got brown yarn for hair and purple button eyes. It ain't finished, but . . . shit, I think it's you, Kallie. You okay, short stuff? What's goin' on?"

Kallie drew in a long breath.

Cielo nosed at the screen door, then glanced at Jackson, her eyes—one blue and one brown—full of expectation. Unlatching the hook, Jackson swung the door open. His dog bounded out into the night-blanketed yard, her tail curved over her back.

"Kallie?" Jackson asked again, her silence filling him with apprehension. "You still there? *Is* somethin' goin' on?"

"I don't know," Kallie replied, her voice edged with frustration. "But I need to find out. Did you know that Gabrielle sent Dallas to keep an eye on me here?"

Jackson frowned. "What the hell for? She knows you ain't an innocent virgin or nuthin' needing to be protected from pervs." He felt his muscles kink up in his shoulders as he considered another possibility. "Maybe Dallas is lying and just watching you for himself. Wouldn't put it past the boozed-up bastard."

Kallie snorted. "I know how to handle Dallas Brûler.

Don't worry about that. But I think he's telling the truth about Gabrielle."

"Makes no sense, *chère*." Jackson trailed a hand through his hair, uneasy. He thought of the unfinished violet-eyed poppet. "Why would Ti-tante do that?"

"Look, we'll talk when I get home. You keep that bag on and keep safe, *cher*. No bayou. No smuggling. You keep your promise to Gabrielle about staying home, y'hear?"

A chill touched the back of Jackson's neck. It wasn't like Kallie to mother-hen him. His uneasiness increased. "I will," he said. "You keep safe too."

Cielo started barking out in the yard, but it wasn't her Yay-I-have-a-possum! bark, but a sharp, full-throated alert.

"Gotta go," Jackson said. "See you Sunday. Love ya." He ended the call, then slipped the cell into the back pocket of his jeans before grabbing the baseball bat beside the door. He walked outside.

Augustine examined the plastic box his guards had left on his desk, a box filled with items they'd confiscated during their search of Rosette St. Cyr's apartment. He dug through piles of cloth, sticks, needles, and thread for making poppets; oils and powders and mojo bags smelling of cloves, frankincense, and juniper—among many other things; nails, candles of all colors; small jars of dirt; gnarled roots; and, at the box's bottom, a couple of weathered manila file folders.

Pulling the folders free, Augustine sank back down into his leather captain's chair and flipped a folder open. On top was a printout of a newspaper photo of Kallie

Rivière and a young man standing on a wharf in front of a blue-trimmed white boat named *Bright Star,* their arms around each other's shoulders.

Dressed in jeans and a red short-sleeved blouse, Kallie Rivière squinted in the sunshine, her long, espresso-brown locks trailing across her face in a camera-frozen breeze.

The young man tucked up against her side wore a white T-shirt reading CAJUN HOT RODS stretched across his tight-muscled chest, faded blue jeans, and rubber fisherman's boots. His wavy, coffee-dark hair brushed his shoulders, framing a handsome face. A roguish smile curved his lips and glinted in his slightly tilted golden-brown eyes. He held his hand above and behind Ms. Rivière's head, fingers shaping a V.

Bunny ears, or a profound and admirable wish for peace?

Augustine opted to assume bunny ears. Given the young man's action and the physical similarities to Ms. Rivière—eyes, cheekbones, mouth—Augustine imagined him to be a relative. Most likely an obnoxious one.

And guess who stood, hip cocked, beside them in jeans and a blue plaid button-down shirt and cowboy boots, blue eyes hidden behind sunglasses, a woven-straw cowboy hat tipped over his red hair? One Dallas Brûler, aka Doctor Snake.

Flipping the photo over, Augustine saw that Rosette had scrawled in black Sharpie across the back: *With Dallas Brûler and her cousin Jackson Bonaparte at the launch of his boat—*

Augustine wondered if this was the same cousin with whom Kallie Rivière had been raised. He scanned the copy of the article that had accompanied the photo. It seemed that Mr. Bonaparte had built his boat by hand over the course of several years, a process the small community of Bayou Cyprès Noir had watched with mingled excitement, anticipation, and doubt.

"I always said that Jackson was one determined son of a gun."

"I done tol' Velma, my ol' lady over dere, dat de boy was loco as hell."

"We're all proud of Jackson and what he's accomplished."

Clearly not much to do in Bayou Cyprès Noir.

But the article *did* reveal a couple of very interesting facts. Jackson Bonaparte's parents and siblings had died in a hurricane the same year that Sophie Rivière had splattered her husband's brains on the wall of their home and tried to do the same with her daughter's. Bonaparte was also the same age as his cousin—twenty-three.

The article also mentioned that a celebratory crawfish boil and *fais do do* would take place at the home of Jackson and Kallie's aunt, Gabrielle LaRue.

Crawfish boil. Creatures mucked up out of mud and tossed into a pot. Yes, just the thing with which to celebrate several years' worth of hard and diligent work. And what on earth was a *fais do-do*? It sounded like something else one might toss into a pot to boil.

"I've been informed that Ms. Blue has made arrangements for Mr. Buckland's body to be transported to the DiSario Crematorium ahead of his family's arrival," Felicity said, lowering a rose-nailed finger from her Bluetooth. She'd changed from her skirt and blouse to a purple pantsuit and a tailored white shirt. An amethyst necklace was looped around her throat.

Lovely, as always.

Augustine believed that if he'd been born straight, he would've claimed her as a bride the moment he'd seen her strapped to the spinning wheel in that Cheapside circus all those years ago, her lips curved into a luscious smile as knives skimmed past her face and scantily clad body to thunk into the painted wood of the wheel.

Of course, the now-deceased Mr. Fields might've had a word or two to say about that. Ah, but the fight would've been worth it.

"Offer her any and all assistance," Augustine said. He pushed the photo of Kallie and her cousin across the desk. "I need you to research Jackson Bonaparte. See how he fits—if at all—into this little mystery."

"Very good, my lord," Felicity replied, scooping up the photo.

Augustine glanced at the digital time readout in the lower right-hand corner of his laptop. 8:01 P.M. Time was slipping away, and he had much still to do.

And on the "accomplished" side of the ledger?

1. Arrangements for the care and burial of his body. Obituary written.

2. Transfer of his assets to his living relatives, with a substantial portion going to Felicity and a more modest portion going to the Hecatean Alliance.

3. Good-byes said in multiple awkward phone calls and webcasts.

4. Research done on Kallie Rivière, Gabrielle LaRue, and the murderous Rosette St. Cyr—learning a few intriguing bits of information, but nothing that really explained that morning's events.

Augustine toggled Alt-Tab on the keyboard. The nine-year-old Shreveport, Louisiana, newspaper article popped back into view, its headline declaring: "Woman Shoots Husband and Daughter; 14-Year-Old Survives."

At least he'd solved the puzzle of the thin white scar at Kallie Rivière's temple.

Fell out of a swing indeed.

Sophie Rivière had never offered any explanation as to why she'd murdered her husband, a Cajun with violet eyes named John Rivière, or why she'd tried to murder her daughter and only child, one Kalindra Rivière.

Sophie Rivière, an attractive woman of mixed blood—light caramel skin, tilted amber-brown eyes, black hair—had refused to defend herself. She'd pleaded guilty and was later ruled to be insane and placed in Saint Dymphna's Institution for the Criminally Insane—where she still resided.

Augustine had found nothing more on Kallie Rivière after the media interest had (swiftly) died down and she'd been released from the hospital and into the care of an unnamed relative.

"A bit of supper, my lord. You need to eat." Felicity placed a plate of spicy curry-scrambled eggs, deliciously greasy-smelling fried sausages, and buttered biscuits on his desk. British comfort food. Augustine blinked. Felicity had ordered a meal and he'd been so deep in thought, he hadn't even heard the waitstaff's arrival.

"More tea?" Felicity asked, white porcelain pot in hand. A smile dimpled her cheeks.

"Yes, thank you," he replied. She was right about his need to eat. He needed to keep Valin's body fueled, an efficient and now-hungry body. One he'd dressed in charcoal-gray trousers and a French-blue tailored shirt Felicity had purchased for him, along with black loafers instead of Valin's motorcycle boots—in defiance of Ms. Blue's edict.

And a body he needed to give back. Eventually.

Felicity poured more steaming tea into Augustine's empty cup. Murmuring his thanks, Augustine added milk before taking a sip of the strong brew, savoring the bitter taste of the black leaves gentled by the milk.

Augustine struggled to remember what it was he'd seen in Ms. Rivière's eyes as she'd leaned over him, using her pink bathrobe as a compress against his wound. Tried to remember the words he'd said to her as he'd died. But failed.

Augustine plucked free one of the cigarettes in the opened stainless-steel case on his desk, then hesitated as he remembered the coughing fits his first few attempts had triggered. Apparently, the nomad wasn't a smoker. A pity, really.

He trailed the cigarette beneath his nose. The enticing dark-Turkish-tobacco-and-black-cherry scent, sharp and rich, curled into his nostrils like a favorite lover's cologne. Augustine sighed. Maybe he'd have one just before vacating the nomad's body: the proverbial last cigarette. He tucked the smoke back into its case, then flipped the lid closed.

"It seems Ms. St. Cyr lied during our hallway conversation," Augustine said, resting the maid's file on Kallie Rivière in his lap. He picked up his fork and stirred it through his eggs. "She's originally from Delacroix, Louisiana, not Haiti."

"She *is* a murderer, my lord. Hardly an occupation conducive to telling the truth."

"Indeed. I found very little on her aside from the

usual—parents, school records, a few book reviews on Barnes and Noble—no criminal history. Unless you consider her positive and glowing review of *Going Rogue* criminal. However, I found one very intriguing fact."

Felicity strolled back to his desk, then relaxed into one of the plush chairs positioned in front of it. Crossing her legs in a graceful and elegant motion, she took a sip of her tea, an inquiring eyebrow raised.

"Her father, Jean-Julien St. Cyr, was released from the Louisiana State Penitentiary just a month ago after completing a twenty-five-year sentence for murder. He used to be known as Doctor Heron, a root doctor of some repute, until he went to Angola for poisoning and killing several clients."

"And was Gabrielle LaRue responsible for Doctor Heron going to prison?"

Augustine frowned and skewered a sausage with his fork. "No, as far as I can determine, and that's the problem. Well, or *a* problem. Gabrielle LaRue herself is another issue."

The *bee-dink* of a new e-mail message sounded from his laptop. Glancing at the screen, Augustine saw a message from the board of directors. Irritation flickered through him. His sausage-filled fork clattered onto his plate.

Normally in the event of a master's unexpected death, the board would tie up all loose ends and seek out someone to fill the master's shoes. But since Augustine resided within a Vessel's body and was therefore still present despite being dead, the board had—in pure blasted laziness—elected to leave many of the transition details in his hands. Honestly, he had too much to do as it was.

Augustine clicked open the message.

Have you chosen an interim-master until we can properly choose a replacement?

Sitting forward in his chair, Augustine's fingers danced in a fury across the laptop's keyboard, tapping out a lie.

Yes. Shall inform you of who once they've accepted the position.

He hit Send. A moment later, another *bee-dink*.

It's been a pleasure working with you. Again, our condolences. Please be sure to leave your keys on the desk before you pass on.

Augustine zipped the cursor up to the Delete X and stabbed a finger against the mouse. "Keys, indeed. Bleeding idiots," he muttered. Glancing at Felicity through his lashes, he added, "My apologies for the language, Mrs. Fields."

"No need, my lord. I've had several slips of the tongue myself." Leaning forward, Felicity set her cup on the edge of his desk. Her perfume—fresh-dewed roses—swirled into the air. "Now, what is the issue that Gabrielle LaRue presents?"

"She seems to be a ghost. No records of any kind—DMV, birth, SSN—and nothing to indicate that she actually *is* a member of Ms. Rivière's family."

"My, my, my."

Snippets of his earlier conversation with Kallie Rivière skimmed through Augustine's mind.

"Who is Gabrielle LaRue?"

"My aunt. The woman who raised me and my cousin."

"Ah. So your aunt is a hoodoo too. I imagine she taught you."

"Conjuring runs in the family. For the most part."

Had Sophie Rivière also been a hoodoo?

"However, that doesn't mean that she *isn't* a distant relative from one side of the family or another. Given that Ms. LaRue is also caring for one of Ms. Rivière's cousins, it would seem to indicate a definite connection."

"Or an interest in Ms. Rivière's bloodline."

Augustine went still. He held Felicity's bright gaze, his heart picking up its pace, a gentle gallop. An image of the sultry beauty with the tilted violet eyes flashed through his mind.

Kallie Rivière closes her eyes and leans over him, arms locking as her hands press down on the wad of pink bathrobe piled on his chest. She murmurs a prayer or chant, which ends abruptly when she stiffens, muscles rigid, and . . .

And *what*? What had he seen? The memory continued to elude him.

"Intriguing point, Mrs. Fields," Augustine murmured. "*Very* intriguing." And chilling, if true. A bloodline that her mother and Rosette St. Cyr had both attempted to end. For different reasons? No way to know given that Sophie Rivière had never voiced her motive. One thing it wasn't—a coincidence.

"I'll see if Mr. Bonaparte happens to be a maternal or paternal cousin." Felicity rose to her feet and went to her desk at the other side of the room. As she perched on her chair, her quick and nimble fingers clacked across the computer's keyboard.

Augustine replayed the conversation that had taken place between Kallie and Rosette after he'd died, a conversation memorized by the guards present.

"I just have a few questions for her."

"And I have one for you, Kallie Rivière. How many people are you going to allow to die in your place before you accept your fate?"

"What fate? And who the hell are *you?"*

"An eye for an eye is never enough. Never, never, never."

"You murdered two men who never did you any harm, and for what? Why? You even killed Gage's soul, you goddamned chienne*!"*

"That wasn't supposed to happen. How did you know?"

"That doesn't matter. What does *matter is why."*

"Your fate comes compliments of Gabrielle LaRue, and you can thank her for it. You want answers? Ask her."

Revenge, yes. An eye for an eye. But for what wrong? And why not wreak vengeance upon Gabrielle LaRue instead of her innocent niece? Another intriguing point was the fact that Kallie had been selected for soul death and Brûler for simply a physical one.

Augustine could guess at the motivation behind those decisions. What better way to make your enemy suffer than to destroy those she loves? He closed the maid's file on Kallie Rivière, then tossed it onto his desk.

He glanced at the time on his laptop. 8:40 P.M. He wondered how much time he had before McKenna Blue popped in to demand that Rosette St. Cyr be handed over for clan justice and that Valin's body be vacated. He didn't trust the little nomad to wait until her clan's arrival in New Orleans.

Daoine shena liri.

Clan law of the People. Nomads had nothing to do with squatter courts—mundane or magical—preferring to administer their own brand of justice to those accused of crimes against nomads. Always had and, no doubt, always would.

Most law enforcement agencies were just as quick to arrest a nomad victim as the squatter perp, simply because nomads were regarded as outlaws and thieves and cons—a pagan blend of biker and Gypsy, and just as welcome as both in polite society.

As for himself, he had every intention of delivering the maid to the nomads. Given Gage Buckland's murder and soul death, the woman deserved whatever they meted out to her. It didn't matter one whit that Buckland's death and his own had been unintentional.

But what if Rosette *wasn't* the one responsible? Or the only one involved? Soul-killing magic required immense power, skill, and focus.

"Does Ms. St. Cyr seem capable to you of having created the hex on Ms. Rivière's mattress alone, Mrs. Fields?"

Felicity looked away from her computer monitor, her forehead wrinkling as she pondered his question, a single finger tap-tapping against her chin. "I only saw her briefly in the hall outside Ms. Rivière's room," she replied, "right after Mr. Valin had wheeled the body out. She seemed disturbed and anxious, but I attributed it to her having just seen a dead body wheeled away."

"And?"

"Based on what I saw, no, my lord. She seems too easily rattled to possess the deep well of calm and strength it would take to craft such a hex."

"My thought as well, Mrs. Fields."

"Do we know Jean-Julien St. Cyr's whereabouts?"

"He's listed as having moved to Delacroix. Since he completed his sentence, he's not on parole and doesn't need to check in with anyone."

"So the infamous Doctor Heron could just as easily be here," Felicity said.

"Indeed." Picking up the other file folder, Augustine added, "It's not out of the realm of possibility that we are underestimating Rosette St. Cyr."

"We could be, my lord." Felicity gave her attention back to her computer monitor, her fingers returning to the keyboard. Quiet clicking filled the air.

The second folder, a very thin file on Gabrielle LaRue, contained only two photos and a single sheet of paper. The first photo showed a slender, dark-skinned woman in her fifties wearing a simple green-and-blue-flowered sundress. A green scarf hugged the gray-streaked black curls framing her face. She wore gold hoops in her ears. She stared into the camera, unsmiling, but sunlight danced in her hazel eyes.

Her skin color indicated that she had to be a maternal relative, since Kallie's father was white—but maybe a distant relative, given that she looked nothing like Sophie Rivière.

The second photo was smaller, an old Polaroid shot, its edges bent and worn. A much younger version of the woman from the first photo glanced from beneath her lashes over one smooth, bare shoulder, her black curls unbound, her lips curved into a seductive and playful smile.

Such an intriguing and intimate shot. Either the young Gabrielle LaRue had been posing for a Craigslist "model" job or she was flirting with a lover.

Augustine flipped the photo over. One word was scrawled across the back in a masculine hand: *GABI*. Yearning still seemed to whisper from that long-ago inscribed name, a sweetheart's desire.

Who had earned that luscious smile from Gabrielle LaRue? Who had taken the photo and written her name on the back? And how had the photo come into Rosette St. Cyr's possession?

Augustine couldn't help wondering if Gabrielle LaRue and Jean-Julien St. Cyr had been lovers once upon a time. He glanced at the paper beneath the photos. It held only three words: *Bayou Cyprès Noir.*

Augustine returned the poor excuse for a file to its box. He felt like going for a walk, or perhaps going out for a pint while he was still capable of enjoying one. "Please contact Ms. Brown and find out if Ms. Rivière is awake yet. We need to talk, and time is running out."

"At once, my lord."

NINETEEN

HER FINER QUALITIES

Kallie stared at Dallas. "You *what?*" Her voice cut through the conversational buzz beneath Café Du Monde's green-and-white-striped awning. She thumped her café au lait back down onto the white metal table. Coffee sloshed over the cup's rim, spilling hot on her fingers, but not hot enough to burn.

Dallas set his powdered-sugar-coated beignet on a napkin, then rocked forward in his chair, resting his forearms against the table. "Look, it ain't as bad as it sounds. Gabrielle was worried about you, that's all. She wanted to be sure that you were okay."

"By sending you to *spy* on me?"

"Well, *spying* is a bit harsh, more like *looking out for*—but in a nutshell, yeah."

"And you agreed to do it," she said, voice flat. "Despite the fact that I'm an adult and more than capable of taking care of myself." She tightened her fingers around her thick paper cup and continued to hold his gaze, refusing to give him an ounce of wiggle room. "Even when I was a kid, you never treated me like one. I never expected this from you."

"That's what I said to him too, girl," Belladonna

murmured, a gleeful little you're-in-for-it-now-boy tone dancing in her voice. "Go on, tell her the bit about the brainwashing."

Kallie frowned. "Brainwashing?"

"Christ, Bell," Dallas muttered, slashing a glance her way. "Ain't you supposed to be wielding a tape measure in a swinging-dick competition or something?"

"That's not for two hours, and I'm judging a wet-boxers contest, thank you," Belladonna replied. "You ought to enter," she added, popping a sugary bit of beignet into her mouth. She glanced at Kallie. "What's that saying? 'No fool, no fun?' "

"Pas d'amusement sans bêtise."

Belladonna nodded, blue-and-black curls swaying in the breeze. "That's the one."

Smiling, Dallas leaned back in his chair and stretched his jeans-clad legs out in front of him. Crossed his Durangos at the ankles. Mr. Smooth-and-Sexy. "Darlin', the only fool would be you, cuz the moment I stepped on that stage, the contest would be over."

"With everyone scrabbling for telescopes and magnifying glasses, yeah, it'd be goddamned impossible to continue," Kallie growled. "Now let's get back to the brainwashing."

Dallas groaned. "There *was* no brainwashing." He arrowed one more narrow-eyed glare at Belladonna—who ignored him, a satisfied smile on her plump, sugar-dusted lips—before returning his attention to Kallie. "Just Gabrielle's fears. You know how she feels about carnival and the people who run it."

"She thinks they're all fools," Kallie said, curling her fingers around the *loa* and saint pendants hanging below her throat. "Me too, obviously, and a fool she can't trust to boot." Her muscles knotted, and she felt a dull throb above her right eye—the headache's return.

Dallas trailed a hand through his hair, his expression unhappy. "No, now, c'mon," he said, "don't be like that. You ain't never been to carnival before, and she was—"

"Worried?" Kallie finished. "I heard you the first time, Dallas Brûler. All you're doing is making excuses for her."

"She loves you, Kallie. Wants to be sure you're safe."

"She loves Jacks too, and I know she worried about him like hell the first time he sailed alone, but I'm pretty goddamned sure she didn't hide a stowaway on his boat to spy on him."

Dallas hunched forward in his chair again. He shoved his napkin with its half-eaten beignet aside. "I *wasn't* spying, just keeping an eye out for you. And Jacks wasn't sailing with magic, now was he?"

"No, he wasn't. But what's that got to do with anything?"

"Everything. Magic can backfire. Magic can swallow a person whole."

"So can the sea."

"Believe me, hon, if Jacks had taken to hoodoo and learned to be a root doctor, and then had hauled his skinny ass off to N'awlins to cavort at carnival, your aunt woulda sent someone to keep an eye on him too."

"Boy's ass ain't skinny. Mmm-mmm. One tight end," Belladonna purred. "What?" she said, when both Dallas and Kallie paused to stare at her. "I'm just saying." She made a shooing motion with one hand. "Anyhow, go on—spying, trust issues, denials . . ."

"Lying—add that to the list, Bell," Kallie added,

releasing her pendants and tossing her wadded-up napkin onto the table. She looked at Dallas. "And you've been telling whoppers for Gabrielle, am I right?"

The root doctor shook his head. "Nope, you're wrong on that score, sugar-doll. Your aunt's plain paranoid about the outside world and the people running around in it, you know that."

"So we're back to her not trusting me to protect myself."

"She trusts you, dammit. I talked to her this afternoon while you were sleeping— "

"Comatose," Belladonna said around a mouthful of beignet.

Dallas flicked her an annoyed glance. "*Sleepin'*, and I let her know you were all right. Caught her up on what happened, too."

"Such a good and thoughtful little spy," Kallie said. She felt a mocking smile quirk up one corner of her mouth. "I hope she wasn't pissed at you for getting caught."

Dallas eyed her for a long moment, a hint of anger sparking hot in his blue eyes. "You really can be a pain in the ass, darlin'."

Belladonna snorted. "You just *now* noticing that, Dallas Brûler?"

"Not much of a spy, is he?" Kallie commented.

"Oh, I noticed your pain-in-the-goddamned-ass quality some time ago," Dallas said, "but was too much of a gentleman to mention it."

Belladonna's hand froze at her mouth, the last bite of beignet in her fingers. She stared at Dallas, hazel eyes wide. "Sweet Jesus, Shug, he's serious," she said.

"About not mentioning my finer qualities?"

"About thinking he's a gentleman."

Dallas slouched back into his chair. "Ha-ha, hilarious. You two should take it on the road."

"You shoulda just been honest, Dallas Brûler," Kallie said, voice tight. "Shoulda found me and just told me what Gabrielle asked you to do. I know how she can apply the pressure. I woulda understood."

A smile slanted Dallas's lips. "Darlin', I doubt that. You probably woulda decked me."

"Maybe," Kallie allowed. "But even if I had, I woulda helped you back up onto your feet. I thought we had an understanding, you and me. For now, you'd better keep your distance."

"Sorry, but I made a promise."

"Sorry, but you're gonna hafta break it. Tell me this—did Gabrielle know something was going to happen? Is *that* why she sent you?"

Dallas scrubbed a hand over his face, hesitating, then he said, "No, she didn't. She just wanted to be sure you were safe, that's all."

Kallie studied him, saw doubt in the depths of his eyes. He was hiding something, but what? "How come I don't believe you?" she asked, her voice soft.

"I can't answer that, hon," Dallas replied. "Maybe you should ask your aunt."

"Funny. That goddamned Rosette said the same thing," Kallie said. "I plan to ask, believe you me." Her headache settled in, a steady throb, but nothing like it had been originally when she'd hit her head. Planting her elbows on the tablecloth, she closed her eyes and rubbed her forehead with her fingertips.

"You okay?" Dallas asked. "How's the pain? I can mix up—"

"Not necessary," Kallie said, dropping her hands and opening her eyes. "It's nothing to worry about." She gathered the mass of her hair and tossed it behind her shoulders. The movement stretched her thin black tank top tight across the swell of her breasts. She noticed Dallas's gaze drop from her face to her bustline—and linger.

"You spying on my tits too?" Kallie pulled the neckline of her tank down low enough to reveal rounded cleavage cupped by a deep-blue bra. "That give you a better view?"

Dallas grinned. "Much better, sugar-doll. But maybe you could bend over a little more?" he said, scooting his chair out of punch-throwing range.

"Guess I asked for that one," Kallie muttered, tugging the tank's neckline back where it belonged. She lifted her chin despite the heat rushing to her cheeks.

"That you did, darlin'."

Kallie shoved her chair back across the pavement and stood. She exchanged a quick glance with Belladonna. *Ready to go?* The slim voodooienne nodded, then rose to her feet as well, brushing crumbs from her black leggings and belted purple tunic.

"I catch you spying on me or *looking out for* me or any other goddamned thing, and I'll break your nose," Kallie said, stabbing a finger at Dallas. "You hear me, *podna*?"

"I think the key words in that sentence are '*catch you*,'" Dallas drawled.

"Don't play games with me, Brûler. I ain't in the mood."

"Where you going?" he asked, standing.

"You're off spy duty, remember? So what does it matter?" Kallie replied.

Dallas brushed powdered sugar and pastry crumbs from his jeans. "Hey, can't a friend ask?"

"A friend could, yeah. But since friends don't spy on each other, you don't qualify."

"So that's how it's gonna be, huh?" Dallas said quietly.

"Yup. For now."

A muscle played along Dallas's jaw. "Okay, then."

Kallie turned away from the root doctor and the hurt she'd seen shadowing his blue eyes. Wondered if he'd seen the same in her eyes when he'd revealed himself as Gabrielle's spy. But what hurt most of all was knowing that her *ti-tante* had felt a need to send a spy in the first place.

Why doesn't she trust me?

Belladonna looped her arm through Kallie's. "C'mon, Shug, let's head over to the carnival and have a little bit of fun."

Kallie looked at her friend. Belladonna winked, and Kallie couldn't help but grin despite the cold knot tangling up her heart. "Why the hell not?"

Dallas watched Kallie and Belladonna cross Decatur Street, weaving through the damned near bumper-to-bumper traffic. A heavy combination of springtime tourists and carnival attendees. Both women moved with a natural hip-swinging ease, Kallie in her cutoffs, black tank, and sandals, and Belladonna in her black-belted purple tunic, black leggings, and platform-soled black boots.

Nice view. Very nice.

He had a feeling they were heading for the carnival itself, the whole thing spread throughout the Prestige's massive open-air courtyard—safe from the switched-off public. Maybe he should give Kallie a little bit of space—like, say, the space of one or two beers—before he started tailing her again. The killer was in Hecatean custody, after all.

But, killer in custody or not, he hadn't seen a mojo bag hanging around Kallie's slender throat, and she shouldn't be without one. Not here. Cupping his hands around his mouth, Dallas yelled, "Hey, Rivière! Where's your protection?"

Several heads at nearby tables swiveled in his direction at his shouted question, beignets and paper coffee cups paused at their mouths.

Kallie twisted around, and dipped a hand beneath her tank and into her bra. Dallas's heart danced a happy little jig. Pulling her hand out, she held up a small red flannel bag, cocked her weight onto one hip, and arched a dark eyebrow.

Mmm, mmm, mmm. Lucky bag.

Good enough. Dallas nodded and waved her on. Stuffing the mojo bag back into her bra, Kallie pivoted, all suppleness and sexy grace, and resumed walking.

Dallas worked his way across the street, stopped at a restaurant's booze-to-go window, and ordered an Abita Amber. A twinge of guilt twisted his muscles tight. He'd hated seeing the blend of pissed-off hurt hollowing Kallie's face. Hated knowing that he'd helped put it there. Hated lying to her even more.

The waitress slid a clear plastic cup full of foamy beer across the windowsill. "Thanks, darlin'." Dallas paid, grabbed his beer, and sauntered along the tourist-thronged sidewalk. He poured a long draft of the amber liquid down his throat—malty and smooth, just a hint of caramel, and so cold it made his throat ache.

But it would take a helluva lot more than one beer to wash away the niggling doubts coiling and looping and snaking through his mind. Doubts about Gabrielle. Doubts about everything she'd told him in that courtyard.

After his potion had eased Kallie into sleep, Dallas had corralled Belladonna into a long chat about everything he'd missed during the day's events—the soul-killing hex and Gage's murder.

"The killer? She told Kallie something about an eye for an eye never being enough and that Kallie could thank Gabrielle LaRue for everything. Psycho bitch."

That had stunned Dallas, the killer knowing Gabrielle by name. Troubled him still. And the soul-killing hex iced him down to the bone. Several dark possibilities had flashed through his mind:

1. Revenge for some wrong, vicious and soul-killing complicated, nothing plain or simple about it.

2. Every single word Gabrielle had told him in the botanica courtyard had been the absolute truth: "*A seed done been planted inside de girl, a seed dat can never be allowed to blossom. If it does, Dallas-boy, den somet'ing more wicked den long-fallen Babylon and crueler den hell will walk de earth once more.*"

"How will we keep the seed from blossoming?"

"You keep it away from de t'ings dat make it grow. Dis seed craves darkness and strife and blood. We gotta make sure it doesn't get dem. Gotta make sure de seed ain't fed."

But someone had been working their balls off (or tits off, in this case) to do exactly that, using blood and death and darkness. Kallie had never been the true target, just those around her, blood sacrifices to the seed harbored inside of her.

And his least favorite possibility:

3. Every single word Gabrielle had told him in the botanica courtyard had been the absolute truth. But then she'd decided to do what she believed necessary to stop a ravening evil from awakening and walking the earth, what she believed necessary to spare her niece a living nightmare. She'd found someone—Rosette—to lay down a hex that would kill both Kallie and whatever the fucking seed was. When that had failed, Rosette had kept trying.

But why the attempt on *his* life?

Had Gabrielle been behind the hoodooed poppet? Questions raised by the luscious Felicity Fields drifted through his mind:

"Did anyone besides Gabrielle LaRue know you'd be attending carnival?"

"No. Look, if you're implying that Gabrielle had something to do with all this, you're wrong. She's the one who called me—"

"And did Ms. LaRue's call lead you to your door and the bucket beyond..."

None of it made sense.

Gabrielle was a powerful hoodoo, a woman of strength, but brimming with secrets. Dallas didn't really *know* all that much about her. But he'd trusted her all the years he'd known her as a student, then as a fellow hoodoo and—he liked to think—as a friend.

And he just couldn't believe that there was anything wrong with Kallie. He'd never seen any sign of darkness in her. A quick temper, sure, but nothing that would qualify as "*more wicked den long-fallen Babylon.*"

He wondered if Gabrielle had misinterpreted her cards, despite her denials, wondered if maybe it all came down to her thinking she saw something of Kallie's murderous mom inside the girl. *What other seed could she be talking about?*

Dallas poured the rest of his beer down his gullet, then ordered another cold one at the next to-go window he came to. He examined that afternoon's phone conversation with Gabrielle again, twisted it this way and that, looking for rough edges, dangling threads, something not quite right.

"She safe, boy?"

"She is now. I potioned her up, and she's sleeping. But two people are dead—one of 'em body and soul. The hex on Kallie's mattress was a soul-killer."

"A soul-killer? You sure? Not many can shape a black hex dat powerful."

"True, but you can. And I'm sure about the soul-killing because a nomad Vessel happens to be here too. Which is good, since the Hecatean master died trying to defend Kallie."

"Sir Basil Augustine is dead? Sweet Jesus, Dallas, where were you during all dis?"

"Sleeping off the effects of a jinxed poppet chained into a bucket of wormwood and sulfur water."

"I tol' you to keep yo' dick in yo' pants, boy."

"I did, it is, and this ain't got nothing to do with my dick, dammit."

"So you're saying de death fairy picked you for no particular reason?"

"No, I'm saying someone deliberately *tried to kill me too, and if Kallie and Bell hadn't stumbled across me, I'd be dead."*

*"*Kallie *found you? Did you tell her why you're dere?"*

"Did you hear the 'someone deliberately tried to kill me too' part?"

"I heard, boy. You're talking to me, ain't'cha? Obviously, dey didn't succeed."

"The good news is the woman responsible has been caught. Bad news is she's been laying the blame for everything at your feet."

"Silence, then: My *feet? Who be dis woman?"*

"Bell passed this info on to me—the woman's name is Rosette, and she's a black chick in her midtwenties with beaucoup *short platinum-blonde hair. She was working as a maid in the hotel. Know her?"*

"Rosette? I know a white girl named Rosalinda, but . . ."

"Well, this Rosette knows you, *darlin'. She—"*

"Don't you dare 'darlin'' *me, Dallas Brûler."*

"Sorry, ma'am, no disrespect, just a slip of the tongue. Anyway, she told Kallie that everything came compliments of Gabrielle LaRue. She also mentioned some bullshit about an eye for an eye never being enough."

"From several thousand miles away, Dallas hears a breath catch in Gabrielle's throat as though a realization has sparked through her mind—a realization she doesn't reveal."

"Bête comme une bête a chandelle, *dis girl. Sounds like she be carrying a heavy grudge, but I don't know her."*

"She may be crazy as a June bug, for true, but I seriously doubt she has you mixed up with someone else. Do you think it's possible that Kallie's mother sent her?"

Silence hangs heavy in Dallas's ear; then Gabrielle sighs.

"Anyt'ing's possible at dis point, Dallas-boy. You might even be right about Sophie, but I don't believe she'd try to snuff Kallie's soul."

"Why not? She tried to murder her, for chrissakes."

"Sophie just wouldn't and let's leave it at dat."

And no amount of persuasion and cajoling on his part had earned him a single word more about Sophie Rivière.

The conversation had ended with Dallas promising—since he was a goddamned glutton for punishment—to shepherd Kallie home as soon as possible and to find out as much as possible about Rosette.

Gabrielle's words—"*She safe, boy?*"—circled on an endless loop through Dallas's mind. Odd words if she truly wished Kallie dead and the appropriate ones if she wished her niece protected.

And Dallas wished he knew which way to take them.

The only loose thread he'd discovered in remembering his conversation with Gabrielle was that caught breath followed by calm denial. He had no doubt those words—"*an eye for an eye is never enough*"—had clicked into place in Gabrielle's mind like triple cherries on a slot machine.

What ain't she saying? And even more important, why *ain't she saying it?*

TWENTY

MAY MADNESS

"You gonna have it out with Gabrielle?" Belladonna asked as they walked underneath the circular arch proclaiming MAY MADNESS in black wrought-iron ivy leaf letters.

"Yeah, definitely," Kallie said. She strolled along the crowded fairway, the grass cushioning the soles of her sandals a welcome change from a regular carnival's playground of hard-packed dirt, dust, and dying weeds. "I can't believe she sent someone—let alone Dallas, of all people—to spy on me."

Understanding and sympathy sparked gold light through Belladonna's autumn gaze. "Me either. I mean, hell, if you're gonna send a spy, send Jason Bourne, y'know? At least he's sexy."

Kallie slapped Belladonna's arm. "Pure evil."

"Well, *someone* has to be."

Game booths—SPELL A RING AROUND THE BOTTLE AND WIN!—and demonstration booths—CHAKRA ALIGNMENT HERE—nestled against each other. Drums throbbed and pulsed, a primal and earthy soundtrack against the musical *dings, clangs,* and deep-throated laughter curling into the air from the gaming booths as the women walked past lecture tents—HOW TO USE BOTH RUNES AND TAROT IN YOUR READINGS—holding experts seated at tables lined with pitchers of water and folding chairs filled with note-taking listeners.

The carnival drums pounded in time with the dull pain throbbing above Kallie's right eye. *Thanks, Dallas.* She decided to blame the headache on his spy confession—or partial confession, since she remained convinced he had held something back.

"Maybe Gabrielle chose him because she wanted someone she trusted completely to watch over you," Belladonna said. "I gotta admit her actions surprised me too, but maybe it's like Dallas said—she was just worried about you."

"Maybe, but it don't make it right, Bell." Kallie shoved her hands into the pockets of her cutoff jeans.

"No argument here. Hey, you want some cotton candy?"

"When in carnival, yada, yada . . . Sure. Purple."

Belladonna perched her hand on one cocked hip. Her scent—jasmine tonight—floated in the air, light and sweet. "Girl, please. You *always* pick purple. You need to expand your horizons. Live a little."

Kallie shrugged. "What the hell—let's go with blue, then."

"That's what *I'm* getting, so you get pink."

"What the—? Purple!"

Laughing, Belladonna turned to the booth and placed their order. The guy behind the counter, a skinny teen, red-haired and *beaucoup* freckled, murmured a few words and traced a glyph in air laced thick with the sticky, buttery scents of caramel corn and spun sugar, and two paper cones floated over to the whirling cotton-candy-making machine.

Kallie's thoughts spun back to Layne and the grief she'd seen in his green eyes the moment his gaze had landed on her bed and Gage's bloodied body. Spun back to the feel of his hard chest beneath her hands as she tried to summon him back into his lifeless body and siphon the hex's poison from his soul.

"I am fighting, woman. Quit pummeling me."

And now, like a cherry on top of a nightmare sundae, the nomad had Augustine's uncrossed-over spirit jam-packed inside of him.

Two people are dead because of me. Gage's soul destroyed. How do I ever atone for that?

Kallie tugged her hands free of her pockets as Belladonna handed her a paper cone mounded with purple fluff. "I thought I was getting pink," Kallie said.

"I decided to have mercy." Belladonna plucked a strand of blue from her cone and placed it in her mouth. "Yum. Sugar."

"You just had sugar."

"I stand corrected. Yum. *More* sugar."

"I think I want to attend Gage's funeral. I owe him that much," Kallie said, pinching a piece of purple fluff into her mouth. It melted the second it touched her tongue. Sticky sugar fuzz clung to her fingertips.

Belladonna crossed her arms over her chest and gave Kallie a long and measured look. "Mmm-hmm. And when the pixie tries to kill you like she promised?"

"I'll deck her."

"Y'know, Shug, I hate to break it to you, but slamming knuckles into noses isn't the answer to *everything*, and it's far from accepted funeral etiquette. Oh. Wait. It's a nomad funeral, so maybe it isn't. And that's another thing—I don't think outsiders are welcome at nomad funerals."

"I know, I know," Kallie said; then she sighed. She brushed her hair back from her face. "I'm going to see if I can reason with the leprechaun. Maybe I can convince her to call off the ban long enough for me to attend the funeral—then I'll never bother her or Layne again."

Belladonna snorted. "Good luck with that, Shug."

Never bother Layne again. Never see him again.

Well, no big deal, right? Sure, the man was *beaucoup* easy on the eyes, but she didn't really know him, and he'd be back on the road again soon enough anyway. Yet the thought of never looking into his pine-green eyes again or winning a smile from his lips or catching his sweet-orange-and-sandalwood scent twisted cold around her heart. And even though that puzzled the hell out of her—*do I feel this way because I saved his life?*—she couldn't help but wonder what tumbling into the sack with him would be like.

It'd be good, I'd bet. Loving each other up from sunup to sundown until he rode away again. We'd have our space, our privacy, and would look forward to the next meeting.

She stuffed another sticky piece of spun sugar into her mouth, perplexed by the direction of her thoughts. She remembered the flutter of Layne's pulse as it stopped, remembered the feel of his ribs cracking beneath her hands, the hex's oily taint flowing from him and into her. Remembered the look in his eyes when he'd opened them again—all green heat and light: *I know you.*

We're connected somehow—I felt it the first time I saw him standing outside my door looking all sleep-rumpled. Saw it spark in his eyes too.

"My advice regarding the pixie?" Belladonna was saying as Kallie tuned back in. "Make a poppet of her, and compel it to be nice."

"I like that idea," Kallie replied, wondering if she could stop at just compelling McKenna to behave. "But I'll try talking to her first. If that doesn't work . . . You got poppet-makings in that mambo-scout bag of yours?"

"Nope, but you can buy them in the dealers' room."

"Wonder if they make poppets that small?"

"Girl, please. In *her* case, the poppets are life-sized."

Kallie laughed, and the pain in her head eased a little. "Yup, you are pure one hundred percent evil."

"Kind of you to notice, Shug." Belladonna stuffed a wad of blue fluff into her mouth. "But before you go look up the pixie or start hexing tiny poppets, there's something you need to think about—and think hard."

All the amusement and mischief vanished from Belladonna's face and her somber expression knuckled a fist of apprehension into Kallie's guts. "And what's that?" she asked, keeping her voice level.

"I know you want to say your good-byes to Gage, I totally get that. But you've got to look at it from the other side. How do you think Gage's family will feel about a squatter chick dropping in on the festivities? A squatter chick who also happens to be the last woman their boy slept with and in whose bed he died?"

"Because of a hex intended for her," Kallie finished. Her appetite for cotton candy withered. She crossed to the trash bin stationed between the BEWITCH A MOLE and WHEEL OF DESTINY booths and dumped her cotton candy into its black-plastic-lined interior.

"Think they'd want to see her?" Belladonna asked

gently when Kallie rejoined her. "Think they'd want her to share in their sorrow?"

"No, I guess not." Shoving the heavy mass of her hair behind her shoulders, Kallie sighed. "If Jacks died in some woman's bed because of a bullet or spell or whatever aimed at her, I'd fucking deck her if she dared show her face at his funeral."

"I know you feel bad, Shug, and I know you want to do what's right, but in this case, staying away *is* the right thing."

Throat tight, Kallie nodded. "Yeah."

But she hated to leave it at that. To just walk away from a man who'd made her laugh and whose touch had made her moan. A man who'd died in her place. Her fingers sought out the soothing onyx-and-sterling-silver touch of her pendants and locked around them.

The memory of Gage's fingers slipping across the swell of her breasts to the base of her throat and the pendants that rested against her skin sparked through her mind.

"What's with the coffin? You ain't Goth, so I'm figuring it's a hoodoo thing."

"How do you know I ain't Goth? Never judge a book, yada yada."

"You're right, my bad. Are *you Goth?"*

"Nope, and you're right, it's a hoodoo symbol. The coffin represents Baron Samedi. He's the lord of death, and he stands at the crossroads."

"Is that what the X *is for? Or is that a cross?"*

"Both. It represents the crossroads. The Baron alone decides who crosses over into Guinee*—the realm of the dead—or doesn't."*

"'Or doesn't?' What does that mean, exactly? Sounds kinda ominous."

"Not really. It just means that he's also the loa *of resurrection. A lot of times, he's called upon as a last resort when someone's near death or dying."*

"And this one? The saint medallion?"

"Saint Bernadette, for healing."

Gage traces a gentle finger along the scar at her temple: "Healing. Death and resurrection. Sounds like you faced something pretty rough once upon a time."

"My aunt thought so, anyway. She gave me both of these, and I promised to always wear them."

"Good symbols to wear, you ask me. I know someone who'd love to have a chat with the Baron about open and instant admission for everyone into the land of the dead."

Kallie knew now that Gage had been speaking about Layne. Releasing the pendants, she wondered if she'd at least be able to give the nomad a gift to send with Gage without resorting to binding a McKenna poppet.

"Why don't you help me judge the wet-boxers contest?" Belladonna said. "Have a little fun and get to ogle men's packages with impunity to boot. I'll see if you can be the one who hoses them down."

Kallie felt a smile tugging at her lips. "I hope they plan to use warm water. Maybe. It'd be fun, for true, but first I gotta meet with Augustine and see what he wants."

"Oh, that's right," Belladonna mumbled around a mouthful of cotton candy. "Where did he ask you to meet him again?"

"Some bar on Bourbon Street—The Latex Closet."

Belladonna snorted. "Sounds like a dominatrix fashion boutique."

Kallie grinned. "Well . . . he *is* British."

"And he's in Layne's hot body. Imagine him all decked out in latex."

Heat fluttered through Kallie's belly at the image Belladonna's words invoked. *Nomad in skintight latex. Yum.*

"Go, girl, but make sure you're here for the wet-boxers fun. Hunky conjurers and illusionists in skimpy underthings, you with a hose . . ." A wicked smile danced across Belladonna's lips.

"Wouldn't miss it. I'll meet you at the contest stage when I'm done."

"I'll have a hose waiting for you, Shug."

Kallie blew Belladonna a kiss before turning around and heading for the MAY MADNESS arch; the wrought iron glinted like polished black pearl in the sunlight. She headed back across the courtyard and to the hotel, Gage's words haunting her thoughts.

"Healing. Death and resurrection. Sounds like you faced something pretty rough once upon a time."

Cold fingers closed around Kallie's heart. Nothing she'd faced compared to what Gage had suffered alone, and nothing ever would.

TWENTY-ONE

DOCTOR HERON

Jean-Julien St. Cyr strolled along the scarlet-flowered Persian carpet through the Prestige's spacious, people-thronged lobby. Light from Canal Street filtered in through the bank of floor-to-ceiling windows stretching along the walls on either side of the bustling entrance, sparking soft illumination in the lobby's mirrored columns.

Phones trilled and voices rose into the air, buoyant with laughter. Hotel guests in shorts, T-shirts proclaiming LAISSEZ LES BON TEMPS ROULER or a fleur-de-lis embellished WHO DAT? clustered near a long table covered in a pristine white cloth, spooning complimentary jambalaya into bowls, buttering corn bread, or stirring sugar into coffee while children chased each other with toy fairy wands across the lobby.

"You're a frog!"

"Then you're a fly and I just ate you!"

"Did not!"

Hotel employees in gray uniforms, THE PRESTIGE embroidered in red on their suit jackets, pushed luggage racks toward gleaming elevators, and maids in gray dresses, white aprons, and sturdy rubber-soled shoes whisked along beside them.

A sharp pang pierced Jean-Julien as one young woman with platinum-blonde hair bustled past, shoving a keycard into a pocket of her dress. Throat tightening, he looked away and continued across the lobby toward the room marked STARLIGHT CONVENTION HALL.

"You'll find it in the dealers' room, Papa. Tucked into the dirt of the potted palm tree beside the CREOLE MOJO *booth."*

"I know what it's like to be locked up, baby-girl. I'll get you out of there, safe and sound, as soon as I can."

"I know you will, Papa."

A smiling overweight young man in a gray uniform—one stretched to the seams—perched on the edge of a stool in between the convention hall's open double doors.

"Evening," Jean-Julien said, slowing his pace and smiling.

"Good evening, sir. May I see your badge, please?"

Jean-Julien stopped beside the young man's perch and handed him the visitor's day pass Rosette had mailed to him the day before.

"Thanks." The doorman waved him inside.

Jean-Julien walked into the dealers' room. Booths of all shapes and sizes looped the room's perimeter in diminishing rings. The smell of woody patchouli incense hung in the air, curling around the sweet scent of jasmine and rose and the heated spice of cayenne pepper and pungent anise.

A few people strolled the aisles, but the majority of carnival attendees were most likely at dinner or outside enjoying the May Madness festivities. Derision twisted cold along Jean-Julien's spine. *Carnival.* As though magic was just a game, a plaything for bored children.

He knew better, of course. Magic was a gator submerged just beneath the dark surface of the water. Waiting. Hungry and patient. And it didn't care who or what it devoured as long as it fed.

As for himself, he cared very much that his hex had killed an innocent nomad instead of Gabrielle LaRue's hoodoo-schooled niece. But nothing could be done about the life and soul lost. All the hand-wringing in the world wouldn't change a thing. The nomad remained dead and Kallie Rivière alive. All Jean-Julien could do was move forward.

He walked the circling aisles until he spotted the CREOLE MOJO booth and the potted palm beside it. Painted with flowing grace at the top of the booth's lemon-yellow covering was a picture of a serpent uncoiling up from the ground beside a black pot from which a rainbow arched across the sky—a *vévé* symbolizing Damballah Wedo and asking for wealth and luck.

"*Bonjour*! If you need help finding anything or have any questions, *m'sieu*, please ask, *oui*?" the woman tending the booth said. She was attractive, perhaps in her midforties, her smooth skin darker than Jean-Julien's, chocolate to his butterscotch, her eyes a warm shade of deep brown.

"That I will, *m'selle. Merci beaucoup*," he replied, winning a smile from her as she turned to greet another customer.

Jean-Julien browsed through the racks of prepackaged herbs and roots; examined packages of incense, floor wash, and bath salts, and bottles of oil labeled LADY LUCK OIL and COURT CASE OIL and FOLLOW ME BOY OIL; and surveyed shelves of candles, statues of Catholic saints, and voodoo-doll kits, before purchasing a small packet of powdered St. John the Conqueror Root—after studying it with a critical and practiced eye to make sure it was authentic.

Too many folks out there willing to cheat you in order to make a quick buck. No honor left in the world. Nor trust. All lessons he'd learned the hard way.

Thanking the woman, Jean-Julien walked past the booth to the potted palm. Dropping his purchase, he bent and plunged his fingers into the pot's dark soil, quickly finding the rounded edges of the thing he sought.

"Kallie Rivière's room has been sealed, Papa, but I'm sure they'll give her another. It's also possible that she might stay with her friend, Belladonna Brown, in room 629."

Jean-Julien pulled the keycard free of the dirt; a maid's universal keycard, one that provided access to every non-restricted room in the hotel.

Palming the keycard, Jean-Julien picked up the powdered-root packet, then straightened, and slipped the keycard into his trouser pocket.

He strode from the convention hall and across the busy lobby for the elevators. Each person he passed seemed as insubstantial as an image flickering on a computer screen—bands of light and data, an illusion.

His daughter's words whispered through his memory: *"Once they believe they have the killer, they will have no need to protect or hold the old* sorciere's *niece. They will release her."*

"And you? What will become of you?"

"I am happy to be your sacrifice upon the altar of revenge, Papa."

A muscle flexed in his jaw. If they'd hurt his Rosette in any way . . .

Once inside the elevator, Jean-Julien glanced up at the old-fashioned tin ceiling and punched a floor button at random. When he looked, he saw that the 10 button had lit up. As *bon Dieu* willed.

Jean-Julien would go where the *loa* guided him. Once Kallie Rivière was dead, then he'd concentrate his efforts into freeing his daughter—so much like her mother, his long-lost Babette.

Babette, *ma belle femme, ma morte chère.*

But first a little prep work on his daughter's behalf.

Jean-Julien stopped in front of the first room that drew his eye. Reaching into his trouser pocket, his fingers slipped past the packet of purchased powder and the hard, folded shape of his pocketknife to the vial he'd filled the night before.

Jean-Julien pulled out and uncorked the vial, releasing the pungent odor of bergamot, licorice, and calamus root into the still air—a potent bend-over blend—and carefully tapped a portion of the black powder into the palm of his hand. Stuffing the stopper back into the glass mouth, he dropped the vial back into his pocket.

He rapped his knuckles against the door of room 1013. A moment later, the door was yanked open, revealing a red-haired woman tying a paisley scarf around her hair. She frowned, puzzled.

"May I help you?" she asked.

"Yes." Jean-Julien lifted his palm to his mouth and blew the dust into her face. "My bidding you desire, no will of your own, my word holy fire."

The woman stumbled back a step, coughing, blinking, and fanning the air in front of her shocked face.

Jean-Julien shoved into the room after her, closing and locking the door. The woman stopped coughing. She stood in the entry staring at Jean-Julien with a blank and black-dust-sooted face, her watering eyes unfocused.

"Turn around and go sit on the bed," Jean-Julien said gently.

Obeying, she shuffled to the unmade bed and sank down onto it, hands in her lap. Jean-Julien crossed to the desk and the phone sitting on its polished surface. He dialed room service.

"Fruit plate and coffee, please. Room 1013."

The woman stiffened and glanced around the room, her dust-smudged face anxious. Hanging up the phone, Jean-Julien went to the bed and knelt on one knee on the floor. Grasping her chin, he turned her face toward him.

"It's not for you to bring, not your task," he said. "Your task is to get up, go into the bathroom, and wash your face. Be sure to dry it with one of the towels hanging on the rack, then come back to the bed." Releasing her, he rose to his feet.

The woman stood, her movement rigid, then tottered off to the bathroom like a woman twice her age. A moment later, he heard the sound of water pouring into the basin—a sound that continued even after she shuffled out of the bathroom, her face scrubbed clean of powder and dry.

"Ah-ah. Go back inside and turn off the water."

Wheeling around, the woman teetered back into the bathroom. The blast of running water stopped.

Jean-Julien waited. Nothing. He sighed. *Zombies.* "Come out of the bathroom now," he called. "Return to the bed and lie down."

Once the woman had lain down and curled up on

her side, Jean-Julien instructed her to sleep, murmuring that all she would remember of the evening was a strange dream she couldn't quite recall. Her eyes closed. Within a minute, her breathing had dipped into the slow and easy rhythm of sleep. Jean-Julien pulled the sheet up over her.

Pulling the vial of bend-over powder free of his pocket, he sat down in one of the high-backed chairs beside the French window leading to the balcony. He filled his palm again with the black and pungent powder, and waited.

Rosette's failure to kill Dallas Brûler still rankled. A simple jinx—a tricked poppet—and the root doctor from Chalmette, and Gabrielle's prize pupil once upon a time, should've been dead.

"Papa, she was just there. *It was almost as if the* loa *themselves had guided her to him. I mean, for her to be there at that very moment. And maybe they did—punishing us for murdering an innocent man's soul."*

"No, that man's death is just more blood on Gabrielle LaRue's hands. Another consequence of her actions all those long years ago. You watched your mama die, Rosie. Watched pain devour her inch by inch. Don't go soft on me, girl."

"Never, Papa. An eye for an eye is never enough. Never, never, never."

No truer words existed.

Jean-Julien would deal with his daughter's screw-up and make sure Brûler joined the ranks of the dead. But if it came down to choosing between the root doctor and Gabrielle's niece, he'd choose the one whose death would break the hoodoo woman's heart and spirit and will. Her niece.

He yearned to be a spider tucked into a corner of Gabrielle's ceiling when she learned about her niece's death, yearned to see the devastation on her face when she realized that Kallie Rivière's body hadn't died alone, that her soul had perished as well.

And just when Gabrielle would be thinking nothing worse could ever happen, her nephew, the seafaring and bayou-raiding Jackson Bonaparte, would suffer the same fate.

Then Jean-Julien would make damned certain Gabrielle knew why.

"An eye for an eye is never enough. Never, never, never."

A polite rap on the door drew Jean-Julien's attention away from his thoughts. Rising to his feet, he strode to the door and opened it. A smiling young man in a gray uniform stood in the hall, a plastic-domed tray in his hands.

Jean-Julien ushered the dark-skinned waiter inside, then lifted his palm and blew the dust into his startled face. "My bidding you desire, no will of your own, my word holy fire."

The tray fell to the floor with a loud crash, the plate and glass shattering, splattering the carpet with fruit and black coffee. The sharp scent of pineapple and cantaloupe wafted into the air.

Once the waiter had finished coughing, stumbling, and gasping, and had gone still, his black-powdered face blank, his brown eyes wide and unfocused, Jean-Julien gave him the item he'd need to carry out his soon-to-be-assigned task: a vial containing a black oil—a deadly shadow-work potion—with the pieces of a torn-up paper command floating inside. Using his pocketknife,

Jean-Julien sliced a small piece of fabric from the hem of the waiter's white shirt.

"Put that vial away," Jean-Julien instructed. The young man slipped it into his jacket pocket. "Do you know the name Rosette St. Cyr?"

"Yes."

"In what capacity?"

"She is a maid here, or was until she shot Lord Augustine. Now she's—"

"What?" Jean-Julien stared at the waiter, his pulse thundering in his ears. "Did you say she *shot* Lord Augustine?"

"Yes."

Jean-Julien raked a hand through his close-cropped hair, his thoughts whirling through his mind so fast he couldn't nab a single one. Drawing in a deep breath, he worked on centering himself, calming the frenzy in his mind. His thoughts slowed; his pulse dropped to a canter.

The plan had been for Rosette to turn herself in as the dead nomad's murderer, to name herself as the guilty party in the attempted murder of Kallie Rivière so that the need for protective custody would no longer be necessary. Instead, the girl had shot the Hecatean master, the head of the Alliance. Why? And where in *bon Dieu*'s name had she found a gun?

What had gone wrong? What the hell had Rosette *done*?

Jean-Julien asked, "Is Rosette St. Cyr still alive?"

"Yes."

Relief curled through Jean-Julien. "And Lord Augustine? Is he still alive?"

"We haven't been told."

Jean-Julien mulled over that bit of information. A couple of possibilities for the official silence rolled through his mind. One—the news was bad, Augustine wasn't expected to survive or had already died. Two—Augustine *was* expected to survive, but in fear of another attempt on his life, the news was being kept quiet.

"Do you know where Rosette St. Cyr is being held?"

"Yes."

"Tell me."

"On the fifteenth floor."

"Once you return to the kitchens, you will do everything in your power to make sure you stay on duty until I need you. Do you understand?"

"Yes."

"Once I contact you, you will take food to the guards watching Rosette St. Cyr. Before serving them, you will add the contents of the vial I gave you to their food. Divide it equally among them and mix it up well. Do you understand?"

"Yes."

"No thoughts shall occupy your mind except for the instructions I have given you," Jean Julien said. "My bidding you desire, no will of your own, my word holy fire."

"Your bidding my desire, no will of my own, your word holy fire."

"Yes. Now go into the bathroom and wash your face. Turn off the faucet when you're done and be sure to dry your face with one of the towels."

"Be sure to dry your face with one of the towels," the waiter parroted, turning. He disappeared into the bathroom.

Once the cleaned-up waiter had shuffled back out into

the hall, domed tray once more in his hands, Jean-Julien left the room and headed for the elevator.

All he could do now was wait for the right moment to end Kallie Rivière's existence. In the meantime, he might visit the outdoor carnival, then see where Belladonna Brown's room was located.

Who knew who he might run into?

TWENTY-TWO

LEPRECHAUN'S GOLD

The Latex Closet turned out to be a small blues bar tucked in between a gentlemen's club and a strip joint—both featuring nude males and females. Kallie barely managed to keep from decking the persistent barkers who tried to lure her into both as either a tourist to rip off or a potential new nude dancer.

She slipped into the darkened bar, the door swinging shut on the noise from the street behind her—*"This way, ladies and gents! Live nudes! Sex shows! Smokin' hot! Sexy! C'mon in! You ain't seen nuthin' like this!"*—and searched the crowded and smoky interior for Augustine.

A blues trio performed on a small stage at the far end of the room, their faces—white, black, and in between—lit by a blue spotlight. The music spilling out from their guitars and bass sounded original, an up-tempo walking-out-on-my-baby song, sung by the white guy in a raspy growl.

Ceiling fans swirled the smells of beer and cherry-tobacco pipe smoke and fresh popcorn through the warm, humid air.

Kallie spotted Augustine—well, Layne—sitting at a table near the bar, his dreads knotted back from his handsome face, and her pulse pounded just a little harder. *Augustine*, she reminded herself. *Not* Layne. His attention was fixed on his laptop as his fingers pecked away at the keyboard. A large blue plastic crate and a half-filled beer stein rested beside the laptop.

She worked her way over to the table. "Hey," she greeted him.

Layne-Augustine glanced at her. "I appreciate you coming in, Ms. Rivière. Please sit down. I just need a moment to finish this blasted recommendation for an interim master."

"Look, can we drop the 'Ms. Rivière' bullshit? Just call me Kallie, okay?" The British accent coupled with the nomad's face kept throwing her. She wondered when Augustine planned to leave Layne's body.

"Kallie it is," Layne-Augustine agreed. "You may call me Lord Basil."

"Lucky me," Kallie muttered, pulling out a chair and plopping into it.

A few more pecks at the keyboard, then, "There. Sent." Layne-Augustine picked up his beer stein and sat back in his chair. He saluted Kallie with the mug. "Bureaucracy continues even after one dies, apparently." He took a long swallow of the dark, foamy brew.

"Well, that sucks, for true," Kallie sympathized. A waitress in a red skirt and black apron paused by the table and Kallie ordered the one-dollar strawberry daiquiri special.

Layne-Augustine set his stein back on the table, then stood and dug through the plastic crate. "I just have a few questions for you."

"I've got a few questions of my own," Kallie said. Her gaze swept over him from head to toe, taking in the sharp-fitting French-blue shirt and charcoal trousers. *Mmm-mmm. Cleans up well.* She shook her head, a smile curving her lips. "The leprechaun's gonna kill you."

Layne-Augustine pulled a skimpy-looking manila folder from the crate and looked at her, expression puzzled. "Leprechaun? I haven't stolen a pot of gold."

"Um . . . yeah, you have. The pot of gold's name is Layne, and his ex was pretty clear about you leaving him as is."

"Are you calling Ms. Blue a leprechaun?"

"Possibly."

Layne-Augustine's lips twitched into a smile. "I don't see how she could object to improving Valin's fashion sense—which wouldn't take much." He smoothed a hand along the front of his shirt. A dreamy expression flickered across his face. "So tight," he murmured.

"Excuse me?"

The Brit's hand dropped from his shirt as though scalded, and the dreaminess vanished from his eyes. He cleared his throat. "Ahem. The shirt . . . it's a tad tight. But as to the other matter, I doubt very much that Ms. Blue will kill me. Not while I reside within Valin."

Kallie lifted her eyebrows. Good save, but she didn't believe for a single second that his "so tight" comment had been referring to the shirt, which looked like it fit just fine. "She probably wouldn't," Kallie agreed.

The waitress placed the cheap-ass strawberry daiquiri—*should be the state drink, it's as common as mosquitoes here*—in a frosted glass in front of her. "Thanks." Kallie handed her three ones for the one-dollar drink and told her to keep the change.

With a quick smile, the waitress disappeared into the crowd.

Tapping the worn folder against the table's edge, Layne-Augustine sat back down. "You mentioned that you had questions," he said. "What are they?"

Kallie leaned forward in her chair and rested her elbows on the table. "What have you learned about that Rosette chick? Did you search her home?"

Layne-Augustine nodded. "We did indeed search Ms. St. Cyr's apartment, and we recovered a few items of interest."

"Rosette St. Cyr," Kallie said, kicking the name around her memory. "Never heard of her. What did you find?" She took a sip of her icy drink, the strong taste of rum blotting out the strawberry sweetness. She stirred it with her finger.

"Pictures of you, your cousin, Mr. Brûler, and your aunt, plus information on all of you," Layne-Augustine replied. "It seems that her vendetta against your family is quite personal. But as to the reason why . . ." He shrugged one shoulder.

"Did you find any herbs or potions? How about an altar?"

"Yes, on all counts."

"Show me her conjuring stuff," Kallie said, rising to her feet.

Layne-Augustine nodded at the plastic crate sitting on top of the table. "It's right there, Ms. . . . Kallie. Please take a look."

Pushing her hair back over her shoulders, Kallie peered into the crate. Herbs and gnarled roots and potions in glass bottles; powders; piles of cloth, sticks, needles, and thread for making poppets; mojo bags; candles of all colors, and statuettes; small jars of graveyard dirt and nails; and a mortar and pestle. Nothing unusual, hoodoo-wise.

She reached in and rummaged through the items. The nostril-pinching reek of sulfur mixed with anise wafted into the air.

"Magic tends to be odorous at the best of times," Layne-Augustine said, fanning the air in front of his face,

Kallie sneezed. "No argument here." She lifted a small bottle filled with an amber-colored fluid into the light. Little bits of material—leaves and maybe a tiny chunk of root—floated in it. Looked like an attraction oil. "Have you questioned the bitch yet? All she told me was that I could thank my aunt for my troubles and that—"

"An eye for an eye is never enough," Layne-Augustine finished. "We've tried, but with no success. She refuses to speak."

Kallie returned the bottle to the crate and looked at Augustine. "So how come you ain't cast a truth spell on her?"

"Because forcing the truth via spell can result in brain damage. For the recipient, that is, not the caster."

Applause rippled through the bar as the blues trio ended one song, then started another, this one a low-voiced let-me-back-into-your bed number with a sexy bass throb. Enthusiastic whistles followed.

"Then what's the problem?" she asked.

"Since we might only have one shot at it, I'd prefer to wait until Mr. Buckland's family is present to hear that final truth."

Understanding and sorrow washed through Kallie. She had a feeling that the truth—that Gage had been killed by mistake—would give his family very little peace. But Augustine was right. They should be allowed to hear that truth, no matter how bitter, from the lips of Gage's killer.

"Fair enough," she said. "I'd like to be there as well."

"I don't see why that can't be arranged," Layne-Augustine said. "Do you see anything of interest in the crate?"

"That's the problem," Kallie said, frowning. She held up a Blessed Mother statue—a crowned figure of the Virgin Mary holding an infant Jesus—and pointed it like a finger at the Brit. "What's interesting are the things I *don't* see, and I don't see the components necessary for a hex as complicated as the one on my mattress. She's got a few of the ingredients, like wormwood, sulfur, and graveyard dirt, but not the dark elements needed for a hex like that—like bones and skin and blood."

"She could've hidden those ingredients, and it's possible my guards missed them, but I believe we suspect the same thing," Layne-Augustine said. "That Rosette St. Cyr didn't create the hex—not alone, anyway."

"Who could've helped her?" Kallie asked, replacing the statuette inside the crate.

"I suspect her father. I've learned that he was a root doctor and perhaps he still is, but I have nothing that indicates he's in New Orleans. His last known address was in Delacroix, Louisiana."

"Not too far from where I live," Kallie mused. Finished with her search of the crate, she dusted off her hands and sat back down. "So he's a root doctor? What name's he known by?"

"Doctor Heron."

Kallie stared at the Brit, heart racing. "Holy shit! I've heard of him. My *tante* used to tell me horror stories about Doctor Heron at bedtime, about the evil hoodoo who'd poisoned and killed all his clients. I thought she'd made it all up."

"No, indeed not." An amused light gleamed in Layne-Augustine's eyes. "Jean-Julien St. Cyr was convicted of multiple murders and sentenced to twenty-five years in prison. He was released last month. Do you know if your aunt knew the man? Have you spoken to your aunt about what's happened here?"

Kallie tensed. "Not yet. But Gabrielle never acted like she actually knew Doctor Heron. She only told me stories about him like he was the Freddy Krueger of hoodoo or something." She downed the rest of her daiquiri.

"Would Doctor Heron have the skill to instruct Rosette on how to construct a soul-killing hex?"

"Sure, if even half of what my *tante* told me was true. But she'd still need to possess the strength of will to imbue the hex with power. I ain't sure she's got that level of skill."

"But it's possible that she does?"

"Sure, anything's possible."

Layne-Augustine studied her for a moment before saying, "Is it also possible that your aunt was responsible for what happened to Jean-Julien St. Cyr, possible she turned him in to the police?"

"She's never mentioned anything like that. Never even hinted, so I don't know." She held the Brit's gaze, feeling cold inside. "Is *that* what Rosette thinks?"

What if it's true? What if Gabrielle knew this might happen, but never said a goddamned word, just sent Dallas instead? Maybe that's *what he's hiding.*

"I'm merely making an educated guess. And even if the St. Cyrs do believe your aunt was responsible, it doesn't mean she actually was," Layne-Augustine ruminated. "But there must've been a good reason for them to think her guilty in the first place."

"Dunno about that—a good reason and all," Kallie said. "Rosette seemed a little on the crazy side to me." The waitress pushed through the crowd to the table, and Kallie ordered another daiquiri, her headache all but gone. "What about Rosette's mama? She a hoodoo too?"

"No. Babette St. Cyr died of cancer ten years ago in Delacroix."

Layne-Augustine tossed his head as though to flip his hair out of his eyes—the short hair on the body he no longer possessed—and Kallie choked back a laugh at the startled look on his face when the weight of Layne's dreads pulled his head to one side.

"Bugger," he muttered, rubbing his neck. "I agree, however, with your assessment of Ms. St. Cyr's sanity. For her to dust-drug two guards and steal one of their guns in the hope of shooting you dead . . . hardly seems rational."

"Seems desperate," Kallie said.

"Indeed." Layne-Augustine finished his beer.

Guilt coiled and looped through Kallie. "I'm sorry you're the one who ended up dead instead of her," she said. "What's going to happen to the murdering bitch? Are you handing her over to the nomads?"

"I am," he said. "And the clans will agree with her 'an eye for an eye is never enough' belief. Given what she did to Mr. Buckland, I doubt her death will be pleasant."

"Will they kill her soul too?"

"I couldn't say. I've never witnessed nomads carrying out a death sentence—and, trust me, I'm quite sure that is what she faces."

"She killed you too," Kallie said quietly. "Do you want to see her die?"

Something bleak and cold breezed through Layne-Augustine's eyes. "I believe so. But how that will reconcile me to the fact of my own death, I don't know."

"I can't imagine what you're going through," Kallie said, voice soft. She pulled her hair over her shoulder, sectioned it, then started braiding. The mindless motion soothed her.

"I think that's a lie. I believe you can imagine what I'm feeling quite well. You stared at death point-blank when you saw your mother murder your father, then turn the gun on you. 'Fell out of a swing' indeed."

Kallie's fingers stilled in her hair. She glared at the Brit. "You goddamned sonuvabitch, you just had to go digging."

"I did indeed," he said. "But the maid had a file on you with the same information, so I would have learned about the murder attempt regardless."

"Okay, so you're an honest goddamned sonuvabitch," Kallie muttered. She unthreaded her hair, then shook it all loose with her hands. "But just because my mama shot me doesn't mean I have any idea what *you're* going through. I *didn't* die—in case you hadn't noticed."

"But you *believed* you were about to die just like your father. You believed everything was about to end with your blood sprayed on the walls."

"So what? It's not the same as *being* dead."

Layne-Augustine folded his arms over his chest, looking unconvinced. "I suppose not."

"You have to vacate Layne's body soon. What happens to you then?"

"I don't know," the Brit answered, voice low. "I have hopes that an angelic chorus will be kind enough to guide me. I shall find out in due time."

The waitress delivered another frosty daiquiri to the table, then scooped up Kallie's empty glass and the cash she'd left beside it. Kallie stirred this one first before taking a sip.

"I have a theory that your aunt and Rosette's father were once lovers."

Kallie choked on the daiquiri, nearly squirting it from her nostrils. She launched into a volley of hard, gasping coughs. Layne-Augustine leaned across the table and thumped his hand against her back. "Usually best *not* to inhale one's liquor," he murmured.

Once the coughing stopped and she could breathe again, Kallie wiped at her watering eyes and croaked, "Lovers? My aunt and Doctor Heron? You kidding me?"

"No, just theorizing. Would you care to hear possibilities of what might've happened between them?"

"Christ," Kallie muttered, taking another, careful swallow of her drink. "Go ahead."

Brow furrowed in thought, Layne-Augustine folded his arms over his chest and said, "Possibility one: Perhaps the lovers argue over Jean-Julien's less-than-ethical practice of using high dosages of potentially toxic herbs and roots. The lovers part on bad terms. Jean-Julien's clients start dropping like flies. Maybe the deaths are unintentional, just carelessness on his part, but that doesn't matter. Murder is murder. Gabrielle—whether inspired by spite or compassion—phones the police anonymously and gives her now-former lover up.

"Possibility two: Exactly the same as the first, except Gabrielle doesn't phone the police, doesn't give Jean-Julien up. But he *believes* she has.

"Possibility three: For whatever reasons, the lovers part

on bad terms. Furious at his rejection, Gabrielle adds toxic levels of herbs or roots to Jean-Julien's most popular potions and powders. When his clients die, the police look at the root doctor who had potioned them up. He's convicted of murders of which he is innocent, while Gabrielle remains silent.

"Possibility four: Jean-Julien knows he screwed up the dosages and doesn't place any blame on Gabrielle. But once his daughter grows up, she does.

"And possibility five: None of the above."

"But what makes you think Gabrielle and Jean-Julien were lovers?"

Layne-Augustine slid the worn manila folder across the table to her. "Take a look at those photos. See what you think."

"Okay." Kallie flipped the folder open and picked up the small, tattered Polaroid on top. She studied the young woman captured within it, guessing her to be about her own age, maybe a few years older. The woman gave a sultry glance from beneath her lashes over one smooth, bare shoulder, her lips curved into a flirtatious smile for whoever was taking the picture—a lover, most likely, given the sexiness of the pose and expression, or a soon-to-be lover.

"Look at the back," Layne-Augustine urged.

Kallie turned the photo over. *GABI* was written across the top in black marker, each letter traced over more than once, like a man trailing a finger over a woman's face, memorizing its contours. Or like a hoodoo writing a name or command repeatedly on a piece of paper to complete a spell.

Kallie looked at the front again and studied it. The woman was beautiful and in love.

"The other photo is more recent."

Kallie set the Polaroid down and looked at the other photo. The same woman, but a couple of decades older, her face thinner, her curls more gray than black, the joy leached out of her.

"So who is she?" Kallie asked, looking up.

Layne-Augustine stared at her. "Your aunt. Gabrielle LaRue."

TWENTY-THREE

UGLY POSSIBILITIES

Kallie looked down at the photo, her pulse drumming through her veins. "I don't know who that woman is, but she ain't my aunt."

The blues singer wailed about being a coldhearted cheatin' man. Wailed about needing mercy from a cold-hearted cheatin' woman.

She thought of the name penned on the back of the Polaroid—*GABI*. She tossed back her daiquiri, wincing as brain freeze spiked icicles through her mind.

"But . . . are you sure?"

"Of course," Kallie snapped, rubbing her forehead. "I know what my aunt looks like. That ain't her. In either picture."

"I see," Layne-Augustine said slowly, his perplexed expression making a liar of him. "Maybe she's not your aunt, but she *is* Gabrielle LaRue. Do you happen to have a picture of your aunt?"

Kallie nodded and reached a hand into her back pocket before remembering she didn't have her cell phone. She groaned. "My stuff's still sealed in my room."

"Does your aunt look anything like your mother?"

"Yeah, she and Gabrielle look a lot alike. My *tante*'s older, though."

Relief flickered across the Brit's face. "Then the odds are good that she's truly your aunt and not someone posing as her. It would seem that we have a case of mistaken identity somewhere along the line."

"Yeah, obviously Rosette identified the wrong woman as my aunt. Shit, Augustine, what else *could* it mean?" But even as the words left Kallie's lips, several ugly possibilities pranced through her mind. The first of which the Brit voiced aloud.

"It could mean that your *aunt* has taken on the identity of *Gabrielle LaRue*. Perhaps the original died, or perhaps your aunt simply absconded with her identity."

And there it was in a nutshell, ladies and gentlemen, ugly possibility *numéro un*. *What if my* tante *is a goddamned identity thief?*

Gabrielle didn't drive a car, rarely went into town, and since she believed that banks and credit card companies were the devil's capering minions, Gabrielle always paid in cash; Kallie and Jacks had been homeschooled, since Gabrielle had claimed she didn't trust the inept and inadequate public-school system.

But her aunt's behavior didn't seem typical for a cash-and-expensive-goodies-hungry identity thief. Gabrielle's actions seemed more suited to a person hiding from, say, the mob. Or how about a root doctor framed for murder?

"One thing is certain," Layne-Augustine put in quietly, "Rosette St. Cyr's vendetta *is* against Gabrielle LaRue. What is less certain is *who* that might be. Of course, the possibility exists that there is more than one Gabrielle LaRue."

Step right up to ugly possibility *numéro deux*, ladies and gentlemen: *The woman in the photos is the* right *Gabrielle LaRue, but faulty research led Rosette to my aunt instead—the* wrong *Gabrielle LaRue.*

Kallie propped her elbows on the table and buried her face in her hands. She felt sick. If that was the case, then the hex crafted on her mattress had been a mistake; Gage's murder and soul death, an error; Augustine's violent death, a fumbling accident; and Dallas's near poppet-drowning, all because of a mistaken identity.

"Shit," she whispered into her palms. "Shit, shit, shit."

"Care to share your scatological revelation with the rest of the class?" Layne-Augustine asked, voice martini-dry.

"The wrong goddamned woman," Kallie said, lifting her head and meeting the Brit's gaze. "The murdering bitch mighta nabbed the wrong woman."

Layne-Augustine nodded. "A distinct possibility."

But Kallie wanted more than distinct possibilities. She wanted the truth. "I need to use that," she said, nodding at the laptop.

"Go ahead."

Kallie rose to her feet and walked over to Layne-Augustine's side of the table. The Brit scooted his chair to the side to allow her room in front of the laptop. She bent over the keyboard and awakened the monitor with a tap of her finger against the mouse.

She ran a quick search on Sophie Santiago—her mother's maiden name, looking for a record of relatives and next of kin. Scrolling quickly through the list of hits, her pulse quickened when a genealogy site dedicated to Creole heritage led her to a listing for an André Santiago and his wife, Bethany Santiago—née Hawkins—and their three daughters.

Sophie, Divinity, and Lucia.

Jackson's mama's name had been Lucia. Kallie stared at the monitor as though she could will the name Gabrielle in place of the one she didn't recognize—Divinity.

This can't be right. Wrong Santiago family. Gotta be.

"What is it?" Layne-Augustine asked, concern threaded through his voice.

"I don't have an aunt named Gabrielle," Kallie whispered.

"Is this the first time you've Googled your family?" The Brit sounded bemused. He leaned in to look at the monitor and the information it held.

Kallie nodded. "I never bothered. I think I was kinda afraid of what I might find out." *Looks like I was right.* A dull ache built behind her eyes.

I no longer know who my ti-tante *is. All I* do *know is that she's been lying to me ever since she came into my life after the shooting.* Kallie felt like she was falling, her foundation yanked out from under her. Her hands clenched into fists. *I'm gonna get the goddamned truth no matter what it takes.*

"Another drink?"

Kallie looked up. The waitress nodded at her empty glass, raised a questioning eyebrow. "No thanks," Kallie said. "Hey, what time is it?"

"Almost ten, hon," the waitress called over her shoulder as she melted back into the crowd.

Kallie straightened. "Shit, I gotta get back over to the carnival so I can toss buckets of water on men in their skivvies."

"Men in their skivvies?" Layne-Augustine questioned. Interest glinted in his eyes.

"Wet-boxers contest," Kallie explained. "I promised Bell I'd help. I was looking forward to it, but now with all this . . ." She sighed, trailing a hand through her hair.

"I'll walk with you." The Brit rose to his feet.

"No need," Kallie said. "But thanks."

Layne-Augustine motioned to a guard hidden among the crowd and instructed him to take the laptop and crate back to his office. "Oh, I'm not offering as a gentleman," the Brit said. "Or at least, not entirely. I happen to be going the same way."

"Back to the hotel?"

"No. Since this might very well be my last evening on this mortal coil, I intend to enjoy myself. I'm entering the contest. Or, more precisely, I'm entering *Valin* in the contest." The Brit winked.

Kallie stared at him, her breath catching in her throat, and found herself looking forward to tossing those buckets of water all over again.

Twenty-Four

Follow Me, Boy

Jean-Julien finished the last spicy bite of cheddar-filled chorizo, savoring its garlic-and-smoky-paprika flavor. Licking a smear of tangy brown mustard from his finger, he tossed his wrapper and napkin into a trash bin beside one of the gaming booths.

He sauntered along the carnival fairway, regarding the game booths and the people flocked in front of them with a mix of amusement and contempt, not even sure himself if he felt more of one emotion than the other.

He paused in front of an empty stage, his gaze drawn by the hand-painted sign hanging above it:

WET BOXERS CONTEST 10 P.M.!
IF YOU'VE GOT IT AND WANT TO FLAUNT IT,
SIGN UP NOW!
WET T-SHIRT CONTEST AT MIDNITE.

Rosette's words returned to him: *"It's like spring break for those teaching and learning magic, Papa, all forms of it. They get to cut loose and have fun."*

"Sounds like disaster in the brewing to me, girl. Don't have anything to do with it."

"Yes, Papa."

"Spring break for fools who don't know what they're playing with," Jean-Julien muttered. His hand slid into the pocket of his khaki trousers, his fingers caressing the half-empty vial of black dust. He wished for enough powder to throw into the face of every fool walking the fairway. Then he'd teach them all a few lessons, *si l'bon Dieu veut*.

A smile curved Jean-Julien's lips as he pulled his hand from his pocket and sauntered away from the empty stage. He'd nearly reached the point from which he'd begun his carnival exploration, the black-wrought-iron entry arch, when he saw something that halted him in his tracks.

Kallie Rivière and a dreadlocked nomad passed underneath the arch and into the carnival. A troubled expression shadowed the Rivière girl's lovely face. Tension tightened the line of her collarbone, knotted her muscles. She curled a lock of dark hair behind her ear as she talked to the tall nomad.

She was a beauty and no older than Rosette—a couple of years younger, in fact, if he remembered right. And she herself was guilty of nothing.

But Babette had also been guilty of nothing. Condemned simply for being his wife. Gabrielle hadn't considered killing his clients and setting him up for the blame enough pain. Hadn't considered sending him to prison for twenty-five years for murders he hadn't committed soul-crushing enough. Hadn't considered keeping him from his bride and the child she carried sorrow enough.

No, the coldhearted bitch had made sure he'd never reunite with his bride. Not in this world, anyway. Jean-Julien would return the favor threefold.

Most of the high-spirited attendees milling along the

fairway carried plastic cups full of booze, but the Rivière girl and the nomad wove with ease through the crowd without bumping one elbow or causing a single drop of liquor to spill. They walked with purpose toward the contest stage.

It looked like Jean-Julien wouldn't have to use Rosette's keycard to go into the Brown girl's room to search for a personal item to use in his spell after all. Maybe he could collect it right now.

Jean-Julien turned and followed them.

Dallas's stomach rumbled when he breathed in the sweet and tangy smell of BBQ wafting from the carnival grilling competition. After he'd located Kallie and Belladonna, he just might come back for a plate of ribs. A man couldn't live on beignets and beer alone. Well . . . not and be happy about it, anyway.

Middle Eastern music and rhythmic jingling from underneath an awning to his right drew his attention. A pair of hennaed belly dancers in swirling chiffon skirts and coin-dangling hip scarves performed hip drops with a supple and sensual precision that left his mouth dry.

Although Dallas yearned to stay and watch, he forced his gaze away from their shimmying hips and gold-coin-draped cleavage and resumed walking. Noticing the contest stage just ahead across the fairway, Dallas paused in front of a gelato stand a few booths back and ordered a cup of raspberry ice.

Just as Dallas had slipped the first cold, tart-sweet spoonful into his mouth, he saw Kallie and the ghost-possessed nomad—whatever the hell his name was—working their way through the crowd to the stage. He also noticed a tall and wiry man in his fifties with a close-cropped cap of dark hair and milk-in-coffee-colored skin following behind them, an expression of intense focus on his face.

Dallas stiffened, the hair prickling at the back of his neck, little plastic spoon in his mouth. *Look sharp, podna. Now who the hell is that?*

Tossing aside his spoon and cup of raspberry ice, and ignoring the angry "Dude, what the hell? My sandals!" that followed, Dallas hurried after him.

Kallie bounced up on her toes. She spotted Belladonna standing with three other people between the stage and the first row of metal folding chairs, her head of blue-and-black curls bowed as she conferred with the other judges. "There she is. C'mon, let's get you signed up."

"How many are participating?" Layne-Augustine asked.

Kallie shrugged. "No idea. You'll have to ask Bell." She cut across the fairway and led the way up the grassy aisle to the stage.

Belladonna looked up, and a smile lit her hazel eyes. "Just in time, Shug." She glanced at Layne-Augustine, then back at Kallie. "Is he still that Lord Augustine?" she whispered.

"Yep. And he's entering the contest." Kallie grinned.

Belladonna's eyes widened. "Get the hell out! Seriously?"

"Well, not seriously, of course," the Brit said, "but for fun. It *will* be fun, correct?"

Belladonna's gaze slid over him from the top of Layne's honey-blond dreads to the tips of Augustine's expensive loafers. "Oh, yeah, it'll be fun," she murmured. She shook her head in appreciation. "Mmm-mmm-mmm. Walk your fine ass backstage, and Rudi will fill you and the other contestants in."

"Goody," Layne-Augustine said in a voice dry enough

to spontaneously combust. He climbed the stage, then ducked behind the curtain.

Belladonna grabbed Kallie's arms, fingers curling around her biceps. "Hellfire! How did you convince him to enter the contest?"

"I didn't. He—"

"Excuse me," a man's voice interrupted. "But I'm looking for the chakra-reading booth. Would either of you ladies know where it is?"

Kallie swiveled around to face the speaker—a tall, middle-aged man, but a good-looking one with café-au-lait skin, high cheekbones, and eyes a striking sea shade of pale green. He smiled, a warm and inviting curve of his lips, but she only felt cold seeing it.

The image of a heron, a flopping fish held in its long beak, flared in her mind. The mojo bag tucked inside her bra tingled and burned against her skin.

"There you are!" Dallas exclaimed, trotting to a stop between Kallie and the stranger. "I thought I'd lost y'all." He cut a warning glance at the man, his blue eyes frosty.

A strange expression crossed the stranger's face—an odd blend of annoyance, wariness, and astonishment—and it almost seemed like he recognized Dallas.

Speaking of which . . . Kallie doubled-up her right hand and punched Dallas square in the nose.

Pain lanced through Dallas's skull as his nose cracked with a sharp and sickening sound beneath Kallie's knuckles. He staggered back a step, his hands flying up to his face. Blood trickled hot against his fingers and onto his lips. His eyes teared up, dunking his vision underwater.

"What the *fuck*, Kallie!" he cried.

"Shit, Dallas. I warned you," she said, shaking out her hand and wincing.

"You broke my nose, dammit." Dallas glared at her from over his hands. He wanted to tip his head back to help stop the bleeding, but didn't want to take his tear-swimming gaze off the man standing in front of Kallie and looking *beaucoup* startled.

Maybe he was just another carnival attendee asking directions. Maybe he wasn't. But after the morning's grim events, Dallas didn't feel like taking chances.

Kallie glared back. "Toldja I would. Toldja to keep your goddamned distance."

"Don't blame her, Dallas Brûler," Belladonna put in, adding her two cents. "You're the one who marched over and put yourself in harm's way."

"Like hell," Dallas muttered. Blinking until his vision cleared, he narrowed his gaze on the stranger. "Just who are you, podna? Think it's wise to bother women you don't know?"

"He ain't bothering anyone," Kallie snapped. But Dallas caught a flicker of uncertainty in her eyes underneath all the anger.

Huh. Maybe she picked up some kind of weird energy from the guy. Felt something.

"My apologies, *m'selles*," the stranger said, lifting his hands palms out and eyeing Dallas's damaged face. "I'll just keep looking."

"Good idea," Dallas growled. He wiped blood from his face with the hem of his lilac button-down shirt.

"It's closer to the entrance," Kallie said, shooting Dallas another cold, furious look. She blew a wayward strand of hair out of her face.

"*Merci*," the stranger said. "Much obliged."

"Hold on, podna," Dallas said, dropping his shirt hem and straightening. "Where you from, anyway?"

"Enough, Dallas," Kallie said. "Let him go about his business." She handed Dallas a wad of napkins that Belladonna had fetched from her bag. "And you'd better go too, cuz I don't wanna hafta give your nose another goddamned adjustment."

"I'll be going, all right," Dallas replied, lobbing the napkins unused into a black-bag-lined trash barrel. "Just hold onto your britches."

"Again, *m'selles*, thank you," the stranger said. He sidestepped past Belladonna, brushing against her as a small contingent of jingling and veiled belly dancers sashayed along the fairway.

Dallas watched the man stroll over to the black iron entry arch and pass underneath. Once he was on the other side, his long-legged stride shifted from casual to purposeful.

Wiping at his nose with the back of his hand, Dallas spat the heavy taste of copper into the grass. "Keep away from that asshole, both of you," he said, voice harsh. "Something ain't right about him." Without waiting for an answer and without a backward glance at Kallie or Belladonna, he headed back to the entry arch, breaking into a jog so that he wouldn't lose sight of the man.

Let's see what you're really up to, podna.

Kallie shook out her throbbing and bruised hand. Belladonna was right about one thing—she couldn't keep punching people, not without gloves, at least. She watched the root doctor stalk away toward the black iron arch, body coiled tight, his red hair ablaze beneath the carnival lights. A twinge of regret curled through her.

Ease up, he's only trying to help. And I did feel something off about that man.

"Maybe I shoulda counted to ten before hitting Dal," she said.

"Maybe. But you *did* warn him."

Kallie glanced at Belladonna. "Did you feel anything negative from that guy?"

"No, but I'm guessing you did." Belladonna nodded toward the MAY MADNESS arch. "Dallas too, apparently."

"Man triggered my bag's protective mojo," Kallie said, touching her fingertips to the top of her tank, still feeling the tingling warmth of the flannel bag nestled against the curve of her left breast.

A look of disgust rippled across Belladonna's face. "Probably a perv looking to lay a domination trick on a naïve and nubile young thing without a lick of enchantment-awareness sense. Bastard."

Kallie hadn't seen the heat of lust in the stranger's sea-foam-green eyes, just a skin-crawling intensity that reminded her of a gator's unblinking stare. But that didn't mean Belladonna was wrong. Maybe the supposedly naïve and nubile young thing the potential perv desired had been a tall mambo-in-training and not herself.

In any case, the man was gone.

"Speaking of pervs," Kallie said in a low voice, "I think Augustine is playing with Layne's body."

"Playing how?"

"Molesting him."

An expression dreamy enough to rival the one Kallie had seen on Layne-Augustine earlier floated across

Belladonna's face. "Mmm-mmm. I'd pay to see that. Do you think we could convince him to molest himself onstage?"

Even though the image those words conjured pulsed heat through her veins, Kallie shook her head. "Your tank is still full of one hundred percent pure evil, Bell."

A cat-in-the-cream smile curved Belladonna's lips, and she shrugged. *Whatcha gonna do?*

Thinking of all she'd learned about her aunt—whoever that might be—Kallie's amusement and desire faded. "We need to talk after the contest," she said.

"That sounds serious, Shug." Belladonna studied her, her smile vanishing.

"It is, but later, *oui*? You're supposed to be having fun."

"You're supposed to be having fun *too*, Kallie."

"Shit. I don't even know if I should be doing this." Kallie dragged both hands through her hair, pushed it behind her shoulders. "With everything that's happened—"

"You *need* this," Belladonna cut in, "*because* of everything that's happened. Hellfire, Shug, what if you'd climbed into that bed with Gage instead of running off to the bathroom to puke?"

"I know," Kallie said from a throat gone tight. "But—"

"'But' nothing." Belladonna grasped Kallie's hands in her own, her warm fingers squeezing tight. "You *need* a little fun, Kallie, you *deserve* a little silliness."

"I thought that's what I had you for," Kallie teased.

Belladonna snorted. "Girl, please. I am *much* more than 'a little fun.'"

"Fun? No. I was referring to the silliness part. But maybe *demented* would be more accurate."

Belladonna's hazel eyes gleamed with appreciation. "I

see you're filling up *your* tank with high-octane one hundred percent evil."

"More like siphoning from yours," Kallie said. She wriggled her hands free of Belladonna's, then wrapped her friend up in a quick hug. "So what do you need me to do?" she asked, releasing Belladonna and stepping back.

"Wet the hunks down once they strip to their boxers." A wicked smile parted Belladonna's lips. "Wouldn't break my heart if you used extra water on Layne."

Kallie grinned. "Mine either."

TWENTY-FIVE

COLD AND EMPTY

Dallas strode along the Persian carpet on the sixth floor, uneasiness crawling along his spine. Except for him, the hall was empty. A cart full of linen and cleaning supplies was parked between two rooms, both doors wide open. The high-powered roar of an industrial vacuum rumbled out of one room.

Nothing felt good about this.

He'd tailed the stranger from the carnival and into the hotel, as careful as possible to keep his distance to avoid being spotted. He'd hung back as the man had stepped into an elevator. Then Dallas had watched to see what floor it stopped at—the 6 button lighting up—before jumping into an elevator and slapping the button for the sixth floor.

Belladonna's room was on the sixth floor—hell, so was his. But Dallas doubted that the stranger had any interest in him given that he'd been chatting up Kallie and Belladonna at the carnival.

Oh, sure, the man could have a room on the sixth floor too. Quite a coincidence if he did. And Dallas would stake his life that it was no coincidence Mr.

Could-You-Ladies-Direct-Me now walked the sixth-floor halls.

Question now was—where the hell was he?

How about a process of elimination? See where he isn't?

Lengthening his stride, Dallas headed for Belladonna's room. He paused at the hallway junction and listened. Nothing but the pounding of his pulse and the distant roar of the vacuum behind him. He caught a thin whiff of bitter-orange bergamot in the air. Could be a trace of perfume or tea or . . . The hair prickled at the back of his neck.

Bergamot amped up a hoodoo's personal power and was often used in bend-over potions and oils. *Maybe I'm tailing another hoodoo.*

Of course, if so, it was also possible that most of the hoodoos and root workers attending the carnival had been assigned to the sixth floor—Kallie being an exception—and that he was being paranoid as all hell.

Maybe.

Dallas swung to the left at the hallway junction, slowing his pace to keep his footfalls as quiet as possible as he approached Belladonna's room. Sidling against the wall, he crept up to the door. Drawing in a breath and holding it, he ducked down out of the peephole's line of sight and pressed his ear against the door. Listened.

Silence. No stealthy shuffling or noisy ransacking. Just the distant hum of the vacuum. He listened for several long moments, fighting the creepy feeling that the stranger listened on the *other* side of the door, his ear also pressed to the cold metal.

More silence. More paranoia.

Exhaling, Dallas straightened, still keeping clear of

the peephole, and wrapped his fingers around the door handle. Pulled down. It was locked. His gut told him to ignore the paranoia, that no one lurked unwelcome inside Belladonna's room.

Hell, maybe the guy was just another red-blooded male horndog looking to pick up some good-looking and curvaceous company.

Ain't we all? No crime in that.

Hearing the door across the hall swing open, then click shut, Dallas stepped back from Belladonna's door and turned around. And whirled into someone standing right behind him.

Dallas looked into the stranger's pale-green eyes, saw amusement glinting in their jade depths. The man locked a steel-muscled arm around Dallas's shoulders and punched him in the gut three times with the other hand.

"You ain't worth wasting magic on, boy," he hissed.

The pain of the blows stole Dallas's breath. Shoving free of the man's grip, he staggered back against the wall and stared at the blood-smeared knife in the man's hand. His heart hammered against his ribs, roared like a waterfall in his ears. He pressed his hand against his belly and felt something warm and sticky soaking his shirt. He looked down. Fear poured cold through his veins. His shirt glistened with blood.

Dallas opened his mouth, but no sound emerged. His legs wobbled underneath him, then gave out, but before he hit the carpet, the stranger grabbed him by the shirt collar, hauled him across the hall, and tossed him into the room he'd been waiting in.

Dallas hit the tiled floor hard, shoulder first. His vision grayed. Blood, hot and coppery, flooded his mouth, trickled past his lips. Choking, he spat blood onto the floor. He struggled to get onto his hands and knees, knowing he needed to get up and away before the sonuvabitch planted that knife in his back and finished him, but his blood-slick hands slipped across the tiles.

"You've got your teacher Gabrielle to thank for this, Dallas Brûler," the stranger said. "You're gonna die because of things she did long before you ever knew her."

Grabbing the comforter on the freshly made bed, Dallas reeled himself up onto his knees, but a breath-stealing kick to the ribs knocked him back onto the floor. The comforter slithered down beside him. A pair of binoculars *thunk*ed onto the tiles. He gasped for air. Pain chewed into his guts with sharp, sharp teeth.

"But you're the lucky one. You'll get to keep your soul since you're not a relative of the backstabbing whore. Kallie and her cousin won't be so fortunate."

Keep your soul. Shit, shit, shit. Kallie . . .

Cold sweat slicked Dallas's body, beaded on his forehead. Darkness sucked at his consciousness. Fear coiled through him. *Am I dying? Gotta keep awake. Gotta get your ass outta here. Move and keep moving. Talk to him. Buy time.*

"What happened?" Dallas panted. "Gabrielle and you? Why hurt others?" He rolled over onto his belly and pulled himself along the floor with shaking hands, expecting to feel the hard punch of the knife into his back as he inched his way toward the phone perched miles above him on the dresser.

Instead, the stranger grabbed Dallas by the shoulders and wrenched him back over onto his back. Held him in place on the floor with one strong hand against his chest.

"You're just going to have to find your answers in the afterlife," he said, his voice flat.

He lifted the knife. Street light slanted along its blood-glistening length.

Dallas saw nothing in the man's pale-green eyes that he understood—no hatred, no rage, no satisfaction—just eyes as cold and empty as a flood-ravaged tomb.

"For you, my sweet love," the stranger whispered.

The blade slashed down and across Dallas's throat.

TWENTY-SIX

TIME OF RECKONING

Should he wear his best boxers, or the pair most likely to become translucent when wet? Which would be sexier—expensive silk, or cheap and clinging? And could he keep his excitement from showing when luscious Hoodoo Kallie tossed water on him? Would she be in a bikini in case of backsplash?

Oh, blessed and horny Pan, please-oh-please, let her be in a bikini.

A sudden thought froze Ray Wippler, binocular-spying Wiccan extraordinaire, in front of his room. Not *cold* water, surely? As he slipped his keycard into the slot on the door handle, he realized that not even cold water could diminish the molten heat of his lust for the lovely hoodoo—lust she would finally see and admire.

For once he wouldn't need his binoculars to keep a close eye on her. This time she would be up close and oh-so-personal.

Jiggling ta-tas barely covered by her low-cut bikini top, the nipples hard little pearls beneath the thin material, Kallie's purple-hyacinth eyes widen as Ray's soaking-wet boxers reveal his burgeoning manhood.

"The contest is over," she whispers from red, glistening lips. "I

declare I've never seen a bigger . . . man. Ravish me, Ray, ravish me like I've never been ravished before. Right here. Right now."

But Ray's ravishment fantasy popped and vanished like a finger-poked soap bubble when he realized he heard noise on the *other* side of the door.

Inside his room.

Gurgling. Choking. And underneath it all, a conversational voice, the words too low for him to make out.

Ray glanced down the hall. Maybe the maid . . . ? But a maid would've left the door open if she was busy cleaning his room. A maid also wouldn't be choking, gurgling, or chatting while doing so either. Unless . . .

The TV.

Relief flooded through Ray. He must've left the TV on when he'd left the room. He *had* been watching the National Geographic channel when he'd split for dinner. The ravishment fantasy returned full force.

Kallie swoons against his thick-muscled chest and throbbing member. "So much man," she whimpers. "Take me now."

Ray unlocked the door, pushed it open, and stepped inside. A rush of air thick with a raw, metallic scent washed over him and he froze again, skin crawling. The low murmurs stopped, but the choking and gurgling continued—albeit weaker.

A man in jeans and a purple button-down shirt was sprawled on the floor beside Ray's bed, blood-wet hands grasping his throat while his cowboy boots scuffed weakly against the tiles. Blood spilled in dark rivulets from between his fingers and from underneath his palms, a deep red tide spreading across the gray-and-umber tiles and lapping against the tan, tasseled loafers of a man standing beside him.

Ray's heart pogoed up into his throat and stuck there. He caught a glimpse of khaki trousers above the tasseled loafers, of a blood-smeared knife held in long, brown fingers against the trousers. Panic blurred Ray's vision, and he refused to look any higher. Refused to look into the face of a knife-wielding bogeyman.

The bleeding man choked out a liquid plea. "Run . . ."

Just as Ray whirled to flee, the guy with the knife slammed into him, bulldogging him face-first into the wall. The coppery taste of blood seeped into his mouth. Expecting to be stabbed at any moment by the intruder, Ray dropped to the floor, curled into a tight, muscle-quivering ball, and, following the advice learned in a geeks' self-defense class—*Drop! Curl up like a dead bug! Scream!*—shrieked with everything he had.

A second later he heard the quiet click of the door closing. Ray felt faint. Had the throat-slasher actually left, or was it a ploy to lure him out of his fetal position? Sweat trickled into Ray's eyes.

The choking sounds faded. Stopped.

C'mon, man, lure *you outta your fetal ball? When he could just stab you at leisure? Someone's* dying *behind you.*

Unfolding, Ray sat up and glanced around the room. Empty except for him and the poor sonuvabitch bleeding to death. Pushing himself onto his feet, he hurried over to the bogeyman's victim. The guy's hands lay lax against his sliced throat, his eyes now closed, his face whiter than a vampire's.

Ray yanked the sheet from the bed, tore a strip free, and dropped to his knees beside the red-haired man. Blood soaked warm through the knees of his jeans. His gut clenched. Swallowing back the bitter taste of bile, he shoved the guy's hands away from the wound. A gash had been sliced clear across his throat. Ray knotted the cloth around the guy's throat.

A litany of *who-why-how* kept snaking through Ray's mind. Who was this poor bastard, and why had he been knifed in Ray's room? And how the hell had they gotten in?

Ray pressed both shaking hands against the cloth. Blood oozed, warm and sticky, through the material. He nearly gagged when he sucked down a breath of blood-reeking air.

Focus, or this poor bastard's dead.

Ray closed his eyes, concentrated all of his Wicca-trained energy into his hands, and visualized stitching blue light like thread through the gash. Visualized a red aura full of vitality flickering around the guy's body and radiating out from around the hands he held over the stranger's throat.

Heat pooled in Ray's palms, and sweat popped up on his forehead, and trickled down his back. Energy vibrated from the crown of his head and down along his chakras, sparking electricity down his spine, into his arms, and his hands. Opening his eyes, Ray saw deep-blue and scarlet flames dance against the torn strip of sheet before dimming, then vanishing.

And that will have to be good enough for now.

"Don't die, okay?" Ray begged. "Hang in there, man. Help's on the way." Jumping to his feet, he dashed to the bureau, snagged up the phone, and punched O for the front desk.

Hooves thud against the ground, crunch across fallen leaves.

Dallas opens his eyes. Above him, he sees pale phantom aspens crowned with blood-red leaves against a frost-etched autumn night. A black-veiled woman in a scarlet dress rides a wild-maned white horse out of the moonlit forest and into the room. The horse's nostrils flaring, eyes glowing red embers, its hooves clatter and slip in the thickening and cooling blood pool.

A wind Dallas doesn't feel flattens the veil against the woman's face, revealing the shape of her nose and lips, and flutters her dress against her body, outlining lush and bountiful curves. He notices that her feet and well-rounded calves are bare, her skin the color of sun-warmed caramel.

But the pendant hanging around her throat and glimmering like pale moonlight against her brown skin truly captures his gaze; a vévé *of a heart pierced with a knife.*

Symbol for Erzulie Dantor, the loa *of love, passion, and sex.*

And one helluva fierce defender of women—every last one of them—especially those betrayed by a lover.

Looks like reckoning time, podna. All those broken hearts, all those games, all the empty searching . . .

A blur of movement from one of Erzulie's long-fingered hands, and a knife thunks *into the floor beside his head, point sinking deep into the slate. "You be mine, Dallas Brûler," the* loa *says. "And mine alone."*

Her words surprise Dallas, considering she lost her tongue long ago in an act of violence and has relied on interpreters ever since. He parts his lips to speak, but no sound emerges. Everything within him has spilled out onto the floor. Darkness edges his vision. Numbing cold frosts his veins, ices his heart.

The night sky lowers over him, veiling him in starless black.

Veil, hell, podna. A shroud.

Any regrets? Yeah, one. Dying.

Erzulie's magnolia and dying leaves scent perfumes away the stench of his own blood, and Dallas draws in an easy breath. Shivering, cold to the bone and down to the soul, he wraps himself in the night-woven shroud for warmth and shuts his eyes.

TWENTY-SEVEN

BUCKETS OF WARM WATER

Kallie watched from the wings as Contestant Number One awkwardly stripped down to his boxers to the hip-shimmying rhythm of Shakira's "Hips Don't Lie," revealing a weight lifter's thick-muscled build on a medium frame. He danced with stiff, muscle-flexing movements as though he were posing for a bodybuilders' competition, pausing between moves as though waiting for applause.

The largely female audience shrieked with delirious and rum-soaked—Kallie would bet it was daiquiris—enthusiasm, clapping and shouting encouragement.

"That's right, baby! Take it off! Shake that ass! Make Mama happy!"

Recognizing the voice, Kallie looked across the stage to the four judges seated in the front row—Belladonna, two other women, and a guy in a rainbow tee—and saw Belladonna standing, her hands cupped around her mouth. "Make Mama *real* happy!"

A totally impartial and professional judge.

Oh, for a cell phone camera and an Internet link.

Smiling, Kallie gave her attention back to the stage. Number One dance-posed for a few more moments, then shuffled backward to the crossed-spotlight-beam backdrop.

The music switched to Nine Inch Nails' "Discipline," and Contestant Number Two bounded onto the stage and shucked his clothes like they were on fire.

If he was that quick in the sack, Kallie felt sorry for his girlfriends.

Tall and skinny, but good-looking with long, dark hair, his entire body quivered spasmodically and she thought he was having a seizure until she realized he was dancing.

Of the ten men who had signed up, only seven would actually be participating. One had hurried away for the restroom and had never returned; another had hyperventilated, then fainted; and one was a no-show. She wondered what the ratio would be for the ladies when it was time for the wet-T-shirt contest.

Number Two finished his "dance," then joined Number One at the backdrop. Contestant Number Three strode onstage to N-Trance's "Do Ya Think I'm Sexy?" and given his dancer's tight-muscled build, graceful moves, and his wild, natural Afro, her answer was a definite yes.

The shrieking decibels increased to jet-engine levels, so Kallie guessed the audience agreed with that assessment.

"Back that thing up, baby boy!" Belladonna shouted. Number Three offered her a wink and a slow, sexy smile. Playing dirty. Playing to win.

But the bucket of water would determine the winner, not a playa's smooth moves.

Number Four, a short but gorgeous guy with a ripped physique and dark bedroom eyes framed with long lashes, peeled his clothing down to his boxers and danced to AC/DC's hard-pounding "You Shook Me All Night Long."

Kallie had a feeling that wouldn't be wishful thinking on his part. Lying down, everyone was the same height. And given the slow, sensual way he moved his hips, he knew *exactly* what to do with them.

"Shake me, lover boy, morning, noon, and night!" Belladonna yelled. She blew him a kiss that he pretended to catch. He pressed the captured kiss against his boxer-clad crotch.

Aw . . . a romantic.

Number Five, pudgy and sweating, tripped on his way out to the stage and fumbled off his clothes, his movements completely out of sync with his song, Queens of the Stone Age's "Make It Wit Chu." But then he started dancing. He whirled, all grace and flowing rhythm, popped his hips in belly-fluttering fashion, a sexy beast.

Belladonna jumped out of her chair to call, "More man to love, baby!"

The Pussycat Dolls' song "Buttons" throbbed from the speakers as Number Six, a clean-cut, dimple-jawed guy with a decent but not spectacular build pranced onto the stage and stripped with such military precision that Kallie suspected he did it for a living. Maybe he even worked for one of the clubs on Bourbon Street.

"Shake it, honey buns, shake it hard!" Pro or skilled amateur, Belladonna obviously didn't give a rat's ass.

Gorgeous Number Seven sauntered barefoot out from the wings, winked at the male judge, then unbuttoned his French-blue shirt to Justin Timberlake's hip-swinging "SexyBack." Kallie stared as Layne-Augustine peeled off his shirt, revealing his long, lean torso and the exquisite muscles she had felt beneath her hands when she'd been resuscitating him.

"Give it to me, you hot nomad!" Belladonna yelled once more.

Blue-inked tattoos rippled along his shoulders and down to his biceps, swirled across his chest and belly in Celtic designs; detailed knotwork looped underneath his hard pecs around to his back; shamrocks, spirals, and fanciful animals cavorted on his flesh. Concentric circles curled around both of his nipples, and a dragon's knotwork tail disappeared beneath the waistband of his blue boxers.

Kallie wondered if Layne's nether regions were also tattooed. A beautiful spiral design had coiled around Gage's hard length.

A barb of guilt pricked her. It hadn't even been twenty-four hours since she'd tumbled and played with Gage, then discovered him dead in her bed, and here she was wondering about his best friend's most intimate parts.

What the hell is wrong *with me?*

"Go, baby, go!" Belladonna yelled.

Layne-Augustine unbuckled his belt, undulating with an easy and sexy grace that seared the guilt from Kallie's heart and pooled heat between her legs. He moved Layne's body as if it was as familiar as his own. His dreads worked free of their knot and slithered over his muscle-cabled shoulders to his waist.

He unzipped his pants with a slow, teasing pull on the zipper, then shimmied his hips. His trousers dropped to his ankles.

Belladonna gave a wordless and happy shriek.

The Brit stepped out of the trousers and danced like he

hit the clubs every weekend and most weeknights, moving his hips with mouth-drying suggestiveness, muscles rippling like water. As he danced, he slipped a cigarette out from behind his ear, placing it between his lips. He lit it with a lighter he'd tucked against his palm. The cigarette's end glowed as he inhaled.

Layne-Augustine's grace faltered as he coughed out a cloud of smoke prickly with the scents of lavender and sage into the night. Squinting through watering eyes and still coughing, he traced glyphs in the air with his cigarette.

Layne must not be a smoker. But what the hell is the man doing?

The scented smoke swirled together to form a motorcycle on the stage, a chopper with high handlebars and a sissy bar. Recovering from his coughing faux pas, Layne-Augustine reclined on his smoke-cycle—*how in the name of Houdini is he* doing *that?*—and suggested with subtle thrusts of his hips what might happen if someone were to join him.

Show-off.

"Saddle up, naughty boy!" Belladonna hooted. "Mama's gonna ride!"

With a smug smile, Layne-Augustine rolled off of his chopper and undulated his way to the backdrop to stand beside the other six contestants. When he stubbed out his cigarette, the smoke-cycle vanished.

Rudi, the emcee, a woman with a hairspray-shellacked beehive hairdo and a matronly shelf of a bosom, paused to touch Kallie's shoulder and whisper, "You're up next, sweetie," before bouncing onstage.

"Let's hear it for the men!" she cried. A deafening and lust-filled roar answered her. "Y'all come up here," she said to the contestants once the applause had died down, motioning them to the front of the stage.

Belladonna set up a line of buckets beside Kallie. "Here you go, Shug."

Kallie smiled. "Great."

Belladonna hurried back to her seat and her prime view.

Steam curled into the air from the water's surface. Kallie dipped a finger into the first bucket to test the warmth. She didn't want to accidentally scald anyone. A braided band of guilt and grief and loss snapped her shoulder muscles taut.

Too bad you didn't finger-test the bed before Gage slipped under the sheets. Would've saved him from a helluva lot more than just a scalding.

Kallie closed her eyes and rolled her shoulders in hopes of working the tension from her muscles. *Wallow later. You've got a job to do, no matter how silly.*

"And now the moment y'all have been waiting for! The wet boxers!"

Kallie opened her eyes. *Show time.*

More screams and wild applause. The emcee nodded at Kallie and stepped aside. Wrapping her fingers around the handles of two buckets, Kallie walked across the stage to Number One.

Several males in the audience wolf-whistled, and one yelled, "You can get me wet anytime, darling!" Laughter followed.

Kallie couldn't help but wonder if those particular guys were keeping their wives or girlfriends company or were just curious. "That's what *she* said," Kallie replied. "Or would, if y'all knew how."

More wolf whistles, hoots, and laughter.

Kallie placed one bucket on the stage, then lifted the other in both hands. "Ready?" she asked, her gaze skipping from one boxer-clad man to the next.

Each one nodded. Kallie tossed half of the first bucket on Number One, the weight lifter, soaking him from chest to feet. His wet boxers clung to him.

Huh. So he ain't building muscles as compensation for a small dick. So much for that myth. I don't see nothing for him to compensate for.

Smiling, Kallie moved to the next man and flung the rest of the bucket's warm contents on him. *Eh, average.* She picked up the next bucket as Rudi scuttled up with a full bucket to replace the one she'd just emptied.

Kallie moved down the line. *Three—Average. Four—Oooo, nice! Five—Where is it and what the hell was he thinking by entering the contest? Six—Something to write home about.*

And Seven. Kallie tossed the last of the water on Layne-Augustine. The soaked material clung to his thighs and outlined everything underneath them. Her eyes widened. "Goddamn," she whispered. She peeled her gaze away from the Brit's wet blue boxers and looked up into his eyes.

Amusement danced in his pine-green eyes. "I believe the words I said when I made the same discovery were 'Oh dear God.'"

"Good choice," she murmured, her gaze returning to his wet and clinging boxers. *Layne must know how to use it since his ex-wife is so damned reluctant to let go of him.*

The emcee told the audience that they would be allowed to choose their favorite by applause in addition to the judges' choice of winner.

"Number One," she called.

The applause was healthy, but not overwhelming. The emcee moved to the next man. Kallie heard the tap of heels on the stage and looked over to see Felicity Fields, her freckled face somber, stride toward her.

"Mrs. Fields?" Layne-Augustine questioned as she stopped beside Kallie.

"My lord," she replied as though he stood completely clothed. She glanced at Kallie. "Someone has just tried to kill Mr. Brûler."

Kallie snorted and waved a dismissive hand at her. "Happens all the time. Don't worry about it. Man has more lives than a dozen cats."

Felicity blinked. "My, my, my. Not the response I expected."

"After the first five or ten attempts, you kinda get used to the fact that someone's always gonna be trying to kill Dallas Brûler."

"Really? Fascinating. However, this isn't one of *those* times. He's on his way to the HA medical clinic on the twentieth floor. His injuries are critical, I'm sorry to say, and by the time we get there . . ." With an elegant half-shrug, Felicity left the rest of her sentence unspoken.

But her meaning had been crystal clear: *He might already be dead.*

Kallie stared at her, a cold pit opening up in her belly.

Layne-Augustine scooped up his trousers and fought them on over his wet boxers, then grabbed his shirt from the stage. "Do we have his attacker in custody?" he asked.

Felicity shook her head. "Assailant unknown. We're questioning the guest who discovered Mr. Brûler."

"Right," Layne-Augustine said, voice grim. He headed across the stage in a brisk stride, Felicity in his wake.

Heart drumming hard and fast, Kallie followed. She curved a *come along* finger at Belladonna.

Shit! Please don't let my threat to readjust his nose again be the last words I ever speak to Dallas.

TWENTY-EIGHT

HIDDEN IN PLAIN SIGHT

The primal pulse of palm-thumped drums sounded through the dealers' room in the Starlight Convention Hall, an earthy pulse that echoed deep within Jean-Julien's heart. Seated at a small, round table, he added the final component to the poppet he was constructing—a bit of cloth he'd cut from the waiter's shirt.

"I still command you, I still compel you," he murmured as he stitched the poppet closed with thick black thread. "Mine thou still art and my bidding you still desire, no will of your own, my word holy fire."

Finished with the doll, Jean-Julien sat back in his wrought-iron chair and picked up the to-go coffee cup resting on the table. He took a sip of his cooling mocha, savoring the melted-whipped-cream-and-chocolate taste, and examined his handiwork: three basic cloth poppets with black-button eyes.

One contained the single hair he'd gathered from Belladonna when he'd brushed past her at the carnival. His hope had been to glean a strand from the Rivière girl, but she'd been standing much too close to the suspicious and watchful Brûler for him to attempt it. Deciding to hedge his bets in case Gabrielle's niece proved elusive, he'd created a poppet of her friend as well.

The second poppet contained a strip of paper bearing Kallie's name in place of a personal item, and the third—the waiter's poppet—had been crafted as a remote-control device to help Jean-Julien guide the zombie-dusted waiter in his task.

Preparation for his daughter's eventual rescue.

And speaking of rescue—how about the unfortunate arrival of the room's occupant just as the last of Brûler's blood was spilling onto the floor?

Renewed frustration strummed along Jean-Julien's muscles, stringing them tight. He finished his coffee, then placed the empty cup on the table beside the waiter poppet. Just a minute more and he would've been able to see the light go out in Brûler's eyes.

He believed it impossible that the Chalmette root doctor could have survived. Between the stab wounds to his gut and the knife across his throat, Gabrielle's former student should've bled out before help arrived.

Hell, man had damn near emptied his veins before their interruption. But without seeing the man's lifeless body, Jean-Julien couldn't be positive of Brûler's death.

All he could do now was focus on killing Kallie Rivière, then freeing Rosette. The niece was more important than Brûler anyway—a source of far greater pain for Gabrielle. Still . . . he'd been so close.

Brûler's blood washes across the gray-and-umber tiles in a steaming red tide—the sound a powerful whoosh *as it pours from the wound.*

Jean-Julien had used his keycard to slip into another room to steal clean clothes—too-big jeans belted tight to keep them from slipping down his hips, and a sail of a Hawaiian shirt with a palm-tree motif—and scrub the blood from his loafers. He'd dumped his bloodied clothing in a trash bin on the fourth floor.

Jean-Julien felt safe hiding in plain sight among the patchouli-and-sandalwood-reeking crowds browsing the booths in the dealers' room since he was reasonably certain that the idiot who'd interrupted his deathwatch over Brûler hadn't actually *looked* at his face given that the man's gaze had never traveled north of the knife in Jean-Julien's hand.

The downside of his unplanned attack on Brûler was how it might affect Kallie Rivière's actions—not to mention those of the Hecatean Alliance—especially if she now suspected that Rosette hadn't acted alone. Which would mean his daughter's self-sacrifice would've been in vain.

Foolish to act on impulse.

Jean-Julien glanced at Belladonna's poppet, hoping he wouldn't need to use it, hoping that he wouldn't be forced to harm the pretty voodooienne, but knowing he wouldn't hesitate to do so—if necessary.

Jean-Julien scanned the crowded conference hall for any indication of danger—HA guards or officials walking in his direction with a purposeful stride, for instance. But he saw nothing out of the ordinary. People thronged and milled at the booths and blocked the aisles with their pastry-widened asses. Voices in several languages thickened the air with laughter and greetings, cheerful questions, and enthusiastic sales pitches.

"Lord amighty! Are them there voodoo dolls or hoodoo dolls?" a gravelly male voice asked, its inflection all East Texas.

Frowning, Jean-Julien shifted his attention back to his

own table. A tall man of about sixty with gray-threaded white hair and a red face stood at his table, his thin, whipcord frame dressed in a blue-and-gray-checkered short-sleeved shirt and crisp new jeans. He regarded Jean-Julien with curious blue eyes.

"Voodoo or hoodoo?" he persisted. "We don't use poppets much in my Wicca clan, but I've heard plenty about them dolls, I'll tell you what."

"I'm a hoodoo root doctor," Jean-Julien replied, "not a *houngan*, but there's no difference in how the poppets are used."

"*Houngan*," the man repeated, eyeing Jean-Julien. "Now that'd be a voodoo priest, is that right?"

"*Oui*," Jean-Julien said, forcing a polite-but-you're-boring-me smile onto his lips. "Now, if you will excuse—"

"Are they for sale?"

"No, they're not, and this is not a booth, *m'sieu*. Please—"

"Cuz, I tell you what, Mr. Hoodoo, I sure could use one a them love poppets, if you know what I mean." East Texas winked one good-ol'-boy blue eye. "The missus just ain't been looking at me like she used to, says it's the menopause—if you can believe that." He shook his head, slow and reflective, clearly unable to believe that the menopause should dim his wife's ardor for his sun-baked and ropy hide. "Used to be I had to practically beat the woman offa me with a stick just so's I could get some sleep. And if you'd be willing to help a partner out, I'd be more than happy to pay . . ."

Tuning out the rough-road sound of East Texas's voice, Jean-Julien sighed and stood up. Reaching into the pocket of his borrowed too-big jeans, he pulled his vial of black dust free, unstoppered it, and tapped a small portion into his palm. The sweet, dark smell of licorice mixed with the citrus tang of bergamot curled into the air.

Jean-Julien then leaned across the table and blew the dust into the man's red and startled face. "My bidding you desire," he intoned, annoyed with the necessity and the interruption, "no will of your own, my word holy fire."

Waving his hand in front of his face, East Texas blinked, coughed, then stared at Jean-Julien, eyes unfocused. Black dust peppered his face.

Telling the man to lower his hand, Jean-Julien said, "Go away. Leave this room and go back to your own room, then go to bed. You'll have no memory of our meeting. And you shall never bore me or your wife again. Go away. Now."

East Texas stepped forward, bumping into the table.

Jean-Julien twirled a finger in the air, saying, "Ah-ah-ah. Turn around, then go."

Teetering around in a careful but unsteady circle, East Texas shuffled like an old man into the crowd. Jean-Julien watched him until his white-haired head vanished from view. He blew air out his nostrils, still irritated. Why on earth did some people seem to think they could talk right over you whenever you said something they didn't want to hear, like no? As if all their will-laced words would change your mind?

Like magic.

And speaking of will-laced words and magic . . . Jean-Julien scooped up the Belladonna and Kallie poppets and stuffed one into each front pocket of his voluminous jeans. *Out of tourist sight, out of tourist mind.* He picked up the waiter poppet. Turning his chair around so that its back rested against the table's edge, he sat back down, the poppet in hand.

Closing his eyes, Jean-Julien drew in a deep breath, then centered himself. Tuned out the cheerful noise buzzing around him and focused on the steady rhythm of his heart and the pounding drums from the hall's tribal circle.

Placing the tips of his index fingers over the poppet's black-button eyes, Jean-Julien whispered, "Mine thou art, your eyes, your body, and heart. I see what you see. I hear what you hear. And you do as I do, following each command true."

The darkness behind Jean-Julien's closed eyes faded, and he became aware of another bright room, one bustling with activity as men and women in white uniforms and caps clattered pans onto massive stoves and griddles.

He looked out through the waiter's eyes, and it felt exactly like looking through the eyeholes of a plastic Halloween mask as his vision narrowed down to small dead-ahead spots. He heard the sound of his breath as if it bounced back from the mask's confines.

"Fetch a late snack and drinks for the guards. Do it now."

Obediently following Jean-Julien's instructions, the waiter grabbed bowls of chocolate pudding and swirled whipped cream on top of each. He grabbed coffee cups, a carafe of coffee, sweeteners, and cream, and loaded everything on a metal serving cart.

"Add the special spices contained in the vial secreted in your pocket. My word is—as always—holy fire."

White-uniformed figures danced past the waiter, frowns on their faces as he plowed ahead without altering his course. Shoving the cart through swinging metal doors, he wheeled it along the hallway until he found a quiet and empty spot.

"Now add the special spices."

Jean-Julien moved the poppet's stubby arms in a mixing motion.

"Your will my desire," the waiter whispered as, with slow and jerky movements, he managed to fumble the vial of black oil from his pocket, thumb free the stopper, then tip the vial upside down.

And empty it into *one* bowl of pudding.

Jean-Julien wished he could slap a hand over his forehead. The potion had been intended for several guards—not just one. But perhaps this would work best. The concentration required to keep several zombified guards on task might've proved overwhelming even for Doctor Heron. He continued moving the poppet's arms.

The waiter picked up a spoon and stirred the black liquid with its tiny bits of paper command into the pudding. Then he resumed his journey to the sixteenth floor.

After watching the waiter deliver the snacks, Jean-Julien ordered him to bring the spoon of the guard who ate the jinxed pudding once the man had finished his dessert.

Jean-Julien opened his eyes, tucked the waiter poppet into his pocket on top of the Belladonna doll, and wiped the sweat from his forehead.

The key to Rosette's rescue had been slid into the lock. Now all he needed to do was turn it—when the right moment came.

His stomach rumbled, reminding him of all the energy he'd just expended and needed to replenish before laying any more tricks. He needed every ounce of strength possible to make sure he didn't fail a second time with Kallie Rivière.

Jean-Julien stood. He swiveled his chair back around, then sat once more. He picked up the salami, pastrami, tomato, and olive relish sandwich he'd purchased when he'd picked up his coffee, unwrapped it, and ate with gusto.

As he ate, his thoughts rolled back to his final conversation with Gabrielle, a conversation that had replayed through his mind off and on for the last twenty-five years, the living embodiment of that old saying, "Hell hath no fury like a woman scorned."

"I be fooling myself, oui? *You ain't ever gonna leave Babette."*

"I never told you I would, Gabi. And now that she's pregnant . . . No, love, Babette will always be my wife and the mother of my child. I love her, for true."

"You know nothing of love—just need. You done fooled us both."

"Gabi, ma belle ange, *you're my passion, the fire in my—"*

"The plaything in your bed. I found the poppet, Jean-Julien. I took it apart and removed my name. I burned it."

"What the hell you talking about? There's no poppet."

"Not anymore, there ain't. And there's no longer any us. We're through. Go back to Babette and stay in her arms—if she'll have you, you sorry excuse for a man."

Two weeks later, Jean-Julien had found himself handcuffed and tossed in jail on multiple murder charges when a handful of his clients died of poisoning. At first he'd thought some kind of horrible mistake had been made, had even wondered if he'd mismeasured certain ingredients. But then he'd remembered the good-bye Gabrielle had hurled at him as she'd stood in the doorway of the weather-warped swamp shack known as Doctor Heron's office.

"I'll make damned sure you never hoodoo another woman into your bed again, Jean-Julien St. Cyr."

A dark promise she'd fulfilled, beyond what he imagined even her expectations had been. With Babette so ill with morning sickness that lasted all day, Gabrielle LaRue had been the last woman he'd slept with.

Swallowing the final bite of his sandwich, Jean-Julien wiped his fingers clean with a napkin. He pulled the Kallie poppet from his pocket.

And now I have a promise for you, my bitter and lying Gabi. Those you love most are going to die, and you'll spend the rest of your miserable life alone, locked within the prison cell of your cold, cold heart.

But first, he needed to get Gabrielle's niece away from the hotel and any protection offered her by the Hecatean Alliance. Needed to get her alone.

Bringing the poppet to his lips, Jean-Julien whispered, "I command you, Kallie Rivière, I compel you. Mine thou art and my bidding you desire, no will of your own, my word holy fire."

TWENTY-NINE

THE VOICE OF THY BROTHER

Kallie paced the waiting room's pristine and polished floor, her sandals clacking against the tiles with each step. The air smelled of fresh roses and carnations mingled with the clean scent of lemon—aromas to aid health and healing.

"You're wearing a groove in the floor, Shug," Belladonna said, voice soft.

"Don't care," Kallie replied.

She couldn't believe what had happened to Dallas—stabbed multiple times, his throat cut. No way that was a pissed-off husband. If that guy, Belladonna's spying Wiccan neighbor, hadn't walked in when he had . . . Her throat tightened.

"It's safe to assume that whoever attacked Mr. Brûler is a coconspirator of Ms. St. Cyr rather than the usual disgruntled individual seeking payback," Layne-Augustine said. "So we shall have to place you in protective custody once more."

"Great," Kallie growled. "The last time we did that, you ended up dead."

"Indeed," the Brit murmured. He stood beside Felicity's chair, in damp trousers and shirt, still barefoot.

Kallie shot a glance at the double doors at the end of the hall. "When will we hear something?"

"I don't know," Felicity said. "Given the severity of Mr. Brûler's wounds, I believe the surgeons and healers have their hands more than full."

Kallie also heard what Felicity didn't say: *He may not survive. Prepare yourself.* If Gabrielle—or whoever she actually was—hadn't sent Dallas to spy on her, he'd be in Chalmette right now in one piece. And up to no good with somebody's wife or fiancée, most likely, true enough—but in one piece.

Yeah, and if you hadn't gotten all high and mighty and decked him, he'd still be following you around at carnival, safe and sound and annoying, with all of his blood circulating through his veins. He was only doing as Gabrielle asked.

Gabrielle. Mingled pain and fury burned a hole in Kallie's heart. Maybe Augustine had been right from the start: Gabrielle had set her and Dallas up to be murdered. Although she couldn't come up with a single reason why her aunt would want either of them six feet under.

Gabrielle was a woman more than willing to get her own hands dirty, and possessed a strong DIY work ethic. If she'd wanted Kallie and Dallas dead, they'd probably be gator food at this very moment.

If the woman truly was her aunt and not some impostor.

If? *C'mon, Kallie, she* must *be. Maybe Gabrielle ain't her real name, but who raises someone for nine years, then inexplicably has them murdered—especially when no inheritance is involved?*

But the memory of her mother's voice, her soft words, underscored the power of the inexplicable: *"I'm sorry, baby. I ain't got a choice."*

Kallie's chest tightened. The matter of her aunt would

have to simmer on the back burner for the moment. She had no intention of allowing Augustine to trap her inside a sigil-warded room, helpless and unable to do anything but wait. She also had no intention of twiddling her thumbs like a good little victim and waiting for the goddamned killer to play his next goddamned hand. No, she planned to find the cold-blooded sonuvabitch and stop him.

Uh-huh. And how, exactly, was she planning on doing that when she didn't even know what the goddamned bastard looked like?

Her thoughts tumbled through memory's trapdoor into a storm-lashed night from her past—a night eight years ago.

Wind whips Gabrielle's long hair into knotted, rain-wet spirals as she stands in a tangle of sawgrass and low-crawling peppervine, her face glistening with rain as she stares at the pitiful form sprawled in the grass beneath a white-blossomed dogwood.

Kallie stands beside a Spanish-moss-draped old oak ten yards back, her heart pounding so hard her entire body rocks with each beat. Rain trickles warm down her face.

Rain also drips from the brim of Sheriff Alphonso's plastic-protected hat. "Her name is Sandra Findley, and I called you here first ahead of everyone else, Miss LaRue, cuz the sumbitch who snatched and killed this girl is purest evil, for true," he says, his voice as tight as a coiled whip. His hands grip the gun belt strapped around his hips. "I plan to use every goddamned resource at my disposal to bring this monster to justice. And I'm hoping you can tell me who did this before I take word of her murder to her folks."

"And before de blood washes away," Gabrielle replies. "I'll do my best, Sheriff."

"I'll appreciate anything you can give me."

Gathering her long cranberry-red skirt in one hand, Gabrielle crouches beside the woman's head—no, not a woman, she's probably younger than Kallie, thirteen or maybe twelve, her jeans yanked past her hips, her shirt and bra shoved above her small breasts—a girl who will never draw another breath, let alone become a woman.

Gabrielle murmurs, "Come here, child."

Even though the rain is Gulf warm, Kallie feels cold down to the bone. She pads across the sawgrass, her sneakers squelching in the mud underneath, and stands behind her aunt. Swallowing hard, her muscles so tight they thrum beneath her skin, she looks at the dead girl. The girl's blood, black as oil in a stark flash of lightning, glistens in the grass around her bashed-in head and shines in her dark hair.

Delicate white flowers from the dogwood decorate the girl's body, ghost blossoms in the stormy dark. In the distance, thunder rumbles.

Gabrielle slips a small blue bottle from her skirt pocket, swivels, and hands the herb-filled bottle to Kallie. "Fill my palms, girl."

Unstoppering the bottle, Kallie does as her aunt requests and empties the bottle into her aunt's cupped, rain-wet palms. The green and bitter scent of ragweed and vervain wafts into the air until the rain scrubs the scent away.

"Thy word is a lamp unto my feet and a light unto my path," Gabrielle prays, rubbing the herbs together in her hands, into her skin, consecrating herself as a tool of divination. "Saint Anthony of Padua, Saint Joan of Arc, Saint Gerard Majella, and Saint Moses, I seek de truth in de name of de Father, and de Son, and de Holy Spirit. Baron Samedi, god of the crossroads, please unlock de mystery of dis poor child's death."

Gabrielle leans forward and plants one herb-dusted palm in the blood puddle seeping out from underneath the dead girl's skull, then closes her eyes.

Sheriff Alphonso shifts, his boot soles squeaking against the wet sawgrass—a restless sound swallowed up by the drumming rain.

Twilight-purple light flares around Gabrielle's fingertips, glimmers in the pool of blood. "I be asking de same question bon Dieu *once put to Cain; 'What have you done? De voice of thy brother's blood crieth unto me from de ground.' "*

Bayou-steeped power shimmers into the moist air, lifting the hair on Kallie's arms and goosebumping her skin. She hears the sheriff's boots squeaking against the grass again as he takes another step away from Gabrielle.

"Sandra, chère, *show me who did dis awful t'ing to you."*

"Ms. Rivière? Hello? Anyone in? Anyone at all?"

Felicity's smooth voice hooked Kallie and reeled her up from the past. She focused on Augustine's assistant, her pulse pounding hard through her veins.

"Ah, there you are," Felicity said. "I've been trying to tell you that I have your cell phone. Lord Augustine told me you needed it."

"Great," Kallie breathed, clacking over to where the Bondalicious Babe sat. Felicity handed her the cell, and Kallie tucked it into a front pocket of her cutoffs. She shifted her gaze to Layne-Augustine. "Listen, I need to visit the room where Dallas was attacked—provided that the blood hasn't been cleaned up yet."

The Brit glanced at Felicity and arched an eyebrow.

"No, it hasn't," Felicity said. "I thought it best to preserve the scene in the event that Mr. Brûler either doesn't survive surgery or that he survives, but remains unconscious and incapable of providing us with a description of his assailant."

Kallie blinked. *"Doesn't survive surgery . . ."* To hear her fear spoken aloud chilled her blood. She rapped her knuckles against one of the wood arms of Felicity's chair. Just in case. Little Miss Bondalicious regarded her with an amused smile.

"My, my, my. Perhaps I should knock on wood too, since I'm the one who spoke."

"Couldn't hurt," Kallie agreed.

Felicity politely tapped her knuckles against the arm of her chair.

Layne-Augustine shook his head. "I'm afraid I must refuse your request. It simply isn't safe."

"It wasn't a request, and you ain't got a right to refuse," Kallie replied, shifting her weight onto one hip and folding her arms beneath her breasts. "I ain't gonna let you lock me up again. Sorry. I'll sign whatever waiver you want so you don't hafta worry about being sued, but I'm going to find this asshole before he realizes Dallas *isn't* dead and before he comes looking for me."

"I see. And how do you plan to accomplish that?"

"Blood divination." Kallie decided it was wisest not to mention that it was a method she'd never tried before. "And I need to do it now, before the blood congeals and before that goddamned murdering sonuvabitch gets the drop on anyone else."

"Hellfire," Belladonna breathed. "Do you—"

Staring at her, Kallie jerked her head to one side in a little please-follow-my-lead motion. "No, I don't need any help. You stay here and wait for Dallas, okay?"

"Um . . . good. Okay," Belladonna said. Slipping her black shoulder bag free, she handed it to Kallie. "Just in case you need anything."

Kallie looped the strap over her head and across her shoulder. "You never know," she said, offering her friend a grateful smile.

Layne-Augustine said, "I don't believe a waiver will be necessary, since you signed one absolving the Prestige and the Hecatean Alliance of any responsibility for injuries incurred due to magic or malice when you registered."

Kallie blinked. Oh. She *really* needed to start reading the fine print on stuff. "Okay, great. All I need then is the room key."

"You mean *we* need the room key, since I'll be accompanying you," Layne-Augustine said. "And I believe we need to hurry if we're to get to the blood before it's no longer readable, correct?"

Kallie nodded. "That we do." Even though she would have preferred to go alone, this was a compromise she could live with.

Felicity handed the Brit a keycard. "The sixth floor, my lord. And I'll send a pair of guards to meet you."

"Yes, thank you, Mrs. Fields. Please keep Ms. Brown company until we return."

"Of course."

As Kallie swung around and headed for the elevators at the waiting room's mouth, dizziness whirled through her, spinning her thoughts like a weather vane caught in a tornado. She stumbled and, throwing out a hand, caught herself against the wall.

Faraway voices, small and indistinct as though shouting into a high wind, buzzed against her mind. One sounded like Augustine; the other was unfamiliar and belonged to a man, a voice that somehow made her think of her long-dead papa.

"C'mere, chère. *Where you been,* ma 'tit monde? *How was school?"*

Her headache returned with a vengeance, throbbing behind her eyes and at her temples with a hard and nauseating rhythm. The pungent aroma of licorice filled her nostrils.

A cold certainty iced Kallie's mind and rocketed her pulse into light speed. Someone was trying to *compel* her. Working to dominate her.

Electricity tingled beneath her skin, thrummed in her bones. The mojo bag tucked into her bra burned against her breast, its protective magic triggered. Ignoring the pain pulsing in her head and forcing the nausea back down, Kallie concentrated on surrounding herself with glowing white steel.

"Back to you your spell will bounce, my will ain't giving an ounce," she whispered. "Compel to your black heart's content, my will and desire ain't gonna be bent."

The dizziness slowed to a stop. The voices vanished—well, the mystery man's voice, anyway.

"Ms. Rivière? Kallie? Are you all right?"

Opening eyes she hadn't even realized she'd closed, Kallie looked into Layne-Augustine's concerned face. She nodded, and immediately regretted it when pain knuckled her temples. "Yeah, but someone just tried to compel me, and we can bet our sweet asses we know who that someone is."

A hard, cold smile slanted across Layne-Augustine's lips. "A dead man, I would imagine—as soon as we find him."

"Damn straight. And we ain't got no time to lose." Shoving away from the wall, Kallie trotted to the elevators.

Jean-Julien grabbed the table's edge to keep from falling from his chair. The Kallie poppet tumbled to the floor, the acrid smell of smoldering paper and Spanish moss wafting from its blackening form.

She'd *rebuffed* him—*refused* his command. Jean-Julien kept turning that thought around in his head, looking for flaws in the realization and finding none. A twenty-three-year-old *girl* had bested Doctor Heron's juju. Juju he'd honed to a killing edge in the dark and hellish forge known as Angola.

Not possible.

Or it shouldn't be, but, possible or not, his command had skittered across the surface of Kallie Rivière's mind like a stone across a winter-iced lake. Gabrielle must've loaded her niece up with charms and talismans to keep her safe while in wicked New Orleans. Another thought occurred to him, one that turned his blood to ice.

Gabrielle knew I'd been released. She sent her niece and her former student to carnival as sacrificial lambs to draw me out. She's watching me even now.

Jean-Julien jumped to his feet, heart hammering against his ribs, and scanned the crowd, the hall, from end to end. Feeling heat against his foot and smelling smoke, he glanced down. The poppet burned merrily as though it'd been doused in lighter fluid. He stomped out the flames, then scattered the poppet's ashes across the scorched bit of carpet with the toe of his loafer. He used leftover napkins from his sandwich to fan away the smoke.

Imbécile. *Gabi* isn't *here, and more's the pity,* oui?

Raking his fingers through his hair, he slumped into his chair, pondering his next move. It looked like he wouldn't be able to spare Belladonna after all. But given that Gabrielle had chosen not to spare Babette even after he'd spent a lifetime in the hell known as Angola . . .

As Rosette had said, *"We're fighting a war, Papa. One we didn't start."*

But one they *would* finish.

He'd use a more direct approach with Belladonna than he had with Kallie, and eliminate any possibility that she'd be able to refuse his control. And if, for whatever reason, his spells didn't work, he still had his knife.

The waiter shuffled out of the crowd and over to Jean-Julien's table, a dirty spoon clutched in his hand. He stopped in front of the table, his expression lax, his brown eyes empty. The spoon clattered onto the table.

"Ah, well done. Good boy," Jean-Julien said, vaguely wishing for a treat to give the waiter.

Jean-Julien unstitched the waiter poppet and plucked out the piece of cloth tucked inside. He slipped the cloth into the waiter's jacket pocket, then ordered him to leave the convention hall and find a nice, quiet spot to sleep off the black dust.

After the waiter had toddled away, Jean-Julien busied himself with transforming the waiter poppet into a guard poppet. He worked the pudding-smeared spoon inside, then stitched the poppet shut once again, murmuring, "I command you, I compel you. My bidding you desire, no will of your own, my word holy fire."

Finished, Jean-Julien rose to his feet and stuffed the guard poppet into his jeans pocket. He left the dealers' room, walking from the conference hall to the elevators in quick, long-legged strides. He pulled the vial of black dust from his jeans and tapped a healthy dose of powder into his palm. Then he punched the button for the sixth floor.

Time to find the lovely Belladonna Brown.

THIRTY

CAUGHT IN BLOOD

Murmuring an incantation under his breath, Layne-Augustine trailed a finger around the door's seams, unsealing it. The white light rimming the door winked out. He slid the keycard into the handle's slot, swung the door open, then stepped aside so Kallie could enter.

Two black-uniformed guards in sunglasses, one guy and one gal, stood in the hall on either side of the door.

Kallie paused in the doorway and looked over her shoulder at the Brit. "I need you to wait out here. This is a tricky spell and I—"

"Don't wish for any distractions," Layne-Augustine finished. "A shame, since I am more than a little curious, but I understand. How long should I give it before deciding you're in dire need of assistance?"

Kallie felt a smile brush across her lips. "Ain't dangerous, so I won't be needing assistance. Just wait until I come out again."

Layne-Augustine nodded. "Very good, then. I shall wait here."

Kallie walked inside, then turned and closed the door, making sure it was locked. The coppery stink of blood thickened the air, and her thoughts whirled back to Gage.

He lies on his belly, his face turned to the side. Blood masks his fine features, glitters in his black curls.

She touched the saint and coffin pendants hanging at her throat, the metal cool against her fingers, and tried to resist the image of his fine features and black curls ablaze with white-hot flame once his body was fed to the crematorium's fire.

She pushed the image away, chest tight and aching.

One killer sat in custody awaiting nomad justice. Kallie would do everything she could to make sure that the one who had created the hex that had killed Gage and who had slashed Dallas's throat joined Rosette in her cell—and in death.

Kallie turned back around. Bloody shoe and gurney-wheel prints streaked the tiles leading from the bed to the door. She skirted them as best she could. Her breath caught in her throat when she saw the pool of blood stretching from the bed to the bureau—all of it belonging to Dallas.

Plastic wrappers, bloodstained towels and pads, a comforter marked with bloody fingerprints, a pair of binoculars, and other medical remnants dotted the blood pool like lake floats.

She couldn't believe Dallas was still alive.

Imagining Dallas's desperate fight against his knife-wielding assailant, she dug her nails into her palms.

I ain't giving up on you, Brûler. Don't you give up either.

Kallie knelt beside the blood pool, hoping she wasn't too late. The blood looked thick and tacky already. She didn't know how much time could elapse before blood became silent, inert, as dead as the person from whose veins it had spilled. And she didn't know if the divination would work on the blood of a person who still breathed.

Did the blood of the living cry up from the ground too as it soaked into the soil? Dallas was as close to murdered as a person could get without dying. And if he didn't make it, they'd never know who had killed him until the *fi' de garce* showed up again, a hex on his lips and a blood-stained knife in his hand.

No. Dallas is *gonna make it, and we're gonna stop this bastard. Stop him cold.*

Kallie closed her eyes and tried to still her racing thoughts. The blood stench soaked in through her pores, filling her lungs with each breath she drew. She wished she could open the French windows and let in fresh air, but that would mean she'd have to step into the blood pool, and that thought didn't appeal to her. It would feel like walking on Dallas's body.

She lifted her hands, then remembered that she needed to consecrate herself for the divination. She dug through Belladonna's black bag full of goodies, rummaging through the bottles and tins for something appropriate for the work at hand.

The voice of her *ti-tante*—or whoever the hell she was—sounded loud and clear in her memory.

"Usually we use a Green Blood o' de Earth potion to consecrate de shells before we do a serious reading. To consecrate our bodies too."

"Green Blood of the Earth?"

"Fresh-picked ragweed and bloodweed and pigweed, althea and vervain, child, ain't you been paying attention? I oughta thump yo' head, girl. Dis be important."

"I'm listening, dammit, Ti-tante. *You just ain't called it Green Blood before."*

"Don't get smart with me, Kalindra Sophia Rivière, I'm gonna be as tricky as life and twice as hard to make sure you continue to survive whatever comes your way. So you better pay close heed. If you ever find yo'self in a dark place where you can't mix up a batch of Green Blood, dere be other ways to consecrate de shells."

"So what are these other ways?"

"One of 'em is yo' own blood, girl. Each of us is a holy fount."

No Green Blood of the Earth, but she found a small vial marked holy oil in Belladonna's neat printing. Good enough. At least now she wouldn't have to open a vein.

Kallie unstoppered the vial. Centering herself with a deep breath, she drizzled the oil over her hands and fingers, releasing the sharp scents of cinnamon and cassia, myrrh and calamus into the air. She rubbed the fragrant oil into her skin.

"Thy word is a lamp unto my feet and a light unto my path," Kallie recited, her voice low but steady. "I seek the truth buried in an evil crime. I seek the truth in the name of the Father, and the Son, and the Holy Spirit. Baron Samedi, *loa* of the crossroads, god of the cemeteries, please open the way for me."

A cold breath blew against the back of Kallie's neck as though a tomb had opened behind her, stone scraping against stone. Power surged through her, prickling and electric. Despite the ice trailing the length of her spine, she felt sweat pop up on her forehead.

Leaning forward, Kallie placed her oil-anointed palms in the cold, thickening puddle of Dallas's blood. "I'm asking the same question *bon Dieu* once put to Cain: 'What have you done? The voice of thy brother's blood crieth unto me from the ground.' "

Kallie watched the blood, listening to the steady

rhythm of her own heart, wondering if it would happen the same way as it had with Gabrielle that night in the bayou—*if* it happened at all.

But no flash of purple enveloped her fingers. No voice whispered like it had that night, a thin and girlish sound intertwined with the wind and the thunder and the rain, the words disbelieving and sad.

Words Kallie would carry forever.

"I didn't know him. He said he was visiting relatives and asked if I would guide him to the Llewellyn place. Said his name was Scott. He hurt me. I begged him and begged him to stop . . ."

Nothing happened. Maybe nothing would. Maybe the blood was too cold, too thick, too long dead. But she goddamned wasn't going to give up—not yet.

"A man's blood shed by another who wished him dead," she chanted. "Cold steel and a cold heart. Help me dig up the truth before someone else dies."

Deep gold light flashed out from her fingertips, flared from her palms, and her heart leaped into her throat.

It was working!

The light suddenly dimmed, guttering like a spent candle, and Kallie corralled her wandering thoughts and focused on the task at hand.

"I'm asking the same question *bon Dieu* once put to Cain: 'What have you done? The voice of thy brother's blood crieth unto me from the ground.' "

Power curled into the air like steam above a kettle on full boil. Her skin goosebumped, and sweat trickled between her breasts. Heat kindled at her core, white-hot, a newborn sun. She burned. The blood beneath her hands bubbled.

"Dallas, *cher,* show me who did this awful thing to you."

More power steamed into the air, white and vaporous. A scorched-blood reek pinched Kallie's nostrils, but she couldn't wrench her gaze away from the form shaping itself from the white mist/steam: a heron with a flopping fish held in its long beak.

Doctor Heron. Rosette's hoodoo papa.

Her heart pogoed into her throat. She'd seen the same heron image from the guy who'd spoken to her at the carnival, the tall, middle-aged man with café-au-lait skin and striking pale-green eyes.

The man Dallas had confronted, and she'd broken his nose for the effort; the man whose friendly smile had left her cold.

"Ah, goddammit, Dal," she breathed. "I'm so sorry. You were right all along."

The heron faded, replaced by a mist-shaped image of a slender woman with long, straightened hair and deep-set eyes. She stood in front of a house with a wide front porch bracketed by tall palm trees.

Kallie frowned. What the . . . ? Who is *that*?

The image wisped away as if breeze-blown, and Kallie looked down. She stared at the thin layer of heat-seared black blood now etched into the slate tiles, her pulse roaring in her ears. The pool was gone. She lifted her hands. Dried blood flaked from her skin.

"Shit," she whispered. She didn't know what had just happened or what it meant, but she'd have to worry about that later.

Kallie jumped to her feet and rushed to the door. She yanked it open. Layne-Augustine swiveled around to meet her gaze, his dreads once more knotted behind him. A question lingered in his eyes.

She nodded. "It worked, and it *was* goddamned Doctor Heron," she said. "And it turns out that me and Bell had a run-in with him at carnival, but Dallas shooed him off."

Layne-Augustine's expression turned grim. "I find it chilling that you and Ms. Brown have already had an unknowing encounter with Jean-Julien St. Cyr."

"I owe Dallas big-time for that one," Kallie said, pushing her hair behind her shoulders. A fresh round of guilt nudged at her. "Especially since I broke his nose."

Layne-Augustine shook his head. "You really must stop punching people. Have you considered anger management, or a twelve-step program for quick-fisted pugilists?"

"You made that last one up."

"Perhaps."

"That's not all," Kallie said, the mist-woman's face flaring in her mind. Familiar. "There's another woman involved as well."

"Another?" Layne-Augustine's blond brows knitted together. "Do you know who?"

"No. But I have some ideas that I need to research online."

"I'll have the guards go with you to my office while I stop by my suite," the Brit said. "I seem to be a tad wet."

Kallie smiled. "I think you had fun getting wet tonight, you big show-off."

"I enjoyed myself, yes," Layne-Augustine said. "I've never done anything remotely like that before. Now I can go into the afterlife secure in the knowledge that I've stripped for a horde of screaming, frothing women and won a wet-boxers contest."

"Well, you *would've* won if you'd remained onstage," Kallie reminded him.

"Yes. So the judges selected Number Four in my place, and the audience chose Number Three," the Brit grumbled. "But *I* was the true winner on both counts."

"You mean *Layne* was the true winner."

"Allow me my delusions. I *am* about to pass on or whatever, after all."

Kallie sighed. "Okay. Fine. You were the true winner on both counts."

"Thank you," Layne-Augustine said. "I'll join you in the office after I change clothes."

Kallie looked him up and down, then murmured, "That's a goddamned shame."

"Excuse me?"

"Nothing, Basil. I'll see you in a few." She started down the hall for the elevators.

"Fine, and it's *Lord* Basil."

"Even in the bedroom?"

"*Especially* in the bedroom." Layne-Augustine replied, straight-faced, shoving his hands into his damp trouser pockets and strolling after her.

Augustine strode into his bedroom, unbuttoning his shirt and draping it over the back of a chair. He trailed a hand over his chest. The feel of the hard muscles underneath thrilled him, but also reminded him that the flesh beneath his fingers wasn't his own.

Reminded him that the clock had nearly run out.

Ghost. The word skittered across Augustine's soul like a rat on ice. He didn't feel like a ghost. He didn't feel dead—however that was supposed to feel. Was one *supposed* to feel dead? Weren't the dead *beyond* feeling, period?

And after he vacated the comfortable and natural solidity and warmth of Valin's body, what then? Did he wisp away like a stray patch of fog caught in a breeze? Would light shaft down from the heavens, a celestial escalator into the afterlife?

He'd find out soon enough.

Just as he peeled off his damp trousers, the rumbling roar of a motorcycle reverberated through his skull, vibrated in his ears. Valin's signal that he wished to switch places. The last time they had juggled past one another, he had accidentally snagged one of the nomad's memories and relived it.

He finds himself standing in front of a trailer door. . . .

The squatter answers the door with his right-hand fingers clenched around the grip of what looks like a Colt .38, a sweating can of Michelob Light gripped in his left hand. His brows are squeezed together in what he probably imagines as a menacing glare as he peers into the darkness, but it looks more like a baby's scrunched-up diaper-shitting expression.

"Glad you're home," Layne says.

"What the fuck you want, ass-wipe?"

A quick flick of both wrists, and a blade slides down into each hand. Layne's fingers curl around the grips. "Does the name Poesy mean anything to you?"

"Poesy?" The squatter laughs, voice cigarette-smoke rough. "Should it? That you, sweetheart?"

"Nah, ain't me, and, yeah, the name should mean everything *to you." Layne shoves forward, knocking the squatter off balance and sending him reeling into the beer-and-bean-burrito-scented front room of his double-wide. His can of Michelob Light goes flying, showering the room with beer. Layne smashes the hilt of one blade against the fucker's forehead.*

Said fucker goes down twitching like a Tased car thief after a long chase by uniformed and pissed-off cops. Groaning, he swings up the Colt. Fumbles for the trigger.

Layne sweeps one blade across the inside of the squatter's raised wrist, slicing through flesh, muscles, and tendons. The blade's edge scrapes against bone. Blood streams from the wound, threads the smell of copper into the air.

The squatter howls in pain, the Colt tumbling from his useless fingers to the carpet. Layne kicks the gun away, then kneels beside the squirming squatter, one knee on his plaid-shirt-covered chest, one knife jammed against his fleshy throat.

"Poesy. My sister. You raped her, along with your squatter buddies. Then you beat her to death."

The squatter's tear-glistening gaze locks onto the clan tat beneath Layne's right eye, drinks in the yellowing bruises and scabbed-over cuts on his face. Recognition ignites, sparking a growing terror in the mouth-breather's pale blue eyes. "Oh, shit."

"Yeah, 'Oh, shit' *is right. Shoulda made sure I was dead too."*

That memory had chilled Augustine to the bone. But it had also convinced him that Valin would do whatever it took to protect Kallie Rivière from those hunting her. Still, all of his prowess with knives and guns wouldn't save her from a hex.

Not unless he shot the hexer between the eyes. A feat he had a feeling the nomad could accomplish quite well.

The revving engine noise ratcheted up a roaring notch or two. Standing beside his bed, Augustine closed his eyes and focused his thoughts inward.

<Valin. Is something wrong?>

<What's happening with Kallie?>

Augustine brought the nomad up to speed, telling him all they'd learned about the St. Cyr family and the mystery behind Gabrielle LaRue's identity, and gave him the news about the near-fatal attack on Kallie's friend, Brûler.

<She performed a blood divination and has learned a third person is involved.>

<Time to change places. Your goal is to see your killer get justice, and mine is to protect Kallie. Now scoot.>

In the end, unable to produce a valid reason to deny Valin control of his own body, Augustine agreed to the switch, knowing it wasn't the last time. Not yet.

Just before he closed his safety bubble of static around himself, he heard the nomad say, "What the hell? Why are my boxers wet?"

Augustine grinned. *<Ask Kallie.>*

THIRTY-ONE

NO WILL OF HER OWN

Since Dallas was still in surgery, Belladonna told Felicity she planned to go to her room and fetch her book so she could read while she waited. It beat the hell out of sitting there staring at the ceiling and imagining the worst.

Belladonna paused at a coffee kiosk near the elevators, drawn by the heady smell of fresh-roasted coffee beans, and ordered a double espresso to go. She had a feeling she was going to need it. She told the barista that she'd be back in ten minutes and would pick it up then.

Getting in the elevator, she tapped the button for the sixth floor. Kallie would be in the room across from hers reading Dallas's blood. Unless she'd already finished. Belladonna's throat tightened. The question in her mind was whether or not the Cain-and-Abel trick that Kallie was about to lay down would work on a *breathing* man's spilled blood.

At least she prayed Dallas was still breathing.

She popped out of the elevator on the sixth floor and strode down an empty corridor. No Augustine. No black-uniformed guards. Either they were all inside the room or Kallie had already finished and they were gone.

Wonder what she found out?

She slipped her keycard in the slot, and the light flashed green. But before she could twist the handle, the door flew open and she half stumbled, half fell into the room. “Oh!” she gasped.

A man stood in front of her. The man with the jade-green eyes from the carnival. The one that Dallas had run off.

“*Bonne nuit,* Belladonna,” he said.

Belladonna turned to run back into the hall . . . or *tried* to turn, anyway.

As though she'd stepped into a puddle of superglue on the carpet, her feet refused to budge no matter how hard she tried. In fact, she couldn't even force her feet apart. The electric prickle of building magic lifted the air on her arms, tingled against her scalp. The mojo bag hanging around her throat burned like a red-hot coal against her skin. The burnt odors of lavender, jasmine, and sandalwood wafted into the air as the bag's protective magic was overwhelmed.

Hellfire.

“Sunrise east, sunset west,” the man's voice intoned. “Black yarn will bind her up best.”

Cold fear shocked Belladonna into action. Someone was hexing her, and she sure as hell didn't need to think long or hard on who or why.

She reached a hand for her shoulder bag, thinking about her small bottle of anticonjure saltpeter. Too late, she remembered she'd given the bag to Kallie. She had a feeling it wouldn't have mattered. As though tugged by an invisible string, her hand dropped to dangle uselessly at her side.

“Moonrise north, moonset south, bind her limbs and silence her mouth.”

Belladonna tried to yell for help, but her lips refused to

part. Her trapped scream vibrated in her throat. Her heart battered her ribs.

The man held up a poppet for her to see. Her eyes widened. "By air and earth, water and fire," he said, "so be you bound, as I desire."

Belladonna's heart sank, and the first tendrils of real terror rooted deep into her guts. Black yarn bound the little cloth body from head to foot, and a piece of tape covered its mouth of black thread *X*'s.

Stepping forward, the hoodoo lifted his palm and blew black dust into her face. She tried to close her eyes, but couldn't. The pungent smells of anise and bergamot filled her nostrils. Her eyes watered, stung by the dust.

"I command you, Belladonna Brown, I compel you," he said, his voice low but brimming with power. "My bidding you desire, no will of your own, my word holy fire."

His will muffled her thoughts. Suffocated her sense of self. Her fear vanished. *All* emotion vanished except for the need to keep his jade-green eyes focused on her, his gaze sun and moon and whirling Earth. His voice burned against her mind, her heart.

"Mine thou art, Belladonna," he whispered, unwinding the yarn from the poppet's legs. "And it is time for us to go. You'll drive us to Bayou Cyprès Noir. There's work for us to do and people to see."

Kallie looked up from the laptop's monitor when Layne-Augustine walked into the office, met his pine-green gaze and knew—even before she heard him speak or took full notice of his clothes—that it was Layne, and not Augustine.

A sense of connection rippled into her, a soothing heat

that quieted her troubled thoughts and stirred up certain parts of her anatomy. Her lips parted, but no words came out. He stood in the doorway, staring back at her, something close to panic in his eyes.

Then he looked away, breaking the spell, and said, "Augustine told me about your friend. I'm sorry. I hope he pulls through."

"I appreciate that," she murmured, leaning back into Augustine's leather captain's chair, wishing he hadn't looked away, but not sure what would've happened if he hadn't. She could just imagine the hotel manager leading tourists into the room.

"They've been like that for decades, staring at each other, mouths open. Tragic, really."

Kallie shook her head, a rueful smile on her lips. *Looks like we need to avoid stare-downs.* "Did Augustine tell you what was going on?"

"Yeah, he did." Layne looked at her again, but this time it felt normal, no connection shock. Relief flickered in his eyes. "Whatcha find out?" He nodded at the laptop.

"C'mere and I'll show you," Kallie replied. *Wow. Did I just sound like a dirty old man offering candy to a pigtailed and stacked teenager?* Heat rushed to her cheeks.

A smile brushed Layne's lips. He crossed the room and walked behind the desk to stand beside her chair. He was wearing the black Inferno T-shirt, jeans, and flame-painted scooter boots that he'd had on when Augustine had initially possessed him.

He bent down to look at the monitor, one hand on the arm of Kallie's chair, his dreads swinging soft against her arm and smelling of sandalwood, orange blossoms, and Augustine's cigarettes.

Kallie's pulse leaped through her veins.

"Who am I looking at?" he asked, studying the photo of a pretty black-haired, brown-eyed woman with toffee-colored skin.

"Babette St. Cyr," Kallie answered. "Rosette's mama. The photo's from her obituary."

"If she's dead, then she can't be the third person involved in this, yeah?"

"I think she is," Kallie said, looking up at him. "When I did the blood divination, it showed me a heron for Rosette's papa, Doctor Heron, and that made total sense. I'm sure he's the goddamned bastard who slashed Dallas's throat. But then it showed me a woman standing in front of a house. Babette."

Layne crouched down so he could be at eye level with her. "Maybe that's because Babette is the reason behind everything. Augustine told me that she died while her husband was in the pen. Maybe he blames your aunt, or Gabrielle LaRue or whoever, for her death."

"That was my first thought too," Kallie said, her hand sliding beside Layne's to grip the chair arm. Excitement burned through her like adrenaline. "But then I remembered that I'd asked who had been *responsible* for what had happened to Dallas, and the blood revealed Doctor Heron *and* Babette."

Layne chewed on his lower lip as he considered. "And it showed *her* in front of a house, but not the heron?"

"Right. I looked up the St. Cyr Delacroix address and Googled the house. Wide porch. Palm trees. It's the one I saw Babette standing in front of." Kallie's pinkie brushed against the nomad's thumb. "Layne, what if Babette was so furious over her husband's affair with

Gabrielle that she poisoned his clients, then let him take the fall? And died without ever telling him or their daughter the truth?"

Layne whistled. "More than enough reason for her not to cross over. Hell, if she was that crazy-jealous in life, she might still be that crazy-jealous."

"My thought exactly. And now that her husband's finally come home, maybe she's influenced him or . . . Hell, I don't know what her role in this is or even how big it might be, but I think it's worth a trip to Delacroix to find out."

"If she's the main force behind all this blood and death, then she needs to be stopped, yeah," Layne said, glancing at her picture on the monitor again. "Otherwise, once Rosette and Jean-Julien are dead, she may try to influence others to carry out her revenge."

"*Provided* she's a part of this."

"Blood don't lie." Layne smoothed his hands over his dreads, his face thoughtful. "How far away is Delacroix?"

"Mmm. A hundred and forty miles or so. Couple of hours."

"It's almost midnight and my clan'll be here anytime," Layne said. "But Gage's cremation ain't until late morning tomorrow, so that gives us plenty of time for a trip to Delacroix and back."

"Could Babette shanghai you?"

Layne shook his head. "Not with Augustine still in the cargo hold."

"You don't have to go with me," Kallie said. "I can always lay a talk-to-the-dead trick and—" She quit speaking when Layne laid his warm palm over her mouth.

"Shut up, woman. That sounds dangerous as hell. You ever lay a trick like that before?"

Kallie shook her head, struggling with the urge to kiss his palm.

His gaze dropped to his hand, then back to her eyes. His hand remained over her mouth. "I'm going with you, sunshine. With Doctor Heron loose on the premises, you'll be safer away from this damned hotel anyway."

"Safer?" Kallie pushed his hand away, indignant. "I can take care of myself. I don't need a bodyguard."

"I've seen your right hook, no argument here. But ain't no shame in needing someone to watch your back. This is a man who fights dirty—magic *and* knives. A man who kills souls." Grief flared in his eyes.

Kallie slipped her hand over the top of Layne's. Rubbed her thumb across his scarred knuckles. "I'm so sorry about Gage," she said.

"I know, and it ain't your fault, Kallie."

Before she even knew what she was doing, Kallie leaned over the arm of the chair and pressed her mouth against Layne's, kissed his soft lips.

His breath caught in his throat, surprised, and Kallie half expected him to jerk away, appalled.

What the hell am I doing? I slept with his best friend!

Heart pounding hard and fast, she started to pull away, ready to stammer an apology, but Layne's hands cupped her face. Held her still. And he deepened the kiss. His lips parted beneath hers, his breath coming fast. Their tongues touched.

A lightning bolt of mind-blanking heat streaked from her lips to her nipples, sparked down her spine and between her legs. She slipped her arms beneath his dreads and wrapped them around his neck.

Layne's fingers trailed from her face to weave themselves into her hair. A low growl vibrated in his throat and the next thing Kallie knew, he'd lifted her from the chair with easy strength and set her on his lap. She straddled his thighs, her arms still laced around his neck, her lips still lost to his molten kiss.

He held her tight with one arm around her waist, his other hand cupping her left breast, his thumb circling her hardened nipple through her tank and bra. She moaned her approval against his lips. She felt him stiffen underneath her.

She slid her hands down his sides to pluck at his T-shirt, wanting to peel it off, but that would mean he'd have to let go of her and the kiss would have to stop.

And then coherent thought might kick in again.

With a little sound of frustration, she broke the kiss and tugged at his T-shirt. Layne's fingers locked around her wrists, held her hands in place against his belly. She looked up at him. Hunger and heat glimmered in his eyes.

So did guilt.

And, like she'd feared, coherent thought returned in a rush of shame. Layne opened his mouth to speak, but Kallie jerked her hand free and pressed it against his lips. She shook her head. "You don't need to say it. I understand. Gage."

Then he did what she'd yearned to do earlier and kissed the palm of her hand, his gaze holding hers. Inner light gleamed in his eyes like sunlight through mountain pines—so different from the way Augustine regarded her through those same eyes.

Kallie's head jerked up when she heard the office door creak open. Heard a familiar voice say, "The clan's due within the hour, Augus—"

McKenna, in black jeans and a royal blue blouse underneath a tight-fitting black leather jacket, came to a dead halt in the center of the office, Layne's leather jacket slung over her arm. The blackbird V tattooed beneath her right eye was vivid against skin pale from lack of sleep and, Kallie realized, grief.

She stared at them, her face incredulous as she took in the sight of both of them on the floor, flushed with lust, Kallie astride Layne. Her dark gaze skipped from Layne to Kallie. Fury ignited in her eyes.

"'Keep away or yer a dead woman' *means* 'keep away or yer a dead woman,'" the nomad pixie said, her brogue thickening with each heated word.

"Knock it off, Kenn." Layne eased Kallie off his lap and onto her feet, then stood and turned. His honey-blond brows knit together in a scowl. "You're aiming your rage at the wrong person. Kallie ain't the enemy."

"Aye, she is. She's bloody death in shorts and a tank top, and I warned her to keep her fucking distance. If not for her, Gage would be standing with us right now."

"Wrong," Layne said. "If not for the asshole who made the hex, Gage would be standing with us right now. And I'm working with Kallie to take care of that."

"*Working*? Is tha' what ye call it? Funny. We call it fookin' where I come from."

"Dammit, that's enough," Layne growled.

The leprechaun stalked across the room, stopping right in front of Kallie. Only a foot of tension-thick air separated them. She tossed Layne's jacket at him. He caught it easily, its metal studs and chains jingling.

Kallie met the nomad's scorching take-no-prisoners death glare and held it, chin lifted. "We've found the man responsible for that hex," she said, pleased with the cool, even tone of her voice. "And we're going after him."

"Looks to me like yer going after *Layne*. I guess fooking Gage in every way possible wasn't enough fer you."

"Christ in a bread basket, woman!"

Kallie's muscles coiled and her hands curled into tight fists at her sides. "Stay out of it, Layne. This is between me and her."

"Christ. You too?" Layne threw his hands up in disgust. "Woman-stupid," he muttered, then looked oddly pleased with himself.

Light glinted in the leprechaun's eyes, and a dark smile tilted her lips. "You think those are gonna save you, do you now?"

"Save me—no. Flatten you—yes."

"Count to ten before you throw a punch, Shug. Count slow, like you would between rumbles of thunder."

One Mississippi . . . Ten! Kallie swung up her fists and shifted her weight. Something vibrated against her hip and she looked down, perplexed, until she remembered her cell phone.

"Hey, lassie."

Kallie looked up in time to see the nomad's fist looming in her vision like an incoming asteroid. She ducked, but not quickly enough. McKenna's hard knuckles grazed her cheek, knocking her off balance.

Kallie stumbled against Augustine's desk, bruising her hip against its edge, then caught herself and whirled away from the pixie nomad's next air-swooshing blow. Adrenaline flooded her system, poured through her veins. She spun back around, fists lifted. And barely stopped herself from knuckling a blow into Layne's back.

He stretched his arms out, one hand in front of Kallie's chest and the other in front of McKenna's. "Stop it," he said. "This ain't solving anything, and we're wasting time."

"Get out of the way," McKenna barked.

"No. I need you to listen to me. Gage bought Kallie's life with his own. That should mean something to you. It does to me. If anything happens to her and I trace it back to you—we're finished."

McKenna stared at him. "You don't mean that. You can't."

"Don't test me on this, Kenn. Please."

"You'd actually choose a squatter over clan?"

"Let it go, buttercup, I'm asking you. Let it go."

McKenna's hands unclenched and her expression smoothed into a cool and expressionless mask. She held Layne's gaze for a long moment before pronouncing in a cold voice, "Bewitched, that's wha' ye are."

"Cursed, more like," Layne muttered.

Daggering a last dark look at Kallie, McKenna pivoted around and walked from the room without another word.

"Fuck." Layne sighed.

"You shouldn't give her so much shit about me," Kallie said, slipping her cell phone from her pocket. "I'd feel the same way in her place."

An amused smile flickered across Layne's lips. "Mighty magnanimous of you, sunshine, considering that she's probably plotting your death even as we speak."

"Well, everyone needs a hobby," Kallie murmured as she looked at the caller ID on her cell—BELL. A knot of anxiety tightened in her belly. Must be news about Dallas. Kallie returned the call.

Jean-Julien looked at the ringing cell phone. The caller ID read: KALLIE. A smile curved his lips. He thumbed the talk button. "Kallie Rivière, *oui*? Just the woman I wanted to speak with."

A short pause, then the Rivière girl's voice, low and taut, curled into his ear. "You must be Doctor Heron, the goddamned prick who killed Dallas. Where's Belladonna? She'd better be all right—"

Jean-Julien cut her off. "She's fine, and we're on a little journey. I truly don't want to hurt her, but that's up to you. Give yourself to me, and I guarantee your friend will walk away restored and unmolested."

"*Restored?*" Dark suspicion edged the word.

"At the moment, she and her poppet are mine."

"Shit! Goddamned bastard! So where is all this supposed to go down?"

"Your aunt's house in Bayou Cyprès Noir," Jean-Julien said. "Alone, Kallie, of course. If I catch even a whiff of the Hecatean Alliance or anyone else, I'll *destroy* Belladonna even if it's the last thing I do."

"Wow. How über-villain of you," she muttered. "I ain't gonna risk Bell's life, don't worry."

Jean-Julien chuckled. "I'm *not* worried. But *you* should be, girl."

"We'll see. You know it's going to take a couple of hours for me to get home."

"I know. But if you're not there by two-thirty . . ." Jean-Julien switched off the phone.

So Brûler had died, after all. He wished he could see the look on Gabrielle's face when she received the news of her former star pupil's death. However, he would have the far greater pleasure of seeing her face as she watched her niece die.

Rolling down the passenger window of Belladonna's ancient Dodge Dart, Jean-Julien tossed the cell phone into the night. No excuses. No distractions. No escape.

"I hope for your sake she's a very good friend," he said, looking at Belladonna and touching a finger to her dark cheek. She shuddered, but kept her lovely hazel eyes—well, relatively lovely, considering how unfocused they were at present—on the road beyond the bug-spattered windshield.

Kallie stuffed her cell phone back into her pocket, then shoved shaking hands through her hair. Fury and fear raged through her in equal measure.

She was too goddamned late. The soul-killing goddamned bastard had *already* gotten the drop on someone else. Belladonna. And not only that—the prick had hexed her and bound her to his will.

Doctor Heron. The bogeyman of hoodoo.

And Kallie was pretty damned sure he was hunting the wrong goddamned people.

She swallowed hard and closed her eyes. Her hands knotted into fists at her sides. She didn't want to imagine what Belladonna was enduring this very moment, her every action manipulated, her thoughts suppressed. Kallie hoped her friend was unaware of what had been done to her.

She had no illusions about St. Cyr setting Belladonna free. It hadn't bothered him that an innocent man had been killed, body and soul, by accident. Belladonna's life would also mean nothing to him.

"Kallie? What's wrong?"

Kallie looked up into Layne's concerned face. "Doctor Heron has Belladonna," she said, her voice rough. The nomad's jaw tightened. "He's taking her home. My life for Bell's."

Layne grabbed Kallie's hand and headed for the door in long-legged strides. "That's what he thinks. How far away's home?"

"Nearly as far as Delacroix," Kallie said, hurrying to keep up with him. "He gave us two and a half hours."

"Looks like Babette and Delacroix are gonna hafta wait for another day."

"Looks like." *I'm on my way, Bell. I'll be there soon. Hold on,* chère, *hold on.*

The leprechaun's dark and bitter words circled through Kallie's mind: *"She's bloody death in shorts and a tank top."*

It scared her to think that McKenna just might be right.

THIRTY-TWO

Bayou Cyprès Noir

Layne made it in two hours and ten minutes, his black, low-slung Harley tearing up I-10 West in a steady, high-pitched thrum, his dreads snaking in the wind. Kallie kept her arms locked around his T-shirt-draped waist, her mouth close to his ear to give directions. And as the night cooled down, she was glad she hadn't gotten all woman-stupid and refused his leather jacket.

Layne stopped the bike at the mouth of the rutted dirt drive leading to Kallie's house and killed the engine. The night air seemed to vibrate in the sudden silence. A single cricket sawed a quick song, then quieted. The night-rich smells of moist dirt, green leaves, and muck from the bayou's edge drifted in the air.

Kallie climbed off Layne's bike and unstrapped the black-and-orange-flamed shorty helmet he'd given her to wear. She shook out her hopelessly tangled hair. The nomad took off his own helmet and hung it from the handlebar by its chin strap. He swung his leg over the bike's seat, then stood. He looked up the dirt drive and into the darkness.

"Don't like this," he said quietly.

"Me either," Kallie said, resting her helmet on the bike's seat. "But you gotta stay out of it. I can't take chances with Bell's life."

The night shadowed Layne's face so she couldn't make out his expression. "I hear you," he said. "But *I* can't take chances with *your* life. Not when Gage has paid for it."

"You're gonna hafta, until I call you," Kallie insisted, keeping her voice pitched low. She'd programmed Layne's number into her cell phone with the idea that she'd ring him—well, vibrate him—the moment she'd found Belladonna.

Layne crossed his arms over his chest and grunted. He hadn't liked the plan from the start, but he understood that St. Cyr would be watching to see if she came alone or not, so Kallie decided to accept that as a fine-but-I-still-don't-like-it grunt.

She shrugged out of his leather jacket and handed it to him. It had protected her from the chilly night air, but the damned thing was too heavy and way too large.

"You wanna take a gun or knife with you?" he asked, tugging on his jacket.

Kallie shook her head. "He's likely to use it on me if he finds it."

She slipped off Belladonna's bag of potions and handed it to Layne. No point in letting St. Cyr take it from her. Besides, she had a couple of tricks of her own. Tucked inside her bra was a small bottle of confusion oil. And stuffed into the back pocket of her cutoffs? A hastily stitched poppet bearing Jean-Julien's name and a few powerful herbs.

Two could play the bend-over game.

But first she needed to make sure Belladonna was safe and out of St. Cyr's easy reach and command. Kallie wished she'd had a little more time to put together something truly badass.

"Okay," she said. "I guess I'm ready."

Layne grasped her shoulders, his hands warm against her rapidly chilling skin. "Be careful, sunshine," he said. "I'm gonna be right behind you."

"Waiting for my call, right?" she asked, searching his green eyes.

"Right." He squeezed her shoulders, then—almost reluctantly—released her.

Kallie offered him a smile, hoping it looked more confident than she felt, and started walking up the tree-lined drive—tall cypress, bitter pecans, and oaks.

Headed for home.

The breeze, carrying the honey-sweet fragrance of the button bushes growing beside the water, pushed at the blue bottles hanging from the branches on the oak in front of the house. The bottles clinked and tinked musically, a soothing sound. Kallie hoped they still held luck.

She faced the house, the skin on the back of her neck prickling. A single light burned inside, and the front door was wide open. So quiet—too quiet. The unusual silence sawed at her nerves. No Cielo *whooing* a Siberian husky–style greeting; no earthy C. C. Adcock–crafted swamp-blues pounding from Jacks's iPod station as he worked on his truck or his boat; no creak from the porch swing as her aunt relaxed with a beer and a book.

Of course, normally at this hour, everyone would be asleep. But that one burning light, the open door, and the silence suggested that there was nothing normal about the hour—not tonight. Tension knotted the muscles in Kallie's shoulders.

Jackson's weathered Dodge Ram was missing from its spot in front of their garage. Were Jacks and her aunt safe, or bound just like Belladonna?

Only one way to find out.

Kallie walked up the stone path to the weathered porch. Just as she placed her foot on the first step, a man's voice—St. Cyr's—said from behind, "Don't move."

Something cold pressed against the side of her neck. Kallie held still, fear slicking an icy finger down her spine as she remembered the pool of blood Dallas's slashed throat had created.

"The knife ain't necessary," she said, mouth dry. "Not when you've got Belladonna."

"I think I'll keep the knife right where it is, since the need for survival often trumps loyalty to friends."

"If I was focused on survival, I wouldn't be here."

St. Cyr slid his arm around her shoulders and gripped her left bicep with a hard-fingered hand. His right kept the knife pressed against her neck. "Let's go," he murmured, his breath warm against her ear.

"What about my cousin and my aunt?" Kallie asked. "Are they all right?"

"I wouldn't know. No one was here," St. Cyr grumbled. "Now shut up and walk."

Having no choice, Kallie went with St. Cyr. He led her into the backyard, walking her past the cistern for rainwater and the shed, past Gabrielle's workshop and through the brush to the bayou's edge. The breeze rustled through the trees, carrying the smells of muck and moss and damp rot through the air. An owl hooted.

Kallie's heart skipped a beat when moonlight illuminated a curly-haired figure sitting in the sawgrass underneath a tall cypress next to the water. Belladonna, and only Belladonna. No sign of her aunt or Jackson. Maybe Gabrielle was still away doing whatever and Jacks had ignored Kallie, put Cielo in the back of his truck, and driven into town for a few drinks.

As St. Cyr walked Kallie toward the cypress Belladonna waited beneath, Kallie saw a checked picnic blanket spread out in the grass and weeds.

And when she saw what was on it, her blood turned to ice.

The blanket held a large black X. Just like the one on her mattress back at the hotel.

And Belladonna sat curled right at the blanket's edge. One little movement and the hex would snag her, body and soul.

"You don't need Belladonna," Kallie said. "It's me you want, right? Release her." And though she felt like she'd need the Heimlich maneuver in order to get the word out of her throat, she added, "Please."

"*Oui*, it's you I want, true enough, but you have no say in anything that happens here, girl, no negotiating power," St. Cyr replied. "That said, I plan to release Belladonna as soon as you're dead. So the sooner you get on the blanket and accept your fate, the sooner Belladonna can be freed. She's an innocent in all of this."

"So was Gage. But you killed him."

"The nomad's death was an accident. Tragic, but nothing I can fix."

"And Dallas, you sonuvabitch?"

"As my daughter once put it: He was a sacrifice upon the cold altar of revenge—just as you will be."

"But that's just it. You've tracked down the *wrong* Gabrielle LaRue," Kallie said quickly. "My aunt looks *nothing* like the pictures of the woman in your daughter's files. She's not the Gabi you're looking for. Maybe your wife learned about the affair. Maybe she got mad enough to poison your clients and to let you take the blame."

Fury blazed in St. Cyr's eyes. "Shut up, girl. Enough talk." His fingers squeezed Kallie's bicep so tight that her fingers tingled, then went numb as the circulation was cut off. "Your aunt filled you full of lies." He brought them to a stop in front of the hexed picnic blanket.

Sweat trickled between Kallie's breasts. The sight of the thick black X crossing the checked material twisted cold around her heart and filled her mind with images of Gage's empty eyes and bloodied body.

She tried to measure the distance between her and Belladonna. Tried to figure if she could jump the blanket and knock her friend over at the same time. Belladonna's glassy-eyed gaze remained fixed on St. Cyr, her hands curled lax in her lap.

Odds didn't look good. Maybe if she had a running start . . .

Keeping the knife in place at Kallie's throat, St. Cyr released her arm, then yanked up the back of her shirt. Kallie stiffened as he pulled the hidden poppet free. Her belly sank. Now might be a good time to call Layne. If she could slip a hand into her pocket.

"Look at me, girl," St. Cyr said, removing the knife from her throat.

Kallie turned around slowly. Doctor Heron, aka Jean-Julien St. Cyr, aka Rosette's ex-con daddy, ripped the poppet apart with his knife and plucked out the piece of paper bearing his name. He stuffed it into the pocket of his jeans. The rest of the poppet he scattered in the grass and alligator weeds.

She slid her hand into her pocket and tapped the speed-dial button for Layne.

"Belladonna, stand up," St. Cyr said quietly, his cold pale-green gaze meeting and holding Kallie's. "Hold one foot above the blanket."

Kallie heard movement behind her as Belladonna obeyed Doctor Heron's command.

"I hope your friend has good balance," he commented. "One little wobble . . ."

Kallie kept her gaze on St. Cyr, wishing she could turn him to stone with just a glance. "She does. But you don't need to do this. Let her go."

St. Cyr chuckled. "You sound just like Brûler. Either you take your place on the blanket or Belladonna does."

Kallie swiveled around, giving her back to St. Cyr and facing Belladonna. Her friend swayed on one platform-soled foot at the blanket's edge, her face blank. Kallie's gut knotted with dread. Despite what she'd told St. Cyr, Belladonna wasn't known for her coordination and grace.

"How can I trust you to release Bell when you've sold your own daughter's soul to the nomads? Left her high and dry?"

"The nomads? What are you talking about?"

He didn't know. The goddamned bastard didn't know. Maybe she could throw *him* off balance with a bit of truth mixed liberally with speculation.

"The clan of the nomad you murdered has arrived in New Orleans and they've asked for your daughter," Kallie said, slipping the bottle of confusion oil from her bra and palming it. "Augustine okayed it. But that shouldn't be a surprise, since Rosette murdered him too, right? You ain't the only one who believes an eye for an eye is never enough. The nomads do too, and they're gonna kill Rosette—body and soul."

Hard hands seized Kallie's shoulders and spun her around. St. Cyr searched her face with eyes as hard as green diamonds. "You're lying, stalling for time," he growled. "No more. Belladonna—"

Kallie punched him before he could finish speaking. Doctor Heron staggered back, blood trickling from his nose, his expression stunned.

Pulse roaring in her ears, Kallie uncapped the bottle of confusion oil and tossed the contents into the bastard's face. The nostril-pinching stink of bitter rue and pungent guinea pepper spiced the air. "Your thoughts spin, your purpose you cannot hold," she chanted. "Your evil intentions will not unfold."

But the majority of the oil spattered on the arm St. Cyr had instinctively flung up. "Belladonna," he yelled, his voice thick with blood. "Step onto the blanket! Now!"

Kallie whirled around to see Belladonna slowly lowering her foot.

"NO!" Kallie screamed and, knowing only one way to save Bell from the hex's fatal discharge, she threw herself into the middle of the black-dust X.

A cold and black flood of venomous magic poured into Kallie, oil-slicking her veins and shocking all thought from her mind. Choking, she struggled to breathe as the hex's power coiled like a hungry python around her heart and squeezed. Sucked at her soul like a black hole drinking in a star's brilliant essence.

White-hot pain wracked her body and short-circuited her mind. She felt hundreds of tiny fists battering her from within, hammering with increasing strength.

"I'm sorry, baby. I ain't got a choice."

Her breath stopped; then, a moment later, her heart quit beating.

THIRTY-THREE

HORSE WITH NO NAME

The Rivière girl's body convulsed violently on the blanket, her long mane of dark hair whipping around her face. Blood poured from her nose and mouth, her eyes and ears. Her fingers twisted into the blanket's fabric, a blanket Belladonna's booted foot now rested upon.

Kallie Rivière's body stopped thrashing. With a soft sigh, she died in every way.

Bitter disappointment curled through Jean-Julien. *Should've brought a camera and filmed the girl's death so Gabrielle could see the consequences of her actions from all those long years ago.*

Grateful that the girl had cared enough for her friend to make sure she took the brunt of the hex's power and not Belladonna, Jean-Julien raised a shaking hand to his forehead and wiped away the sweat. He caught a whiff of bitter rue. The girl's confusion spell would've worked if he hadn't anticipated her pulling a stunt like that and doubled his protection.

Close. Too close for comfort.

"Belladonna, turn around, walk to the dogwood behind you, then sit down."

The voodooienne paused for a moment, her eyes glistening with tears; then she turned around, as stiff and slow as an old woman, and tottered across the grass to the dogwood tree. She plopped down at its base.

Jean-Julien frowned. Dust or something must've gotten into Belladonna's eyes to make them tear up like that, since it was impossible for her to comprehend what had just happened—Kallie's sacrifice for her sake.

But before he released Belladonna, he needed to follow up on Kallie's words. Desperate words, surely, from a girl trying to buy a few more moments of life.

"You ain't the only one who believes an eye for an eye is never enough. The nomads do too, and they're gonna kill Rosette—body and soul."

Now that Gabrielle's niece was dead, it was time for Rosette to escape. Reaching into his pocket, Jean-Julien pulled out the guard poppet. He paused beside the picnic blanket, frowning once more. From what he could see, there was no trace of the black dust that had killed Kallie Rivière.

Only the hex itself should've been absorbed into her body, not the now-harmless powder. Jean-Julien rubbed his chin thoughtfully. Most likely between the girl's convulsions, all the blood, and the night breeze, the black dust had been scattered or liquefied. Part of it could even be underneath her. In any case, it couldn't just vanish.

Jean-Julien continued across the grass and brush and sat down beside Belladonna. The girl's hands were curled lax in her lap, her face pleasantly blank. But tears wet her cheeks, and her unfocused attention seemed to be on the Rivière girl's small and motionless body. Which wasn't possible, of course.

Closing his eyes, Jean-Julien drew in a deep breath, then centered himself. He placed the tips of his index fingers over the poppet's black-button eyes and whispered, "Mine thou art, your eyes, your body, and heart. I see what you see. I hear what you hear. And you do as I do, following each command true."

The darkness behind Jean-Julien's closed eyes faded and he became aware of a well-lit hall, heard voices in conversation. He looked out through the guard's eyes, his vision narrowing down to small dead-ahead spots. His heart leaped into his throat when he saw the cluster of people gathered in front of the guard: four female nomads and one male nomad, along with a red-haired woman in a purple pantsuit.

Fear sliced through him, slivered his heart with ice. Gabrielle's niece had told the truth. His Rosette *was* to be handed over to nomad justice.

"Where will we kill her?" a teenage girl says, her dark skin glimmering with highlights from the overheads. "Will we do it here, or take her somewhere else?"

"Here, of course," the red-haired woman answers, her voice bearing a lacy, high-class British accent. "Outside of the Prestige, you'd be subject to local laws and could find yourselves accused of murder."

Jean-Julien felt sick. His beautiful and courageous daughter was about to be slaughtered. How would he ever explain that to his Babette? Atone for it? That he'd gained his revenge, but destroyed their daughter?

A possibility occurred to him, a dark and heartbreaking possibility. One he knew he would have to take, for Rosette's sake.

Jean-Julien focused on the guard's open and compliant mind. Filled it with his instructions—instructions to be followed the moment the guard was asked to fetch the prisoner.

"Your will my desire. Your word holy fire"—looped on endless repeat through the guard's mind.

The redhead glances at the guard and says, "Please bring out Ms. St. Cyr, Rudolph."

Rudolph nods, his instructions triggered. He shuffles over to the warded cell door, unlocks it, and goes inside. Rosette, curled on her neatly made bunk, bluish shadows under her eyes, looks up from the newspaper she is reading.

She scans the guard's face and smiles. "Papa," she breathes.

"I love you, Rosette," the guard mumbles. "I have no choice but to send you to your mother. Please forgive me."

Rosette's eyes widen as the guard pulls his gun from its holster. She presses herself against the wall. "Papa, no," she chokes out.

The guard empties the gun into her body. Shouts ring from the hall.

Jean-Julien pulled away from the guard's mind. Chest aching, he plunged his knife into the guard's poppet and with several quick slices, disemboweled poppet and man, killing both. He tossed the poppet's remains into the grass.

Bending over, elbows to knees, he rested his head in his hands.

Rosette is in her mama's arms now, her soul safe. The nomads can no longer touch my little girl. Hold her tight, Babette, ma chère.

Sucking in a ragged breath, Jean-Julien lifted his head and straightened. He would release Belladonna, then leave. His work for the moment was done. All that remained was Gabrielle's nephew, Jackson Bonaparte—a project already in process.

Not wanting to chance harming Belladonna when he unmade her poppet, Jean-Julien sprinkled it with a simple uncrossing powder, a blend of sandalwood, five-finger grass, myrrh, and frankincense.

"Free thou art, your will once again your own," he murmured, as he unstitched Belladonna's poppet, removing and scattering its insides. "Free thou art, your will once again strong as bone."

Belladonna sucked in a breath and rubbed her eyes. "What the hell?" she muttered. "Where am—"

Jean-Julien rose to his feet and walked away. Behind him, Belladonna's anguished scream shattered the bayou's silence.

"*KALLIE!*"

The jarring thud of hooves against the ground vibrates along Kallie's spine, jolts her body with each ground-swallowing gallop. Rough hair rubs against her cheek, twists around her fingers. She smells horse musk and, underneath her thighs, feels the powerful flex of muscles. She realizes the pain has stopped.

<*Hold on,* m'ame-soeur, *and ride.*>

A woman's voice, low and determined; a voice as familiar as her own even though she's certain she's never heard it before.

The image of a heart bound in chains made of pale bones and surrounded by black X's flares behind her closed eyes.

Kallie opens her eyes. Purple fills her vision, and coarse hair tickles her nose. She sneezes. She lifts her head and sits upright, realizing she's astride a black horse, her fingers wrapped in its flowing purple mane. Panic surges through her.

Where's the blanket? Is Belladonna safe? Wait. Am I goddamned dead? And wait one more time—there's sneezing *in the afterlife?*

<*You be awful chatty for a dead girl, Kallie Rivière,*> *the horse replies, managing to sound dry and witty and nothing like Mr. Ed.* <*Our body's dead, but nothing says it has to stay that way—especially*

since we *ain't dead, not yet. Not if we win this race and claim what be ours.*>

<*Wait.* Our *body? Who the hell are you?*>

<*Your horse. For now.*>

<*And does my horse have a goddamned name?*>

<Oui, *My name be Shut-Up-And-Look-Already-Will-You?*>

One Mississippi . . . Two . . . Kallie's count stops when she looks as her goddamned horse has so subtly suggested and realizes she— they—*are still in the bayou and on an* iceberg-dead-ahead *course for the checked picnic blanket.*

And Belladonna.

Kallie's breath catches rough in her throat as Belladonna, her face wet with tears, performs CPR on her *blood-smeared body.*

Sorry, Bell. I'm so sorry.

<*I think my name is now You-Need-To-Look-Up-Okay?*>

<*I never asked for a goddamned horse, let alone a* sassy *goddamned horse,*> *Kallie grumbles. She looks up, and what she sees stuns her into silence.*

A *huge black-dust* X *jeweled with ruby skeleton keys glimmers against the night-shadowed canopy of trees sheltering the bayou.*

Black and red, keys and crosses. A gift from Papa Legba, loa *of the crossroads, the intermediary between spirits and humanity.*

<*We need to claim that,*> *her horse says.* <*Drink it in and make it a part of us. Or you do, anyway. It's the only way for us to win.*>

<*Win what?*> *Kallie's gaze remains locked on the* X *undulating in the moonlight.*

<*The right to breathe again.*>

Kallie wrenches her gaze away from the X *and looks at her grieving friend.* <*All right, but how?*>

<*You'll know when we get there.*>

<*Great. That's goddamned helpful. Is there some kind of talking-horse rule stating that they must be as vague as possible at all times?*>

<Maybe.>

Kallie rolls her eyes. <Then let's get this show on the road.>

The horse's hooves gouge chunks of sod from the ground, and it splashes water up from the bayou, then strikes clods of night sky and stars from the air as it leaps over the blanket and Belladonna and into the sky. With her knees to the horse's ribs and her hands in its purple mane, Kallie guides it toward the X's shimmering center.

Fear ripples through Kallie as memories of the pain she just suffered sweeps through her mind and, for a second, she considers stopping and accepting her fate.

"Sorry, baby. I ain't got a choice."

"She's bloody death in cutoffs and a tank top."

"The sooner you get on the blanket and accept your fate, the sooner Belladonna can be freed."

But the image of Belladonna's anguished face shoves Kallie's fear and doubts aside.

She'll always blame herself for my death. Because of it, she'll never be free.

Can't stop now.

Breathing in the hex's pungent odor of bergamot, black licorice, and sulfur, Kallie decides to ask one more time. <What's your name?>

<Don't have one. Not yet, anyway.>

<Fine. Be that way, then.>

The X fills Kallie's vision. Power radiates from it, cold and razor-thorned, prickles against her skin, her face. Her essence. Kallie kicks her heels against the horse's sides, and they leap into the X.

Each tiny barbed bit of black dust, each and every cold molecule, pours into Kallie through her sternum like boiling oil into a funnel.

This time the pain is worse. Much worse.

She screams.

THIRTY-FOUR

CHAINS MADE OF PALE BONES

Layne was crouched in the backyard of Kallie's aunt's house, examining a line of white, green-flecked powder stretching across the stone threshold of what looked like a workshop, when his cell phone buzzed in his jeans pocket. He held his breath, waiting to see if it buzzed a second time. It didn't. Kallie's signal.

Layne straightened, the toe of his left boot nudging the line of powder, and suddenly he found himself walking briskly through the grass back to the rutted dirt drive, thinking, *Maybe someone will be home tomorrow.*

He came to an abrupt stop. *Shit. Shit. Shit. Virgin Mary in a ceiling crack. A fucking spell.* Whirling, he raced back to the shadowed yard. His leather jacket creaked as he pulled one of his blades free from its inside sheath. Just as he ran past the workshop, careful to skirt the powder guarding it, a heartrending wail sliced through the air.

"KALLIE!"

Layne barreled through the thick brush, vines slapping him in the face, thorns scratching his jacket and snagging his dreads. His heart drummed a light-speed cadence against his ribs, one that pounded out Kallie's name with each beat. He quickly scanned the dense undergrowth and tree-shadowed depths. But, seeing no one, he bolted in the direction he thought the scream had come from.

A shape stepped out of the darkness from beside a lightning-shattered cypress. Layne skittered to a stop, his boots sliding in the dew-slick sawgrass, and just missed smacking into the startled-looking man. Doctor Heron.

“Hold it right there, asshole,” Layne growled.

But the asshole refused to hold it right there. Instincts drenched in adrenaline, Layne swung his knife under and up in time to parry the blade punching for his own belly.

Edged steel *thunk*ed together, scraped apart.

Layne jumped back and out of easy reach. Relaxing into a knife-fighter’s half-crouch, he circled the hoodoo slowly.

An expression of intense hatred flickered across St. Cyr’s caramel-brown face, icing his pale-green eyes as his gaze locked with Layne’s. Or—more accurately—locked onto his clan tat. “My daughter’s dead because of nomad trash like you,” he spat.

Clang! Clang! Clang!

“Not now,” Layne grated under his breath. “I know who the fucker is.”

Clang! Clang! Clang!

Movement at the bayou’s edge tugged at Layne’s attention. Risking a quick glance away from St. Cyr, he saw Belladonna kneeling, her arms locked together and stiff as she compressed . . .

Layne stared in deepening horror as Belladonna performed CPR on a prone form in the grass. Kallie stood beside Belladonna and the prone form she labored over, but her skin glittered as though dusted with black mica, and her hair flickered black flame. Her head turned, and she looked directly at him.

"Oh, fuck," he breathed, despair cracking his voice. "Kallie . . ."

CLANG!!

Layne wrenched his gaze away from Kallie just in time to see Jean-Julien St. Cyr leap forward, his knife slashing at throat level. Layne spun away, his own blade swinging in a defensive uppercut as he evaded a literal close shave.

Close, hell. Woulda been fatal. Focus, dammit. Dying ain't gonna help. Kallie's gone. Just like Gage. You can't do anything for her now.

<*Except avenge her,*> Augustine sent.

Layne switched his blade to his left hand and reached into his jacket to unsheathe another. With a knife in each hand, he went after St. Cyr again.

<Layne. I need to help Layne,> Kallie says. Black-dust mojo crackles like lightning within her, a wild storm of power corralled within her motionless heart.

Her horse with no name no longer looks like a horse. Instead she looks like a woman her own age with café-au-lait skin and long cinnamon curls. A vévé *hangs at her throat—the image of a heart bound in chains made of pale bones and surrounded by black X's. It's a* vévé *Kallie has never seen before.*

A guardian angel, maybe?

<Ooo. Yum. He be cute, for true. But you can't help him until you get us back into our body.>

<There's that our body *thing again. Okay. How?>*

<It be simple. Just lay us down on yourself. Like making a sand angel but minus all the flapping. Hurry up before it be too late.>

<Great. Not only sassy, but bossy, too. I liked you better as a horse.>

Kallie kneels beside her blood-spattered body.

Kallie opened her eyes. She tasted blood in her mouth, felt it sticky on her eyelashes. Rib-cracking pressure hammered down on her sternum.

"Bell," she whispered. "Stop."

Eyes wide, Belladonna froze on her last compression, her gaze shifting to Kallie's face. "Oh, *bon Dieu,*" she sobbed, and grabbed Kallie up in a bear hug. "Thank you, thank you, thank you."

Pain lanced through Kallie's chest. Looked like it was *her* turn for broken or cracked ribs. Touché, karma. "I can't breathe," she protested. "Kinda defeats the whole purpose of CPR."

Belladonna released Kallie and rocked back on her heels. "I thought I'd lost you," she said, wiping the tears from her face. "Hellfire. I *did* lose you."

"You sure you're okay? That bastard didn't hurt you?"

Belladonna shook her head. "I'm fine. But . . ." Her words trailed off as her gaze fixed on something past Kallie. "Hellfire. Layne!"

Layne.

Looking over her shoulder, Kallie saw the nomad fighting with Doctor Heron, both men slicing knives through the air. She struggled to her feet, pain stabbing into her sternum with the movement. Her vision grayed. She hurt everywhere as though her skin had been turned to glass, then shattered. A dull ache throbbed at her temples.

"What are you doing?" Belladonna asked.

"Helping Layne."

"Oh, hell no."

Blinking her vision clear, Kallie pressed a supportive arm against her aching ribs and trotted—albeit unsteadily—across the lawn. A memory tickled at the back of her mind, something about a purple-maned horse and black dust, a memory she couldn't quite grasp. A dying and/or resurrection dream, maybe?

Just as she reached Layne, he whirled on her, knives arcing through the air and aimed for either side of her throat, his pine-green eyes cold as winter-frosted stone.

Kallie skidded to a stop, her pulse thundering in her ears. *Smart, Kallie. Run at a man engaged in a knife fight.*

Stunned recognition melted the frost in his gaze. "Shit!" His blades stopped just shy of their target. Kallie felt the muscles in her neck twitch.

St. Cyr swung his knife at Layne's exposed back.

"Behind you!" Kallie choked out.

Layne dropped, dreads flying as he spun around on his knees and drove both blades hilt-deep into St. Cyr's belly. The root doctor gasped. His knife tumbled from his fingers into the grass. The color drained from his face as he looked down at Layne.

"For Gage and Kallie both," Layne snarled, twisting both knives.

St. Cyr dropped to his knees. His mouth opened, but no sound emerged. He collapsed into the grass. Layne slid his blood-glistening blades free of St. Cyr's body and sat back on his heels.

The root doctor's mouth kept opening and closing like that of a drowning fish and Kallie realized that—even dying—the man was trying to cast a spell.

Give the goddamned man back what be his.

Power crackled like ice beneath her skin. Stars wheeled through her vision.

Kallie knelt beside St. Cyr, and his pain-dilated eyes widened. He shook his head in silent denial and tried to scoot away from her. Before she knew what she was doing or how, she grabbed him by the front of his Hawaiian shirt and forced him to face her. He stared at her, his expression stark with mingled disbelief and fear.

"Black dust mambo," he whispered, his words bubbling with blood.

What the hell's he talking about? But even as she wondered, she felt power rise within her like a gator from beneath cypress-shadowed water. Words flowed through her mind.

"Graveyard dirt, black salt, sulfur, rattlesnake skin, sand, pigeon shit, and the bitterness of an empty heart, ingredients all in a hex to kill body and soul," Kallie chanted. "Back into you they flow."

Kallie cupped her empty palm and blew into it. Her breath caught in her throat as black dust actually flowed up from beneath her skin and streamed from her palm into St. Cyr's face. The glittering onyx powder rushed into his mouth and down his throat.

Drums pounded in time with the throbbing in Kallie's skull, the rhythm fast and primal and hungry. Shadows rippled at the edges of her vision. Cold frosted her veins. And still the black dust poured from her into St. Cyr—mouth, nose, ears, and eyes—in a violent rush of power that scraped against her heart and threatened to yank her under.

How the hell am I doing *this?*

Blanketed in blackest juju of his own making, St. Cyr's body convulsed, then went still. A second later, a shape dusted in black powder pushed its way out of the root doctor's lax mouth.

Kallie stared, her heart thundering in her chest as St. Cyr's hex-oiled soul slithered out into the night from between his lips.

"Hellfire," Belladonna and Layne said together.

Doctor Heron's black soul spiraled up into the air, a triumphant expression sparking across his face.

"No, goddammit," Kallie said. She jumped to her feet and grabbed the spirit's ankles. St. Cyr struggled to kick free of her grip. "Eye for eye, life for life, soul for soul. You shall pay what you owe. For Gage." Letting go of him with her left hand, she cried, "Return to me!"

"Kallie, no!"

Kallie looked in the direction of the voice and saw her aunt and another woman standing beside the old lightning-blasted cypress. She recognized her aunt's companion as the true Gabrielle LaRue, or one of them at least, the woman from the photos in Rosette's file. She watched Kallie with a calm and curious expression, a red scarf covering her curls.

Kallie's aunt, however, regarded her with the exasperated, hands-on-hips expression she usually wore before grounding someone for the rest of their natural lifetime. She shook her head. "Don't do it, child. It ain't yo' place."

"It wasn't his either," Kallie said, throat tight. "And I don't know how you can tell me right from wrong when you can't even tell me your name."

Her aunt blinked, then said, "I had my reasons, girl, but now dat you know, you need to get over it."

One Mississippi . . . A muscle flexed in Kallie's jaw. She returned her attention to the slippery St. Cyr and growled, "Return to me, I said."

The black dust coating St. Cyr's soul rippled, then flowed backward and down, back into Kallie's waiting palm. The root doctor's spirit unraveled inch by inch, molecule by molecule, until the air was empty.

"Hellfire," Belladonna repeated, her voice stunned.

Her aunt tsked in disgust.

"I guess an eye for an eye *is* enough," Layne said.

The last speck of black dust melted into the palm of Kallie's hand and she stumbled, drained and aching. Strong arms looped around her, scooped her up against a hard, leather-jacketed chest. She felt the tickle of dreads against her face.

"Gotcha, sunshine," Layne said, voice husky.

Kallie slipped an arm around his neck and closed her eyes.

What just happened? And how did I do it?

THIRTY-FIVE

Gros Bon Ange

Kallie walked out of the bathroom, smelling of Ivory soap, her face and hands scrubbed clean of black dust and her own drying blood. Pain throbbed in her sternum and every muscle prickled and ached like she had the flu. A little sleep, and she'd be fine.

But before she could sleep, she needed the truth.

Slipping her cell phone from the pocket of her cutoffs, she noticed a text message from Felicity and opened it.

DB out of surgery. Expected to live.

Relief nearly drained the last of the strength from Kallie's legs. She tucked the cell back into her pocket and hurried into the living room to share the news.

Belladonna shook her head. "I don't know if I can ever mock the attempts on his life again after this. Damned man. Glad he's alive."

"Me too," Kallie said.

"I t'ink we all could use a drink," her aunt said. She circled the room and passed out ice-cold bottles of Abita, her long lavender gypsy-style skirt sweeping the hardwood floor as she moved. "It's been a helluva night, for true."

Kallie didn't know about anyone else, but she had a feeling *one* drink wasn't going to do the trick.

"Thanks," Layne murmured, accepting a bottle. He leaned against the wall beside the open front door. Light-mesmerized moths fluttered against the screen door as cool night air filtered into the room.

Kallie pressed the cold bottle of Abita against her face, hoping it would chill the ache in her head. It didn't. Sighing, she decided to give drinking it a try and poured a long, frosty swallow down her throat.

She wanted to pace the goddamned floor, but was too exhausted to do much more than plop down onto the floral-patterned sofa and prop herself up against one corner. Belladonna slouched at the opposite end, looking just as drained.

Gabrielle LaRue, the woman from the photos, sat in one of two cherrywood rockers opposite the sofa. A carnation-red scarf hugged her curls, matching the button-down, three-quarter-sleeve blouse she wore over a pair of tan corduroy jeans. She tipped her beer bottle against her lips, her curious gaze on Kallie.

How can she look so calm after watching me destroy a man she once loved? And why—how—*is she here? She doesn't seem upset about St. Cyr* or *the loss of her identity.*

"So let's hear it," Kallie said, shifting her attention to her *tante*. "Who are you, really, and why did you lie to me and Jacks? Who are you hiding from?"

From the second cherrywood rocker, her *tante* flapped a hand at her. "Don't be foolish, girl. I be your aunt."

"I know that. You look like Mama." Shoulder-length black hair, light cocoa-colored skin, tilted eyes more green than hazel. "I'm betting you're Divinity."

Her aunt nodded and took a sip from her beer. "Dat I am."

This was going to be like wrenching nails from an old board with only fingernails. Kallie forced herself onto her feet. "You planning on answering me sometime *this* decade?"

"I was getting to it, girl," Gabrielle—her aunt, Divinity—chided. "Where be yo' patience? I didn't lie to you kids, I just didn't tell you my true name."

"Why not? Why all the goddamned subterfuge?" Kallie asked. "Dallas was nearly *killed* because Doctor Heron confused you with the real Gabrielle, and Layne's clan brother *was* killed."

Divinity looked at Layne, sympathy and regret on her face. "My heart goes out to you," she told him. "If I'da known . . . if I'da had any idea . . . I woulda chosen a different identity to steal. My only intention was to protect Kallie."

Layne just nodded, jaw tight. He drained a good portion of his beer.

"Protect me from who?" Kallie folded her arms under her breasts and shifted her weight onto one hip. "Mama's locked up." A dark thought occurred to her. "Ain't she?"

Divinity returned her attention to Kallie. "*Oui*, girl, your mama's still in Saint Dymphna's."

"So then why did you need a new identity?" Kallie prodded. "And why did you choose Gabi's?"

"She knew I'd left Louisiana for Haiti after everything that had happened with Jean-Julien," Gabi cut in, her voice musical with island rhythm. She fixed a fierce gaze on Divinity, her handsome face hard. "She thought I'd never find out and, in truth, she might've been right, since I don't use credit cards or banks."

Kallie glanced from Gabi to her aunt. Divinity sat rigid in her chair, looking uncomfortable, but far from contrite with her lifted chin.

Whoops. Seems I was beaucoup *wrong about Gabi not being upset.*

Divinity met her former namesake's eyes. "Nine years ago, when de need came up, I asked around to see if you'd come back and I learned you were still in Haiti. So . . ." She lifted a shoulder in an eloquent shrug.

"So you stole my name and eventually drew Jean-Julien's attention," Gabi said. She placed her empty Abita bottle on the candle-cluttered end table situated between the rockers. "When I knew him, the man wasn't a killer. A womanizer, yes, but not a murderer." She sighed. "That changed in prison, it seems. But being convicted of crimes you never committed and then being denied parole for refusing to express remorse for those crimes would take a toll on anyone."

"Don't make it right," Layne said. "Go after the one who framed you, yeah. But why kill people who had nothing to do with it?"

"*Did* you frame him?" Kallie asked Gabi quietly. "Or was it Babette?"

Surprise rippled across Gabi's face. She studied Kallie, head tilted thoughtfully to one side. "Much more than just pretty, aren't you, girl? I always believed that Babette had been the guilty party and, no matter how furious I was with Jean-Julien at the time, he hadn't deserved what happened to him. But I had no proof of his wife's guilt. I'd even spoken to the sheriff, but it was a closed case as far as he was concerned." She looked at Layne, sorrow shadowing her face. "I had no idea

Jean-Julien or his daughter blamed me for his imprisonment. I'm so sorry."

Layne's muscles tensed and flexed underneath his T-shirt, along his arms. He nodded. "Thanks," he said, voice husky.

Kallie joined him against the wall. He glanced at her, a rueful smile on his lips. She offered him a smile in return, wishing she could just kiss him instead.

With a soft sigh, Kallie shifted her attention back to her aunt. "How did you figure out what was happening?" she asked. "And how the hell did you find Gabi?"

Divinity took a long swallow of beer, then shook her head. "Dat's just it—I *didn't* piece it together right away. When Dallas called, he tol' me that a girl named Rosette tried to shoot you and dat she mentioned my name and—" Pausing, she glanced at Gabi. "*Yo'* name," she corrected, "dat she'd been talking about revenge."

"'An eye for an eye is never enough,'" Kallie murmured. "Then what?"

"I remembered my readings from dat morning—de cards and de shells," Divinity replied. "De cards had revealed jail and imprisonment, bad luck caused by a man, and de shells had laid down de pattern for death and night, ancestors, and a destiny about to be disrupted. When I added de readings to what Dallas had tol' me . . . well, it got me to t'inking dat maybe de '*imprisonment*' didn't mean Saint Dymphna's, and dat de '*ancestors*' didn't mean yo' mama. Got me to t'inking dat maybe it wasn't *me* dis Rosette wanted revenge upon."

"So I got a phone call," Gabi put in.

"True dat," Divinity said. "I'd heard a rumor dat Gabi had moved back from Haiti a couple of weeks ago and settled in Lafayette—meaning I'd hafta change my identity again soon—so I started askin' around. When I found her, I draped a mojo bag around Jackson's neck—and I got an earful waiting for dat boy when he gets his ass home, for true—den I walked into town and took the Greyhound to Lafayette." She glanced at Gabi. "What I had to say couldn't be said over de phone."

Gabi's hands curled around the rocker's arms. Her jaw tightened. "No," she agreed. "After the initial shock of everything your aunt told me, I realized that Rosette had to be Jean-Julien's daughter. I'd heard he'd been released from prison, but I didn't want to believe he was involved."

"What convinced you?" Kallie asked.

Gabi's sympathetic gaze flicked back to Layne. "The soul-killing hex," she replied. "I couldn't imagine Jean-Julien's daughter possessing that kind of power. But Jean-Julien? Oh, yes. But I never dreamed . . ." Lips compressed, she shook her head.

"Since Gabi hadn't yet stocked up on all de herbs and roots Customs forced her to leave behind in Haiti, we came back here to lay a crossing trick against Doctor Heron—one powerful enough to stop de man dead in his tracks."

"But you and your nomad friend had already put Jean-Julien down with steel and black dust," Gabi said, her attention focused on Kallie, her hazel eyes looking deep. "Special child," she murmured.

Kallie shifted, uneasy beneath the woman's scrutiny. "What do you mean?"

"Of course she be special," her aunt said indignantly. "She's my niece, ain't she? And I don't regret what I've done." She looked at Kallie. "I did what I needed to do to keep you and Jackson safe. But I *do* regret not being more careful."

"Again—keep us safe from what?"

"From dose who would want to finish what yo' mama started."

"Kill me," Kallie said, stating a fact.

Layne sucked in a sharp breath of air, and shifted against the wall, and Kallie had a feeling Augustine hadn't mentioned her past to him.

"Hell no. Yo' mama *never* wanted to kill you," Divinity said.

Kallie stared at her aunt, incredulous. "She *shot* me. In the *head*."

"But she wasn't trying to kill you, girl. She was trying to awaken what's inside of you."

"*Inside* of me? What?" A chill shuddered through Kallie as the image of a heart bound in chains made of pale bones filled her mind. "Are you loco?"

"No, you sassy child, I ain't loco." Divinity slammed her bottle of Abita onto the coffee table, rose to her feet, then stalked across the room to her worktable. She picked something up from its root-and-herb-cluttered surface and carried it over to Kallie. She shook a violet-eyed poppet in Kallie's face.

"Dere ain't nothing I wouldn't do to help you, Kalindra Sophia. Teach you. Guide you. Lie to you. *Bind* you, if it be necessary. Because a big wrong's been done to you."

Kallie pushed away from the wall, her hands clenched into fists. Her pulse pounded hard through her veins. "I didn't notice 'tell the truth' in that list," she said, voice tight. "Where does that fit in . . . *Divinity*?"

Fire burned in her aunt's eyes, a controlled blaze. "It don't, *child*. Because de truth be too much for you to bear."

"How can you know that when you haven't *told* me the truth?"

"Foolish girl," she muttered. "T'inking de truth be a white knight on a beautiful pony. Well, it ain't. T'inks she knows what be best. Well, she don't. Don't care what people do for her. Ungrateful."

Kallie rolled her eyes. "Yeah, yeah. So what *wrong* has been done to me?"

Divinity dropped her hands to her generous hips and drew herself up to her full five foot seven. Even though she was only two inches taller than Kallie, she somehow always managed to loom. Like she was doing now. She fixed her stoniest Medusa glare on Kallie. "You want de truth? Fine, den. How do you t'ink you survived dat hex tonight?"

Kallie frowned. "Belladonna did CPR on me."

Divinity lifted a knowing eyebrow. "Mmm-hmmm. Dat she did—on yo' *body*. How do you t'ink yo' *soul* survived? Yo' *Gros Bon Ange*?"

"I . . . uh . . ." Kallie lapsed into silence. Already she could barely remember what had happened beside the bayou. A dream pulsed through her memory.

The jarring thud of hooves against the ground vibrates along her spine, jolts her body with each ground-swallowing gallop. Rough hair rubs against her cheek, twists around her fingers. She smells horse musk and, underneath her thighs, feels the powerful flex of muscles.

She looked at her aunt and shook her head. "I don't know," she admitted. "I had this dying dream . . . something about a horse and a chained heart."

"No dream, girl. You be alive because when you were born to your mama and papa, yo' soul was removed to make room for the *loa* placed inside yo' infant body. The same *loa* dat your mama tried to awaken with blood and darkness by murdering your papa and shooting you."

"Fuck," Layne whispered.

Kallie felt like she'd just been pummeled by a heavyweight with lead in his gloves. She stared at her aunt, her brain scrabbling for something—*anything*—to say beyond "*Huh?*"

Quick-witted Belladonna said nothing, because the gentle buzz rising from the sofa indicated that the voodooienne had fallen asleep. Kallie envied her. She didn't think she'd ever sleep again.

"Dere," Divinity said, hands still on her hips. "You feel better now?"

"Yes," Kallie lied. "Absolutely. One hundred percent."

Divinity snorted. "Well, you can be grateful for de fact dat yo' *Ti Bon Ange*, yo' consciousness, will, and stubborn personality, be still in place."

"But . . . *why* was a *loa* put inside of me?" Kallie asked. "Who did it? How? And why the hell would Mama want to awaken it?" She felt strong, supportive fingers curl around her forearm, and she darted a grateful glance at Layne.

Divinity blew out a weary breath. "You taking up journalism? Questions for another day, Kallie-girl. You be dead on your feet and de story's too long." Her expression softened. "But I promise you de answers—later, after you've slept."

Kallie wanted to argue, wanted to demand those answers now, but her aunt was right—exhaustion blurred her thoughts, dulled her focus. "*D'accord*, but I'm gonna hold you to that. Tell me this at least—where's my soul, my *Gros Bon Ange*?"

"Well, see, dat be de problem," Divinity said. "We don't know. Your mama was de last one who had it, and she ain't talking."

"Great," Kallie muttered. She lifted the bottle of Abita to her lips and drained it.

Layne straddled his Harley and strapped on his matte black shorty-style helmet. His green-eyed gaze held Kallie's. "I'll be back to help you," he said. "After Gage's cremation and after Augustine passes on."

A smile brushed Kallie's lips. "I appreciate that, I really do. But you ain't obligated. You've got your clan."

"Shut up, woman," Layne said. "I know I ain't obligated, and I'll never be so far from my clan that I can't find 'em again."

"Where's home for you?" Kallie asked.

"Wherever my clan is."

Kallie glanced behind her toward her aunt's house. "Family is everything," she murmured. "Even if you want to strangle them."

Fingertips brushed Kallie's jaw, turned her head. She met Layne's warm gaze. "That's the thing about family," he said. "You're always adding to it."

Or subtracting from it.

Kallie reached back and unfastened the coffin pendant's clasp. She handed Layne the necklace, coiling the body-heat-warmed chain into his palm. "I want you to burn this with Gage. It represents the *loa* of the crossroads, something we talked about . . . *that* night . . . and he . . ." Her words stuck in a throat suddenly too tight. She folded Layne's fingers over the pendant, then closed her hand over his. "Please," she whispered.

Renewed grief washed across the nomad's face. She felt his hand squeeze tight around the pendant. He nodded. Lifting their joined hands to his lips, he kissed her knuckles. Kallie slid her hand away from his and stepped back.

"Hey," he said. "Augustine told me to ask you why I found myself in wet undies."

"Interesting suggestion, given that it came from the man who entered you in a wet-boxers contest, stripped you down like a pro, and proudly displayed everything you had to a crowd of *beaucoup* appreciative women. And men."

"Christ in a teacup," Layne muttered. "Man has no shame. So . . . who won?"

"Who do you think won?" Kallie asked innocently.

A wicked smile slid across the nomad's lips. He winked, sending flutters through Kallie's belly. He kick-started his bike and it roared to life with a powerful rumble. "I'll be back, sunshine," he promised. "We'll find your soul."

Kallie hoped so. Though she'd be okay if the search went no farther than underneath his clothes. *Sheesh. Looks like I can give Bell a run for her money on the pure-evil title.* She watched Layne ride down the dirt drive into the waning night.

Turning, she trudged back to the house. As she climbed the steps to the porch, a flash of red caught her eye. She paused and scanned the ground beside the stairs. She bent and scooped up a mojo bag, its leather cord snapped as if it'd been yanked from someone's neck.

Jackson's voice curled through her memory.

"I don't know where she is, Kal. I got in from Grand Isle this

mornin', and she was beaucoup *worked up about somethin' . . . put a mojo bag around my neck and made me promise to stay home until she got back."*

Dread dropped like cold stones into her belly. Jacks *hadn't* driven into town. And someone had torn the mojo bag from him. As she straightened, she saw moonlight glinting upon something metallic just under the button bush beside the porch.

A baseball bat—the one Jacks kept beside the back door.

Kallie's heart kicked against her ribs. She ran up the steps and into the house. "*Ti-tante!* Jacks didn't take Cielo and go into town." She held up the mojo bag. "His baseball bat's out in the yard too."

Divinity's eyes widened. Fear flashed across her face. "Sweet Jesus," she breathed. She hurried over to Kallie and took the red flannel bag from her. The woodsy scents of dog rose and sandalwood curled into the air.

Cupping the bag in her palm, Divinity trailed her fingers across it as though she could read Jacks's fate from the flannel itself.

And maybe she could. But whatever had happened to Jacks had occurred *hours* ago. And that fact scared Kallie. What if he was already . . . ?

No. She squelched the thought, refused to give it voice.

"Could this be connected to Jean-Julien too?" Gabi asked, joining them.

"I ain't sure," Kallie said, hating how helpless she felt. She knotted her hands into fists. "But given that his truck is gone, I doubt it. Why would St. Cyr have stolen it or hidden Jacks? I think he'd've just killed Jacks and left his body where it could be found."

Gabi nodded. "I think you're right about that."

In truth, Kallie suspected her cousin's disappearance could be blamed on his work. Jackson had made enemies with his Robin Hood–style bayou pirating, and it didn't matter one goddamned to them if the goods and cash he gained was given to those most in need, or used to help rebuild hurricane-devastated areas the government continued to ignore.

More than one unhappy outlaw wanted Jackson dead.

But why rip the mojo bag from around his neck and drag him away when a couple of bullets into the head would solve the problem named Jackson Bonaparte?

Something felt off and, despite the adrenaline rush lighting up her mind, Kallie had a feeling she was missing something obvious, something important.

"Boy's still alive," Divinity said, relief thick in her voice. "But I can't get a fix on him. No images. No sense of place. I don't know where he be, but we're damned sure gonna find out. Go get your cards, girl."

Kallie raced to her bedroom and scooped the silk-lined bag holding her cards up from her altar. In the living room once more, she knelt in front of the sofa and shook Belladonna's shoulder. "Wake up, Bell. I need your help."

Belladonna slivered her eyes open and regarded Kallie suspiciously. "Did you just say you *needed* me or am I still dreaming about pod-Kallie?"

"It's Jacks," Kallie said, ignoring her friend's comment. "And his ass is in the fire, for true."

"Hellfire." Belladonna sat up, wide awake. "Then we gotta pull his fine ass out."

Kallie felt a tight smile pull at her lips. "Goddamned

straight." She freed her cards from their bag and shuffled them, the last words her cousin had said to her a mantra looping through her thoughts.

"Gotta go. See you on Sunday. Love ya."

Love ya back, and I'm goddamned holding you to Sunday, Jacks.

Kallie flipped over the first card.